THE LANE

BY

—FRAN HOPPER—

Copyright

Legal Notice

This book is a work of historical fiction. Names, characters, places, and incidents are either a product of the author's imagination or are used fictitiously. Any resemblance to actual people, living or dead, events, or locales is entirely coincidental.

Courtesy
Published by Pacific Publishings
5101 Santa Monica Blvd, Suite 8#221
Los Angeles, CA 90013
USA

ISBN 978-1-965490-68-6

DEDICATION

*I dedicate this book to my **wife, Sylvie,***

*My two sons, **Antoine and Oisín**,*

*My sister **Brenda** and to my family*

*and **dear friends** past and present.*

A special mention also for my martial arts teachers over the years -

Jim, John, Tommy, Frank, Jaff and Daniel.

At times, silence is the best music.

—F. Hopper

Do nothing that is of no use.

—Miyamoto Musashi

Table of Contents

Chapter One Dublin 1990 Summertime 1

Chapter Two Rotunda Hospital, Dublin 1956 7

Chapter Three Dublin Present...11

Chapter Four 1961 The Early Days, Marino School 15

Chapter Five Dublin present 23

Chapter Six Dublin present 47

Chapter Seven Present day – Little Italy, Manhattan, ...76

Chapter Eight Saturday morning – Clontarf 87

Chapter Nine Okinawa eight years previous 96

Chapter Ten Dublin Summer present 117

Chapter Eleven Okinawa, 7 years previously 157

Chapter Twelve Little Italy - Manhattan, New York, present day .189

Chapter Thirteen Dublin - present day 195

Chapter Fourteen The trial 213

Chapter Fifteen Manhattan - present day................................232

Chapter Sixteen Okinawa – 6 years previous 238

Chapter Seventeen Back to Dublin, Autumn 1990 256

Chapter Eighteen Okinawa 6 years previous 285

Chapter Nineteen Back to Dublin - D-day 296

Chapter Twenty Palermo - Italy 318

Chapter Twenty-One Dublin – Ireland 325

Chapter Twenty-Two California, Maryland – USA......................344

Chapter Twenty-Three Okinawa – Japan 1984 347

Chapter Twenty-Four Dublin, present day - November 353

Chapter Twenty-Five Okinawa 1985 387

Chapter Twenty-Six Dublin 1990 December 390

Chapter Twenty-Seven Trapetto, Sicily, 1991 April 396

Chapter Twenty-Eight Tokyo 1991 March 399

Chapter Twenty-Nine Manhattan 404

Chapter Thirty Okinawa 406

Chapter Thirty-One Manhattan 420

Chapter Thirty-Two Okinawa - present day 426

Chapter Thirty-Three Okinawa – 4 years ago 445

Chapter Thirty-Four Back to Palermo 451

Chapter Thirty-Five Dublin 467

Chapter Thirty-Six Okinawa 481

This Page is Left Blank Intentionally...

CHAPTER
One

Dublin 1990 Summertime

Jack awoke from a drunken stupor at exactly 11 a.m. His head pounded. How many drills were jackhammering in there? His mouth felt as though it was filled with cotton wool and sandpaper. He needed water and a Disprin, and in that order. He slung himself out of bed and headed for his modern, well-equipped kitchen, poured himself a long, cool glass of water, and downed it in one gulp. Christ, that felt good, he thought to himself. He then found a Disprin, which he popped into a half glass of water. He stared at the bubbles fizzing up like a cheap school science project. When it had completely dissolved, he tossed it back.

Jack felt better, but knew it was only a psychological fix. He would have to wait a few more hours before the toxins left his body. Why did he do this to himself each year on the anniversary of Akiko's death? Was it to forget, or just to ease the pain?

But how could he forget? Akiko had been savagely raped and left to die from her horrific wounds two years previously. Now, on the date of her anniversary, he lit joss sticks in the Buddhist tradition and got pissed with his mates in the Irish tradition.

Akiko had spent the last days of her life in a Buddhist monastery, as the doctors had explained to Jack that they could do no more for her. She had passed away peacefully in Jack's arms as they both watched their last sunset over Okinawa Bay.

Since Akiko's passing, Jack felt empty, as if thrown into a void from which he couldn't return. Their love had been pure; they had been connected in mind, body, and soul. But life carried on, and Jack just got on with his daily routine as best he could.

He stepped out onto his balcony overlooking Dublin Bay. It was a fine Summer's day. The seagulls screeched and circled, heralding the incoming tide and their daily lunch. Life was good.

Jack rented a nice apartment in Clontarf, an upmarket region of northern Dublin. This was where the Irish chief Brian Boru had defeated the Vikings in the Battle of Clontarf, 1014. The place was steeped in history. He loved the area—the view, the fresh air, the daily jogs along the seafront and the Bull Wall, and of course, the proximity to the city centre.

Yet there were two things Jack loved above all: sunrises and sunsets. He had come to appreciate these unique phenomena during his six years in Okinawa with Akiko. Each time he experienced one or the other, he felt a cleansing of his soul and spirit, felt in harmony with the universe. In the same breath, he felt centred—*kokoro*, the heart of the universe.

Settling into *kiba-dachi*, the horse stance, Jack began his daily abdominal breathing exercises, designed to oxygenate the blood cells, eliminate the stale air accumulated in the lungs, and stimulate the *ki*, the universal energy. Most people used only 45% of their lung capacity; Jack was around the 95% mark thanks to his years of martial arts training. The average total lung capacity of an adult male is about six litres of air, but Jack was around ten litres.

So, a new day had started. He had planned to go jogging around four in the afternoon, after a small lunch in the Yacht Bar, his local pub, and maybe catch up with a few familiar faces. On Saturdays, the place was always buzzing.

Jack took a refreshing power shower after his workout, put on a fresh blue denim shirt, blue jeans, and white sneakers. He was about to go out the door when the phone rang. He picked up the receiver.

"Hello, Mr. Hopkins?"

"Yes, speaking."

"Mr. Jack Hopkins?"

"This is he. What can I do for you?"

"My name is Johnny Tanaka. I'm here on holiday, checking up on my Irish ancestors." Jack recognised the thick New York accent. Not many Irish with the name Tanaka, he thought. But maybe it was on his mother's side.

"So how can I help you, Mr Tanaka?"

"I read an article about your dojo in *The New York Times* a while ago, and I'd like to check out one of your classes and do some sparring."

Jack remembered meeting an American law student in Trinity College called Laura two years back. She used to write a few articles for the American press to help pay for her studies. They had met over a drink in O'Donoghue's pub, and she had said she'd like to do an article about Jack and his dojo. It was called "An Irish Samurai." They had slept together, but nothing had evolved from their night of love.

"No problem," said Jack. "You can work out with one of my black belts."

"You don't get it, man. It's with *you* I want to spar. I'm a fifth dan black belt." Jack was a bit taken aback by the sheer brass neck and lack of respect of the man.

"The class starts at 7 p.m. on Monday and ends at 9 p.m. We'll be able to work out together when the dojo is empty."

Strange character, thought Jack. Anyway, it would be a good experience to meet a high-grade black belt. In Ireland, you could count them on one hand. Master Saito had bestowed the 6th dan on Jack in the style Shōrin-ryū before leaving Okinawa. This was the highest technical degree possible; all the following dans were honorary for services rendered to the Art.

Shōrin-ryū (小林琉), as in the Shaolin Temple of China.

Ryu means "style." Shōrin-ryū is one of the major modern Okinawan martial arts and one of the oldest styles of karate. It was named by Choshin Chibana in 1933, but the system itself is much older. "Shōrin" means pine tree. "Ryu" means school. Shōrin-ryū combines elements of the traditional Okinawan fighting styles of Shuri-te.

Jack strolled down to the Yacht Bar from the apartment—it was less than half a mile away—and the fresh air from the incoming tide, along with the smell of iodine, invigorated him. The sun glared off the whitewashed walls as he popped his head inside the lounge bar and was met by a hovering haze of cigarette smoke. The extractor fans weren't turned on. Some publicans were too stingy to switch them on, and others were too stingy to buy them. This was something Jack hated, as the smoke left a very unpleasant smell on your clothes. Hard to imagine today, with smoking banned inside all public houses. He looked over to the corner and saw a few familiar heads from the previous night— Anto, Lenny, Danger, and Bradley. They all looked hungover and were already on the pints.

"Over here, Jack!" bellowed Anto. He had an easy, welcoming face with a ready smile and was always up for some fun—the gang's comic, and not an ounce of badness in him.

"Hiya lads, what's the craic? Jaysus, yez all look like death warmed up," laughed Jack.

"Where the fuck did you guys go last night?" shouted Danger. "I had to get a taxi home on my own—cost me a fuckin' fortune." He was one of the two redheads among the lads, the other being Lenny, whose hair was a lighter shade.

"I hope you were nice to the taxi man," taunted Bradley.

"Don't start, ye bollocks," retorted Danger.

"Stop being cranky," shot back Bradley.

"What are you havin' to drink, Jack?" asked Lenny, stabbing out a fag.

"Don't worry about me for the moment, Lenny. First, a bit of grub and a glass of cool milk."

"The tuna salad is good," said Anto.

Some things never changed, thought Jack. Always a bit of banter and slagging when the lads were around. It was always good to see them. Jack ordered a tuna salad and a plate of chips on the side from the lounge girl, and a pint of cold milk. It wasn't exactly haute cuisine, but it would do the job.

"So, where's the craic tonight?" asked Jack.

"Don't know," said Danger. "I'm skint."

"Nothin' new there," said Bradley, pulling a hand down his face in a mock gesture of despair.

"Skint already?" hissed Anto. "Sure, we'll sort you out." One for all and all for one was what Jack was thinking. A bunch of good heads.

"So, how about O'Donoghue's?" asked Jack. "The craic is always good. Say around 9 o'clock?"

"Jaysus," hissed Anto. "Better tell Trigger 7 o'clock—he's never on time."

"Don't be slagging," sneered Bradley. "You know he hasn't an easy job as a night-owl plumber."

Trigger, another regular in the gang, was notorious for his bad timekeeping. He worked for himself as a plumber, and his day could start between 10 and 11 a.m., depending on the night before, and go on until all hours of the night. Of course, it was always a great subject of discussion with Bradley, who was always amazed that people would tolerate tradesmen in their homes up until 10 p.m.—and sometimes after. Hence, the slogan Bradley had suggested for Trigger's ad in the Yellow Pages or local papers:

"Trigger—your very own night-owl plumbing service."

Trigger hadn't seen the funny side of it.

"Okay, see you tonight," said Jack. He stood up, called over the barmaid, and asked her for the bill. He paid cash and left her a decent tip, which brought a bright smile to her young face. He pushed open the stylish glass-paned doors and stepped out onto the pavement. The sun was still blazing, and there wasn't a whiff of wind. So, Jack decided to make the best of the good weather and go for a stroll along the Bull Wall before returning to the apartment. The walk would stretch his legs before his daily run.

To serve and to be served are two folds in the same garment

Buddhist monk

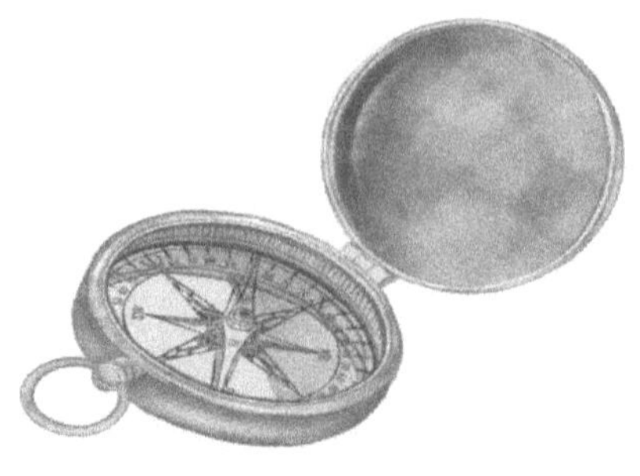

CHAPTER
Two

Rotunda Hospital, Dublin 1956

Congratulations, it's a baby boy, Mrs. Hopkins." Fiona opened her arms as the nurse gently passed her their first child. She held him to her breast and felt a love she had never thought possible. It was Easter Monday. What better gift could she receive than a beautiful baby boy?

And so it was, Jack was born on this day in the Rotunda Hospital, Ireland's busiest maternity hospital, churning out hundreds of babies every week. The Catholic Church were, of course, over the moon with these new recruits, but the Minister for Finance was more than distraught trying to find the funds to support the growing burden of children's allowances.

The Rotunda was founded in 1745 by Bartholomew Mosse as a charitable institution and was designed by architect Richard Cassels, who also designed Leinster House and Powerscourt Terrace. In 1889, the first caesarean section carried out in Ireland was performed at the Rotunda.

With no system of contraception tolerated in the Republic of Ireland by the Church, there were many large families and countless unwanted pregnancies. The Church at the time had the State by the scruff of the neck. No democracy can operate efficiently and righteously unless the Church and the State are entirely separate entities.

Fiona couldn't wait until Tom arrived. He would be so proud—his first child, and a boy to boot. Tom had received a phone call that morning from Sister Philomena at the hospital, announcing the good news: he was the father of a baby boy.

He had to negotiate some time off with the head overseer, who just happened to be his father, the one and only Tom Hopkins. There was no such thing as paternity leave in those days. Tom Hopkins Sr. was very strict and unbending when it came to punctuality or taking time off. After all, one couldn't run two daily newspapers without being stringent about timekeeping. However, this was a very special occasion.

Tom tread light-footed down the stairs as the bell on Christchurch chimed out 1 p.m. and slipped out the back door of "The Irish Independent Newspapers Ltd." or "The Indo," as it was fondly known, onto Prince's Street. His head was in the clouds. He popped a John Player into his mouth and lit it with a Friendly match. Today was a good day indeed.

He then crossed Henry Street into Moore Street, where the hawkers were selling their goods, their heads covered in scarves, with shawls over their shoulders to keep off the morning chill.

"Apples and oranges! Anyone for apples and oranges, two pence a pound!"

"Some apples or oranges, love?" cried a hawker.

"Yeah, give us two pounds of oranges, love," said Tom. He handed over a shilling and told her to keep the change.

"Jaysus, you're an angel, love. Today, you have a twinkle in your eye," she laughed.

For Christ's sake, thought Tom, I nearly forgot—I need some flowers.

He knew most of the hawkers on Moore Street, as he bought fruit and veg there at least three times a week, along with his Christmas decorations. He saw Imelda at the next stall and asked what flowers she had to offer.

"What's the occasion?" says she.

"I've just become a dad," says Tom.

"Jaysus, Tom, I'm delighted for ye! Now take this bunch of crocuses and give my love to your wife."

Tom took the purple and yellow flowers, which were wrapped in newspaper, and handed Imelda a few coppers.

"Would ye feck off, Tom—they're on the house. Skiddle off now and see your wife and child!"

These people were salt of the earth, thought Tom. He was radiating with happiness and walking on air. The weather was fine—unusual for this time of year. Ireland could be notorious for its ever-changing weather; one could experience all four seasons in a single day. Dirty Dublin never looked better, he thought.

Further on, another hawker sold fresh fish laid out on newspaper sheets—yesterday's news from the Indo, of course. The presentation wasn't exactly appetising, and the smell was a bit nauseating, but the fish was fresh.

Tom arrived at the Rotunda Hospital and stubbed out his fag. Smoking was still allowed in public places but frowned upon in hospitals. Funny how times change. He glided merrily up the flight of stairs to the maternity ward on the first floor. He was a beacon of happiness. One of the sisters told him which room his wife and child were in.

He entered the room to see his beloved with his son in her arms. She glowed with happiness. Fiona shared the room with two other women; there were just curtains pulled around each bed to give some semblance of intimacy when treatments were being administered. It was a far cry from today's private rooms equipped with TV, showers, and toilets.

The two other women hadn't drawn their curtains and were deep in conversation with Fiona. They were on their second child and were sharing their past experiences—sleepless nights, breastfeeding, and nappy changing.

When Tom came to the side of the bed, he immediately caught their attention. He was a striking-looking man: five foot eleven, with dark hair and a slim build, smartly dressed in black slacks, a shirt and tie, and a beige jacket. Of course, he was a big fan of Humphrey Bogart.

Fiona handed him their son, whom he took very carefully—even awkwardly—not really knowing how to handle the little bundle of joy. Having one's first child has to be experienced; the sensations are hard to describe. It's a very intense and intimate moment.

"What will we call him?" asked Fiona.

"I'd like to call him Jack, after my grandfather."

"But what will the parents say? That isn't a saint's name," replied Fiona.

"To hell with that!" bellowed Tom. "I think we've done our bit for the Holy Catholic Church."

And so, Jack it was.

Eaten bread is soon forgotten ...

F. Hopper

CHAPTER
Three

Dublin Present

Jack returned to his apartment around 3:30 p.m., still feeling the remnants of the night before lingering in his muscles and mind. He decided to straighten the place up a bit before heading out for his usual five-mile run. A light hoovering, some dishes in the sink, and the bins to be brought down in time for Monday's collection — small domestic tasks that grounded him.

"This place could really use a woman's touch," Jack muttered to himself as he carried the rubbish down the stairs. Though he was in a casual yet increasingly comfortable relationship with a French woman named Sophie, whose every visit brought with it an air of femininity — a new throw, a handpicked bouquet, a quirky flea market find — her presence, however delightful, was still intermittent. The apartment, like Jack's life, hovered between solitude and possibility.

Sophie had her own key and a painter's instinct. She'd pop in unexpectedly, leaving behind traces of warmth: a fresh tablecloth from Stephen's Green, a vintage vase, the scent of her citrus perfume lingering in the hallway. Jack appreciated her spontaneity, even if he wasn't ready to define what they were.

He changed into his running gear: light shorts, Adidas trainers well-worn with miles, and a thin vest. This was his season — the time of year when the air was crisp but not punishing, when a coastal run didn't feel like survival. As he made his way toward the Bull Wall, the sharp tang of iodine filled his lungs — a scent that was both cleansing and oddly nostalgic.

The Bull Wall was more than just a local landmark to Jack. It was history underfoot. Built at the advice of Captain William Bligh — yes, *that* Bligh, of *Mutiny on the Bounty* fame — it had been conceived as a solution to the silting of Dublin Bay, a way to deepen and protect the harbour. Bligh's 1801 survey had led to a wooden bridge in 1819 and, eventually, a stone wall designed by George Halpin.

Construction began in 1820 and wrapped up in 1825 at a cost of £95,000. A marvel of engineering for its time, the wall stretched over 3,000 yards and stood proud even against flood tides. But Jack wasn't thinking about measurements or history as he pounded along the stones — he was thinking about Akiko.

It had been a slow, steady run — not a record-breaker by any means. His personal best was thirty-five minutes, but that wasn't the goal today. He was still sweating out last night's grief, the kind that clung to anniversaries like a fog.

Back at the apartment by a quarter to four, Jack peeled off his clothes and stepped into the shower, cranking the heat until his skin tingled. The stream pulsed against his back, washing away tension, while memories of Okinawa floated just beneath the surface of his thoughts. He ended with a blast of cold — a discipline his sensei had drilled into him: open the body with heat, seal it with ice.

Wrapped in a towel and wearing his handmade *zori* — traditional Japanese thongs he had brought home from Okinawa — Jack stepped out onto the balcony. This view never got old. No matter the season, it offered something: a sense of scope, a reminder of place. Today, under a flawless sky, the city shimmered.

To the right, the twin red-and-white smokestacks of Poolbeg stood tall against the skyline, like soldiers keeping vigil over the south side of the bay. Beyond them, the hazy outlines of the Dublin Mountains and the jagged peak of the Sugar Loaf. To the left, Howth Head stretched out into the sea, its silhouette resembling a grand cruise ship permanently docked on the horizon. A wealthy man's retreat, but Jack never envied it — his treasure was this peace.

Still, peace was temporary. Jack's thoughts shifted to Monday — to Mr. Tanaka, the American martial artist who'd called out of the blue. Something about the man's tone had rubbed him the wrong way, but also intrigued him. Jack had sparred with arrogance before, but every match was a test — and tests were how he measured progress.

His dojo in Fitzwilliam Square had come a long way since those uncertain early days after Okinawa. He'd started with just five students. Now he had over fifty on the books, with four classes a week and around twenty students in each. Word of mouth had done the heavy lifting — the dojo's reputation spread not through marketing but through sweat and bruises.

The basement space couldn't hold everyone at once — not that Jack wanted it to. He preferred small groups, where each student could be observed, corrected, and refined. He wasn't interested in turning out belt collectors. He wanted warriors with discipline, heart, and humility.

The dojo alone didn't pay the bills, though. Jack picked up occasional work as a bodyguard for politicians, celebrities, and international visitors. The pay was decent, the risks minimal — the biggest threat usually came from overeager journalists or fans with boundary issues. With his background in martial arts and journalism, Jack was a rarity. He had spent three years studying at the school of journalism and emerged with honours — sharp, articulate, respected.

As a freelancer, he still submitted the occasional piece to *The Indo* or *Evening Herald*, which kept his name in print and his vintage Fiat Spider on the road. Yet even now, his father — and Jacky

Gilroy, *The Indo*'s general manager — hadn't quite gotten over his abrupt decision to leave it all behind and move to Okinawa.

"For Christ's sake, Jack. Okinawa? It's not exactly down the bloody road," his father had said.

"It'll break your mother's heart."

The truth was, Jack's departure came six months after the end of his four-year relationship with Molly — his first real love. They had been engaged, bought a home, and built a future on promises and good intentions. But something had cracked beneath the surface.

Molly believed in waiting until marriage. "If you love me, you'll respect my wishes," she'd said often, deflecting Jack's frustration with references to faith and virtue.

"I'm here. I'm real. And I love you," Jack had once said in desperation. But she wouldn't — or couldn't — hear him.

He couldn't understand how a doctrine could outweigh a living, breathing person. In time, the tension broke them. Jack, unwilling to betray her or lie to himself, ended it. One-night stands had filled the physical gap, but never the emotional one. Ireland was full of sacred contradictions, and he had decided not to build a marriage on silence and shame.

Now, standing on his balcony with sunlight on his shoulders, he felt the stirrings of anticipation.

"Let's see what Mr. Tanaka has to offer," Jack thought. "It should be... interesting."

The two most important days in a man's life are the day he is
born and the day he discovers why ...

Mark Twain

CHAPTER
Four

1961 The Early Days, Marino School

Jack started school in "High Babies" in the autumn of '61, enrolled by his mother at Marino School on Griffith Avenue. It was an all-boys institution, naturally—boys and girls were separated even at that tender age in Ireland, a division that would echo through their turbulent teenage years. The school was run by the Sisters of the Presentation, a congregation known for its rigid discipline.

At first, Jack didn't know what to make of these women in stiff, penguin-like habits, with expressions carved from stone. They seemed like creatures from another world—silent, severe, and ever watchful. The whole scene unnerved him.

Thankfully, the presence of lay teachers brought a sense of normality and warmth. Their gentler demeanour offered young children a softer landing into the intimidating world of school. It was this balance between rigidity and compassion that helped Jack through those early days.

On his first day, Jack's mother walked him into the school, gently coaxing him forward to meet the teachers and nuns. He was neatly dressed, his hair freshly trimmed, although his mother's final touch—flattening the cowlick with saliva from her tongue—made his skin crawl. He hated that.

They were introduced to the head nun, Sister Anne, whose cold, piercing gaze seemed to scan Jack's soul. He wasn't sure if the twist of her lips was a smile or a sneer. He would later come to learn the full measure of her authority—and her cruelty.

The first day passed without incident. The teachers smiled, refreshments were served—cakes, tea, and orange squash—and Jack even spotted a couple of familiar faces from the neighbourhood. That helped. He wasn't entirely alone.

As time passed, Jack completed what was called "First Babies," the school year for children aged five to seven. He was lucky— his cousin Molly, four years his senior, attended the girls' school just a short distance away. Every lunchtime, she'd come visit him, bringing his hot soup in a flask and sandwiches—always either salmon or ham. She fussed over him like a little mother, and he adored her for it.

Jack's heart always lifted when he saw her little blonde head bob through the doorway. She'd sit beside him, and they'd chat and laugh over lunch. If the weather was kind, they'd take a walk together in the schoolyard. When it was time to go, Molly would dash off down the sloped path, the pleats of her uniform swirling and her white socks flashing with every step. To Jack, she was a burst of joy in a world that often felt grey.

But that joy was tempered by the daily torment from Aidan L.—a mischievous boy who never missed a chance to needle Jack. The jokes about his surname were relentless: "Hop over here," "Hop up," "Hop down." Then there were the pranks—yanking his cap from behind, hiding his gloves or coat. What began as teasing soon turned cruel.

Then one day, it all came to a head.

School let out at 2:30. As usual, there was a mad dash to the cloakroom, where coats were hung two or three to a peg. Jack was sure he'd left his coat on peg 42, but it was nowhere to be found. As the room emptied, he finally spotted it—on peg 13. And standing beside it, smirking, was Aidan L.

Jack had always been mild-mannered. But something inside him snapped.

When Jack confronted him, Aidan didn't back down. "Fuck off," he said, loud and clear.

Jack struck fast. A flurry of punches, one landing square on Aidan's nose. Blood gushed. The smirk vanished. And right on cue—Sister Anne stormed in, her voice echoing like a siren down the hall.

She didn't want explanations. Judgment was immediate, as was her fury. The boys were hauled off to her office, where she reached for the dreaded stick. Jack caught a gleam in her eyes—a cruel satisfaction.

Aidan went first. "Hold out your hand," she barked.

He hesitated, whimpering.

Whack. Whack. Whack. On one hand, then the other. He was sobbing now, fat tears streaking his cheeks.

Jack stood next. He looked her straight in the eye. He would not flinch. He thought of Molly—her bright smile, her golden hair. He found his centre.

The blows came—three on each hand. But he did not react. His face was stone. In that moment, without knowing it, Jack entered a different state—focused, unshaken, almost meditative. It was the first sign of something deeper stirring in him, an instinct for control, perhaps even a warrior's discipline.

Sister Anne was furious. She had never seen such defiance, especially from a boy so young. Her face reddened. Her voice rose to a shriek. She spat insults like venom.

Jack, now back in himself, watched her in silence. She was livid—but he had won.

The episode disrupted his routine. He missed the last bus home. He'd have to walk—two miles—but that was fine. He'd save the bus fare and spend it at the Pear Tree sweet shop tomorrow. Aidan had gone home bloodied and disgraced. Sister Anne had been defied.

Yes, Jack thought, it had been a good day.

It was April. Jack had just turned seven. He was now in High Babies and would be making his First Holy Communion the next month. There'd be visits to relatives and plenty of pocket money to collect. He was looking forward to it.

Neither Aidan L. nor Sister Anne bothered him again. But of course, new adversaries would always appear. Fortunately, a breath of fresh air entered Jack's school life in the form of a middle-aged teacher named Mrs. Silk.

She was exactly as her name implied—gentle, elegant, and serene. She never raised her voice. In every way, she was the opposite of the penguin-clad sisters. Her handwriting was graceful, looping across the blackboard like calligraphy. Her silk scarves, light makeup, and kind blue eyes gave her an air of warmth and quiet dignity.

She radiated care. There was no corporal punishment in her class, only encouragement. For Jack, she became a beacon in the school's stormy climate.

But Mrs. Silk suffered from poor health. Every few months, she'd vanish for weeks at a time. Jack dreaded those absences, which nearly always meant one thing: Sister Anne would return to the classroom. It felt like swapping cotton for barbed wire.

Thankfully, there was also Mr. MacDarby. When Mrs. Silk was out, Jack often ended up in his care. A small man of fifty, his trousers too short, his coat too long, his hat comically oversized— he looked like a character from a storybook.

And the children adored him.

He was funny, patient, and deeply respected. He never used the leather strap. He didn't need to. His kindness earned obedience, and his teaching got results.

For the first time, Jack found himself actually looking forward to school.

Jack started school in high babies in the autumn of '61 with the nuns in Marino School on Griffith Avenue. An all-male school, of course, even at this early age, boys and girls did not mix in Ireland. This would, of course, have repercussions later on during their difficult teenage years.

The order of the nuns was the Sisters of the Presentation, a fairly strict congregation altogether. At first, he didn't know what to think of these women dressed up in penguin-like uniforms and stern countenances. The whole scene was a little bit scary. Luckily enough, there were also lay teachers present. This offered some kind of normality and warmth which young children needed on their first steps into this unknown and mysterious world of education.

And so it was Jack's mother brought him to school on his first day to meet teachers and nuns alike. He was all dappered up, the hair nicely trimmed despite his mother's efforts to keep his calf's lick in place by wetting her hand with her tongue, something that Jack abhorred. Presentations were made to the head nun, Sister Anne, whose eyes seemed to bore through Jack.

He thought he deciphered what was a very slight smile or grimace. Later on, he would incur the wrath of this head nun and realise that her cruelty had no bounds. The day, however, had been good. Smiles all around from the teachers. Cakes, cold beverages, and tea had been offered. Jack saw one or two buddies from his neighbourhood, so things weren't too bad after all. He wasn't alone. So, time passed on and Jack got through what was known as "First Babies" for children from 5 to 7 years.

He was lucky to have his cousin Molly, who was 4 years older, only 100 yards away in the all-girls' school also run by the nuns. She would come by every lunch time and make sure Jack got his hot soup from the flask and had his sambos, either salmon or ham. She was a real little mother to him.

Jack was always elated when he saw her little blonde head bob in through the door and take place beside him at the desk. They would have a good little natter and a laugh, and sometimes, weather permitting, go for a little walk in the yard. Then she would leave him running down the tarmacked slope and out the grilled gates, the pleats in her school uniform dancing to the movement and her little socks an immaculate white.

So, all was rosy in Jack's little world until the day that Aidan L. pushed things a little too far. This guy was a daily thorn in Jack's side. Apart from the usual jokes about his surname: Hop over here, Hop up, Hop down, etc. … there came the physical aspect, pulling off his hat from behind, hiding his gloves and coat in the locker room. Some would call him a real little wanker.

And came the day when the cork exploded. School finished at 2.30 and, as usual, there was a big scurry for the cloakroom. Most times, the coats were stashed two to three on one hanger, so it wasn't easy to find the corresponding garment. Jack couldn't find his coat; he was certain he had left it on the number 42.

So, little by little, as the other kids found theirs, he eventually saw it down the other end of the locker on number 13. And of course, who was scoffing and laughing, no other but Aidan L. Jack was a mild-mannered kid, but this was it; he had had enough. He confronted the little wanker only to be told to fuck off in no uncertain terms.

Jack moved so quickly that Aidan L. didn't know what hit him. A sharp flurry of punches, with one hitting the target square on. He was rewarded with a nice bloody nose. But who was there right on queue, only Sister Anne, the head nun. She stormed in, shouting and bellowing and asked Jack what was going on. Explanations seemed pointless as they fell on deaf ears. She had already judged and condemned. They were both frog-marched down to the head office, where she produced her big stick. Jack could perceive a vicious glee in her eyes as she branded her weapon.

 Aidan L. was up first, told to stretch open his left hand. He was very reluctant and was already whinging in a very annoying manner, which amused Jack immensely. One, two, three whacks on his little red hand. The right would receive the same treatment.

He was balling at this stage, the tears flowing endlessly down his rosy cheeks. So, Jack's turn came. He was determined to defy this Sister Anne, look her in the face and not even blink. His hand didn't matter to him; he thought of his cousin Molly, her little blond head and her roguish smile.

One, two, three on each hand and his countenance was unchanged. Little did Jack realise it, but his martial arts training had already begun. He had entered an alpha state of mind or an altered state of consciousness. Of course, Sister Anne didn't take too kindly to this phenomenon; she had never witnessed anything like it.

Young boys of this age always cried when they received the big stick. Jack, coming back to his normal state of consciousness, thought the nun looked redder than he had ever seen her before, and she was shouting insults at an accelerated rate as if she was spitting feathers.

That was it, no big deal, thought Jack. The only thing was that his timetable was completely disturbed; this was one thing that he hated. It meant that his last school bus home was long gone; he would have to leg it home. Ah, what the heck, it had been a good day, AidanL. Went home with a bloodied nose, sore hands and had humiliated himself in front of Jack and Sister Anne had been defied.

Yes, a good day indeed, he was going to run it home and save the two pence bus fare and buy some sweets in the Pear Tree the following day.

The two-mile run would do him good and clear his head. It was April and Jack had just turned 7 and was now in high babies. He would be making his First Holy Communion the following month. He was looking forward to it as there was plenty of pocket money to be collected while out visiting the relatives on a marathon day.

Sister Anne or Aidan L. never bothered him again, but others would take their place. There was a welcome breath of fresh air in Jack's school life, and this came in the name of a middle-aged teacher called Mrs. Silk.

She was everything her name suggested. Soft-mannered, silken-tongued, and she moved with ease and grace. Her voice was never raised; this was in stark contrast to the Sisters of the Holy Immaculate, the penguin-clad squad as they were known. As far as Jack was concerned, she abounded in softness and femininity.

Her writing on the blackboard alone was something to behold; it was perfect, depicting her personality and showing it to all who cared to observe. She always wore silk scarves, and her make-up was tastefully done, bringing out the blue and the kindness in her eyes.

She gave affection and love. Corporal punishment was unheard of in Mrs. Silk's classes. However much to Jack's sadness, Mrs. Silk suffered from ill-health and was prone to sickness and prolonged absences.

She would be absent practically every three months for one to two weeks each time. These were periods that Jack detested as she was inadvertently replaced by a nun, and most often by none other but Sister Anne.

Talk about replacing cotton with barbed wire. Luckily enough, when Mrs. Silk was absent, Jack had Mr. MacDarby to fill the empathy gap. He was a small, fifty-year-old man whose trousers were too short, his hat too big, and his coat too long.

All the kids loved him as he was funny, kind and was a great teacher. He got results without ever taking out or using the loathed leather. Jack, for the first time in his life, actually looked forward to going to school.

"The man who conquers himself is superior to him who conquers a thousand men in battle."

Buddha

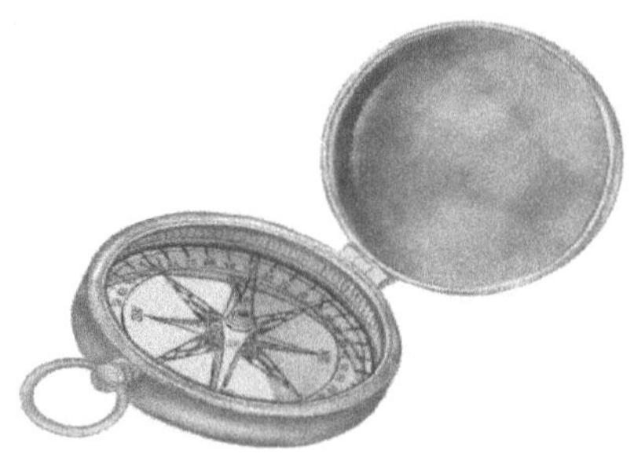

CHAPTER
Five

Dublin present

Jack burst down the stairs from the first floor of his apartment, keys jingling in hand, and into the car park where his pride and joy—the Ferrari-red 1979 Fiat Spider— waited under the golden hue of evening light. Sleek, low-slung, unapologetically bold, it was more than a car—it was a statement, a moving sculpture. Jack never tired of admiring it. If machinery could be poetry, this was it.

He dropped into the snug leather bucket seat, turned the key, and the engine growled to life. The 2-litre twin-cam powerplant, with its throaty twin-choke Weber carburettors, sucked in the summer air with a sound that made Jack's skin prickle. Music. Pure mechanical music.

He unlatched the convertible top, stepped out, and folded the black hood back with swift, practised hands. Back behind the wheel, he switched on the broadband radio. Four Pioneer 15-watt speakers flickered to life just as Bill Withers crooned *Ain't No Sunshine When She's Gone*. Jack grimaced and jabbed the tuner forward. That song cut too deep—memories of Akiko, of Okinawa, of heat and regret.

He landed on *Satisfaction*. Mick Jagger's snarl filled the cockpit.

"...And that man comes on the radio

And he's tellin' me more and more

About some useless information..."

"Now that's more like it," Jack muttered as he pressed the accelerator. The engine responded in kind, purring into a scream as it hit 5,000 RPM, pressing him back into the seat like a jet on takeoff. The Fiat wasn't just a car—it was a mood, a medicine, an escape from anything he didn't want to feel.

He eased off near the traffic lights at Malahide Road. Fairview Park rolled by on his left, scattered with tulips and daffodils. Couples walked hand in hand on grassy paths, and teenagers shouted over Gaelic football and hurling matches. Summer had Dublin glowing.

Jack turned down North Strand Road. The breeze tangled through his hair, scented faintly with iodine from the coast. It cleared his mind. On the radio, *In the Summertime* by Mungo Jerry burst through with its carefree strumming:

"You got women, you got women on your mind

Have a drink, have a drive..."

He smiled. It was almost too perfect. Dublin, when the weather held, could feel like anywhere in the world—Paris, Barcelona, even California.

Crossing the Liffey over the Matt Talbot Bridge, the city shimmered below twilight. Streetlights blinked on like tiny stars reflecting in the water. Outside the riverside pubs, men clinked glasses, laughter bouncing from the cobblestones. There was something continental about the night. Jack turned into Lime Street, then Erne Street, and finally Holles Street, past the famous maternity hospital. He pulled up at Merrion Square. It was quiet here—safe. And he had no interest in finding the hood of his Spider sliced open by some jealous drunk.

He locked up the car and headed on foot toward Merrion Row, planning to swing by the Unicorn Restaurant to say hello to Sophie, his girlfriend. She was working the evening shift.

As he stepped inside the restaurant, the warm murmur of conversation washed over him—voices layered in half a dozen languages. Sophie spotted him instantly and lit up, her weariness momentarily forgotten as she danced toward the door.

"Comment ça va?" Jack asked, grinning.

"Oh, *j'en ai marre*," she replied with a tired smile. "Wrecked. Milo O'C and Paddy D. nearly came to blows earlier—over absolutely nothing. Too much wine, as usual."

She laughed, but it was tinged with fatigue. Some of the city's more colourful characters were known to make an entire day out of lunch—wine, digestifs, arguments, repeat.

"You alright though?" she asked.

"Grand," Jack said. "Meeting the lads next door. We'll catch up after, yeah? Oh, and I got a weird call this morning—but I'll fill you in over a jar later. *À toute à l'heure*, chérie."

Merrion Row pulsed with life as Jack crossed to O'Donoghue's. Outside the iconic black-and-white facade, he spotted his crew just ducking in.

"Lads!" he called.

"There you are, Jack!" Anto replied, waving him in.

O'Donoghue's was electric. The hum hit you before the door did. The first set of doors gave you a muffled preview—but open the second, and the place exploded into your senses: music, chatter, the low clink of pints, and a heat that wrapped around you like a wool coat. Packed to the rafters.

The pub's narrow corridor pulsed with bodies. A grand mirror hung above the bar, reflecting a kaleidoscope of faces. The wood-panelled walls bore black-and-white portraits of Dublin's musical royalty. At either end, the pub opened into cosy, living-room-like spaces where traditional music played nightly—songs and sometimes poems filling the air like incense.

At the bar stood Con, the legendary barman, perched atop his usual wooden box like a general surveying a battlefield.

"What are ye havin', lads?" Con barked.

"Jaysus, Con, you're on the ball tonight," Anto fired back.

"Just tell me what you fuckin' want!"

"Alright, alright—four pints of the black stuff."

You couldn't not meet people in O'Donoghue's. You were practically dancing around strangers from the moment you stepped in. The place was more than a pub—it was a living tradition. Tourists came here chasing Ireland; locals came to be themselves. Americans especially—searching for their roots, drinking in the music like it was something holy.

Just before eleven, Trigger showed up—two hours late, as usual. "Night Owl Plumbing," they called him, and the name fit. Instantly, Bradley and Anto pounced.

"Jaysus, Trigger—did you just finish the plumbing or are you still covered in the client's shampoo?"

"Don't start, ye bollocks. Order me a pint and stop flappin' your gums," Trigger fired back, grinning.

Danger, Lenny, and the rest roared with laughter, tossing in their own barbs to keep the banter rolling. It was what they did. It was a ritual.

Then Jack spotted Sophie entering at the far end of the pub, wading through the shoulder-to-shoulder crowd. Predictably, a few lads tried their luck.

"Hey, gorgeous, what's your name?"

"Can I get you a drink?"

Most of it was cheeky and harmless. But some crossed the line. In a place packed this tight, gropers were a constant hazard. Jack clenched his jaw but let her handle it—Sophie was no pushover.

She finally reached the group, flushed and grinning, where she was greeted with the usual round of mock-French cheek kisses and exaggerated gallantry.

"*La vache*, it's like a bloody sauna in here! And the noise!" she laughed, her French accent slicing through the din.

One of the lads' favourite pastimes was mocking Sophie's French accent, asking her to repeat tricky English words just for the laugh. She had arrived just in time—the bell was ringing for last orders. Official closing time was 11:30 p.m., and the bell chimed at 11:20. Of course, the whole system was more theatre than rule. Most patrons would double or even triple up their orders, some finishing with three pints and a short in front of them—a mountain of drink to conquer in minutes.

Lenny, true to form, was already clinging to the bar like it was a lifeboat on the Titanic.

"What are ye havin', lads? Hurry up, for fuck's sake! Sophie, what'll you drink, love?"

"I'll have a gin and tonic, please."

"Comin' up, *ma belle*," Lenny slurred with a wink.

Behind the counter, the barmen were run ragged—pulling pints, pouring shorts, juggling whiskeys, gins, vodkas, Bacardis—you name it. The place was chaos, but beautiful chaos.

Con, now back on his box to be seen above the crowd, shouted over the din: "Ladies and gents, we must clear—finish your drinks, please!"

The bar began to empty, patrons drifting out onto the street, many of them nursing their final drinks in plastic cups, unwilling to let the night end just yet. A jovial crowd gathered outside, filling the pavement with banter, laughter, and smoke trails curling up into the warm night air.

Not far from the group, a young couple was locked in a heated argument. Voices escalated. Suddenly, the tall, broad-shouldered man began slapping his girlfriend—open-handed, aggressive, and cruel.

Jack's spine stiffened.

Injustice always lit a fuse in him. His mates called him *the Sheriff* for a reason—he couldn't turn a blind eye.

He stepped forward, positioning himself between the man and the woman, shielding her from another strike. The aggressor snarled and landed a blow to Jack's head. It was clumsy, drunken, but solid.

Now seething, the man barked, "Fuck off, ya bollocks! Mind your own business. I'll fuckin' do ye!"

From behind, the lads were calling out—"Jack, leave it! Not your fight, man!"

But Jack's focus was razor-sharp. He raised both palms in a calming gesture and spoke quietly, trying to de-escalate. When it seemed the storm had passed, he turned his back, intending to leave them to their mess.

Then it happened.

The sharp crack of glass breaking.

Jack turned instinctively—a pivoting tenkai movement so fluid it seemed choreographed. He spotted the flash of a shattered pint glass, its jagged edge coming straight at his face.

He reacted without thinking.

A swift upward block—Jodan Uke—with his left arm deflected the attack, and in the same breath, he stepped forward with his right foot, driving a powerful Shotei palm-heel strike into the man's solar plexus.

The thug lurched back, his face twisted in shock, then collapsed to the pavement—gasping for air like a lifelong smoker sucking his last breath. Jack had deliberately avoided the head—one blow to the temple that could've killed him.

This was control. This was training.

Haragei—total awareness—had saved him. Jack's senses had absorbed the tension behind him, and his body had responded with lethal precision. His muscles, his reflexes—honed by years on the makiwara board, forged through bruises, blocks, sweat, and will— moved on instinct alone.

"For fuck's sake, Jack, come on! Let's leg it before the boys in blue show up asking all sorts," the lads yelled in unison.

Sophie clung to his arm, pulling him back.

"Leave it! Don't go checking on him—you had no choice. It was either you or him. He's okay, just winded."

Jack didn't answer. His jaw was tight. Since Okinawa, his greatest fear was taking a life by accident—especially over something so petty.

Across the street, cloaked in shadow, a figure named Johnny Tanaka observed the whole incident silently, a flicker of interest in his eyes.

They left quickly and made their way to Barbarella's—a trendy nightclub tucked away in Fitzwilliam Lane, just a stone's throw from O'Donoghue's. Jack never had a problem getting in. One of his students, James, worked the door.

The same couldn't always be said for the lads. More than once, they'd been turned away for being a little too "merry." But tonight, fortune smiled, and they were waved through the golden gates.

Barbarella's was a feast for the senses—plush interiors, neon lighting, and its signature waterfall bar. Go-go dancers in barely-there outfits swung across a shimmering pool on high swings. It was excess incarnate.

Jack remembered his return from Okinawa. That infamous night with the lads had ended not just at Barbarella's—but in the pool itself. James, mortified at the time, hadn't yet met Jack. Now they were friends—sensei and senpai. Time had a way of smoothing over chaos.

The lads wasted no time ordering Bacardi and Cokes. Sophie stuck to her gin and tonic. Jack, however, opted for a Britvic orange.

"What's wrong, Jack—your stomach at ya?" Anto shouted over the music. "Don't have too many of those Britvics now—they'll fry the auld neurones!"

Jack laughed, sipping the orange soda. He was at ease. The slagging, the noise—it all felt right.

The sound system erupted with the Stones' *Brown Sugar*:

"Brown Sugar, how come you taste so good.

Brown Sugar, just like a young girl should... ”

The place was a riot of colour and energy. Two Black men in bowler hats and canes strutted across the dancefloor like old-school showmen. Around them, mini-skirted girls swayed, twirled, and twisted—leaving little to the imagination.

The Bacardi was kicking in. The lads were in stitches. Lenny was in rare form, firing off jokes faster than anyone could breathe, drawing belly laughs from all corners.

The night was young. The city was alive. And for now, at least, all was well.

“Did you hear the one about the guy who thought an itchy gee was a Japanese motorbike?”

Needless to say, the gang collapsed in laughter, especially when Jack was given the awkward task of delicately explaining the essence of the joke to Sophie, whose English still wasn’t fluent. Anto was in his element, eyes watering from his own punchline.

The clock struck 4:00 a.m.—closing time was upon them. Jack excused himself to use the gents before leaving. As he approached the restroom, a man of Asian appearance and athletic build politely held the door open, offering Jack a glance and a nod. Jack took note, as he always did.

Outside, the group said their goodbyes on the pavement, parting ways into the sleeping city. Jack and Sophie took the short walk back to the Fiat, relieved to find it untouched. It wasn’t uncommon for sports car roofs to be slashed open by drunk thugs or envious passersby.

The coastal drive home was blissfully quiet. Dublin had surrendered to sleep. The warm air allowed Jack to pull the soft top down, exposing them to the open sky. They drove in peaceful silence, the only sounds being stray dogs overturning bins, cats yowling over territory, and the faint whisper of the sea.

Up ahead, Howth Head jutted into the black sea like a stone finger, dotted with lights—some from people returning home, others from insomniacs or early risers. The wind in Jack’s hair and the salty air in his lungs were the perfect antidote to the loud, smoke-filled pub.

Jack and Sophie didn't speak. They didn't need to. Carpe diem.

Suddenly, Jack's thoughts turned to the man who had opened the restroom door. Thanks to his training in Getsumei no Michi—*the moonlit path*—his middle consciousness began retrieving precise details. It wasn't just memory; it was a practised, subconscious decoding of every sensory impression.

The man was likely Japanese, with a strong European influence. Around 5'11" and about thirteen and a half stone, he was athletic, V-shaped, broad-shouldered, with jet-black hair. He wore wide-belted Levi's and a sky-blue Lacoste T-shirt with white armbands. His arms were powerful, and a tattoo marked the inside of his left forearm.

Getsumei no Michi, honed through daily discipline in Okinawa under Sensei Saito, allowed Jack to recall without *trying* to remember. The technique was not meditation, but rather a passive awareness—absorbing every detail into the unconscious, which could be accessed later like a photographic archive.

Jack had mastered it. And now it had kicked in, unbidden.

Could that man have been Johnny Tanaka? Dublin didn't have a large Asian population—mostly a small Chinese community, working in restaurants. Jack made a mental note: wait and see.

Back at the apartment, Jack and Sophie made love with an intensity only found in the early hours, before drifting into a deep, dreamless sleep that carried them well into Sunday morning.

They enjoyed a light breakfast on the terrace overlooking Dublin Bay—freshly squeezed orange juice, piping hot tea, and toasted brown bread slathered with coarse-cut marmalade. The view was peaceful; the day stretched ahead.

Jack never trained on Sundays. Though no longer a practising Catholic, he respected the idea of a day of rest. He looked forward to it: no phone calls, no students, no physical strain—only deep breathing and meditation.

Sophie, humming a Charles Aznavour tune, cleared the table:

Jack adored Sophie's humour—it was uplifting, and God knew he needed it after the trauma of Okinawa and Akiko's brutal death.

He lowered into a kiba-dachi horse stance and began his fifteen-minute deep breathing routine. To the untrained eye, it looked like nothing more than controlled breathing. But anyone who tried holding kiba-dachi for five minutes or more would quickly discover the burning pain, trembling muscles, and collapsing will.

Jack called it a dynamic-static exercise—designed to dissolve tension and free the mind. Sophie had long learned never to disturb him during this ritual. He would often enter the Theta state—7 to 8 Hz—an altered consciousness tied to spiritual insight.

There had been one occasion when she playfully jumped on him mid-session. The reflexes Jack had cultivated almost snapped her neck. She'd never done it again.

She didn't always understand his martial or esoteric side—but she loved him, so she accepted it.

Later, after ablutions, they decided to take a trip to Howth and walk the Loop Head trail. The Fiat Spider purred into life at the first turn of the key. The twin Weber car burettors inhaled air like hungry piglets on their mother's teats. Jack maintained the car religiously—regular spark plug and point changes ensured it never let him down.

He vividly recalled his father's old Fiat 1100, which would routinely stall—especially on rainy mornings when Jack had to accompany him to work. Often they'd end up on the dreaded C.I.E. bus, notorious for its tardiness. His father would arrive late to the Independent Newspapers, cursing the car under his breath.

But good old Paddy Murphy always sorted things out by evening.

"Jaysus, Tom!" Paddy would shout. "Do you even know how to open the shaggin' bonnet? It was just a loose plug lead!"

"Good man, Paddy," Tom would reply, "How much do I owe you?"

"Would you shag off, Hopkins. Buy me a pint in the Rendez instead." The Rendezvous, their local pub.

Jack often had to jog the half-mile to Thatch Road, where Paddy lived, to report the latest car or house issue—since there was no phone in the house at the time.

Paddy was a jack-of-all-trades. A former army man who cycled thirty miles daily, he had become a taxi driver, a plumber, a mechanic, a welder, an electrician—you name it. Sharp as a tack, he should've been an engineer, but a modest background made university out of reach.

Jack was always welcome at the Murphy household. Tessy, Paddy's second wife, always greeted him warmly, her inner-city roots evident in her humour and spirit. Helen, their daughter, was another reason Jack enjoyed visiting. She was three years older than him, fifteen, and stunning. Her miniskirts—fashionable in the 60s—showed off long, silky thighs that made Jack blush crimson.

Paddy loved teasing him about it.

"Jaysus, Paddy, leave him alone—he's only a child," Tessy would say, laughing. "You're embarrassing him!"

But Paddy would chuckle from his leather armchair, pipe in hand.

"Hello, Jack! What tale of woe brings you this time? The car is acting up again, is it?"

Jack would shuffle awkwardly. "The car won't start, Mr. Murphy."

Paddy exhaled a cloud of blue smoke. "Is the motor turning over, Jack?"

"It is, Mr. Murphy."

Paddy would lean back, pipe between his lips—a picture of Sherlock Holmes in deep thought.

"Right then. Probably pitted points, or the gap needs adjusting. Might be condensation in the distributor cap."

To Jack, it was all double Dutch—but he nodded anyway.

"Tell that aul fella of yours I'll swing by later. I'm heading to the Rendez for a pint anyway."

Jack would sprint the mile back home to deliver the message—and his father would wait, confident that Paddy would, as always, work his magic.

Paddy was never long in turning up. He'd arrive in his beige Hillman Hunter, pulling up like a cavalryman to save the day. Jack would hear the familiar double-beep of the horn, then the car door slam shut. Moments later, Paddy was at the front door, pipe clenched between his teeth and toolbox in hand.

"Right so, Tom—let's have a gander at this bollox of a car."

Jack would often tag along to observe, although the mechanical process remained a mystery to him. The bonnet would pop, the tools would clatter, and within ten minutes, Paddy had diagnosed the fault. Usually a worn contact, a dirty spark plug, or a loose wire. Nothing too grave, but enough to throw Jack's father's day into chaos.

"She'll start now," Paddy would declare with a self-satisfied puff of his pipe, "if she doesn't, I'll eat my hat."

Sure enough, the engine would sputter, then hum back to life.

"Good man, Paddy," Tom would say, his mood instantly lifted.

"Ah, it's nothin'—I'll take a pint of Guinness in the Rendez, and we'll call it square."

Jack always admired Paddy's easy charm and competence. He was the kind of man who made you feel things were never beyond fixing. As a child, Jack often wished he could be more like him—unshakable, grounded, always knowing what to do.

The memories stirred as the Fiat Spider cruised toward Howth. The road curled gently along the coast, sunlight flickering off the water. Sophie's scarf fluttered in the breeze, her hair swept back like something from a French film. She was singing softly again—another Aznavour number—lost in her own world.

Loop Head was their destination—a favourite of theirs. The sea cliffs, the salt-tinged wind, the steady rhythm of waves crashing against the rocks—it had a way of cleansing the mind. Jack parked near the Summit Inn and took Sophie's hand as they began the walk.

The path wound along the edge, daring them to peer over the cliffside. Below, the Irish Sea stretched endlessly, moody and blue. Seagulls wheeled and called above them as the distant ferry crossed toward Wales.

Sophie squeezed Jack's hand.

"You seem pensive today," she said gently.

Jack smiled but didn't respond immediately. How could he explain the weight of memory? The man in the restroom. The reflexive violence in front of O'Donoghue's. The ghosts of Okinawa that never really let go. Even Paddy Murphy's laughter seemed distant now, a comforting echo of a world long past.

"Just remembering," he said finally.

Sophie nodded. "Good memories or bad?"

"A bit of both."

They stopped at a bench overlooking the bay. Jack exhaled deeply, the wind pulling at his jacket. Sophie leaned her head on his shoulder, and for a few minutes, neither of them spoke.

Below them, the sea kept moving, as it always had.

Jack ran down the stairs from the first floor of his apartment into the car park. There, his 1979 Ferrari red Fiat Spider was waiting for its pilot. Jack never tired of looking at his car; if there was such a thing as art in motion, then this was it. He installed himself in the leather bucket seat and fired up the engine.

The two-litre twin overhead cam engine equipped with twin choke Weber carburettors revved up and sucked in the air like a massive bellows. This was music to Jack's ears as it heralded all the driving pleasure that would follow. He undid the clips on each side of the cabin, got out and folded back the black hood. Sitting back behind the wheel, he turned on the broadband radio with the four inbuilt

Pioneer 15-watt stereo speakers.

As he exited the car park, Bill Withers was singing *Ain't No Sunshine when she's gone*, Jack immediately changed stations looking for something more rock 'n roll, not songs that brought bad memories flooding back … Akiko and Okinawa. He found Mick Jagger belting out Satisfaction

…And that man comes on the radio; And he's tellin' me more and more; About some useless information; Supposed to fire my imagination; I can't get no, oh no no no.

That was more like it, thought Jack as he pressed down on the accelerator. The engine responded immediately, revving up to 5,000 rpm and pushing Jack back into his bucket seat, a spine-tingling, exhilarating sensation. The little Fiat was a real pleasure machine. He slowed as he approached the lights and the junction of the Malahide Road. Fairview Park was on his left, dotted here and there with tulips and daffodils and plentiful with lush green grass where lovers walked and courted.

Young teenagers were playing ball, either soccer or Gaelic football and hurling, the park was buzzing on this beautiful Summer's evening. Jack continued down into the North Strand Road, feeling the breeze in his hair and breathing in the iodine-filled air. It felt good. The Pioneer radio was blasting out Mungo Jerry's in the Summertime.

In the summertime, when the weather is hot, you can stretch right up and touch the sky; When the weather's fine, you got women, you've got women on your mind; Have a drink, have a drive; Go out and see what you can find.

The evening traffic was moving smoothly as he arrived at the Five Lamps, a famous landmark in Dublin City and then into Amiens Street. He crossed the River Liffey over the Matt Talbot Bridge and continued down City Quay. Street lights were just being turned on, and the effect all down the river was both cosy and fairy-like. There were lots of people outside pubs drinking their beers and shorts, chatting away and making the most of the good weather and solving all the problems of mankind.

The whole atmosphere felt very Continental. He turned right up

Lime Street and into Erne Street before arriving at Holles Street, Holles Street Hospital being another famous baby factory in Dublin. He arrived at Merrion Square, a nice green area of the city where he had decided to park his car. It was only a short walk to O'Donoghue's pub, and it was a fairly quiet area at night; he didn't want to risk having the hood of the Fiat being ripped open with a knife by some drunken or jealous gouger.

He had intended to pop his head into the Unicorn Restaurant and say hello to his girlfriend Sophie, where she worked as a waitress. Jack arrived in Merrion Row and proceeded to walk up the lane to the Unicorn Restaurant. He popped his head in the door to a throng of voices holding different conversations. Sophie immediately saw him; she released a big smile and skipped down to say hello. *Comment ça va? How is it goin',* says Jack

Oh, j'en ai marre, I'm fed up, been on the go all day. Milo O'C and Paddy D. were arguing and nearly came to fisticuffs over something stupid. Too much wine, I suppose she laughs. It wasn't uncommon for certain known personalities to stay the whole day from lunch time onward, sipping wine and digestives. And how are you, Jack?

"I'm grand in fine form. Meeting up with the lads next door, so we'll catch up together after work. Yeah, one thing though, I got a strange phone call this morning, but I'll tell you all about it later over a jar. A toute à l'heure chérie, see you later."

Jack made his way to O'Donoghue's pub and came across some of the lads just entering the main entrance. The black and white exterior was a well-known landmark in Dublin city. It was the birthplace of many famous traditional music bands and musicians such as The Dubliners, Christy Moore, the Bothy Band, The Fureys, and the list goes on, not to mention the famous people who had visited the pub over the years, from sports personalities to politicians. It was a melting pot of culture and race where locals and tourists mingled and chatted.

In some cases, it was the place where love stories began. "Hiya lads", shouts Jack. "There you are, Jack", echoes Anto. O'Donoghues was as packed as ever. For anyone who had never been to the pub before, it was certainly an experience not to be missed. On opening the first door, one could hear a kind of low baritone drone.

However, on opening the second door, the noise exploded into one's ears with the sound of music, voices engaged in different conversations and an overwhelming heat. It was packed just like the proverbial sardines in a tin. There was a very cosy sensation, however, just like coming to someone's house for a party. The *craic,* fun was ninety.

The main artery of the pub was quite narrow, with a huge mirror as the central showpiece and wood-panelled walls. Black and white photos of various musicians and famous people adorned the walls. Both ends of the pub opened up into what one could consider as living rooms, this was where the music was played, songs were sung and where poetry on certain quieter occasions was recited.

As usual, Con, the barman, was standing on a box behind the bar just at the entrance. It made it much easier to place an order, as trying to get to the bar was an exercise in itself.

What are ye havin', lads shouts Con. Jaysus, you're on the ball tonight, hisses Anto. Just tell me what you fuckin' want roars Con. Okay, cranky four pints of Guinness it is. One couldn't help meeting people in O'Donoghue's; you literally bumped into them. The place was electric, nothing but good vibes.

Everyone was there to enjoy themselves and the traditional Irish music. It was like a magnet for tourists, especially Americans eager to catch up on their Irish heritage and culture. True to form, Trigger "night owl plumbing" showed his face at a quarter to eleven, just nearly two hours late. This gave plenty of ammunition to Bradley and Anto to start a fierce and unrelenting slagging match, which everyone enjoyed immensely. It was harmless fun but great free entertainment.

Jaysus Trigger, are you just out of the shower, or did you just finish plumbing one? Sneers Anto. Don't you start your bollocks, shut up and order me a pint and make yourself useful for once retorts Trigger. Of course, Danger, Lenny and Bradley were lapping all this up, throwing in the occasional caustic remark to keep the slagging going. Jack spotted Sophie coming through the door at the far end of the pub and trying to beat her way through the throng of patrons.

She was the butt of remarks such as "Hey, gorgeous, what's your name? Can I offer you a drink"? Most of the time, it was innocent fun, but there were also the guys who went overboard, and of course, the gropers, which was made very easy by the inevitable close body contact. She eventually made her way to the end of the bar, much to the lads' delight, where she was greeted with eager smiles and, of course, the inevitable French custom of kissing both cheeks, which they had become accustomed to and insisted upon each time they met her.

Yeah, real French gentlemen! La vache, it's like a sauna in here and the noise, says Sophie in her strong French accent.

One of the lads' favourite pastimes was slagging Sophie over her accent and asking her to repeat difficult words in English. Sophie had arrived just in time as the bell was ringing for last orders. Official closing time was 11.30 pm and the bell rang for last orders at 11.20. The whole thing was a farce, as most people doubled or tripled their orders, and some guys finished up with three pints and a short to imbibe in a very short space of time.

So Lenny, who was the best advertisement for last orders, was already clinging to the bar as though his life depended on it.

What are ye havin' lads, hurry up for fuck sake?

Sophie, what do you want to drink, love? I'll have a gin and tonic, please. Comin' up, my belle. The barmen were literally run off their feet. From pints of all sorts to shorts, whiskeys, gins, vodkas, bacardis, etc. It had to be seen to be believed.

At this stage, Con the barman was back up on his box shouting: "Ladies and gents, we must clear, finish your drinks please". The bar started to empty as the patrons trickled out slowly onto the path, most of them carrying their precious beverages with them to be finished outside and thus prolonging the festivities. A fair crowd had now gathered on the pavement with the usual banter and good-natured fun.

Not far away, a couple in their twenties were having a heated argument. One thing led to the other, and the guy who was tall and broad-shouldered started slapping his beloved around the place. Of course, this immediately caught Jack's attention, who hated any form of injustice and always defended the underdog. His friends referred to him as the sheriff for obvious reasons.

Jack decided to intervene as the girl risked serious injury from such a violent onslaught, and the fact that alcohol had been consumed made things worse. He stood in front of the girl to protect her and took a blow to the head for his troubles. The boyfriend was now blue with anger, and Jack was the object of an avalanche of bad language and curses :

Fuck off, you bollocks and mind your own business. I'll fuckin' do ye.

The lads were calling to Jack, telling him to leave them to their problems. Jack, however, managed to calm down the situation and decided to turn on his heels and leave them to their privacy. No sooner had he turned his back than he heard the unmistakable sound of breaking glass. Jack immediately spun on himself *tenkai* just in time to see the broken pint glass coming straight into his face.

He performed a powerful upper block *Jodan Uke* with his left arm, and stepping forward with his right foot, slammed a powerful palm heel strike *Shotei* into the man's solar plexus. The man rocked backwards and fell heavily onto the pavement. He was left gasping for his breath like someone who had smoked twenty Woodbines every day all his life. He deliberately avoided striking the man's head, knowing that it could have been a fatal blow. *Haragei,* or total awareness, had allowed Jack to detect movement behind him, and his body had responded accordingly.

The movements which he had practised over and over were ingrained into his body cells so that the technique became a natural movement. His body had been forged by the fire of his will and conditioned by thousands of repeated movements on the *makiwara* punching board and hours of bruising and painful blocking techniques with his colleagues.

Come on, for fuck sake, Jack, let's beat it before the boys in Blue show up asking all kinds of questions shouted the lads in unison. Sophie was clinging to Jack, making sure he didn't go back to check on the guy's well-being. You had no choice; it was either you or him.

Anyway, he's okay, just catching his breath. After the incidents in Okinawa, Jack's deepest nightmare was taking another man's life, especially in such a minor incident as this. On the other side of the street, hidden by the shadows, a certain Johnny Tanaka had observed the entire incident with great interest.

They headed off to finish the night at Barbarella's, a trendy nightclub in Fitzwilliam Lane, a stone's throw from O'Donoghue's Bar. Jack never had any trouble gaining admittance, as one of his students, James, was among the doormen. The same couldn't be said for the lads, though, as they usually had difficulty gaining entrance, usually due to the consumption of too much alcohol.

But tonight, everyone got past the golden gates. Barbarella's was well known for its lavish décor and, of course, the waterfall bar where scantily clad gogo dancers swung across the pool on a swing. On Jack's return from Okinawa a few years back, the lads had gone out on the town and had not only finished the night in the club but in the actual pool itself, much to the embarrassment of James, whom Jack didn't know at the time.

But the dust had settled, and they had become the best of friends and at the same time sensei, teacher and senpai, senior student. The lads got stuck into the Bacardi and Cokes while Sophie sipped her Gin and tonic. Jack had decided to take it easy and had ordered a Britvic orange, much to the scorn and slagging from the gang, especially Anto :

"What's wrong, Jack, is your stomach at ye? Don't have too many of those Britvics now, they're bad for the auld neurones!" Jack was enjoying the banter and was feeling totally relaxed. The sound system blasted out the Rolling Stones' Brown Sugar: *"Brown Sugar, how come you taste so good Brown Sugar, just like a young girl should"*

The place was in a frenzy. Two blacks in bowler hats and canes strutted like peacocks on the dance floor, along with mini-skirted young women who didn't leave much to the imagination. The lads were having the crack, and the Bacardis were having the required effect. The auld Lenny was in great fettle and was telling jokes to beat the band.

Did you hear the one about the guy who thought that an itchy gee was a Japanese motorbike?. Needless to say, the gang fell about laughing and even more so when Jack was given the ungrateful task of delicately explaining the essence of the joke to Sophie, whose English wasn't quite fluent. Anto was having a ball. The clock struck 4.00, so closing time was imminent.

Jack went to the gents to relieve himself before leaving the premises. A man of oriental extraction and athletic build kindly held the toilet door open as Jack approached and looked him up and down.

Everyone said goodbye outside on the street before heading their separate ways. Jack and Sophie had a short walk back to the car, which they gladly found in one piece. It wasn't unusual for canvas roofs on sports cars to be ripped open by drunk thugs or jealous passersby. The drive back along the coast was pleasant and quiet,

Dublin was asleep. It was warm enough for Jack to let the hood of the Fiat down, which made it easier to appreciate the complete calm that the city provided at the early hours of the morning. The only sounds were stray dogs turning over bins and fighting over scraps of food, and cats marking their territory.

Up in the distance, Howth Head jutted out into the sea like a sore thumb, house lights lit up randomly, either people coming home from a night out or someone doing their ablutions or maybe insomniacs. The cool wind in the hair and the smell of the sea were more than welcome after a noisy smoke filled environment. Jack and Sophie didn't exchange a word; there was no need to, carpe diem.

Suddenly, Jack's thoughts were filled with the image of the man who had so kindly held open the toilet door earlier on. Thanks to his enhanced powers of observation, along with the technique of *getsumei no michi* – the moonlit path, all the details came back one by one as his middle layer of consciousness deciphered every detail very vividly.

The man was of Asian extraction, probably Japanese, with a strong European influence. About 5 feet 11 for thirteen and a half stone. He was an athletic V shape, trim with broad shoulders and jet black hair. He was wearing wide-belted Levi's jeans with a Lacoste sky blue tee-shirt with white armbands. He had powerful arms and a tattoo on the inside of his left forearm.

Getsumei no michi, practised regularly, eventually became automatic. The technique involved letting go of one's imagination and thus not focusing on any detail in particular, but on the contrary absorbing everything into the unconscious mind, which would later on be emptied detail by detail just as Jack was doing. He had practised the moonlit path daily during his training in Okinawa, having been initiated by Sensei Saito. He had explained that in no case should it be compared to mediation, but simply letting go of the mind and absorbing everything that one observed.

Jack now mastered the technique, and it kicked into place naturally. So, could this be Mister Johnny Tanaka? Dublin wasn't swarmed with people of Asian extraction, apart from a small Chinese community, all working in the restaurant business. Let's just wait and see, Jack thought to himself.

On arriving at the apartment, Jack and Sophie had made passionate love before falling into a deep comatic sleep, which brought them into the late hours of Sunday morning. They had a light breakfast on the terrace overlooking Dublin Bay, starting off with freshly squeezed orange juice and followed by a pot of piping hot tea and toasted brown bread with butter and marmalade, coarse cut of course. Jack refrained from doing any physical activity on Sundays, preferring to rest the body and respect the Lord's day, even though he was no longer a practising Catholic and had little or no time for religion.

The idea of a day off pleased him immensely, and he actually looked forward to it. Doing nothing, except for his daily deep breathing exercises and meditation. Sophie cleared off the breakfast table in her usual good spirits, humming a song of Charles Aznavour :

Emmenez-moi au bout de la terre, Emmenez-moi au pays des merveilles, Il me semble que la misère serait moins pénible au soleil.

Jack adored Sophie's good humour; it was contagious, and God knows he needed it after his traumatic experiences in Okinawa and Akiko's murder. He sank into the *kiba-dachi* horse stance and began his deep breathing and meditation, which would last 15 minutes. It was a cleansing and replenishing exercise. To the neophyte, it appeared to be a simple breathing exercise.

One just had to adopt the position and try and hold it for five minutes or more. After a certain time, it becomes very difficult to maintain the stance as the muscles begin to tremble and finish by collapsing. It was what Jack called a dynamic static exercise, which was designed to dissolve tension and free the mind. Sophie knew from experience never to disturb Jack when he was practising this exercise, as he was in an altered state of consciousness, usually in the third level known as Theta between 7 Hz and 8 Hz and a state of spiritual enlightenment and exceptional insight.

The one and only time that Sophie had literally jumped on him jokingly, she had almost lost her life. Jack had been dragged out of his second state of consciousness and had just stopped short of breaking her neck. She always found it difficult to understand his esoteric and martial side, but she loved him, and so she accepted it totally.

After their ablutions, Jack and Sophie decided to take a trip out to Howth and do the walk around Loop Head. The Fiat Spider fired up on the first turn of the key, and the twin carbs sucked in the air like hungry piglets on their mother's teats. Jack serviced the car regularly and made sure that the spark plugs and points were changed at regular intervals.

One of the most annoying things is a car that won't start due to a lack of servicing or negligence. He had vivid memories of his Father's Fiat 1100, which always decided not to start on mornings when Jack would be accompanying him to work, and it was lashing rain. Sometimes, I ended up taking a C.I.E. bus, which was notorious for its bad time-keeping, which meant arriving late at work in the Independent Newspapers.

Of course his Dad's good friend and excellent mechanic Paddy Murphy would be always on hand that evening to sort out the Fiat's mechanical issues. "Jaysus Tom", he'd shout "do you know how to open the shaggin' bonnet. It was just one of the plug leads that was undone"."Good man Paddy", would retort Tom, how much do I owe you. "Would you shag off Hopkins, you can get me a pint down in the Rendez."

The local pub being known as the Rendezvous. As there was no phone in the family house at the time, Jack remembered only too well the numerous occasions when he would have to run around to Thatch Road, a half a mile or so, where Mr. Murphy resided, to relate the latest mechanical issues or domestic problems.

Paddy Murphy was a man of all trades, who could turn his hand to anything. He had spent several years in the army. He would do the daily cycle to the barracks, there and back, a gruelling 30-mile cycle in all kinds of weather. It was character-forming. He had learnt to drive in the army, among other things.

From a taxi man to a mechanic, plumber, welder, electrician, Paddy had touched at most trades in a small space of time, and to boot, he was extremely intelligent. He should have gone on to third-level education and become a qualified engineer, but alas, as he came from a modest working-class family, this was not to be. Jack was always greeted at the door by Tessy, Paddy's second wife, his first wife having died prematurely, as was the case with Tessy herself, losing her first husband at an early age.

They had two children each from their first weddings and Helen from their own union. Jack liked being called by the Murphys. Tessy, who originally came from the inner city, was the salt of the earth, was always in good humour and gave a great welcome. Another reason was Helen, who was there on most occasions. Jack found her very pretty; she was 15 and 3 years his senior. As was the fashion in the 60s, she wore miniskirts showing off her long, silky, soft thighs. Jack always went scarlet red at such a pleasing sight. Paddy, of course, knew this and got a great kick out of it, throwing in innuendos and remarks here and there.

Tessy would have to interject."Jaysus, Paddy, leave him alone, he's only a child. You're embarrassing him".Paddy always got a great kick out of it. He was sitting in his favourite leather chair beside the fire with the pipe in his mouth and his thumb pressing down on the bowl."Hello Jack, how are you? What tale of woe brings you by this time? I suppose that banger of a car is causing problems again", shouts Paddy, "or there's a problem in the house"

"The car won't start, Mr. Murphy", says Jack coyly. Paddy blew out the blue smoke, "Is the motor turning over, Jack?"

"It is Mr. Murphy."

With that, Paddy would sit back in his chair, taking a draw from his pipe. At that particular instant, Jack always thought of Sherlock Holmes in a deep and pensive mood, trying to find the solution to a mysterious crime."Right, Jack", says Paddy, that's either due to pitted points or the gap that may have to be reset.

There may also be a bit of condensation in the distributor cap."Of course, this was all double Dutch to Jack, who knew little or nothing about mechanics.

"Tell that old fella of yours that I'll be around later on this evening on my way to the Rendez for my pint."Jack would always run the mile or so back to the house and give his father Paddy's message.

When the ego dies, the soul awakens ...

Gandhi

CHAPTER
Six

Dublin present

The radio blasted out Michael Jackson's *Thriller* as the Fiat coasted along the coast road toward Sutton Cross. The hood was down, and the wind caught Sophie's long blonde mane, *twisting and flicking like serpents in a storm.* Jack couldn't help but smile at the sight.

They drove through Sutton Cross, famously the only crossroads in Europe where all four directions lead to the sea. It was just after midday when they arrived in the small fishing village of Howth. Jack managed to find one of the rare available parking spaces on the pier. With the fine weather, it seemed like half of Dublin had the same idea as Jack and Sophie.

Dressed casually, they set off for the 6.5 km walk around the headland, which at a leisurely pace took about two hours. Jack and Sophie, seasoned walkers, usually did the round trip in an hour and a half. Being a talented cook, as many French women were, Sophie delighted in picking the wild thyme that grew abundantly among the heather on the head.

They never tired of the sweeping views and the rich palette of colours spread across the heather-strewn landscape. It was both invigorating and spiritually soothing. Since Jack's return from Okinawa and the trauma he'd carried back, Howth Head had been his sanctuary. He'd run its trails in rain and wind while others sat snug by their firesides. It gave him the balance he needed to keep moving forward.

After the walk, they returned to the car to change into more comfortable shoes before heading to the King Sitric fish restaurant with its iconic red facade. Nothing like a brisk walk to stir the appetite—something the French seemed genetically attuned to, with "Bon appétit" a ritual before every meal.

The King Sitric was renowned for its fresh fish dishes, with a menu that shifted daily based on the morning's local catch. From monkfish to plaice, cod, turbot, sea trout, and magnificent prawns—the selection was always mouthwatering. It was one of Jack and Sophie's favourite restaurants, a treat they afforded themselves once a month. Not only was the food outstanding, but the clientele often included Dublin's social elite, journalists, and media personalities, which gave the restaurant a unique buzz.

Sophie enjoyed people-watching, especially the women, taking note of expensive brand names and the details of high-end fashion. Jack nudged her discreetly.

"Look over your shoulder—Gary Byrne's here with his family, sipping Bollinger," he whispered.

Jack also spotted Charles Heaney, one of Ireland's most controversial and charismatic socialites. A former Minister for Health and Finance, he was now Taoiseach. Seated at a large circular table with an entourage, Jack couldn't help but wonder if it was an unofficial cabinet meeting or just a well-lubricated Sunday lunch. Bollinger flowed there, too.

Jack had met Heaney the previous year when he was assigned as the personal bodyguard to French President François Mitterrand during his three-day visit to Ireland. Mitterrand and Heaney were old friends.

Jack ordered a bottle of Chablis. They both opted for the fresh crab salad to start, followed by sea bass and seasonal vegetables, finishing with strawberries and cream for dessert and a round of coffee. The drive home in the late afternoon, hood down, wind in their faces, was pure delight. Moments to be savoured—carpe diem.

They ended the evening on the terrace, sipping tea and watching the sun melt into Dublin Bay—a sight Jack never tired of. The combination of fresh sea air and a good walk left them with a pleasant, healthy fatigue. They turned in early, wrapped in each other's arms, their day ending as serenely as it had begun.

The following morning, Jack rose with the dawn. He opened the terrace doors just in time to watch the sun peek over the horizon. It was 5:30 a.m. These were the moments when he felt most privileged, most alive. Something almost sacred washed over him. Naturally, memories of Akiko and Okinawa surfaced—all those sunrises and sunsets shared over his six years on the island. Eternal soulmates.

He downed a glass of freshly squeezed orange juice, slipped into a t-shirt and shorts, and set off for his daily five-mile run. At this early hour, the seafront was deserted, save for the occasional car. Jack believed the day belonged to those who rose early.

His thoughts drifted toward his upcoming encounter with Johnny Tanaka. It wasn't every day one got to measure himself against a 6th dan black belt.

Returning to the apartment, Jack collected his copy of the Independent from the letterbox. He always enjoyed his morning read. Sophie was still asleep, her golden hair strewn across the pillow in a Medusa-like swirl. An angel in repose, he thought.

He stepped into the Italian shower, first steaming hot, then ice cold. The bracing finish fired him into high gear. After towelling off vigorously, he prepared breakfast: fresh juice, a pot of tea, toast with butter and coarse-cut marmalade. Sophie adored being served in bed and reading the morning headlines. She waited on others five days a week; pampering her brought Jack great joy.

Serving and being served were, to him, two halves of the same whole.

Sophie stirred, stretching and groaning softly as she brushed the hair from her eyes. Jack placed the tray on her lap.

"Bon appétit," he smiled.

"Merci, ma chérie," Sophie whispered. "Oh non, pas encore," she groaned, glancing at the newspaper.

The headline announced flash strikes by C.I.E., the national public transport company. Sophie, a frequent bus commuter, was directly affected.

"Looks like you'll need your running shoes," Jack chuckled. "Or I can drive you in, no hassle."

Sophie opted to walk—the weather was fine, and she figured an hour's stroll would do wonders for her figure, not that she needed to. Still, like many women, she remained conscious of that particular area, as did the male gaze.

Jack decided to take the day slow with a long walk down the Bull Wall, soaking in the summer sun. He planned to arrive at the dojo early to ensure everything was spotless. A 5th dan black belt wasn't an everyday visitor.

Usually, students arrive 15 minutes before class to clean the dojo. Today, however, Sensei Jack had already taken care of it.

Their guest, Johnny Tanaka, arrived just before 7 p.m. as Jack stepped onto the dojo floor. The students were already seated in the seiza position. Tanaka entered without bowing, which infuriated Jack, though he maintained composure and directed him politely to the changing room.

Tanaka re-emerged in a black keikogi typical of American Kenpo, his worn black belt displaying five red tips. Jack's imposing gaze left no room for interpretation. The visitor bowed before stepping onto the mat and was invited to sit in the front row, far right, among the senior ranks.

Class began with twenty minutes of warm-up and breathing exercises. Jack integrated techniques he had learned from Tibetan monks in Okinawa, routines he swore by for their health benefits. They moved on to kata for thirty minutes, focusing on posture and form. Though often associated with martial arts, kata are used in various Japanese traditions, from kabuki theatre to tea ceremonies.

They transitioned into modern self-defence techniques before ending with light sparring. Jack grew increasingly displeased with Tanaka's heavy-handedness. He was striking too hard, clearly enjoying the pain he inflicted.

At 9 p.m., the class concluded with bows of respect. The students filed out, leaving Jack and Tanaka alone.

Now the real fun begins, Jack thought.

Both men bowed politely before assuming their fighting postures. Jack settled into a right neutral bow position, while his opponent adopted a left-footed cat stance, neko dachi. The man attacked swiftly, powerfully, and with surgical precision: a left front snap kick followed by a straight reverse punch. This guy meant business.

Jack shuffled back, blocking both blows with his right arm. He then stepped into a left bow stance to intercept the long right front kick and a sharp back-knuckle strike aimed at his head. With a double knife-hand block, he caught the strike, seized the man's sleeve with his right hand, and drove a powerful backhand into the rib cage with his left.

The man gasped under the blow's impact, then spun using tenkan, driving a vicious elbow between Jack's shoulder blades. Simultaneously, he swept Jack's leg out from under him, sending him thundering onto the tatami and leaving him momentarily breathless. The introductions were made.

Jack now knew this wasn't a friendly sparring session. This was real. This was war.

He leapt to his feet. A slimy grin smeared across his opponent's face told Jack the fight was far from over. They returned to their stances — Jack in his favoured right neutral bow, the other man mirroring him with that same smirk.

Suddenly, his opponent lunged forward with two brutal backhands aimed at Jack's temple. Jack blocked the attacks with his right arm, but in doing so, left his ribs exposed. An explosive side kick lifted him clean off the ground, slamming him into the stretching rail on the dojo wall.

The man pressed forward with a strong mae geri keage, a front snapping kick, which Jack barely blocked with his left forearm. Spinning on his left foot using irimi tenkan, Jack drove a right elbow strike into the attacker's back. Transitioning into a left stance, he followed up with a tetsui, a hammer-fist blow to the base of the neck. His opponent crumbled to the floor, semi-conscious.

Pain surged through Jack's ribs. He knew at least one was cracked, but adrenaline was his ally.

"Let's call it a draw," Jack shouted.

"Fuck you, man. I'm here to put you six feet under and see you whinging for mercy."

"But why, for Christ's sake?"

"You'll know soon enough, asshole," the man hissed.

Sweat dripped from his face as he stripped off his black keikogi. His muscular torso glistened, and Jack's eyes fell on the tattoo over his left pectoral: five stars — i punt della malavita. A Sicilian mafia brand.

Jack froze.

Memories assaulted him. The same tattoo. Joey Falconetti, the drug-dealing marine he'd left half-crippled in a bar in Okinawa after Akiko's brutal death. Falconetti, one of her attackers.

The nightmare had returned. Standing before him now as Johnny Tanaka, mafia hitman.

Jack realised this fight was going to the bitter end. He despised violence for its own sake. Shorin-te was a martial art of defence. But now, this was survival. His life was on the line.

His master, Sensei Saito, had been clear: deadly force was justified only in defence of life. And now, it was.

He centred himself.

Concentrating on his seika tanden, the core of his being, he summoned his ki, his inner energy. Physically, it was the body's centre of gravity. Spiritually, it was his source of power.

"Where attention goes, ki flows."

By placing awareness there, Jack deepened body-mind integration and grounded his spirit in the moment.

They squared off. Right neutral bow stances. Jack knew only one of them would walk away.

His opponent lunged: a uraken back-knuckle strike to the temple, then a ketomi thrust kick. Jack blocked both, but couldn't evade the lightning-fast mawashi geri roundhouse kick to the head. It sent him crashing to one knee.

Smelling blood, Tanaka followed with a left kick to the sternum. Jack flew backwards onto his back.

But Jack was ready.

As the man rushed in for the kill, Jack hooked his right foot around the attacker's ankle, simultaneously slamming his left foot into his opponent's knee. With a pull-and-push motion, he sent him sprawling.

Jack rose in one fluid motion. He allowed Tanaka to stand. He wanted to finish it clean.

The smirk returned to Tanaka's face.

Jack remained calm, focusing his ki into the seika tanden in preparation. Tanaka charged with a flurry of punches, screaming:

"Fuck you, pal, you're a dead man!"

Jack absorbed the onslaught, stepping into a left neutral stance, ai-hanmi, and countered with a devastating ketomi thrust kick to the solar plexus. He unleashed a kiai shout.

Tanaka flew backwards, crashing into the dojo wall. The very walls trembled.

Blood trickled from Tanaka's lips.

The kick had caused internal bleeding. He now knew he was outmatched. This was the end.

Desperate, his eyes darted to the katana mounted on the wall — Jack's farewell gift from Akiko's father, Ichiro, who had taught him kenjutsu. Tanaka seized the sword.

Jack's heart froze.

The way the man held the blade showed experience. This wasn't a bluff.

There could be no hesitation now. Jack had to be flawless.

The sword's edge gleamed, razor sharp.

Jack sank into the void. The no-mind state: mushin no shin.

No anger. No fear. No ego.

Not calculation, but instinct.

A mind like water. Flowing. Still. Waiting.

Because in swordplay, hesitation meant death.

His opponent assumed the guard *Hasso no Kamae*, the katana held vertically at the right side of his head. Jack moved into a neutral stance. The blade came down with blinding speed toward Jack's head, but he was already stepping into his opponent's space, using *irimi tenkan*—entering and turning on his right foot—while simultaneously delivering a powerful *hiji-zuki* (elbow strike) to his opponent's solar plexus. Johnny Tanaka dropped onto his left knee, gasping for breath, his face twisted in a slimy smirk.

He quickly got back to his feet and assumed *Hidari Gedan no Kamae*, a left-side guard with the sword held low. The man lunged forward with *chudan tsuki*, a mid-level thrust aimed at Jack's abdomen. Jack narrowly avoided it by leaping to his left, grasping Tanaka's right wrist and smashing his own right fist into the man's face. Seizing the opportunity, Jack applied *kotegaeshi*, a powerful wrist lock that flipped Tanaka onto his back and sent the katana flying across the room, embedding itself in the dojo wall.

Scrambling toward the wall in a desperate attempt to retrieve the weapon, Tanaka charged wildly, slashing in all directions. He had lost control—but remained deadly. The katana could slice through bone like a hot knife through butter. Jack braced himself. This would be the final act. He had to wait for the right moment—to blend with his opponent's movement. The man slashed horizontally (*yoko giri*), cutting through Jack's *keikogi* and drawing blood. Just a flesh wound.

"You still don't know who sent me," Tanaka yelled. "Does the name Joey Falconetti ring a bell?"

It rang a very big bell indeed. Jack had left Falconetti half-crippled and killed his sidekick in a bar fight the night before he fled Okinawa—on the same night he discovered who murdered Akiko.

"Let's get it on," said Jack. "I've no time to waste."

Tanaka came in fast with *shomen uchi*, a vertical cut aimed at Jack's head, but Jack was already moving to his right, blending with the attack and landing a spear-hand thrust (*nukite*) to his opponent's pancreas. Tanaka cried out in pain, then lunged forward and to his left with a powerful *chudan tsuki*, another mid-level thrust. Jack dodged to his own left, parried with his right forearm, and stepped in with his left foot to seize the hilt (*tsuka*) of the katana in a reverse grip.

He followed through with a lightning-fast *jodan tsuki*, a high punch to Tanaka's head. The man's head snapped back under the force of the blow. Maintaining his grip with his left hand, Jack pushed down on the *mono uchi*, the part of the blade nearest the tip, carefully avoiding the cutting edge. Using the push-pull motion of his hips and changing guard (*kamae*) by stepping back with his left foot, Jack drove the blade through his opponent's trachea. Blood erupted from the mortal wound.

Jack then gripped the katana with both hands. Advancing with his left foot, he used *yokomen uchi*, a diagonal side strike, to slice through the man's carotid artery with the *mono uchi*. Blood gushed violently from the second strike.

Tanaka's face filled with panic. His hands shot up to his throat and the side of his neck in a futile effort to stop the crimson torrent. Shock and disbelief shone in his eyes as he gagged on his own blood. He dropped to his knees and then collapsed face-forward, his life force spilling out across the bright red tatami.

Jack still held the bloodied katana in both hands. Slowly, he emerged from *mushin no shin*—the "no mind" state. The reality struck him like a sledgehammer. A corpse now lay in a pool of blood on the dojo floor. A nightmarish sight. Jack showed no outward emotion. Calmly, he walked to the corridor, picked up the phone, and dialled the Store Street Special Branch number, asking for his good friend Joey Maloney from homicide.

"Hiya, Jack, I recognised the voice. This is Fintan. How's the body? I hope you're not in a spot of bother?"

"To put it mildly—yes," Jack gasped.

"Ah, for fuck's sake. I'll put you through to the boss. I saw him head back to his office a few minutes ago. Take care."

"Hi, Jack. To what do I owe this pleasure? You must've forgotten that pint of Arthur G you still owe me," snorted Joey.

"I wish to fuck it were only a question of a few pints," sighed Jack. "I have a dead body lying on the dojo floor."

"For fuck's sake, Jack! If you're gonna start killing off your students, it's not going to be great for business. Sit tight, son, and don't touch anything. I'll be there in thirty minutes with the white coat forensic brigade."

Joey Maloney was a detective sergeant in the homicide division of Store Street Police Station and one of the best in the job. Once destined for a professional football career with Liverpool FC, a nasty motorbike accident had ended that dream at age 17. Now 38, he'd played amateur football until 32. Despite a pronounced limp, he could still spread the ball with precision using his famous left foot.

Back in the dojo, Jack sat in *seiza* on the blood-soaked tatami and sank into deep meditation. Thirty-five minutes later, a series of thundering knocks brought him back to the present. He opened the door. Joey Maloney stood there in his Crombie coat and hat, flanked by a plainclothes sergeant detective, two uniformed Garda officers, and three forensic technicians in white coats, hoods, and gloves.

Jack's face was grave. Joey wanted to offer his friend a comforting hug—but protocol forbade it. He was here as a detective, not a mate.

"OK, lads, let's have a look at Jack's handiwork," shouted Joey.

The scene was gruesome. Crimson blood had pooled around Tanaka's corpse. Joey immediately noticed the five-star tattoo on the dead man's chest. He took off his hat and scratched his receding hairline.

"Jaysus, Jack. You didn't take any chances. That is one very dead person."

"I had no choice," Jack replied grimly.

"Right, so, let's leave the rest to the forensics. You and I need a good old heart-to-heart. I'll see you down in the 'office' in forty-five minutes. You can buy me that pint."

Joey fondly referred to Mulligan's Pub on Poolbeg Street as "the office." It was his refuge—a place to unwind after tough cases, to forget for a while the dark side of human nature. The pub served the best pint in Dublin. Arthur G was practically medicinal.

Jack pushed open Mulligan's swing doors around 10 p.m. It was Friday and packed as usual. A cloud of cigarette smoke clung to the low, yellow ceiling. His eyes stung. He spotted Joey in one of the cubicles, waving him over.

"Sean!" bellowed Joey. "Two pints of your best!"

"No problem, Joey. I'll send them over," replied the barman.

"For fuck's sake, Jack, come over here and put me in the picture," Joey urged.

Jack now recognised his friend—not the sergeant detective from earlier, but the man he trusted.

"Okay, Jack, my son. Let's start from the beginning—because we're dealing with some serious shit."

Jack started at the very beginning, revealing intimate details of his personal life—his arrival in Okinawa after what seemed like an endless trip, his meeting with Akiko, and their love at first sight. He rarely spoke her name, as the memories were too painful and the scars left behind still unhealed. He told Joey of his idyllic life in Okinawa, where he had spent six years discovering the island and falling in love with its people. He explained how he had reached the very coveted rank of 6th dan in such a short period, training six days a week, six hours a day.

Joey had been familiar with some details of Jack's stay in Okinawa, but was completely unaware of Akiko, the love they had shared, and the tragic events that had followed.

And finally, Jack revealed the gory details of that fateful night in a bar in downtown Naha, where the marines liked to hang out, drinking and playing pool. He spoke of the fight with the two Marines who had brutally raped Akiko and left her for dead with atrocious injuries. The wounds were too horrific to describe—they had used a baseball bat on her orifices. On that terrible night, Akiko had finished work late and was cycling home to tell Jack the good news of her pregnancy. She had taken the test that morning before work.

The Marines, drunk and high on coke, had spotted Akiko. They drove her off the road and dragged her screaming to the beach, where they raped her repeatedly. She had begged them not to hurt her, saying that she was two months pregnant. But they just sneered. It excited them even more.

Salty tears began to flow uncontrollably down Jack's cheeks—streams of pain and sadness—as he told Joey that it was on that night he had learned Akiko was pregnant with their first child.

They had talked about starting a family, and she had planned to share the great news with him that very night. She died a month later in his arms, watching their last sunset over the bay. Akiko hadn't had the heart to tell Jack that she had lost their baby. The Buddhist monks at the hospice had done all they could to make her final days as comfortable and peaceful as possible.

He told Joey how Akiko had painted a graphic picture of her attackers, especially noting the five-star tattoo that one of the marines—the "Tank"—wore on his left forearm.

When Jack had entered the bar that night, it was as if Falconetti had been expecting him. He had stopped playing pool and stood with the cue in his hand, leering at Jack.

"Well, look who it is—the Karate Kid himself—and he's all fired up. What's wrong, Jack? Don't you like your girlfriend's new face? You know, she begged us on her knees not to hurt her—said she was carrying your gook baby."

At that instant, all the blood had left Jack's face, and his head began to spin.

Falconetti smirked. "Oh, you didn't know she was carrying your half-breed? This gets even better."

It was then that Jack exploded. He turned into a killing machine. He broke the neck of the bigger man, took out Jimmy "the Weasel," and left Joey Falconetti half-crippled—completely ignoring his ties to one of New York's most notorious mafia families and the drug-dealing operation he ran through military bases on the island. The front was perfect. From Okinawa, they could easily supply drugs to mainland Japan, South Korea, Hong Kong, most of Southeast Asia, and, of course, the USA. Jack had received this information months after his hasty departure from the island in a letter from Ichiro, Akiko's father. Ichiro had learned of it from his friend Jiro, the local police chief inspector, *keibu*, at the time.

Ichiro and Jack had shared a deep bond, often practising kendo and kenjutsu—the way of the sword—together. The bonds forged between two people through martial arts are difficult to explain to a neophyte. In some cases, they are even stronger than blood ties.

Jack took a large swig from his perfect pint of Guinness. Now that the adrenaline had worn off, his rib cage hurt like hell. He was certain he had a broken rib from Johnny Tanaka's powerful side kick, which had literally lifted him off his feet.

Joey's heart went out to his dear friend as he listened to this tale of love and desperation. He thought of the pain Jack must have endured in silence over the past few years, unable to share his grief. It was—and always would be—a deeply private matter.

Joey shouted to the barman, "Sean, send us over two glasses of your 12-year-old Redbreast Whiskey—we're both in need of a pick-me-up." No sooner said than done, the bright golden nectar with its silky, oily texture arrived at the table with the inevitable glass of water. The water was never added to the whiskey—that would be sacrilege. It was only for hydration and to avoid a bad head the next day.

Both men brought the precious liquid to their lips. Aromas of crème caramel, toffee, and dried fruits invaded their nostrils, and their palates were titillated with flavours of roasted nuts and exotic spices. Whiskey tasting in Ireland was a ritual—nearly religious— and had to be taken seriously. Just like any vintage wine, it demanded respect.

"The best fuckin' single pot still in the country, my son," laughed Joey as he tastily smacked his lips. "The Guinness and the whiskey were made for each other."

When the lads left Mulligan's, the moon had taken over from the sun on this bright August night, and its beacon illuminated the River Liffey, casting a fairy-like ambience. "Come on, Jack," said Joey, "I'll treat you to the best fish and chips in Dublin."

Joey was referring to Leo Burdock's chipper, considered the oldest and best chip shop in Ireland had to offer. The story began in 1913 when Liberties residents Bella and Patrick Burdock opened the first Leo Burdock's in Christchurch, Dublin. Over the years, the Burdock family grew their business, opening a number of Leo Burdock's Fish and Chip shops around Dublin, such was the popularity of their food.

From a young age, their son Leo was a regular face at the early morning Dublin fish markets, rising at 5 a.m. most days to source the freshest catch. Travelling back by horse and cart with his haul, he would pick up fresh potatoes and coal for heating the pans—a fuel used until 1991 to cook the freshly prepared fish and chips. At that point, they were the last chip shop in Ireland—possibly the world—to use coal-fired pans.

Many generations of Dubliners grew up carrying away a 'great oul feed,' known for generous portions of the freshest quality fish and the tastiest chips in Dublin. The proof of its success was in the almost never-ending queues.

The short twenty-minute stroll to the chipper on Werburgh Street was beneficial to both men, allowing them to chat about more frivolous subjects and forget—if only briefly—the evening's ghastly events. Joey was always one for cracking jokes and sharing amusing anecdotes from his police work. It was his escape from the often glaucous routine. Jack appreciated the light-hearted company.

As they arrived at the chipper, the bells of Christchurch chimed eleven times. Of course, there was a queue more than 20 yards long—such was Burdock's popularity with famished Dubliners, especially after a few pints. Joey nodded to a few familiar faces in the queue—taxi drivers, Gardaí, and ordinary Joe Soaps who recognised Joey Maloney. Even old Judge Campbell was there. Now retired, he never missed his fish and chips at least three times a week. He lived just a few blocks away.

"Hello, Joey, it's been a long time," shouted the judge. "When are you goin' to invite me for a pint and spend all that money you have?"

"Go wan outta that," roared Joey. "Even with your pension, you sure earn twice as much as me."

You couldn't beat a good bit of slagging—it was a favourite pastime in Dublin and, funnily enough, created strong bonds between people regardless of their social status.

When they finally got inside the shop, a strong smell of oil and batter filled their nostrils. Jack was starving. His taste buds began to flow.

"Jaysus, how's it goin', Joey? Haven't seen you in ages. What can I do for you?" shouted Peter behind the counter, perspiring profusely from the heat of the deep-fat fryer.

"Give us two fresh cods and two large singles—and I hope that fuckin' cod of yours is fresh," taunted Joey.

"Couldn't be fresher, Joey. Sure wasn't I down at the markets first thing this morning just for you—to pick out the finest catch."

Joey explained to Jack that the only thing that had changed about Burdock's over the years was that food orders were now wrapped in paper sheets. Originally, the food was wrapped in day-old newspapers, so it used to be said that you could eat and read the news at the same time.

"Salt and vinegar, lads?"

"Yeah, lash it on," Joey grinned without hesitation.

"Just a pinch of salt for me," Jack murmured. "Careful with the salt, my old pal—it kills slowly."

Joey snorted and gave him a crooked smile. "Ah, fuck that, Jack. If it's not the salt that gets me, it'll be something else. Might as well go out with flavour."

The steam from the hot chips rose around them like incense, curling into the night air as they stepped outside with their wrapped bundles in hand. The brown paper glistened with fresh grease, releasing the scent of fried batter and sea salt into the warm August breeze.

They found a quiet stone ledge across from Christchurch and sat in comfortable silence, unwrapping their meals. Jack tore off a chunk of flaky cod with his fingers and savoured the crunch—the contrast between the crispy golden skin and the soft, steaming flesh inside was exactly what he needed.

"You know," Joey said between bites, "there are nights when this city gets to you. The rot, the lies, the blood on the floor. But then there's this—hot chips, fresh cod, the bells of Christchurch keeping time like they always have."

Jack looked out across the Liffey. The water shimmered under the moonlight, the reflections broken by a gentle current. For a moment, it felt like the world could still be stitched back together.

"Thanks, Joey," he said quietly, not just for the food.

Joey nodded, wiping his hands on the paper. "We'll sort this mess. The bastard's gone, and whatever shadow he brought with him— we'll put it behind us."

They sat a while longer, two old friends sharing food and quiet in a city that never stopped moving, never stopped remembering. And for just a moment, the weight of death, vengeance, and pain gave way to warmth, laughter, and salt on steaming chips.

The two men walked down the quays, talking merrily and enjoying their late-night snack. A cold northeasterly wind whipped down the Liffey, prompting both men to stop and turn up their collars in an effort to fight off the night chill.

"Okay, I'll leave you here, Jack. Say hello to your belle," said Joey as they arrived at the Ha'penny Bridge. "And as they say in the movies, don't leave town—the Superintendent will want to have a chat with you. It's not every day we get an American-Asian hitman from the New York mafia in the neighbourhood. The chief'll be looking for a bit of positive publicity from this— probably wants his photo in tomorrow's paper."

"Okay, Joey. Fancy coming for a jog around Howth Head tomorrow morning?"

"No thanks. I'll stick to my weekly game of squash. At least there's a pint after it and you don't get your balls blown off, ye madman."

"Alright then. Slán agat—goodbye."

Jack made his way across the cast-iron bridge, one of Dublin's oldest and most iconic. Before the Ha'penny Bridge was built, seven ferries operated by a certain William Walsh crossed the Liffey. When the ferries deteriorated, Walsh was ordered to either repair them or build a bridge. He chose the latter and was granted the right to extract a ha'penny toll from anyone crossing it, for one hundred years.

The bridge's manufacture was commissioned by the then Lord Mayor of Dublin, John Claudius Beresford, from the Coalbrookdale Company of England. They cast the ribs of the bridge in 18 sections and shipped them to Dublin. The design and erection were supervised by John Windsor, one of the company's foremen and a skilled pattern-maker.

Jack had promised to pick up Sophie at the Unicorn Restaurant at closing time. It was approaching midnight, and she would soon be finishing her shift. He walked at a brisk, athletic pace—it felt good, especially after the day's traumatic events. But how was he going to explain everything without giving her a panic attack? Jack felt composed, but he knew that taking a life would leave an indelible mark on the subconscious. It always did.

When Jack arrived at the restaurant, the last customers were just leaving, bidding their goodbyes and complimenting the chef on the fine fare and Sophie on her excellent service. She noticed Jack, and a smile illuminated her face.

"Salut ma chérie, comment ça va?"

"I'm grand, babe. Any chance of a nice cup of coffee?"

As usual, the manageress, Ms. Dom—who lived above the restaurant—greeted him warmly. She had a soft spot for Jack.

After a short exchange, Jack sat at a small table at the back of the restaurant. Sophie arrived moments later with two steaming coffees.

"So, how was your day?" she asked.

Jack explained everything, sparing her the gory details. Sophie's face filled with astonishment, fear, and horror. She squeezed his hand tightly and kissed him tenderly, a teardrop tracing its way down her high-boned cheek into the corner of her lips.

He tried to reassure her that he was okay and that everything would be fine. But somewhere in the back of his mind, he knew it wasn't over. This was just the beginning. That, however, he couldn't tell her.

They left the restaurant arm in arm. The bright moon had disappeared behind dark, rolling clouds, and only a handful of stars managed to pierce the gloom. The little Fiat was parked near the dojo in Fitzwilliam Square, where Irish and English prostitutes offered their charms to kerb-crawling punters—some hungry for sex, others simply for company and a chat.

As Joey Maloney would say, "They're just like social workers, Jack—except they part their legs as well."

"Here are the keys, Sophie. You're driving. I had a few drinks with Joey Maloney, and I don't want to risk being stopped by one of the boys in blue on the way home."

"Ah, super, j'adore!" cried Sophie. Her joyful spontaneity always warmed his heart.

The little Fiat fired up instantly on the first turn of the key, the twin carbs sucking in the cold night air. The radio came on, and Marvin Gaye filled the car with his sensual groove:

Get up, get up, get up, get up!

Wake up, wake up, wake up, wake up!

Oh, baby, now let's get down tonight…

Jack smiled to himself. I could do with some of that healing, he thought, after the day's chaos.

They drove silently through light traffic under warm orange streetlights. The night was black as tar, heavy clouds rolling in over the bay. The wind had changed—it was now northwesterly.

A double-decker bus, lit up like a Christmas tree, bolted past them as they reached the crossroads at Fairview and the Howth Road. He's in a hurry, Jack thought, anxious to get home after his shift. Maybe he needs some healing, too.

The only healing Jack received that night came in the form of sleep. No sooner had his head hit the pillow than the lights went out—he plunged into a deep, comatose slumber.

He awoke at 6:30 a.m. on Tuesday morning. Rising from bed, he opened the sliding doors and stepped onto the balcony, completely rejuvenated. The bluish-green sky was cloudless, and the wind had completely died down. The moon hadn't yet clocked out, while the sun was beginning its ascent over Dublin Bay, sending bolts of white light across the water. The tide was high.

What a spectacular sight, thought Jack. He never tired of seeing it. Sunrises and sunsets—gifts from the heavens—had become his opium.

He sank down into kiba-dachi, the horse stance, and began his breathing exercises. They had become part of his daily life, just like brushing his teeth.

Fifteen minutes later, he was in the kitchen squeezing two fresh oranges. He poured the juice into a glass and added a spoon of honey. He sipped his concoction and watched the sun rise steadily over the water.

He slipped into his tracksuit and laced up a pair of Adidas running shoes. Sophie was still fast asleep as he gently closed the front door, skipped down the stairs, and started up his Fiat. The twenty-minute drive along the coast road to Howth Head was relaxing—there was little or no traffic.

Jack parked the car at the marina and set off for his run around the Head. The complete loop was about seven miles, steep in places with uneven terrain. It made for excellent cardio training. Jack usually finished the run in about an hour and a half at a brisk pace.

The Head offered spectacular views of Lambay Island, Ireland's Eye, and Dublin Bay. The cliffs were a haven for bird watchers, and grey seals were often seen basking on the rocks.

Jack paused at the summit and assumed seiza for meditation. He needed to heal—to cleanse his mind of the previous evening's trauma.

Fifteen minutes later, he descended to the marina. By the time he reached his car, he was perspiring profusely. It felt good. He felt cleansed.

Jack thought of his misogi shinto practice of ritual purification in Okinawa, where he would stand for long periods under a cold waterfall. This morning run had been the next best thing.

He watched several fishing trawlers set off from the harbour toward the Irish Sea, their bright green, blue, and red hulls gleaming in the morning sun. The tuk-tuk-tuk of their diesel engines echoed as they cut through the still air, blowing thick plumes of smoke.

Seagulls screeched their joy, escorting the boats out to sea—they knew they were guaranteed a meal today.

Jack reflected on the fishermen and the simple life they led. For a fleeting moment, he envied them. But he knew the truth—it was all very romantic: the boat, the sun, the sea. Reality was different. The weather could be cruel and unforgiving. While most people sat comfortably by warm fires, these men battled cold winds and rough seas, tossed about for hours, often soaked to the skin.

And of course, no catch meant no pay. Not so romantic after all.

Jack arrived back at the apartment and opened the letterbox in the corridor to retrieve his daily mail and, of course, the daily newspaper—the *Indo*. He flicked open the paper to scan the headlines, and much to his horror, big bold Helvetica capital letters forced his jaw to drop:

"DOJO DUEL ENDS IN DEATH."

What the fuck, thought Jack. Someone had leaked the story to the press—and they hadn't wasted any time. Of course, it wasn't uncommon for detectives or staff at Store Street to sell information to the press. It could be quite lucrative, depending on the buzz or sensation it created. This was all he fucking needed—and bad publicity to boot. His good friend Joey Maloney would go bananas. Whoever was responsible was going to receive a serious bollocking.

Sophie's reaction was to be expected when Jack threw the newspaper on the table. She read the headline out loud in her best French accent.

"Putain bordel de merde!" she screamed.

It somehow seemed less serious—almost sexy—when Sophie repeated the heading. Jack caught himself thinking just that.

Sophie jumped as the shrill ring of the phone shattered the silence. It seemed louder than usual. Jack immediately knew who to expect on the other end.

"Hello, Jack here."

"Jack, it's Joey. How are things?"

"For fuck's sake, Joey, what the hell happened?"

"I know, my oul' skin, calm down. I read the headline in the *Indo* this morning and was hit by a ton of bricks. I tell ye, there'll be wigs on the Green when I get to the bottom of this. Whoever leaked the info—I'll have him strung up by the bollocks."

"How are you so sure it's a male?" retorted Jack.

"Yeah, very funny, Jack. Listen, Superintendent Branagan wants to see you tomorrow morning at 9 a.m. sharp. I've more or less smoothed things over with him, so think of it as protocol."

"Not sure I like the 'more or less' part, Joey."

"Just get your arse here tomorrow morning, my lad—and for fuck's sake, don't be late. He's a stickler for punctuality."

The next day, Jack was up early at 6 a.m. and completed his usual ablutions. He arrived at Store Street at ten to nine, sharp. He was spick and span, dressed in a smart grey suit, white shirt, and black tie. Very conservative. He wanted to keep a low profile.

Joey arrived, wearing his best Ultra Brite smile, and guided him upstairs to the first floor into Superintendent Branagan's spacious office. Branagan was a big, burly man from County Galway in his early sixties. He had a big red face, long ears—hence his nickname *Lugs Branagan*—and hands like hams. I wouldn't like to be on the receiving end of those, Jack thought.

Branagan had started his career as a young Garda walking the beat in Dublin's inner city, where he earned a reputation as a hard man—yet one who was fair and honest. He gained the respect of most people in the tougher parts of the city. He rendered his own justice, which usually ended with a few clouts and a kick up the bum. He never even carried a baton—something unheard of these days. He gave Jack a virile handshake—the man had hands like shovels—and beckoned him to take a seat.

"So, son, you're the famous Irish ninja who can apparently kill a man with one precisely aimed blow?" he bellowed from across his desk.

Branagan had immediately noticed the callouses covering Jack's knuckles and the knife-hand—or *shuto*—area of his hand. From his own boxing experience, he knew those hands bore witness to years of practice and pain. Forging the body in the fire of the will, he mused.

Jack wished the floor would open up and swallow him whole. He tried to catch eye contact with Joey, who was sitting in the corner to Branagan's right. Jack noticed a slight smirk on Joey's lips, though his eyes stared dead ahead at the wall. The little bollocks, thought Jack. He's enjoying every minute of this.

Jack cleared his throat. "Well, Superintendent Branagan, that's a nickname the press branded me with a few years ago. I wouldn't consider myself in that category."

"Well, based on your handiwork the other night, young man, you seem to be extremely skilful—and deadly—with your hands and feet," said Branagan, pressing back into his leather Pullman chair, his massive hands entwined across his stomach.

"Yes, sir," Jack replied, the words whispering from his mouth. He didn't know whether Branagan was serious or just taking the piss.

Branagan nodded toward Joey Maloney, who seemed to freeze in place.

"Maybe you could show me a few moves. I've done a bit of boxing in my time. But according to Detective Maloney here, a boxer wouldn't stand a chance against a man of your talents."

"I wouldn't go as far as to say that, sir. Every man has his own specific talents and skills."

For the moment, things were going better than Jack had imagined. It felt more like a job interview than a cross-examination in a homicide case.

"A nasty piece of work, this Johnny Chink—or whatever his name is."

"That's Tanaka, sir. Johnny Tanaka," Joey called from the corner.

"According to our intelligence and contacts," Branagan continued, "he was involved with a mafia family by the name of Falconetti in New York—who you apparently already had dealings with in Okinawa." He leaned forward and planted his huge hands on the desk. "Now listen, son, I like ye—and believe me, coming from me, that's good. You've an honest face. Years on the beat have taught me to be a decent physiognomist. But you'll have to keep your nose clean until this case is done and dusted. I don't want any more ninja duels on my turf. I hope I'm making myself clear."

The mention of the Falconetti family sent blood pulsing through Jack's body. He could taste metal in his mouth.

Branagan rose to his full height—straight as a beanpole, an imposing six foot three.

"Now, son," he said, extending his ham-like hand, "I don't think things are going to stop here. I can say with certainty that this is only the beginning. For that reason, I'm placing you under discreet surveillance—24/7—for your own safety. Joey's already filled me in on the events in Okinawa. So as far as I'm concerned, this is a revenge vendetta. They've been tracking you for some time. That Irish Ninja article in the *Indo*? A nail in your coffin, son."

Jack bid the big man goodbye and promised to remain available in case of further questioning. He didn't relish the idea of a watchdog on his heels every day. As he walked down the corridor, he heard Joey calling him.

"Hang on, Jack, son—I'll stand you a coffee."

"You enjoyed that in there, you little bollocks. I saw you smirking away in the corner," scorned Jack as Joey caught up.

"I can't say I didn't enjoy seein' the head on ye in front of the big man. First time I've seen Mr. Cool-Hand Jack look ill at ease," laughed Joey.

"Anyways, let's leg it out of here and head up to Bewley's—for the best cup of coffee Dublin can offer—and a homemade scone."

They bantered joyfully during the short mile walk to Bewley's Café, chatting about this, that, and the other. Jack knew that with Joey, he had a sincere friend who would go through thick and thin for him—and more. They had their differences of opinion, and didn't always see eye to eye—but their friendship was rooted in mutual respect and was an unbreakable bond.

Bewley's Oriental Café was busy as usual, filled with people from every walk of life sipping tea or coffee, chatting, and reading the paper. Bewley's was unique—especially in décor, like being thrown back a full century. It had been founded by the Bewley family, French Quakers, in 1840 and was a major landmark in Dublin, with three cafés in all.

Upon entering, one was immediately struck by the rich smell of roasted coffee beans—a coffee connoisseur's paradise.

The décor was of another era: high vaulted Georgian ceilings, enormous colourful leaded windows, grand chandeliers—some copper—old wooden chairs, and marble tables. A host of famous personalities had passed through those wooden doors—from Robert Emmet to the Duke of Wellington. The ambience was such that one almost expected to see Sherlock Holmes ensconced in a quiet corner, drinking coffee and smoking his pipe, deep in thought, trying to unravel the latest murder mystery.

The two coffees arrived in white china cups. The scones were served with Kerrygold butter and a choice of homemade jams—strawberry, raspberry, blackcurrant, or marmalade. A thoroughly enjoyable and relaxing experience. Without spending a fortune, one felt both important and privileged.

Jack appreciated and enjoyed these intimate moments with his good friend Joey. They'd chat about more frivolous subjects—football, travel, women, and life in general. Jack loved teasing Joey about his favourite football team, Shamrock Rovers, who were going through a rough patch, although they had dominated Irish soccer for decades.

Despite a motorbike injury that had ended his chances of a professional career, Joey still togged out every Sunday morning for his local amateur side, Stella Maris, in Drumcondra. Even though the accident had left him with a prominent limp, he could still spray the ball around from his midfield position with surgical precision, always releasing the ball just before being tackled. The man had natural ability and amazing vision.

This was one of the reasons for their mutual respect. Jack admired his friend's football talent and courage. Joey had enormous respect for Jack's extraordinary martial skills and unwavering self-discipline. To some extent, they could be called the original odd couple.

"Fuck me!" exploded Joey. "Is that the time? Already half past twelve. I'll have to love ye and leave ye, my favourite ninja. I'm havin' lunch with Judge Patterson."

"Okay, hop along then, my friend. Talk to ye soon."

Joey nimbly rose from behind the marble table, rubbed his stiff leg, and limped out through the famous push wooden doors steeped in history. Jack decided to pop into The Unicorn for lunch and surprise Sophie. He wanted to get there before one o'clock to grab a table on the terrace and make the most of the summer sunshine. Ireland not being drenched in sunshine, the tables on the terrace were in great demand on fine days.

Certain personalities, such as government officials, journalists, and actors, had them booked on a permanent basis. Jack knew he could always rely on the manageress, Ms. Dom, to find him a spot no matter how packed it became.

Summer was certainly in the air as Jack strolled up Grafton Street towards Stephen's Green. Young women strutted along in miniskirts, some of them leaving little to the imagination—much to the delight and darting retinas of males on the hunt. Most of the girls wore designer clothes and carried expensive bags. The competition was fierce. Jack couldn't help noticing their spray-on tans covering legs, arms, and faces.

He smiled to himself, trying to visualise the sight as the clothes were peeled off, revealing the true, natural chicken-white skin beneath. It wasn't really Jack's cup of tea. He preferred the natural hue.

He immediately thought of Sophie, who turned a delicious golden colour after a few days under the sun's rays—at times obtaining an overall tan thanks to their daring nude sunbathing in the quieter parts of Dollymount Beach amid the sand dunes.

Grafton Street was certainly buzzing. Street artists were out in force, and passersby had their pick of entertainment: singers, musicians, mime artists, statue performers, dancers, jugglers, and doomsday prophets.

As Jack passed through the main gates of Stephen's Green, his ears were pleasantly alerted to the laughter of children. They seemed to be everywhere—laughing, shouting, chasing each other across the immaculately kept greens. Elderly people were feeding the ducks at the pond. Young lovers were stealing kisses on benches, their sandwiches wrapped in tinfoil resting on their laps. The sense of harmony was palpable. Jack gladly breathed in the scent of tulips and daffodils and reached the exit gates in no time.

He arrived at the restaurant and saw that Ms. Dom was in busy bee mode, directing customers and chatting with the local clientele. Sophie was busy as hell, so Jack blew her a kiss from the bar as Ms. Dom approached with a wide, welcoming smile.

"It's great to see you, Jack. You look fantastic—so fit and strong," she said, planting a kiss on his cheek. "I'm sure you want a table outside on the terrace. Come with me, young man, and I'll find you a place in the sun."

She seated Jack at a table for two under a brand-spanking-new Perrier parasol.

"Today's special is tagliatelle à la crème with the best of fresh smoked Irish salmon."

"That's exactly what the doctor ordered," smiled Jack, "and a nice cool glass of your rosé wine." She whisked off, seemingly floating on air. Customers were piling in, and she had to stay on her toes. She was the main cog in the wheel when it came to running the restaurant, and it turned over with clockwork precision—much to the satisfaction of the owners, the Costa family.

Most people were asking for tables outside. It wouldn't be long before the terrace was saturated. Jack noticed a few local celebrities from political and entertainment circles being seated nearby. Ms. Dom was making a big fuss—these regulars were big spenders. They could spend an entire afternoon at the table, polishing off bottles of wine and brandies to help with digestion.

Sophie bounced out, wearing a big smile, with Jack's tagliatelle and a glass of rosé. She placed a big smacker on his lips.

"Monsieur est servi," she said laughingly.

"Merci, ma chérie."

Envious heads turned in their direction. Ah, yes, one of the perks—having a waitress as your girlfriend.

Jack finished his meal with a cappuccino. The restaurant served the best cappuccino in town—at least according to the press. Nothing like a feature in the Daily Mail to boost sales. The Unicorn turned out a staggering number of cappuccinos daily, serving regular customers and nearly all the offices within earshot.

At the nearby table, Hennessy brandy had been served—nothing but the best for local celebrities. Cuban cigars were out. The air was filled with bluish-grey smoke rings floating delicately upwards. Jokes were being told at a rate that not even Danger could have matched. The craic was ninety.

Jack was in good spirits on this Monday evening as he drove his Fiat Spider through Fairview on his way to the dojo on the other side of town in Fitzwilliam Square. Jack's dojo, Dojo Zanshin, had been closed for three weeks by court order pending investigations. He parked his car in his usual spot and walked to the entrance. Much to his astonishment, there was a queue of at least sixty people standing in the street before the gates.

Jack had feared the closure would be bad for business, but the number of potential students proved otherwise. His loyal students—twenty in all—were present and showed sincere admiration and respect for their sensei. Most of the others displayed a mixture of fear and awe. The headlines in the Herald covering the dojo duel had certainly made him a reputation, whether good or bad.

Jack wondered how he was going to fit everyone into his humble dojo if they all signed up for the season. But from experience, he knew only half would stick it out. Winter was a telling factor, as many people preferred their slippers and a warm fire.

Statistics showed that for every 10,000 people who start martial arts, half drop out within the first six months. Of those remaining, about 1,000 would complete one year, then quit. 500 would study for two years, and only 100 would make it to three. On average, only 10 would earn their 1st-degree black belt. Only one or two would achieve 2nd degree. And only one would go on to become an instructor and teach others the way. That person is the black belt. That one is 1 in 10,000.

So, the path is long and hard. A lot of sacrifice and self-denial is required to reach yudansha, or dan black belt grade.

Don't judge each day by the harvest you reap, but by the seeds that you plant.

Robert Louis Stevenson

CHAPTER
Seven

Present day - Little Italy, Manhattan,

Present day – Little Italy, Manhattan, New York, tension was thick in the back room of Caesar's Diner as the Falconetti family discussed the death of their loyal soldier, Johnny Tanaka.

"Shouldn't have sent a chink to do the job," scoffed Big Toni Falconetti. Big Toni was aptly named, standing an impressive 6 feet 5 inches and weighing over 17 stone. He was an imposing figure who frightened the hell out of most people he met. A long scar down the left side of his face, like a grotesque trophy from a past brawl, made him all the more fearsome.

The man who gave him that scar had spent six months in the hospital, nursing broken bones and learning to walk again—a consequence of Toni's baseball bat, his weapon of choice. In fact, next to his Smith & Wesson, Toni was a sixth-dan master in the brutal art of baseball whacking.

"What the fuck, Toni, show our brother a little more respect. He did a lot of good work for the organisation, and don't you forget that," shouted Pretty Boy Paolo. With jet-black hair and hypnotic green eyes, Paolo was a magnet for women. He often bragged he'd lost count of the number of women he'd bedded since he was sixteen. But beneath that charming exterior was a ruthless killer with a savagery that shocked even his enemies.

Joey Falconetti puffed slowly on his favourite Cuban cigar, listening to the twenty men gathered in the smoke-filled room. He leaned back into his leather chair and blew a cloud of blue-grey smoke into the air. Everyone knew what that meant—just like in a papal conclave, the smoke signalled a decision had been made.

"Okay, listen up, guys," Joey growled. "I'm sick to my fuckin' gut hearing about this so-called ninja Jack Hopkins. That fucker left me half-crippled and killed Tommy 'The Tank' and Jimmy 'The Weasel' back in Okinawa."

Joey now walked with a pronounced limp. His dancing days were over.

"So, here's the game plan. Big Toni and Paolo, you two schmucks are gonna hop a transatlantic flight next week and finish what Johnny Tanaka started. I want that fuckin' ninja in a concrete suit. We got contacts over there — solid people managing our drug operations, and a plainclothes detective on our payroll, name's Shaun Doherty. Find that bastard and end him so we can get back to our business. That little island is our stepping stone to Great Britain, where the market's blowin' up. Now get off your fat asses and don't come back till that gook-lovin' bollocks ain't suckin' air anymore."

Joey's plan was met with nods of approval. Not that anyone had a choice. Some of the elder members silently disapproved—Joey's personal vendetta threatened to cloud his judgment and, more dangerously, the family's interests. But no one dared voice that out loud.

Little did Jack Hopkins know what awaited him just around the bend.

Our two New Yorkers touched down in Dublin Airport via Shannon on a rare sunny August afternoon at 4:00 PM. The flight had been long and gruelling, especially for Big Toni, whose massive frame couldn't find comfort in airline seats built for smaller men. What struck them immediately was the size of the airport. Compared to New York's JFK, it felt like a bus station.

They were also a bit stunned by the friendliness of the people. Strangers smiled and struck up casual conversations like they were old friends. The thick Dublin accent was new to them and would take some getting used to.

As they approached the taxi rank, they spotted a few lads laughing and smoking. "Who owns this fuckin' dinky?" bellowed Big Toni, pointing at the small blue Datsun Bluebird at the front of the queue.

"Oh, that would be mine," replied Dominic, the red-haired taxi driver, visibly startled by Toni's sheer size.

Big Toni made his way to the front seat but instinctively walked to the left side of the car—and found himself face to face with the driver. "What the fuck, man? They put the fuckin' steering wheel on the wrong side!" he grunted.

He finally wedged himself into the seat and adjusted it as far back as it would go. "Fuck me, man, is that it? How the hell do you drive these fuckin' dinkies? Must be made for midgets. They weren't built for real men."

Dominic chuckled, used to dealing with loud, ill-mannered Americans. "Ah, sure, we're all leprechauns over here," he replied with a grin.

"So where can I take you lads?"

"Bring us to the best hotel in Dublin, dude," said Pretty Boy Paolo.

"Alright, lads, the Shelbourne Hotel it is. Hope you've got a few bob in your pockets, it's the' place to be."

"What or who the fuck is Bob?" asked Big Toni.

"Money, my friend. Dinero. Moolah," Dominic laughed.

The drive into town was a comedy show in itself. Anyone overhearing the exchange between the garrulous Dominic and the New Yorkers would have been thoroughly entertained. The pair couldn't believe how provincial Dublin seemed. No skyscrapers, no honking horns, and cars they considered toys. Dominic just smirked at their astonishment.

At the Shelbourne, Dominic helped them retrieve their luggage. Big Toni slapped him on the back with a hand like a shovel and handed him a $20 tip—a generous gesture by any standard.

"You're alright, man. You Irish guys got a weird sense of humour, but you're cool."

"Thanks, lads. Glad I passed the test."

Pretty Boy Paolo waved him over. "Hey, carrot head, can we get broads in this joint?"

"You mean prostitutes?" Dominic replied, grinning.

"Yeah, pussy, man. You know what that is?"

"I'm sure if you ask at reception, they'll be more than happy to accommodate your every wish," Dominic said, barely holding in his laughter. He couldn't wait to imagine the hotel staff's faces when these brash New Yorkers asked about hookers at check-in.

The duo caused a sensation as they strolled into reception and asked for a double room without a reservation. The staff were visibly flustered.

"Sorry, sirs, we only have a suite available at present, with a view of the Green," the receptionist offered nervously.

"So what the fuck? Do we look like schmucks? We'll take it. It better be what it's cracked up to be," Toni growled. The staff, clearly uncomfortable, struggled to remain professional. The pair's tattoos, scars, and bombastic energy unsettled everyone.

"How will you be paying, gentlemen?" asked Mr. Walsh, who had stepped in to assist the overwhelmed staff.

"Cash, buddy," Paolo replied. "That gives you a hard-on, pal?"

"Very well, gentlemen. Olivia will show you to your suite," Walsh said, maintaining his poise.

Once inside the Shelbourne's grand halls, the two men were impressed. The luxury and old-world elegance of this 19th-century establishment, founded by Martin Burke in 1824, stood in stark contrast to the flashy, fast-changing trends of New York.

Fashion fades. But class? Class endures.

Once in their room, Toni headed straight to the shower. The trip had been long, and he needed a good, hot scrub down. He was as happy as a pig in shite — it was one of the few showers where the big guy could actually turn around. Toni was in heaven, impressed with the shower gels and expensive Hermès soaps the hotel supplied to its VIP guests.

The after-shower accessories were just as impressive: luxury talcum powders, Serge Lutens perfumes, and top-quality Egyptian cotton towels embroidered with the Shelbourne logo. Yeah, this was the life, thought Toni. The Italian-made bathrobes were also top-notch, though even the XL size was a tight fit for the big man.

"What the fuck, they must've had midgets for models," he scoffed.

After their ablutions, the two bad apples arrived in the lobby, freshly scrubbed and looking sharp, and left their key with the receptionist.

"Shall you be dining in tonight, gentlemen?" she asked politely.

"No, honey, we're gonna paint the town tonight. Where can we get a good burger in this little town of yours?" The receptionist was happy to direct them to Captain America's on Grafton Street, a local favourite specialising in American-style burgers just a few hundred yards from the hotel. She felt it would suit their "modest" requirements and save the hotel's dining room from potential chaos.

"Okay, thanks, babe. Don't wait up for us," winked Big Toni. As the two men exited, she rolled her eyes skyward. Thank God they didn't decide to dine in, she thought. They didn't exactly blend in with the Shelbourne's usual clientele. A potential crisis averted.

The two New Yorkers were not disappointed upon entering Captain America's Cookhouse. It was, to all intents and purposes, a slice of Manhattan. The Stars and Stripes hung across the beam, accompanied by photos of American folk heroes. Fictional icons from Marvel comics adorned the walls: Captain America, Superman, Spiderman, and Batman all stood sentinel.

A young woman in her early twenties greeted them, flashing a stunning Colgate smile. She wore a checkered shirt, the buttons straining under the weight of her ample chest, a pleated black mini-skirt, and white mid-calf boots, completing her outfit. Pretty Boy Paolo's eyes practically undressed her as he imagined cupping her curvy, milky-white breasts with their large, cherry-red nipples.

She guided them to a private leather-upholstered booth and handed them menus. The men didn't take long to decide — triple burgers with fries and every imaginable dressing. They ordered two pints of Harp lager and were served a plate of peanuts and olives to nibble on while waiting. "Eye of the Tiger" by Survivor blasted from the Bose sound system. It was 7:30 PM, and the restaurant buzzed with patrons, mostly students and professionals from nearby Trinity College.

The burgers arrived, garnished as requested, each bun pierced with tiny American and Irish flags. The guys wolfed them down, followed by two more beers. For dessert, they chose pêche melbas and finished off with American coffees and two Cuban cigars, drawing glares from nearby tables.

But no one dared say a word. An air of unease and menace surrounded them, especially Big Toni. They were used to dominating rooms, used to getting their way — usually through violence.

What better way to digest a meal than a leisurely Friday evening stroll down Grafton Street? Buskers and street entertainers were out in full force. Guitarists, harmonica players, singing "Blowin' in the Wind," fiddle players, acrobats, jugglers, fire-eaters. And, of course, the famous Diceman held court.

"How the fuck does he stay still so long?"

"He must have a broomstick shoved up his ass," scoffed Big Toni.

Eager to soak in Irish culture, they veered off Grafton Street into South Anne Street and discovered Kehoe's Bar, one of Dublin's oldest traditional pubs. First licensed in 1803, its Victorian interior boasted stained glass doors, old Irish snugs, and worn mahogany partitions.

The walls were lined with portraits of James Joyce, Samuel Beckett, Oscar Wilde, Yeats, Shaw, and Stoker, alongside revolutionary heroes like Pearse, Connolly, and Collins.

The bar drew intellectuals, journalists, actors, students, and sports figures. It was said Kehoe's poured the best Guinness in town — though patrons of Mulligan's might disagree. Toni and Paolo ordered two pints of Guinness and two shots of Jameson on the rocks.

The pub was packed. Elbowing your way to the bar was a must — no problem for Big Toni, who barely squeezed through the door. The bar staff wore rolled-up white shirts and protective aprons.

Cigarette and cigar smoke hovered like a cloud. The yellowed ceiling testified to decades of smoking. Ceiling fans merely swirled the haze; air conditioning was deemed too expensive by the owners.

Non-smokers left with burning eyes and reeking clothes. Straight to the washing machine the next morning.

The boys struck up a conversation with two women in their late twenties — one blonde, one brunette. Paolo was especially drawn to Mandy, the blonde, whose ample assets and long legs held him captive.

Irish girls often swooned for Mediterranean men. Was it the swarthy looks, dark eyes, or that intense Italian attention they lavished on their conquests? Paddies were seen as less attentive, more complacent, leaving some women starved for affection.

To Paolo, it was all or nothing. Panties off or walk.

Italians were often nicknamed "greasers" by Dubliners, thanks to the cooking oil from their popular fish and chip shops. These shops, born of Italian immigration during the Mussolini era, offered the famous "one and one" — one fish, one bag of chips. Cheap, filling, and a post-pub tradition.

Others worked in construction and the car trade.

To their delight, the women suggested ending the night at Zhivago's nightclub on Lower Baggot Street, then the hottest spot in town. "Where love stories began," claimed its slogan. With a cover charge of 3 pounds, including a meal, it was a bargain.

Huey Lewis and the News were belting out "The Power of Love" as our four would-be lovers entered the club. Big Toni, as usual, made quite the impression as he strolled past the four bouncers, who exchanged quick, nervy glances as if to say, "Let's hope this guy doesn't cause any trouble tonight — he'd be a fuckin' handful."

The guys, playing true gentlemen, paid the cover for their female companions and dropped their coats at the cloakroom. It was just after midnight, and the place was absolutely hopping. Next up was Whitney Houston's "Saving All My Love for You," which enchanted the two New Yorkers — a perfect slow number for body-hugging.

'Cause tonight is the night for feeling alright

We'll be making love the whole night through

So, I'm saving all my love for you

The dance floor was a sea of tangled bodies — breasts fondled, buttocks groped, and languorous kisses exchanged. The bar, as always, was mobbed; you had to practically fight your way to the counter for a drink. But that was no problem for Big Toni, who waded through the crowd and returned with four margaritas.

The girls waved at him from a corner table they'd claimed — a perfect nook for drinks and dirty laughs.

The margaritas flowed as our Italian-Americans got better acquainted with their companions. The girls went off to grab "tonight's special" — spaghetti bolognese — which, needless to say, pleased the boys immensely. They were surprised to find it legitimately good.

The night rolled on until the bartenders began calling out: "Last orders, ladies and gentlemen! We must close soon — last orders, please!"

"What the fuck?" shouted Pretty Boy Paolo. "In New York, it's 24/7, man!"

"Yeah, well, this is the Dirty Old Town, not the Big Bad Apple," replied the barman coolly.

"You some kinda comedian, pal?"

Before tensions escalated, Toni stepped in: "Relax, Paolo, baby. He's just doin' his job. In that case, give us two more margaritas and two scotches on the rocks, my good man."

The 2 a.m. closing time came as a surprise to the Americans, more used to clubs running till dawn. But this was Irish law — nightclubs serving alcohol past 2 a.m. faced heavy fines or forced closures. Some spots had private rooms for VIPs to keep partying, but for the average Joe Soap, 2 a.m. meant time's up. Of course, by the time everyone finished their drinks and bouncers ushered them out, it was closer to 3 a.m.

Crowds spilt through the exit under the watchful eyes of the bouncers — always a tense moment. Many were drunk, testosterone in the air. A small group of young men, early twenties, had gathered just yards from the door. Boisterous and bold, they threw out bait.

"Hey, blondie, the big greaser's gonna give ye the baldy fella tonight!"

Laughter erupted among the group, except for Big Toni and Dolores, his date.

"Ye little shit," she fired back.

"Ah, yeah? Well, fuck you, ye cunt," the loudmouth sneered.

Big Toni didn't tolerate disrespect — especially toward women. Despite Paolo's and the girls' protests, he strode over to the group, his expression dark.

"Ye got a foul mouth, punk. Should wash it out with soap," he growled.

"Fuck you, greaser — go back to where ye came from!"

Without missing a beat, Toni grabbed the young man by the collar, yanked him forward, and smashed his forehead into the guy's nose. The sickening crunch of broken cartilage echoed, and blood gushed from both nostrils.

The kid collapsed, semi-conscious. Game, set, and match.

His five friends didn't move — frozen in place. Their mouthy leader was down for the count.

The bouncers watched with thinly veiled amusement. Not their jurisdiction, and they weren't about to tangle with Big Toni. One went off to call an ambulance. Saturday nights kept Dublin's emergency rooms busy.

It was only a short walk back to the hotel, though progress was slow, punctuated by French kisses and body-grabbing.

By the time they arrived, the night porter — a man in his sixties named Tom — barely had time to say a word before Big Toni flashed a crisp ten-pound note under his nose.

"Hope ye ain't gonna cause us any trouble, old man. Take that and get back in your little box. Ye never saw us. Capito?"

"Yes, sir, whatever you say, sir. Thank you, sir," Tom stammered.

Hotel policy strictly forbade bringing back guests at certain hours, but Tom knew better than to argue. He didn't have the build or the salary to take those kinds of risks. Discretion was the key — and as long as other guests weren't disturbed, everything would be hunky-dory.

The two girls giggled nervously as they ascended the grand staircase. When they entered the suite, their jaws dropped. The room oozed luxury — a real palace. Neither had seen anything like it, nor expected to again. A once-in-a-lifetime moment.

The bar was stocked with the best — Bollinger champagne, premium spirits, and top-shelf liqueurs. Paolo popped a bottle and poured it smoothly into exquisite crystal glasses.

The girls felt like they'd stepped into a movie scene. Sipping bubbly they'd only seen in Bond films, they were giddy — drunk on alcohol and fantasy. Shirts were unbuttoned, skirts unzipped. Body heat rose; bodies intertwined.

The lovemaking was intense and physical — especially with Big Toni. Debbie had never been with a man of such size. Not every position worked, and some were downright uncomfortable.

Paolo finally unclipped Mandy's bra, latching onto her large, cherry-red nipples like a newborn. He'd seen his share of breasts — but these were a masterpiece.

The night turned into a blur of lust and liquor until both couples passed out from exhaustion and intoxication.

The morning would come with pounding heads and a fog of memory.

I learned that courage was not the absence of fear, but the triumph over it. The brave man is not he who does not feel afraid, but he who conquers that fear ...

Nelson Mandela

CHAPTER
Eight

Saturday morning - Clontarf

Jack, as usual, arose at 6:30 a.m. to begin his daily exercise routine, careful not to wake Sophie, who was in a deep, peaceful sleep. As he stepped out onto the terrace, the scent of iodine and the incoming tide filled his nostrils. Here, he had installed a makiwara — a traditional Okinawan punching post. Three hundred punches with each fist was his daily ritual, except on Sundays, which he reserved for breathing and isometric exercises only.

Three hundred was a far cry from his Okinawan regimen, which had required a thousand tsuki punches per fist, seven days a week. That was old-school training — something many modern karate schools scoffed at. Sure, the target was static, but it built tremendous resistance and wrist strength. As Jack's sensei used to say, "Forge the body in the fire of your will."

It created enormous power — one punch could mean instant death. This wasn't a game or a sport; it was a martial art. Many failed to grasp the difference. Years of daily practice were needed to comprehend the deeper essence — mind and body uniting, transcending pain and ego, to produce a flawless, pure, and powerful movement. Eventually, it became art in motion.

"The mind controls the body. Never forget this, Jack, and you'll be one step closer to the summit," his sensei's words rang in his ears.

He finished his training and stepped into the shower, ending with a cold rinse — a ritual he had become accustomed to. In Okinawa, he had regularly practised misogi — purification through exposure to icy waterfalls. Most serious martial artists performed misogi frequently. Jack had often gone with his sensei and fellow students to Todoroki Falls, also known as "Ice House Falls," near Nago Bay.

The water temperature was around five degrees, and it took serious mental strength to meditate beneath the torrent for more than five minutes. The reward was worth it — a profound feeling of cleansing and oneness with the universe. Elders claimed it was a natural shield against illness. Jack had come to believe they were right; he was rarely sick since adopting the practice.

He pressed a few oranges, enough for two glasses of fresh juice, set the kettle to boil, and dropped slices of Brennan's loaf into the toaster. Nipping nimbly down the stairs, he retrieved a copy of the Irish Independent from the letterbox. Jack always served Sophie breakfast in bed on Saturday mornings. She adored the tradition — a relaxing start to the day, made perfect with a copy of the "Indo" to browse through.

Jack took as much pleasure in serving as she did in being served. He always remembered his sensei's words: "To serve and to be served are two folds in the same garment."

An hour later, Jack had changed into his tracksuit and was ready for his usual run down to the Bull Wall, which jutted over a mile into Dublin Bay. It was a route he particularly enjoyed — though in winter, running into a cold easterly wind could be brutal. As his dad used to say, "Would blow the feckin' cobwebs off ye."

He had arranged to meet the lads for lunch at one o'clock in the Yacht Lounge, their regular haunt. Sophie had made plans to go on a shopping spree with Jack's sister, Brynn. He laughed to himself, knowing no shop would be spared in their quest for the bargain of the day. It would be Penneys, Dunnes, Arnotts, Switzers, and so on. "Best of luck to them," thought Jack. Shopping and window shopping were things he utterly detested.

As Jack pushed through the bar's doors, he spotted his buddies seated in their usual corner, having the craic.

"There's the Hop," smirked Anto.

"You're looking well, Hop. That little Froggie must be treating ye right with all that home cooking."

"I don't think it's just the cooking, Anto," blurted out Bradley in his usual sarcastic and smirking tone.

"Sure, they're ridin' like fuckin' rabbits," scoffed Lenny — and with that, the whole gang burst into laughter.

"Would yez ever fuck off and tell me what ye want to drink, ye shower of wankers," said Jack, peeling off his jacket to reveal a powerful, fit frame.

The pints arrived, and the banter began — varied as always, from the usual slagging between Danger and Bradley to the antics of Anto and Lenny. Stories and jokes flew across the table, and no one was spared. Jack relished these moments — always unpredictable, always fresh.

Someone always ended up as the butt of the group's jokes and razor-sharp wit. Today, it was Bradley, the civil servant's turn. But he was no pushover. No matter how clever or devious his adversaries were, Bradley could hold his own.

He had a lightning-quick wit, a spontaneous sense of humour, and the ability to strike soft spots in one's armour with precisely measured remarks, taunts, and observations. With Bradley, the verb had met its master. It was usually Danger who ended up on the receiving end of his crafted innuendos — causing him to fly off the handle and lose his cool.

The lads loved it. They couldn't get enough of it.

"So where was the craic last night, lads?" asked Jack.

"We all went to Zhivago's. Big Bob, Domo, and Tumbo were there too," said Bradley. "We had to do a whip-around for Danger, of course — the poor fecker was already broke, and he only got paid Thursday."

"Fuck off, ye bollocks," snapped Danger.

Some things never change, thought Jack to himself.

"Jaysus, Jack, you missed it. Some lad got destroyed outside the club — a big fucker smashed his nose in with the most powerful headbutt I've ever seen. Poor bastard went down like a rag doll.

Big, powerful man. He'd have given you a run for your money, Jack. There were two of them — greaser types, with broad New York accents," added Danger.

Alarm bells rang immediately in Jack's head. He tried to keep his expression neutral, showing no signs of the tension that suddenly surged inside him.

He recalled Inspector Branagan's words: "This affair isn't over, Jack. There will be more to come."

"Did someone walk over your grave, Hop? Or has that little waitress got your head all fuzzy?" teased Anto.

The young bar girl, in a mini skirt and tight-fitting tank top that flaunted her feminine attributes to the fullest, came to serve their drinks. She was no more than eighteen and was clearly a student doing a summer job, trying to earn a few bob for holidays, clothes, or whatever else she fancied. A sexy outfit and a big smile always guaranteed good tips from the male punters— the tips were often better than the wages. For Jack, she was a breath of fresh air, momentarily jolting his mind away from worry and grim thoughts. She certainly set temperatures rising and testosterone flowing. As soon as she pocketed her ample tips and turned on her heels, male humour was unleashed.

"Would ya look at the arse on that! What a bottle of Bass she has," shouted Lenny. "I'd eat chips out of her knickers."

"For fuck's sake, Lenny, a bit of decorum is called for here. Poor young innocent girl, probably a virgin too," retorted Bradley in his usual sarcastic tone.

"And that coming from the biggest whoremaster among us," butted in Danger. "She wouldn't be a virgin for very long with you, ye bollocks."

"Ah, now, Danger, you know I have the utmost respect for the fairer sex and would never do anything ungentlemanly. Just like yourself, I'm sure. But then again, when was the last time you enjoyed female companionship? What a terrible waste—a hunk of a man like yourself on a forced sex diet. Ye must be tired beating the bishop."

"Don't start, Bradley. I'm fuckin' warnin' ye," snorted Danger.

"Of course, your attire in itself should be a magnet for women—especially that perfectly ironed and unique t-shirt that bears the catchy 'bull shit' slogan and that you seem to wear day in and day out," scoffed Bradley.

And so, the verbal table tennis continued for the next thirty minutes, with Bradley the master of ceremonies and the verb in his element—prodding just enough, like an expert surgeon, to ensure that Lenny or the fiery Danger lost their cool. One could always count on Danger blowing a fuse fairly quickly.

The mob's contact in Dublin, Sergeant Sean Doherty—a Store Street detective in his forties, of burly build and red, raving hair—walked through the doors of The Shelbourne Hotel on Monday morning at 10 a.m. He proceeded to the lounge bar where he was to meet the two New Yorkers.

Though they had never met before, he spotted the Italian Americans immediately. Both men were seated in comfortable leather armchairs, drinking cappuccinos, of course. Big Toni was enjoying a long Cuban cigar—an Upmann Magnum 50. Nothing but the best for the big man.

Sean waved and walked over to their table. "Good morning, gentlemen. Welcome to the Emerald Isle. I'm Sean Doherty." He stuck out a ham-like hand, and both men stood as they exchanged virile handshakes. Sean was immediately impressed by the sheer size of Big Toni and his shovel-like hands.

He couldn't help but wonder—if everything was proportional, many a woman must have gotten a shock when he dropped his jocks. Both men were impeccably dressed in Gucci suits and shoes. Paolo opted for black and had enough gel in his jet-black hair to satisfy a whole soccer team. Toni wore a grey suit with a matching waistcoat. Must pay well to be a mobster, thought Sean.

"Nice to meet ye, Red," bellowed Toni. "What does an Irishman drink at 10 a.m.?"

"A large coffee and cream is fine for me."

"Bartender, bring our friend a large coffee and cream, will ye?" shouted Paolo in his best Manhattan drawl. "Sit down, make yourself comfortable. Don't suppose ye getta chance to have a coffee in a palace very often, Detective?"

Big Toni took a draw from his large Cuban cigar and blew rings of blue smoke into the air. "So, what ye got for us, Red?"

"My name is Sean."

"Red'll do us fine, pal. Let's just say it's your code name—like in those spy flicks," scoffed Big Toni. Sean didn't want to get off on the wrong foot with these guys, and he certainly didn't want any aggro with the big man.

With that, he reached into his inside pocket and placed a large kraft envelope on the mahogany table. The envelope contained photos of Jack, Sophie, his family, and even his friends. There was detailed information about his daily comings and goings, his home address, and the dojo's location. Sean pointed out that Sophie worked just a stone's throw from the hotel at the Italian Unicorn Restaurant, which was run by the Costa family.

Paolo seemed to be enjoying his cappuccino. "We'll have to check out this restaurant—and what's her name? Sophie? I hope they make lasagne as good as Mama's."

The spick-and-span bartender brought Sean's coffee. It was served in the finest china with fresh cream, white and brown sugar, and a side plate holding a biscuit, a chocolate, and a cake. Fuck me, thought Sean, one could easily get used to this kind of lifestyle. How much could a coffee like this cost, he wondered— probably as much as he paid for his daily lunch at the pub near Store Street.

Both men were impressed with the in-depth information the detective had provided. It would certainly make their work that much easier. Big Toni leaned forward. "Good work, Red. You've been a busy boy. The Boss'll be pleased with ye."

As they departed, Toni pulled a thick envelope from his pocket and placed it in Sean's right hand. "Thanks, Red. Nice doin' biz with ye. Don't contact us—we'll contact you if and when we need anything. In the meantime, keep your ear to the ground."

Sean had explained to the two men that Jack was a personal friend of Detective Captain Joey Maloney, his colleague and senior officer.

Sean exited The Shelbourne Hotel and turned left onto Merrion Row, stopping in front of number 15 — the legendary O'Donoghue's Pub. Originally built in 1789 as a grocery store, the building was transformed into a full-time pub in 1934 when the O'Donoghue family took over. These days, it was more than a watering hole — it was a shrine to traditional Irish music, with its distinctive black-and-white exterior and small, stout windows known the world over.

The pub's international fame had been cemented by The Dubliners, who started gigging there in the early 1960s before becoming icons. Other household names like Seamus Ennis, Joe Heaney, Andy Irvine, Christy Moore, and Paddy Ryan had all found their footing in O'Donoghue's smoky backrooms. For tourists — especially Americans tracing ancestral roots — it was a bucket-list stop for a pint and a story.

Sean knew the place well. In his younger days, he'd been part of its furniture. The craic was electric, the music real, and the female tourists — well, let's just say they were more liberal than the Irish lasses back then. Birth control and less Catholic guilt made for unforgettable summers.

Pushing open the familiar door, he gave a nod to Con, the barman who'd served longer than most politicians stayed in office.

"How's it going, Con? Any gangsters hiding in the snug today?" Sean smirked.

"Same shite, different day. What can I get you?"

"Twelve-year-old Redbreast. Feeling flush today."

Glass in hand, Sean made his way down the narrow passage to the back lounge, still one of the quietest corners in the city. The walls were a gallery of nostalgia: black-and-white photographs of JFK grinning atop a donkey during his famous Irish visit, Irish sports legends, old-time movie stars, and musicians who'd once called this room their stage.

Sean removed his coat and hung it on a wooden hook, the kind worn smooth by decades of elbows and raincoats. He slid into a well-worn seat, took a sip of Redbreast, and exhaled like a man finally off the clock.

Then he pulled the envelope from under his arm. Tearing it open, a thick wad of crisp fifty-pound notes peeked out. He thumbed through the stack.

One hundred notes. Five grand. All earned before noon. Not bad for a morning's hustle.

The whiskey went down sweeter the second time, the honeyed liquid warming his chest and loosening his thoughts. For once, life didn't feel like a bloody uphill battle.

Being a detective didn't pay what people thought — not with a mortgage that kept him up at night and three kids aged five to fifteen. Every time interest rates crept up, it felt like a punch to the ribs. And with Ireland still stuck in the economic doldrums — pre-Celtic Tiger — paychecks didn't stretch far. Jobs were scarce, the cost of living high, and morale lower still.

But today? Today, Sean Doherty felt like a king on Merrion Row.

He began mentally spending the cash: a few grand into savings for a rainy day, no doubt. A proper night out for Molly — she deserved it. The King Sitric in Howth came to mind, with its fresh seafood and discreet glamour. With luck, they'd spot a few minor celebrities and pretend not to care. The kids? Ice cream and a film. And young Conor would finally get those Adidas football boots he'd been nagging about — no more ribbing from his teammates over the worn-out pair he'd outgrown.

Feeling buoyed, Sean stood and made his way back to the bar. He leaned his head through the hatch.

"Line me up another one of those golden beauties, will you, Con?"

"On the double. Jaysus, you're in rare form today. What's got into you?"

"Day off, my friend. And I'm treating myself. And hey — one on me."

"A bit early for me, but I'll save it for the end of the shift. Nothing better than a good whiskey and the Indo in peace."

"Fair play to you. Cheers."

Sean downed the rest of his Redbreast, adjusted his coat with a contented grunt, and slipped out through the back door into the cool, narrow laneway. He was a man on a mission now. He had the day off, a pocketful of illicit cash, and a night to plan.

First stop: booking that table at The King Sitric. Tonight, he'd make it one to remember.

Forging our bodies in the fire of our wills ....

Sensei Saito

CHAPTER
Nine

It was on a cold and wet November morning when Jack bade farewell to family and friends in the Sky Lounge at Dublin Airport. The night before, he'd been out with the lads, celebrating his imminent departure in true Irish fashion. He was still feeling the aftershocks of a hangover—the festivities had stretched well into the early hours, and sleep had been in short supply. Nobody had enjoyed much pillow time. As glasses were raised in his honour, a bittersweet atmosphere settled over the group. Jack knew this was it — it would be years before he'd see their ugly mugs again. And it was certainly *au revoir* to Arthur Guinness; he planned to purify body and mind through a year of misogi, the ancient Japanese practice of spiritual and physical cleansing.

Frankly, it wouldn't do him any harm. Since breaking up with Molly, Jack had hit the bottle hard. Pints of the black stuff had become his nightly companions, six nights a week without fail. It had gone on for a full year, and his body had started to protest. He was sluggish, flabby, and two stone overweight — the beer belly wasn't just a suggestion anymore, it was a statement. Although he held a first-degree black belt in Kenpo Karate, he'd let all physical activity slip away. His only cardio came from pub crawls with his loyal drinking mates. They had even started warning him that he was teetering on the brink of alcoholism.

The wake-up call came one morning, dragging himself out of bed in his parents' house with no memory of how he'd gotten home the night before. His skull throbbed; his memory refused to cooperate. That was the morning he decided it was time to change. To halt the slippery slide into oblivion.

Jack had just completed a four-year journalism degree and shown real promise. So much so that Jacky Gilroy, the manager at the Irish Independent, had told Jack's father there was a position waiting for him as a sub-editor in the sports section. Both men were stunned when Jack announced he was walking away from it all — packing his bags and heading to the other side of the world on what they considered a wild goose chase.

But the decision was made. And so, amid cheers, hugs, and a few tears, Jack boarded his plane and waved goodbye to his little farewell party. He had no idea what the future held — what karma had in store for him.

He finally arrived in Naha, the capital of Okinawa, after a gruelling journey: Amsterdam to Shanghai, then Tokyo, and a connecting flight the next day. It was his first long-haul flight and the first time he experienced the peculiar fog of jet lag — he'd only read about it before.

His overnight stay in Tokyo was a revelation. The culture shock hit him like a sledgehammer. The city was lit like a carnival — thousands of neon lights flickering beneath a damp autumn sky. It felt like stepping into a giant pinball machine. Rain fell steadily, catching the fluorescent glow and painting the streets with colour. Jack thought it was beautiful. Compared to it, "dirty old Dublin" seemed a bit dim. The electricity bill alone made his head spin.

He made his way to Shinbashi — one of Tokyo's famed *hanamachi*, or "flower towns," where geishas could still be found. Walking along the noisy, bustling streets, he rubbed his eyes, certain he was dreaming, as three geishas in full traditional regalia glided past in their geta — raised wooden sandals. They were elegance personified. Completely feminine from head to toe.

Jack half expected to see a samurai round the corner next, katana in hand and kabuki mask glaring. It was like walking through the set of *The Seven Samurai*, Akira Kurosawa's 1954 masterpiece. Of course, the film had been reimagined by Hollywood as *The Magnificent Seven* in 1960 — same story, just set in the Wild West. That one had a star-studded cast and was a runaway global success.

There were plenty of Westerners in Tokyo, too — especially Americans. Jack overheard a boisterous group of U.S. Marines on weekend leave bragging about their night out in Roppongi. So, naturally, he decided to investigate — if that was where the action was, he wasn't about to miss it.

Fortunately, Tokyo's signage was bilingual, and many locals spoke some English thanks to the post-war American presence. Japan had undergone a massive cultural shift since WWII, though core traditions remained deeply rooted. Jack set off on foot, strolling the two-and-a-half miles to Roppongi, taking in the sensory overload with every step.

Tokyo was a vast, living organism — nine million strong — and compared to Dublin's half a million, it felt like a different planet. Jack bounced along the shimmering pavement under a soft drizzle, the kind the Irish might call a *grand soft day*. Surprisingly, he reached his destination in what felt like the blink of an eye. In the city, time and space seemed to warp. As Einstein said, it's all relative.

Roppongi was buzzing when Jack arrived around midnight. The streets pulsed with energy. The neon glow gave the district a fairytale quality — a surreal, fleeting beauty. He sensed that come morning, it would look like a completely different place. Dr. Jekyll by day, Mr. Hyde by night.

There were massage parlours, karaoke joints, and go-go clubs as far as the eye could see — a far cry from Dublin's charming old pubs. Jack ducked into one of the karaoke bars, catching a glimpse of several hammered office workers belting out a disastrous version of *My Way*, ties wrapped around their heads. Their off-key crooning had a group of rowdy Marines in stitches.

"Hey man, come grab a beer! You look kinda lonely," one of them hollered through the haze of cigarette smoke.

Jack sauntered over and took the offered beer, joining six loud but friendly Marines around a cluttered table.

"What do we call you, and where are you from?" asked one, slapping Jack on the back.

"They call me Jack. I'm from Ireland."

"Sergeant Joey Falconetti, at your service. These assholes are Ray, Don, Max, Giovanni — and that gorilla over there is Tommy the Tank." Standing at six-foot-six and weighing over sixteen stone, Tommy lived up to his nickname. Jack also noticed a five-star tattoo on the sergeant's forearm.

"Where the fuck is Ireland?" Ray asked, squinting at him.

Giovanni burst out laughing. "You dumb son of a bitch. Ireland is that little island next to Great Britain. I should know — my mom's Irish. Your geography teacher must've had great tits, 'cause you sure didn't learn anything else. You know, there's like forty million Irish-Americans, right? They built half of New York and Boston, for fuck's sake."

One beer led to another, and soon the partygoers decided to move on — the karaoke bar had run out of novelty. They swaggered down the boisterous street until they came across a go-go dancing club, its bright neon sign beckoning them like a lighthouse to drunken sailors on a stormy sea. The doorman, built like a sumo wrestler, greeted them gruffly.

"No entrance fee, but no trouble either," he warned in his best broken English.

"Don't worry your big ol' head, big man," sneered Joey in his thick Manhattan drawl. "We're just here for the poontang, man."

As they stepped inside, a wave of smoke, perfume, and testosterone hit them like a wall. Most of the dancers were Asian

— likely from Thailand, Hong Kong, or Vietnam. It was rare to find native Japanese women working in such venues. In Japan, courtesans catered discreetly to wealthy clientele, hidden behind layers of tradition and language barriers. For most *gaijin* — foreigners — this world remained cloaked in secrecy and far removed from the in-your-face culture of the West, especially that of Americans.

The waitresses wore identical uniforms: black leather mini-skirts, knee-high boots, and tight white tops knotted above the navel, revealing ample cleavage. Every inch of their attire was designed to inflame desire — and loosen wallets. With smiles practised to perfection, they made each customer feel special — like a boyfriend in a daydream.

Joey slapped one of the waitresses on the rear.

"Bring us some saké shooters, honey — and step on it!" he shouted, letting out a deep, lecherous laugh.

The young woman, likely in her mid-twenties, flinched. She clearly didn't appreciate the Sergeant's hands-on style.

"Bet she's got a tight little ass. I'd sure like a piece of that poontang," he added crudely.

Jack stiffened. He couldn't stomach that kind of behaviour — not toward women, not toward anyone.

"Ease off, pal. Her job's hard enough without being groped by a drunken asshole," he snapped.

Joey set his beer down slowly and wiped his mouth. His expression tightened — a predator sizing up its prey.

"Oh, get a load of this guy," he said with mock surprise. "We got ourselves a moralist here. Mr. Irish Goody-Two-Shoes. Lighten up, man, I'm just havin' a bit of fun. Unless that ain't okay with His Fucking Holiness here."

He leaned in, grinning.

"So what brings you all the way to Tokyo, Redneck? Sightseeing? Or sampling the local delicacies?"

Just then, the waitress returned with a tray full of saké shots.

"See, Mr. Goody, she came back. Must like me, huh? Or maybe it's the twenty-dollar bill I'm about to tuck down that cleavage."

He handed Jack a glass.

"Now spill it. What's an Irish boy doin' all the way out here in the Far East?"

Jack downed the shooter in one go.

"I'm headed to Okinawa. Going to join a traditional karate school."

"Oh, listen up, boys!" Joey roared. "Mr. Do-Gooder here does martial arts! Should we be scared?"

He laughed so hard he slapped the table.

"That's great news, man — we're being transferred to Camp Foster. We'll be neighbours! We'll knock back some beers and screw some gook ass together!"

As the waitress turned to leave, Joey reached for her again.

She approached cautiously, wearing her best forced smile. Joey slipped a twenty-dollar bill into her top, spun her around, and grabbed both buttocks with both hands.

"See, Mr. Goody? She *loves* it."

She winced and struggled against his grip, tears beginning to form in her eyes. That was all Jack could take. He lunged forward and yanked Joey's hands away.

Joey stepped back, smirking.

"Well, well, the knight in shining armour to the rescue. Okay, buddy — how about we take this outside? Let's see what those karate skills are worth."

At that moment, the doorman — who had been keeping a wary eye — strode over with the weight of authority.

"Told you. No trouble," he said in a low, firm voice.

"Don't worry, big guy," Joey replied, knocking back two more saké shots.

"We're just leaving. Mr. Goody and I got some *fun* to finish outside."

The group split out into the neon-lit chaos of the Tokyo night. The street was alive with music, laughter, and wandering souls — the perfect stage for a showdown.

Joey stretched and cracked his knuckles.

"Alright, Irish boy, show us what you got. Let's give the folks a little entertainment."

Jack stepped forward, bracing himself — but Joey backed off.

"Nah," he said, sneering. "Tank — teach this punk a lesson in manners."

Jack's stomach dropped. He hadn't seen that coming.

Out stepped Tank — a mountain of a man — and Jack's heart sank. He hadn't trained properly in over a year. He was out of shape and knew this wasn't going to be a fair fight. A crowd began to form. The bouncer watched silently from his post; he had no jurisdiction beyond the doorway. Under Japanese law, once it left the premises, it was a matter for the police.

Jack took his stance. But before he could react, Tank bulldozed into him with the force of a rugby prop. Jack slammed to the ground, landing hard on his back. Pain radiated through his ribs — at least one was cracked, maybe two. He'd played Gaelic football as a teen, but he'd never been hit like that. Tank was a battering ram in human form.

Pinned beneath the man's massive thighs, Jack could barely move. His arms were trapped, and the pummelling began. Tank's fists, like concrete hams, smashed into Jack's face again and again. Blood poured freely.

Then, something unexpected happened.

The waitress Jack had defended suddenly ran to him, her eyes wide with panic. "Leave him alone!" she cried in broken English, hammering her tiny fists against Tank's back. They may as well have been raindrops on a rhino.

That's when the bouncer made his move.

Because a staff member was now involved, he had the right — and the duty — to intervene. He stormed over and jammed his powerful fingers into the nerve clusters just below Tank's collarbone. The pain made even the giant flinch and jerk back.

Jack gasped for air, grateful for the reprieve.

Tank snarled, ready to retaliate, but before he could act, the bouncer locked him in a kamakubi — a painful chicken-wing hold used by Japanese police and security. It was brutally effective.

Once the chaos had settled, the bouncer released him, stepping back slowly.

"Enough. Time to go. Now," he commanded.

Tank glowered. Joey seethed. But they knew better than to push their luck any further.

"Hey, talk about the fuckin' fighting Irish — that dude's a pussy, a real wimp. But don't worry, Mr. Goody, this is just a time-out. We'll finish our business in Okinawa. If I were you, I'd learn a few moves between now and then, 'cause Sumo-boy won't be there to save your ass. And I *hate* unfinished business — it's bad for my reputation." He spat in Jack's direction. "Mr. Fuckin' Goody — see ya soon, asshole." With that, Joey swaggered off, barking, "C'mon, guys, let's get the fuck outta here — there's plenty more pussy in this city."

Jack was helped back into the club, where the waitress quickly attended to his wounds. She fetched the first aid box from the staff changing room and began cleaning the blood from Jack's battered face, dabbing gently with alcohol-soaked cotton swabs. It stung like hell, thought Jack.

She introduced herself as Noriko and explained that she worked at the club to pay for her law studies at the University of Tokyo. The money was good, and the tips were even better. The downside? The groping — mostly from drunk Western tourists.

Luckily for Jack, she had taken several first aid classes and was able to strap his ribs and offer some support to his back. He'd be in pain for weeks, no doubt. And the timing couldn't have been worse — he was scheduled to arrive in Okinawa the next day and, if all went well, begin his intensive karate training at a local *ryu*. But with one or two cracked ribs? It wasn't going to be easy.

Noriko, grateful for Jack's gallant intervention, offered him a shot of saké in thanks. He gladly accepted — he needed the pick-me-up. He hadn't seen his reflection yet, but he imagined he probably looked something like the Elephant Man from David Lynch's 1980 film, with John Hurt's unforgettable performance. Thankfully, his nose wasn't broken — though everything else *felt* like it was.

Noriko gently examined his face and confirmed a fractured cheekbone and possibly a slight break around his eyebrow.

The Sumo-sized bouncer passed by, sipping coffee from a tiny paper cup that looked ridiculous in his massive hand. In halting English, he asked Jack how he was.

"American military — bad news," he muttered.

Noriko gave Jack a gentle farewell. "Sayonara," she said warmly, wishing him luck in Okinawa.

"Okinawa — best karate," the big man added with a nod, offering to call Jack a taxi. He wanted to make sure Jack got safely back to his hotel — and didn't run into his soldier friends again.

The taxi whisked Jack away through the city streets beneath a murky Tokyo sky. He needed to rest — he had a red-eye flight to Naha the following morning, and his entire body ached, especially his ribs.

The taxi driver was surprisingly chatty — or at least tried to be, using the bits of broken English he knew. Jack was too weary to entertain him and offered only a vague explanation, pointing to his bruised fists.

"Boom boom," he muttered.

The driver's eyes lit up. "Ah, okay, John-san — boom boom!" He grinned. It seemed most Japanese referred to foreign men as "John" if they didn't know their actual names.

Jack woke early the next morning, dragging himself painfully from bed. Every movement sent sharp stabs through his ribs. But once he was on his feet and moving, things eased. A hot shower helped, followed by a cold one to snap him into gear for what was sure to be a long day.

As with everything in Japan, the flight to Naha departed precisely on time — 8:00 a.m. sharp. Jack made the most of the three-hour journey by grabbing some much-needed sleep. He was the only white foreigner on board. The rest of the passengers, mostly elderly Okinawans returning from visits to the mainland, quietly filled the cabin.

Not surprising, Jack thought — there weren't many work prospects on the island unless you were a fisherman or a civil servant. Still, the flight attendants smiled brightly and were eager to help. Their fluent English was a relief.

Jack retrieved his oversized suitcase and stepped out into the Okinawan sun. The sky was cloudless, and the air felt cleaner, calmer — softer. A far cry from Tokyo's noise and density. There was a sense of stepping back in time — the pace was slower, more grounded. It reminded him of home in a strange way. Yes, he thought, I could settle here just fine.

But first things first — he needed a place to stay and a way to earn money. His initial plan was to visit the local university and offer private English lessons. He'd need someone to translate and pin a notice on the university's bulletin board. Lots of foreigners made ends meet this way without needing teaching credentials. That was then — things were a bit different now.

Jack knocked on the window of the first taxi in the queue. A short, stocky, cheerful man in his sixties greeted him with a formal bow and offered to load his suitcase.

Jack climbed into the front seat of the old Toyota Corolla, immediately warmed by the man's energy. His weathered face, tanned like cured leather, told a story of a full life. The driver assumed Jack was another American military recruit en route to one of the island's many bases. Jack smiled and introduced himself, explaining the true reason for his visit.

The driver nodded enthusiastically. "Ah, hai, hai — Jack-san, I understand."

He explained that he often worked with the military — hence his decent grasp of English, which was essential for business.

Jack had planned to head into central Naha, find cheap accommodation, and locate the address of the Shorin-ryu dojo run by the great Sensei Higa Minoru — a lead provided by Sensei Nakayama from the Shotokan dojo back on Gardiner Street in Dublin.

The driver introduced himself as Sato Uehara and offered an alternative plan: his friend Ichiro-san — a fisherman — rented out a small wooden cabin on the picturesque Mibaru Beach, about three and a half miles from Nanjo town. The cabin was modest — just a bedroom, a combined kitchen-living space, and a small bathroom. But it was clean, functional, and came with breathtaking views of the sunrise and sunset from a surrounding wooden terrace. It was quiet, a bit remote, but peaceful.

An American biology student had been renting it for the past two years and was just about to vacate.

Jack was sold.

What better way to begin a new chapter than with a cosy hideaway on one of Okinawa's most beautiful beaches?

"Ah, super, Jack-san! You won't regret it," beamed Sato.

"If you like, we can go now — maybe Ichiro-san is home."

They set off on the 35-minute drive. Jack couldn't stop admiring the lush landscape and, above all, the spotless cleanliness of the island. It was a welcome contrast to the grime of his old Dublin streets.

Just outside of Naha, as they waited at a traffic light, Jack's breath caught.

There she was — poised atop an old Dutch-style bicycle with high handlebars and a front basket. Her flowing black hair cascaded down her back over a pristine white traditional Okinawan kimono. She looked regal, ethereal — like something from a dream.

Jack was utterly gobsmacked. Sato chuckled knowingly, catching his reaction instantly.

The light turned green. She pedalled away gracefully.

Jack blinked. Was that real? A vision? A trick of the light?

Sato nudged him gently.

"Ah, Jack-san — very, very beautiful girl. Her name is Akiko-san. She is Ichiro-san's only daughter. Probably on her way to university. She studies English and Economics. Maybe… if you have spare time, you could give her some English lessons," he said with a wink.

Jack's face flushed as he realised just how visibly he'd been distracted by her beauty. Trying to mask his reaction, he turned toward the road ahead as they continued their drive. The small truck hummed steadily until they pulled up to Ichiro-san's home — a low-slung, traditional Okinawan wooden house with a wraparound terrace, nestled just steps from the shoreline. It was modest, but beautifully maintained, its sliding shoji doors opening onto a sea breeze.

Jack followed Sato to the entrance, where the two men greeted one another with the deep, formal bows typical of Japanese custom. Respect was passed between them without a word. Ichiro's eyes, sun-darkened and calm, assessed Jack with quiet curiosity.

He gestured toward the terrace and invited them to sit. "Tea or beer?" he asked in Japanese. Sato translated, but Jack needed no help choosing.

"All of us will take a beer," Sato grinned, already reaching for the chilled cans of Orion, the local brew. Ichiro joined in the smile as he handed them out.

As they sipped, Sato began to explain Jack's story. A young man, fresh from Ireland, had come halfway across the world to train in traditional Okinawan karate — a journey Ichiro found as unlikely as it was fascinating. He listened intently, his face unreadable but his silence full of weight.

"You're in luck," Ichiro finally said. "The American student moved out just yesterday. Akiko has been preparing the place."

At the mention of her name, Jack felt a new flush rise to his face. He hoped no one noticed.

Ichiro went on, explaining that he'd be honoured to rent the little beach cabin to someone who had travelled so far to embrace their traditions. His tone softened. "It's not much, but it's yours if you want it."

Jack bowed deeply. "It would be a privilege."

Ichiro nodded, the deal sealed. Then, smiling, he invited both men to stay for dinner. "You'll meet Akiko and see your new home."

Jack could hardly believe how perfectly things were unfolding. It felt like fate — or karma, as the Japanese might say.

The rest of the evening drifted by in the golden light of the setting sun. The men chatted and laughed on the terrace, Sato cheerfully interpreting Jack's thick Dublin accent. Jack learned that the beach cabin was just 500 yards down the road. He would be Akiko's neighbour of sorts — and Ichiro insisted she would be happy to help him get settled.

Just as the sun dipped below the horizon, Ichiro looked toward the road. "Akiko should be home soon. She studies four days a week at the university. It's a long ride — nearly an hour each way — but she enjoys the exercise."

He hesitated, then added, "Her mother, Yu Yan — which means 'beautiful smile' — passed away six years ago. Akiko was just sixteen. It changed her. She's still healing."

He paused again, this time more thoughtfully. "She's cautious. Careful with her heart. But strong."

As if summoned by the conversation, Akiko appeared in the doorway. She stepped gracefully out of her sandals and into a pair of simple *zori*, then moved toward the terrace. Jack sat upright.

She was tall by local standards, maybe five feet six, with straight black hair that fell down her back like a silk ribbon. Her features were delicately defined — high cheekbones, soft jawline, luminous skin — and her eyes, jet black and glinting in the dim light, seemed to look straight through him.

Catching sight of the unfamiliar Westerner, she stopped briefly, then bowed formally.

"Hajimemashite," she said politely. "It's nice to meet you."

Jack struggled to find his voice. The only Japanese words he knew were *konnichiwa* and *domo arigato*, and neither seemed appropriate. Instead, he bowed in return, hoping his silence read as respectful.

The older men exchanged amused glances. Jack was clearly smitten.

For someone who had just cycled nearly twenty miles, Akiko looked untouched by the effort — not a single strand of hair out of place. She moved with quiet, poised confidence, as if she were gliding. Jack couldn't take his eyes off her.

Ichiro gestured for her to join them. "Set the table for four, Akiko. Jack-san and Sato-san are joining us for dinner. And afterwards, please show Jack to the beach house."

Jack thought he noticed the faintest smile flicker on her lips. It vanished as quickly as it had come.

"What shall we serve our guests?" she asked her father.

"A good question," Ichiro said. "Let's start with sashimi and sushi — and our finest saké. Then I think we'll offer him some *rafute*."

Jack listened, nodding along politely, though the list of dishes was almost entirely unfamiliar. Sato, watching him, chuckled.

"*Rafute* is braised pork belly," he explained. "Cooked in *awamori*, a strong rice liquor. Melts in your mouth — goes well with beer."

Jack gave an enthusiastic nod. "Sounds great."

In truth, he'd never eaten raw fish in his life, and the thought made his stomach turn a little — but there was no way he was going to decline. Especially not in front of a fisherman and his beautiful daughter.

He'd learn, in time, that refusal — even subtle — was a dangerous misstep in Japanese etiquette. In a culture where *face (mentsu)* mattered so deeply, turning down hospitality could cause shame to the host and to oneself. To make someone "lose face" was no small offence.

Akiko returned with the food, and Jack was stunned. The dishes were exquisite — arranged with the precision of a painter, colourful and delicate. Everything looked so light, so refined, so intentional. He thought of meals back home: pork chops and mashed potatoes, maybe carrots and cabbage, piled high on a plate without ceremony. This, by contrast, was a feast for the eyes before it reached the tongue.

There were no forks or knives. Akiko returned and gently laid four pairs of *hashi* — chopsticks — next to their plates. As she placed his pair, Jack noticed the trace of a smile.

He picked them up awkwardly, unsure how to even hold them.

Akiko noticed and, without hesitation, came to his aid.

"Jack-san," she said softly, "like this."

She reached out and positioned his fingers — one chopstick resting between thumb and ring finger, the other held between thumb and forefinger, guided by the middle finger. Her touch was featherlight, her skin warm and smooth. Jack barely heard her explain that crossing the chopsticks was improper — a small but meaningful faux pas.

With great concentration, Jack attempted to lift a slice of sushi. To his amazement, he succeeded. He placed it carefully on his plate and looked up, grinning like a child.

Everyone laughed warmly.

"Itadakimasu," Akiko said sweetly, bowing her head. *I humbly receive this meal.*

Jack echoed the phrase in his mind, savouring its grace — and the company he found himself in. Everything about this moment felt surreal, as if he had stumbled into a dream. A dream, he hoped, that wouldn't end anytime soon.

Jack savoured every morsel of food, each bite washed down with the finest saké. Though he had only been in Okinawa a few hours, he already felt remarkably at home, sensing a strong bond emerging with his newfound friends. It had been ages since his taste buds had been so tantalised, and his eyes so delighted. Yet it was Akiko's presence that uplifted him most—he now understood what it meant to feel light as air. He realised, with thrilling certainty, that he was in love. He had been smitten the moment he'd first seen her at the traffic lights—that was love at first sight, a notion he'd thought only existed in movies. He could only hope the feeling was mutual.

The meal ended with a unified "gochisōsama deshita!", a heartfelt thanks for the feast.

Ichiro and Sato-san shared a knowing smile.

"Would you like a nightcap, Jack-san?" Sato asked, grinning broadly.
Jack, as an Irishman, was well-acquainted with whiskey's charms—and its warnings. He accepted graciously.

Ichiro returned with an impressive bottle, his expression glowing. Jack read the label, both in English and Japanese, and realised why the men were beaming: "Ichiro's Malt – Hanyu 15-Year Single Malt." He would learn later that the whisky was extremely rare and expensive, intended only for special occasions. This generous offering transcended hospitality—it was a gesture of true friendship.

Akiko placed four delicate glasses on the table. Jack was pleasantly surprised that she would join them. Ichiro poured with formal care. They raised their glasses in unison—"kanpai!"—and drained them. Jack then taught them the Irish equivalent: "Sláinte!" The pronunciation was a challenge, and the laughter that followed was warm and genuine. The whisky was exceptional—proof that when the Japanese set their minds to something, they strove for excellence.

The glasses were refilled, and again came four heartfelt toasts— kanpais and sláintes—in a relaxed, joyful atmosphere. Jack realised he couldn't remember the last time he had felt so content so effortlessly.

Sato-san stood with a respectful bow.

"Oyasuminasai—I must leave; I'm up again at six."

They all looked at the clock; it was already thirty minutes past midnight. Sato shook Jack's hand.

"We'll see much more of each other soon."

With a final bow, he whispered "oyasuminasai" and departed.

Ichiro spoke to his daughter softly,

"Akiko-darling, please show Jack to his room. He must be tired."

She bowed and invited Jack to follow her. Jack slung his bag over his shoulder and stepped into the quiet, star-filled night. The sky's vastness humbled him. Akiko smiled gently as they walked toward the cabin.

The rhythmic lap of waves against the shore was soothing under the luminous moonlight. The cabin stood just 150 yards from Akiko's home. Jack admired its small terrace—complete with a wicker table and chairs. He could imagine summer evenings there, shorts on, cool beers in hand, Akiko by his side.

She opened the cabin door and said softly,

"Dōzo, Jack-san."

Though the space was small—about 90 square feet—it felt unexpectedly spacious. It was sparse, purposeful, almost zen in its simplicity. The cabin held every essential: a fridge-freezer, a bottled-gas stove, and a double futon—a new sleeping arrangement compared to the camping trips with his friends. A sliding door led to a compact toilet and walk-in shower. Everything was spotless and smelled faintly of cedar. The terrace and exterior wood carried subtle notes of cypress and pine.

Akiko showed him a paraffin heater, which she explained would make cool winter nights comfortable—though temperatures rarely dropped below 15°C. She pointed out a closet stocked with linens and towels and told him about a village launderette for his laundry. She then bowed deeply, saying "Yōkoso, Jack-san"—welcome— and slipped away into the night like a graceful spirit.

Unsure whether to bow, shake hands, or hug, Jack simply said,

"Thank you so much for your more-than-kind hospitality, Akiko-san."
He began unpacking his clothes into the wardrobe beside the futon. He'd brought a few personal items—photos and some

good-luck talismans—including a Claddagh ring from his mother. She had told him it would protect him.

On the dining table lay a small note:

"Welcome—whoever you are. I hope you enjoy your stay as much as I did. There are cold beers in the fridge. Enjoy. I miss the place already. —Mike from New York."

Jack dropped onto the futon, but found sleep elusive. Jet-lagged though he was, it didn't seem to matter—his mind was racing with thoughts of Akiko and the adventure ahead. When sleep finally came, it was deep and uninterrupted. He awoke the next morning around 10 a.m. to the gentle sound of waves lapping the beach.

Stepping onto the terrace, he paused—the view took his breath away. Fishing boats bobbed in the distance against a radiant sunrise.

Jack stretched deeply and inhaled the salty morning air. The sharp tang of iodine hit his nostrils, and the freshness filled his lungs— it was invigorating. Little did he know that it would become addictive, even primal, a vital part of his daily rhythm.

He thought of breakfast but realised there was absolutely nothing in the cabin. A trip to town was in order—and an interesting one, at that. Thankfully, Mike, the American, had left a map annotated with post-its marking places he'd found helpful and enjoyable. Jack felt sincerely grateful. It would be an excellent guide.

His beach hut was located on Mibaru Beach, about three miles from Nanjo, the nearest town with a population of around 40,000. Mike had marked a small supermarket on the map, noting that it sold practically everything—from fresh vegetables to seafood.

Jack threw on a tracksuit and shoved a handful of yen into his pocket. He decided to start the day with a run along the beach and see where it led. The sand was fine and golden, and the stretch ran just under a mile, eventually connecting to Hyakuna Beach.

At the far end, he spotted a signpost pointing inland to a café named Café Yabusachi, just 200 yards or so away. He decided to check it out.

Climbing the stairs to the entrance, he was met with a view that took his breath away. The ocean sparkled endlessly under the morning sun. The little café was bustling, filled with young people—mostly students, he guessed. This must be their favourite hangout.

As with most places in Japan, it was immaculately clean. On the counter sat pitchers of freshly squeezed juice alongside an inviting display of home-baked breads, pastries, cold cuts, and fresh vegetables.

A young girl behind the counter, impeccably dressed in a black uniform and matching cap embroidered with the café's name, greeted him with an elegant bow.

"Konnichiwa, yōkoso—hello, welcome."

Jack bowed in return and tried, somewhat awkwardly, to indicate he wanted breakfast. He pointed to the pitcher of orange juice.

"Ah! Orenjijūsu," she said cheerfully.

Well, that's easy to remember, Jack thought.

He recalled that the Japanese writing system comprised hiragana, katakana, and kanji, with katakana used to write foreign loan words, many of which were recognisable to English speakers. Still, ordering a meal was proving to be a bit of a challenge.

Just then, a familiar voice called out:

"Jack-san!"

He turned swiftly and saw Akiko, beaming, her dark eyes glittering like black diamonds. She wore sky-blue jeans, sandals, and a snug, midriff-bearing white T-shirt that revealed her toned belly and a pierced navel. Her body was sun-kissed and athletic— she radiated health and vitality.

Though simply dressed, she exuded elegance. Jack was momentarily stunned.

Akiko walked over and smiled.

"I'll help you finish your order," she said kindly.

Soon, a tray was placed before him—freshly squeezed orange juice, a small pot of tea, toast with butter, and an assortment of jams. She invited him to join her at a table where she sat with her university friends. They had the day off and were relaxing together.

They welcomed Jack warmly. The group—four girls and two boys from various universities around the island—were delighted to meet an English-speaking foreigner, especially from a far-off country like Ireland.

"We've never met someone from Ireland before," one girl exclaimed.

"And you don't have red hair!"

Jack laughed heartily at the cliché.

"Not every Irishman is a red-haired leprechaun with a beard, you know."

They all laughed, though most of them struggled with the word "leprechaun," and Jack, for his part, found it difficult to explain.

They introduced themselves and their areas of study—economics, philosophy, marine biology, and English. While not all were fluent in English, they communicated well enough to make Jack feel welcome.

They were curious about what had brought Jack to Okinawa. He explained his journey and his dream of being accepted into a traditional *karate ryu*.

Tatsuo, one of the boys, lit up with excitement.

"Jack-san, I practice *Shitō-ryū*, a traditional Okinawan karate style. I've been training since I was a child. I'm a *yūdansha*—a black belt."

He leaned forward, eyes gleaming.

"I'd be honoured to introduce you to my sensei, Master Saitō. I can't guarantee admission—that's entirely up to him. He's very strict but also warm-hearted. Once you're accepted into the dojo, you become like family."

Jack could barely contain his excitement.

"Tomorrow is Tuesday," Tatsuo continued, "and adult training begins at 6 p.m. sharp. Come at 5:30—I'll introduce you."

To say Jack was thrilled would be an understatement. He was over the moon at the thought of being welcomed into a true Okinawan dojo. That night, as he lay in bed back in his beach hut, he could hardly sleep—his thoughts alive with anticipation for what the next day might bring.

Under the sword lifted high, there is hell making you tremble.
But go ahead, and you will have the land of bliss.

Miyamoto Musashi

CHAPTER
Ten

Dublin Summer present

It was Friday, and as usual, Sophie was working her weekly late night. The clock read 11:10 p.m., and she was the last to leave the restaurant—except for Ms. Dom, who had arranged accommodation nearby. Sophie kissed Dom good night, closed the door, and stepped into the crisp night air. From O'Donoghue's pub next door came laughter and song—Jack would normally be there to collect her on Fridays. They'd slip into the pub for a final drink before closing, sharing gossip she'd picked up during her shift. But tonight, Jack was with the lads at The Yacht, competing in the final of a darts tournament. The pub had extended its bar hours until 1 a.m., and the crowd was in fine form.

Sophie walked down the narrow lane toward Merrion Row. Suddenly, a massive, ham-sized hand clamped over her mouth and face from behind. She was lifted off her feet with terrifying force and shoved into the back of a black Mercedes S-Class. Baby-Face Paolo sat there, bag in hand; he pressed it over Sophie's head and forced her to the floor. Her wrists were bound tightly with duct tape. She was gagged and told to stay quiet.

The chauffeur was none other than corrupt detective Sean Doherty, who flashed his badge to onlookers—convincing them this was official business, not a kidnapping. "Yeah, she must be involved in something serious… drugs or murder," they murmured as she was driven off.

Sophie was taken to an abandoned flat on Gardiner Street in Dublin's north side—not exactly a romantic hideaway. They dragged her up a crumbling staircase and threw her unceremoniously onto a battered sofa. Paolo yanked off the bag from her head and was amused by her terror-stricken expression.

"Don't worry, sweetie—we'll take good care of you. Right, Toni?"

"You bet," sneered Big Tony.

"You're about to get a bit of Italian hospitality."

Sophie sobbed and shook with fear. The humiliation fueled their twisted excitement. Paolo's eyes roved over her—full cherry lips, round breasts, long tanned legs in that polka-dot dress.

"OK, sweetie, let's call lover boy and set up a meeting. What do we tell him?"

"That his bit of French skirt is clean and unhurt… for now. Cheer up, baby—we might even have a ménage à trois with Big Tony."

"Shut up, you piece of shit," Sophie spat out. The words felt good—she summoned inner strength and bided her time.

Sean spoke up:

"I'm done—my part ends here. I don't want any part in this violence or gang rape."

Big Tony grinned.

"Come on, man—just having a bit of fun. Besides, who knows? Maybe the little demoiselle would enjoy a couple of Italian stallions."

He slipped an envelope into Sean's hand.

"Here's €2,000—nice driving money. You get €5k upfront, €5k when we trap Hopkins. The choice is yours—morals or money.

From what I hear, you prefer the latter. Stick around. We'll contact you with drop-off details. And Sean—act normal. We don't want Deputy Dog sniffing around, do we?"

Sean tucked the envelope away and left.

Meanwhile, at The Yacht Pub, the mood was electric. Danger and Jack had just clinched the darts final, winning two tickets to a U2 concert at Croke Park. Pints flew as last orders rang out. Lenny dashed to the bar, ordering double Jamesons and Pepsis on rounds—almost as if stockpiling for winter. They intended to carry on back at Jack's flat—just down the road.

They arrived at the apartment quietly—Jack motioning for silence as they opened the door, careful not to wake Sophie. Danger and Lenny giggled, the clinking bottles louder than intended.

Jack flicked on the light and immediately sensed something was wrong: Sophie's shoes weren't in the hallway—she never wore them inside. Her handbag was missing from the table. Panic flooded him. He raced to the bedroom, calling her name—only to find it empty.

"What's wrong, Hop? Froggie not here? Maybe she met friends?" Anto offered, trying to reassure.

"Yeah, she'll drop a message, Jack—no need to worry," Bradley added.

Jack nodded and reached for the phone—she'd at least left a message, he hoped.

At that moment, the phone rang—a shrill, piercing tone that made everyone jump—except Jack. He picked up with steely calm, expecting the worst.

"Hello, lover boy," Baby-Face Paolo sneered.

"Don't worry—we've got your French skirt. She's safe in our protective care. Listen carefully, Jacko: do exactly what we tell you, or you'll never see Froggie again. She's quite the turn-on— you've got a real mover in her. Pickup is tomorrow at midnight, down at Dollymount Strand. Come alone—be ready when the headlights flash."

Jack placed the receiver down with mechanical precision, feeling its weight in his hand. His friends watched, faces awed with fear. Jack collapsed onto the couch, hand over his face—he wished it was all a nightmare. He longed to wake up to Sophie calling from the kitchen:

"Le petit déjeuner est prêt, chérie."

But grief was real, a sword poised over his life. The die was cast—the game had begun. Professional assassins, no bluff—this required courage, cunning, and composure.

He shared everything with the lads. They immediately offered to help—but Jack refused. "This is my fight. I can't risk any of you." They persisted—"I'm there whether you like it or not, Jack. You're our buddy—and so is Sophie."

He regretted even telling them the drop-off time and location, but it was too late—they insisted. He'd have to protect both his friends and Sophie—and hope he wasn't too late.

The lads left reluctantly at about 4 a.m., promising to return the next morning to hatch a plan. Jack went to bed, but sleep eluded him—his mind was a restless pinball machine that no meditation from Okinawa could silence. Despite the short, fitful night, he rose at 11 a.m. and performed his daily breathing exercises on the terrace, connecting to kokoro, the heart of the universe.

After callisthenics, he downed a glass of freshly squeezed orange juice and pulled on his jogging gear, determined that a hard run would clear his mind and sharpen his thinking. He pushed himself through the final mile until his lungs threatened to burst—a familiar metallic taste signalling extreme exertion or anxiety.

Back at the apartment, he took a power shower, ending with a blast of cold water. He emerged calm, composed, and fully alert, brewed a coffee, and stepped outside just in time to see the lads arriving as promised. "Fuck that," he thought—they weren't backing down. The fab six—Danger, Bradley, Lenny, Sonar, Anto, and Trigger the plumber—ambled over, mugs of steaming coffee in hand. Plans were discussed, ideas swapped.

Lenny explained he'd convinced his boss, Arthur at the transport company, to lend the lads three Mitsubishi Pajeros, rugged 4WDs equipped with heavy-duty halogen lamps and sirens—originally used for weekend hunts. With Lenny's gift of the gab, Arthur had agreed.

Everything was organised: they would pick up the Pajeros that afternoon, then hide them in the dunes at night, waiting for the main event. Jack thought the concept was sound—they needed surprise and illusion to confront hardened criminals, not local youth from Sheriff Street.

Meanwhile, Joey Maloney had been monitoring colleague Sean Doherty. Suspicious of Sean's behaviour for months, Joey noted a dramatic change—Sean was no longer the easygoing man who shared whiskeys and pints with him at Kavanagh's. His wardrobe had upgraded, his demeanour altered. Joey wondered, "Where's the extra revenue coming from? Is he selling intel to the mob, or just looking the other way?" Despite Big Toni's warning to keep a low profile, Sean had upgraded his meals, clothes, and shoes.

Perhaps a mistress? Joey thought, so he began tailing Sean weekly to uncover the truth. On Saturday morning at 8 a.m., he parked discreetly about thirty yards from Sean's semidetached Tallaght house and waited. After a long watch, Sean emerged at 10 a.m. looking sharp, climbed into his ageing Ford Cortina, and drove off. Joey tailed him in his official Ford Sierra. Unknown to Joey, Robbie Maher, in a shabby Escort, was also following, carrying two Smith & Wessons bound for the New Yorkers. Robbie trailed about fifty yards behind Joey.

Sean headed toward town, avoiding typical midweek jams. Thirty-five minutes later, he pulled up on Gardiner Street, which was still quiet—most weekend shoppers were sleeping off last night's hangovers. Joey watched as Sean parked and entered an abandoned, dilapidated building, beside which sat a black S-Class Mercedes rental. Joey thought, "If that's a piece on the side, she's not living the high life."

Hungry, Joey walked into "The Queen of Tarts" opposite the derelict building. He lit a John Player and vowed to quit the fags—"killing me," he mused—and ordered a full Irish breakfast with soda bread and tea. The waitress was friendly; Joey scored a window seat with a perfect view. When his breakfast arrived fifteen minutes later, his mood soared.

As the café filled, he prepared to light a third cigarette—just then, he saw Sean exit, accompanied by a huge, menacing man, at least six-foot-six and over 260 pounds, clearly of Italian descent. Sean looked small beside him—Joey thought, "That's definitely not a fish-and-chip guy." They spoke briefly, with Sean looking uneasy. The big man slapped him on the back, and they parted ways.

Joey's mind was racing like a Formula One engine at 10,000 rpm. *What the fuck* had Sean gotten himself into? His immediate thought was drugs—Dublin's cartels had deep Dutch connections. One of the most notorious, Christy "the Dapper" Kelly, trafficked ecstasy and heroin in massive quantities. Joey was torn: follow Sean now or stake out the place. He exhaled a long drag of cigarette smoke and resolved on the latter—the action was happening *here*. Sean would return, and Joey would be ready.

He stepped outside for fresh air. The day stretched long before him, whether he liked it or not. Two boys, not yet twelve, hurtled past on battered bikes held together by hope. They didn't seem to mind—they were free. Joey didn't relish spending hours in a café when there was a pub on Talbot Street calling his name.

"Hey lads," he called. "Fancy earning a few bob?" They skidded to a halt and turned, eyes bright. The words "a few bob" were magic. They wheeled around and walked back, curiosity evident.

"Sure, mister—what's the job, and how much?" the taller one asked.

Joey rummaged in his pockets. "How about a quid each—half now, the rest when it's done?" The boys grinned ear to ear, already picturing sweets and Cokes.

"Now listen," Joey whispered. "See that house across the road, dark green door? When a tall red-haired man enters, sprint down to O'Shea's pub. I'll be in the bar. No messing—go straight in. Got it?"

They nodded. The older was Aido—dark hair, hazel eyes, square jaw. Joey thought, *he'll break hearts*. The younger, Gerry, had blond hair, pale blue eyes, and a face still innocent. But they were street-wise—knew everything about the neighbourhood. Joey dropped fifty pence into each palm. "Off you go—remember: as soon as you see him, get moving."

Aido and Gerry sped off on their patched-up bikes.

Before heading to the pub, Joey paid a visit to the Paddy Power next door. His brother-in-law, Tom, had tipped him the night before: *"Fire in the Sky" at 30/1*. Joey slipped five ten-pound notes across the counter, his smile widening at the prospect: a £1,500 return.

Next door, he pushed open the pub's double doors—smoke and stout aroma hit him immediately. It was 12:30 p.m., and the bar was busy. He checked the clock—racetrack action at 1:30 p.m. Ordered a pint, took a seat with a clear view of the TV, and grabbed the Irish Independent on the bar. The headline—"Divorce poll in October tipped"—made him smirk. *That'll stir the pot in Holy Catholic Ireland*, he thought.

The bartender set down his beer with a friendly nod. The pub's clientele—dockers, drivers, tradesmen—were catching up on the morning's banter, others darting next door to the bookies. The 3 p.m. FA Cup Derby between Liverpool and Everton flickered on the screen, a draw for local fans. Today, though, all eyes were on Cheltenham.

With his second pint, Joey watched the TV volume crank up. The seven-horse flat race began; Maggie's Farm was the favourite. Joey's best horse, *Fire in the Sky*, lagged at the start. The pub moaned. When the underdog lurched into view on the third lap, whispers rose. By the final stretch, *Fire in the Sky* surged—neck and neck with Maggie's Farm. The commentator bellowed, *"It's unbelievable—they're level!"* Joey's heart pounded. The pub exploded when Joey's horse edged ahead at the line—photo finish!

Cheers erupted. Pints and whiskeys were snapped up. Next door, the bookie braced for wave after wave of punters. It was a miserable day for the bookie but a jackpot one for patrons. Joey soaked it in, the creamy pint in his hand—and his mind raced again: £1,500. Was this day turning out grand after all?

The derby between Liverpool and Everton lived up to expectations, as was customary. At the halftime whistle, the score was one apiece. Immediately, punters surged to the exit to collect their winners and continue the festivities next door. Joey joined the throng. The payout desk was bustling. "Nice win, sir," the bookmaker smiled. "Twenties or fifties?" Joey was savouring every moment. He requested twenties.

His eyes gleamed as the clerk counted out 75 twenty-pound notes, placing them in a large sealed envelope. "Pleasure doing business. Enjoy your day—and we're always here for your next wager." Joey tucked the envelope into his inside pocket and returned to the smoke-filled bar.

The second half had just kicked off, and the atmosphere was effervescent. The bartender struggled to keep pace with the flood of pints and shorts. Joey, absorbed in the match, was on his third pint. The referee checked his watch several times—injury time was near. The screen showed ninety minutes plus four added. At that moment, local hero and Irish international Ronnie Whelan surged forward, weaving past two defenders with perfect balance, and unleashed a booming strike into the top-left corner—net bulging.

The entire pub erupted. Everton's keeper and defenders were stunned. More pints and shots were ordered; punters happily reinvested their winnings. The bartender was drenched in sweat; his shift partner arrived and stared in disbelief at the beer taps. "At this rate," he thought, "the casks'll be dry by midnight."

Suddenly, the bar door burst open as though hit by a gale, and Aido and Gerry raced in with beet-red faces. They scanned the room feverishly until spotting Joey at the bar, pint halfway to his lips. "Mister! Mister! He's arrived—the redheaded man—with takeaways!" The bar stared in disbelief—about as subtle as a marching band in a library. Joey nearly choked on his drink. "Jesus, lads—easy now!" The boys held out their hands for their reward. They certainly didn't waste time, thought Joey, as he handed each 50p. "Good job, men." He downed his pint, licked his lips, and strode out the door. Discretion was now vital.

He headed straight to his parked car near the apartment and slid into the driver's seat, praying he wouldn't be spotted. He had a gut feeling things were about to escalate. Minutes crept by; Joey felt drowsy—a belated hangover from earlier drinks. Stakeouts were such a pain—he'd endured plenty over his 15 years on the force and always hated them. Hanging around doing nothing—what a bollocks! Thankfully, he had the radio—Gary Byrne kept him company through much of the late afternoon.

The car clock read 6:20 p.m. and hunger gnawed at him—he could "eat a child's arse through railings," as Dubliners said. But he dared not leave. Larry Gogan had replaced Gary Byrne, playing golden oldies from the '60s and '70s—perfect. He tapped his fingers to a favourite tune. Then, through the passenger mirror, he spotted Aido and Gerry pedalling toward him. Just the distraction he needed!

He slipped out of the car and waved them down. They skidded to a stop.

"Got a job for you lads," he whispered.

"What's in it for us?" the taller asked.

"A quid each—go to Mario's for a large chips and a cod. Keep the 50p change. Sound good?"

"No bother, mister—want salt and vinegar?"

"Salt, not too much vinegar—and a 7UP. Here's the cash. And be quiet, coming back." Joey passed over the coin.

They bolted toward Mario's, famous citywide for its fish and chips.

Left alone, Joey watched the apartment intently. Something was going to happen—soon. Fifteen minutes later, the lads returned with steaming parcels.

"Well done, lads. Here's another 20p."

"Piece of cake, mister—call on us anytime."

They sped off again as Joey unwrapped the chips and cod. The aroma hit him—pure bliss. He bit in—"fuckin' gorgeous." The radio played "Waterloo Sunset," his all-time favourite. He smiled—simple pleasures, he thought. Full moon and dusk combined to bathe the street in soft light. Sleep threatened, but Joey bumped up the radio volume. He splashed water on his face—no slumber tonight.

At 11 p.m., Noel Andrews took over, self-styled "Night Owl", just as a black car swept past and then stopped. Sean emerged nervously, flanked by the giant Toni and Baby-Face Paolo, escorting a young woman in a dark hood. "Fuck me," Joey whispered—her silhouette matched Sophie. They shoved her into the Mercedes' back seat. Sean jumped in, and the V8 roared to life.

Joey waited for about 50 yards before following—silent, resolved. The cards were now on the table.

Being a detective, Joey drove his own car—a 1985 Ford Sierra XR4i powered by a thirsty 2.8-litre engine. Joey didn't foot the petrol bill, so fuel consumption was hardly a concern—it was one of the perks of the job.

He loved that car. With 160 bhp under the bonnet, it had plenty of poke, and today it came in handy. As with all Garda and Special Branch cars, it was painted bright blue—a sore thumb, so discretion was essential. The department had secured a deal for a fleet of matching vehicles—budgets being what they are, every penny counts.

Joey decided to radio Store Street for backup; the situation warranted it. He reached for the centrally mounted Motorola car phone beneath the dashboard and dialled. No dial tone—the line was dead. *"Fuck this,"* he thought. He yanked the handset, and the cord snapped cleanly—held together only by invisible tape.

Someone had sabotaged him while he was cosy in the pub or café earlier. But who? Had the saboteur tipped off Sean and the Italians? Perhaps it was a warning. Fords were notoriously easy to break into—and cutbacks had left them without alarms. As one sergeant had quipped, "All Fords should be hung by the bollocks." Nearly seventy percent of stolen cars were Fords. Owners had resorted to anti-crook steering locks, padlocks, cut-off switches— they'd tried *everything*. Joey got a chill. He was alone.

He rummaged through the glovebox and found his Sig Sauer P226—his service weapon. Whoever had ransacked the car hadn't thought to remove it. Joey had drawn that gun only once—just a warning shot. He didn't like firearms, but sometimes there was no choice.

The destination lay 20 minutes away. Joey kept well behind, driving with sidelights only. Traffic was sparse—ideal for tailing, but he was equally visible. The Mercedes crossed Ballybough Bridge into Fairview, heading toward Clontarf—where Jack lived. *"Where the hell are they going?"* he wondered.

He flicked on the radio—noir jazz to calm his nerves. Noel Andrews followed "Thriller" with The Doors' ominous "The End":

"This is the end, beautiful friend... The end of everything that stands..."

The song sent an icy chill down his spine. He switched to Sinatra's "New York, New York." *"That's more like it—I don't plan to kick the bucket tonight,"* he thought.

They continued past Fairview Park, turned onto Clontarf Road by The Yacht Pub—Jack's local—and passed Dollymount Wooden Bridge. The Causeway Road, which led to Bull Island, now loomed ahead. Sean abruptly veered onto it, switched off the lights—and they plunged into darkness. Not a streetlamp in sight. The only sound: the call of a stone-curlew wading through the marsh. *"So this is the drop-off,"* thought Joey.

He parked discreetly, killed the engine, and drew his Sig's holster. The gun felt safe against his left shoulder. Right-handed, he fastened the straps. He decided to walk the final stretch—no headlights, no sirens—through marshland to the dunes. The Mercedes eased to a stop near the sand dunes at precisely 11:30 p.m.—thirty minutes before the showdown. But two cars were parked nearby: one 30 yards away, the other 50.

"Courting couples," Sean said. "We'll have to get rid of them."

"Leave it to me," Toni declared. He asked Paolo for a hockey mask from the boot—a Halloween-issue replica from *Friday the 13th*. The effect would terrify ordinary folk.

Toni exited the Mercedes. As the suspension rose, the car felt "260 pounds lighter." He opened the boot and pulled out his trusty baseball bat—the very one he had breezed through customs in his luggage. Customs had just smiled and waved him through after he explained it was a birthday gift for his Yankees-mad nephew.

The Ford Escort occupants were a young couple in their early twenties, making out. Only the courtesy lights illuminated the cabin. Toni strode forward, bat lowered in his right hand—a terrifying presence. Most people would have shit themselves at the sight of this giant wearing a hockey mask. He approached the car unnoticed, parked on the left side of the road with its boot facing him.

He headed for the front left door—but realised it was the passenger side. It was a right-hand-drive vehicle, as are most cars in Ireland. He'd briefly forgotten he wasn't back in the States. Through the window, he saw a young, nearly twenty-year-old girl, topless, her boyfriend sucking greedily on one big pink nipple. *"Nice rack,"* Toni thought. *"I wouldn't mind a piece."*

He walloped the bat against the door, crouched close to the window. The effect was instantaneous. The girl screamed, her arms flailing to cover herself, panic etched on both their faces. The boyfriend fumbled blindly at the dashboard, eventually finding the ignition. He started the engine and, in his terror, shifted into first gear without using the clutch. The car screeched away, revving high—no headlights on.

Seconds later, Toni spotted another vehicle: a white Austin Mini about twenty yards ahead, its boot also facing him. The occupants must have heard the commotion—the Escort's revs, the girl's scream—because the Mini's lights flicked on just as Toni began walking towards it at his calm, unstoppable pace. The moonlight was faint but enough to reveal the hulking figure wielding a bat in their rearview mirror. The driver violently dumped the clutch, tyres spinning briefly before the Mini screeched off into the night.

Toni checked his watch—10:50 p.m. Just then, a small sports car appeared in the distance, turning toward him. *"That could be Jack Hopkins,"* he thought. He spun on his heel and strode back toward

Sean and Paolo, covering the ground in massive, purposeful strides.

I want to see Sophie, Jack shouted defiantly. At his words, the giant Toni struck the Mercedes bonnet. The back-left door swung open, and baby-faced Paolo, wearing another terrifying mask, yanked Sophie out by the shoulder.

Take off the hood, demanded Jack. Paolo removed the black hood, revealing a terrified and disoriented Sophie, sobbing uncontrollably and staring at the ground.

Don't be shy, sweetie—look up, your hero's here, sneered Paolo. Upon seeing Jack, Sophie burst into tears and wailed, « Oh mon amour ».

Jack clenched his calloused fist as rage surged within him like a pressurised steam boiler.

Robbie, hidden among the dunes, watched the exchange through night-vision binoculars. He had strict orders to assist the Italians discreetly—no shoot-outs, no police entanglements. His boss, Christy, had expanded the cartel's smuggling routes to Mexico, Colombia, and Russia; Robbie's language degrees in Spanish and Russian, earned in prison at taxpayer expense, were now invaluable.

Outnumbered and outgunned, Jack prayed the diversion tactic conjured by his friends would succeed.

Hands in the air, and start walking, Jack, barked Toni. The massive silhouette beside Toni stayed silent—Jack recognised the shape.

We meet halfway, and you let her go, Jack suggested, stepping forward. Paolo shoved Sophie ahead, Smith & Wesson aimed at her temples. Guns were pointed at Jack from Toni and Sean; the scene felt pulled from an old Western.

Walked fifteen yards to a midpoint. Sophie trembled, murmuring, « Oh mon pauvre chérie ». Paolo shoved her once more, then trained his weapon on Jack.

Just get in the car, love—don't look back, Jack implored. Paolo sneered, Our turn now, lover boy. If you hadn't shown, we'd have taken our frustrations out on your chérie. Might've been fun, though.

They escorted Jack back to the Mercedes, pausing to reveal their true complexions—only the silent third man kept his mask.

They marched onto the empty beach.

« Party time," Toni announced, returning the bat to his grip. « Message from Joey Falconetti—don't worry, we don't want to kill you. We just want some fun. Think your sweetheart could live with a freak like you when we're done?

Toni swung the bat upward, smashing Jack's upper lip and shattering cartilage in his nose. With a cruel grin, he ripped Jack's shirt off, revealing shredded muscle and zero fat. The bat's next blow crushed Jack's sternum—he heaved for breath but stood, supported by Sean and Paolo's vice-like grips.

Five hundred yards away, Lenny climbed onto a Pajero's roof, scanning with night-vision binoculars. « Go—now! They've got Jack! » he ordered. The three Pajeros roared toward the beach in a spearhead formation.

Back on the sand, Toni, jacket off, unleashed a brutal flurry: two bone-crunching blows to ribs, a savage strike to the shoulder and collarbone. Jack felt his ribs crack, cartilage shatter. It felt like hanging from a butcher's hook—no slicing, just breaking. He prayed fiercely, clutching hope.

More blows to his right side. Toni was enjoying his craftsmanship, each swing precise. Knee smash—Jack's joints screamed.

Then chaos erupted: blinding headlights, wailing horns, roaring engines from the Pajeros as they encircled the gang, conjuring a mini-sandstorm.

Paolo and Sean released their grips, reaching for their guns. Toni shielded his face from the sand and lights.

Jack sprang forward like a panther, fueled by adrenaline that surged through his battered body. A killing machine was in motion. He unleashed a lightning-fast morote chūdan tsuki—a double-fisted midsection blow—first to the giant's solar plexus, then the left.

Though Jack was just under six feet one and giving away nearly eight inches, targeting the head would've reduced his power. These brutal body shots hit their mark, forcing the giant to double over in agony.

With the height advantage gone, Jack followed with a powerful right circular palm-heel strike (teishō-uchi) to the man's lower left jaw. The blow staggered him. Jack then delivered an enpi uchi, an elbow strike to the side of the head, injecting his formidable hip power. His hours at the makiwara had paid off—the head snapped sideways, winded.

Next came an upward reverse spear-hand strike to the groin. The giant's right knee hit the sand as he dropped the bat and reached— too late—for his holster. Jack seized his moment, driving a double teishō-uchi: one palm smashed Toni's left temple, the other crushed his right jaw. The shock rattled the giant's brain.

Not finished, Jack slammed his right elbow into Toni's temple, snapping his head to the left. Then, with brutal precision, he grabbed a wristful of hair and tetsui-hammered the base of Toni's neck. In a horrifying instant, the blow broke the cervical vertebrae, severing the spinal cord. The giant's massive form collapsed face-first into the sand, bouncing twice—game over.

Jack stood, breathing hard. His fight-or-flight chemistry was vivid: boosted strength, numb pain, heightened senses, surging energy, deeper breaths—a perfect storm.

Meanwhile, the other two men drew their weapons, firing wildly at the arriving Pajeros. Sean, mask off, looked frantic, completely unhinged. Jack's lightning assault—nine savage strikes in under six seconds—had turned the tide.

Jack's gaze locked on Paolo, who was just about to take aim at a Pajero. Jack struck preemptively with a right mawashi geri (roundhouse kick) to Paolo's abdomen, disarming him. Paolo doubled over, retching in agony. Jack's fists were instruments of calculated pain.

From a low stance, Jack hammered Paolo's right kidney with a left hammer fist. Paolo collapsed to his knees. Jack then delivered a right shuto (knife-hand strike) to the side of Paolo's neck, targeting the carotid and snapping his head sideways. Within seconds, Jack slipped behind him, clasped his head, and twisted—crack! A final kick in the back sent Paolo slumping into the sand, head-first, lifeless.

Two down. One to go.

Jack pushed himself upright, the effort agonising—his ribs felt shattered, and his sternum protested with every breath. He stumbled toward the Mercedes, scanning the drawn faces of his friends. All of them stood still, stunned by what they'd witnessed. None had ever realised Jack could unleash such lethal force. They approached, wrapping him in gentle embraces—tears shimmering in every eye. Last came Joey, rubbing his head, muttering, "Fuckin' hell, Jack—fuckin' hell, man."

Joey made his way up the dune, then descended toward the two lifeless bodies—an eerie battlefield. He pulled on rubber gloves from his pocket, determined not to compromise the forensic evidence. He grasped the giant's hair, tilting the head to reveal a smashed face and a broken neck. The bloodied baseball bat lay nearby. Searching for his Sig Sauer, Joey realised it was missing—"I'm up to my neck in shit," he thought.

He wiped clean the Smith & Wesson he'd retrieved from the giant's hand and carefully placed it back into the corpse. The other body revealed a similar broken neck—and no Sig Sauer. Joey scanned for bullet casings but found none. "They'll be buried deep in the sand… good luck finding them," he muttered.

Danger draped a blanket over Jack's battered frame and handed him a bottle of water. "Christ, Lenny—don't ye have anything stronger?" Jack quipped, collapsing into the back seat. Joey sank in beside him. One Pajero sported a shattered windscreen; another bore two bullet holes. Lenny sighed—Monday morning would be painful. "It was for a just cause," he said, though the adrenaline high would take a while to fade.

The trio of Pajeros rolled slowly down Causeway Road. Two hundred yards ahead, Jack spotted his Fiat Spider, parked half on the pavement—Sophie was still inside, frozen in grief. She'd heard the chaos, feared the worst. Lenny pulled in behind her, and

Jack climbed out, stumbling toward her. Gently placing a hand on her head, he whispered, "Doucement, doucement, ma belle… c'est fini."

Sophie looked up at his shattered visage, then threw herself into his arms. Their embrace was fierce—two hearts that nearly died, now clinging to each other. Their kiss was endless, pure, witnessed only by seven silent men—all with tears on their cheeks. Jack gave a tired wave, helped Sophie into the passenger seat, climbed into his Fiat, and started the engine. 2:30 a.m. Saturday. A night that would live forever in memory.

Not far away, a certain Robbie Maher sat in his old Ford Escort, parked in the Yacht Pub's car park. He had inclined the passenger seat and gotten some welcome shut-eye. After all, the night had been quite emotional and exhausting. He wiped his eyes and took a plastic bottle of water from the glove compartment. Unscrewing the cap, he lifted it to his lips and took a large gulp of cool water. Then, he poured some into his left hand and splashed it on his face—it was cool and refreshing. He was now ready to contact the press and put the preconceived plan into action.

He pulled his mobile phone from his haversack and scrolled through his contact list. He pressed on the letter "I", and a list of five contacts appeared. The one that interested him was the Irish Independent Newspapers. The edition he was particularly focused on was the Evening Herald, published by the Independent Group. He wanted the article to appear in that Saturday evening's edition. It would send a shockwave through Dublin's organised crime community. The number corresponded to the head office. Robbie had already used their services to leak fake news and, at times, to pass along useful information.

He had been in previous contact with the up-and-coming crime reporter Zack Cohen, who was fast making a name for himself among the drug cartels, both in Ireland and across Europe. Crime had become his speciality. The drug barons both hated and needed him. What better way to spread information—whether true or false—about your archrival than through a national newspaper?

Robbie rang the number using a masked caller ID and waited for a reply.

"Hello, Irish Independent Newspapers. How can I help you?"

"I'd like to speak to Zack Cohen about a shootout."

"Oh, my God. I'm sorry, but Mr. Cohen is out of the office at the moment. He should be back around 9 a.m. Can I say who's calling?"

"No," said Robbie. "I'd prefer to remain anonymous. Maybe you could give me his mobile number. I'm sure he has one."

"Oh yes, certainly. I forgot about that. He's actually covering a news story at the moment." The person rummaged through some papers and came up with the number Robbie had been seeking. He took a pen from the glove compartment and scribbled the ten digits onto the palm of his hand.

"Thank you," he said and ended the conversation.

Mobile phones were still quite new to the Irish market, and not everyone possessed one. Robbie had usually called anonymously from public pay phones whenever he wanted to contact the press or the police. For now, only people in essential public services, businessmen, or high-rolling executives carried mobile phones. The devices—and their subscriptions—were expensive. But the trend was catching on, slowly but surely, among the general public. Prices, eventually, would come down. It wasn't like the twenty-first century, where ninety-six percent of the population was connected.

Robbie dialled the number. The response was practically immediate.

"Zack Cohen here. Who am I talking to?"

"No names. Just call me Pablo," Robbie replied, enjoying the pun that referenced the infamous Colombian drug lord, Pablo Escobar. "I'm going to make you even more famous, my dear Zack."

"I recognise that voice. We've spoken before," said Cohen quietly.

"Maybe we did, my amigo. Now listen up. There's been a shooting down at Dollymount Strand involving a bent detective from Store Street with connections to the Gallagher gang. And two

Italian hitmen are lying dead in the sand. Now there's a nice juicy story for tonight's Herald, Mr. Cohen. A page-one blockbuster, guaranteed nationwide sales."

Cohen was absorbing the information. "You seem very well-informed, Pablo. How come?"

"Don't be greedy now, my amigo. If you get your ass down there ASAP, you might just arrive before forensics cordon off the area—or maybe at the same time. By the way, the guy heading the investigation is Detective Sergeant Joey Maloney. Oh, and a man by the name of Jack Hopkins was also involved. You might want to look him up. Don't thank me yet—but maybe you can do me a favour sometime in the near future, my amigo. Adiós, Zack. I'll be in touch when I have more juicy information for ye."

Robbie pressed the red button and ended the call. A slow smile crept across his face and reached his eyes. "The perfect scenario," he thought. His boss would be more than pleased. Buckling his seatbelt, he fired up the old Ford's engine and cruised happily toward his home in Finglas, on the north side of Dublin. A good rest would be more than welcome.

Zack Cohen was gloating. An exclusive front-page crime story— what could be better? He was currently on the south side of Dublin, in Blackrock, to be exact, an upper-class area of the city. He had been investigating a well-known Dublin businessman by the name of Robert Maxwell for the past three months. Maxwell, a financial wizard, had made his fortune on the stock exchange and through carefully calculated real estate deals. He had been arrested for the brutal murder of his wife, Elaine, in their luxury home in Castleknock three months prior. After a much-publicised court case, he was acquitted due to a lack of tangible evidence.

Cohen was convinced of Maxwell's guilt and was still searching for concrete proof that could justify reopening the case. Maxwell's ex-wife had held forty percent of the financial company's shares, valued at a total of five million pounds. Upon her death, the shares had automatically passed to Maxwell. A tidy little sum in anyone's language.

On an anonymous tip-off, he'd followed Maxwell to a luxury apartment in the Blackrock area. Cohen had taken photographs of Maxwell emerging from his sleek Mercedes, opening the passenger door for a striking blonde woman in her late twenties—at least thirty years his junior. But now, it was time to move. He rang Andy, the newspaper's chief photographer, and explained the situation. Urgency was paramount. He instructed him to get to Dollymount Strand without delay and wait for him there.

It was just pushing 5 a.m. when Joey set off with forensic team chief Tony Jones and two uniformed guards in his Ford Sierra toward the crime scene. The other three members of the team followed close behind in their specially equipped Toyota Hiace van. Forensic work required a substantial amount of equipment.

When they arrived at Dollymount Strand at 5:20 a.m., dawn was just breaking. The sun—pink and gold—was barely visible on the horizon, just to the right of the iconic Poolbeg Chimneys. The sky glowed with pastel hues, casting long shadows across the bay and bathing it in a crimson wash of light. There was complete stillness—nothing stirred, nothing breathed. It felt magical, almost divine.

Two ambulances from Jervis Street Hospital were already on-site, their blue flashing lights pulling Joey out of his reverie. The men stepped out of their vehicles and greeted familiar faces. Unfortunately, this wouldn't be the last time their paths would cross under such grim circumstances. Joey gave the ambulance crews strict instructions: nothing was to be disturbed or touched until the forensic team had completed their work.

The forensic officers began by inspecting the Mercedes S-Class. Sean Doherty remained in the passenger seat, his head slumped backwards grotesquely. They had just started dusting the door handles and windows for fingerprints when a small Triumph sports car came screeching to a halt. Out jumped Zack Cohen and photographer Andy, the camera already flashing in the pale morning light.

Joey's heart skipped a beat. What the fuck—who leaked this? He instinctively touched the back of his still-throbbing head, then reached for his holster. Empty. Of course. Whoever had taken his gun had tipped off the press. Joey's head spun.

Zack Cohen approached confidently. "Detective Maloney, I'm Zack Cohen. What can you tell me?"

"I know who you are," Joey snarled. "I've nothing to tell ye. You shouldn't be here. I can have you arrested for obstructing a police officer in the line of duty."

"Come on, Joey. Give us a break. We're just doing our job—same as you. Is it true your colleague was mixed up with a local drug lord? And who are the Italians?"

Joey's jaw clenched. "What the fuck? Where are you getting this information? You seem very well informed."

"You know I can't reveal my sources, Detective Maloney. Look, just let us take a few photos. You won't even know we're here. In and out—quick as a flash."

The Canon camera continued to flash, unbothered by the tension.

"Okay," Joey muttered reluctantly. "When forensics finish, you can have your pictures before the bodies are moved to the morgue. That's it—take it or leave it. But don't expect any quotes from me."

Joey knew he owed Cohen one. The journalist had once passed on vital intel that cracked a homicide case wide open. Without it, the trail would have gone cold. This was the first time they had met in person.

He turned to the two uniformed guards. "Make sure they don't move an inch until forensics are done."

Thirty minutes later, the forensic team completed their work on the Mercedes and Sean Doherty. They moved on to the beach, where the two Italians still lay face-down in the blood-spattered sand. Cohen and Andy returned to the car and resumed snapping photos.

Joey knew his day was just beginning. He still had to call Inspector Branagan and visit Eileen—Sean Doherty's widow—to break the devastating news. No way was he letting her find out through the evening paper. And by 1 p.m., the news would be everywhere.

The forensic lads were hard at work on the beach. The scene resembled something out of a science fiction film—a surreal ballet of evidence gathering—as they moved through the sand in full protective gear: gloves, goggles, face masks, booties, and white jumpsuits. It was now fully daylight, making their job easier. Flashlights could only do so much in the dark.

They photographed footprints and the two bodies. Fingerprints were lifted from both corpses, and bloodstained sand was sealed in evidence bags. The handguns and the bloodied baseball bat were also collected and tagged. They spent a solid hour methodically combing the area before they were satisfied that they had retrieved every possible clue. Protocol demanded perfection.

Zack Cohen and Andy observed from a respectful distance, perched atop a sand dune. The two guards ensured they didn't get too close or interfere with the meticulous work. Still, Andy managed to sneak a few more shots when their backs were turned.

Joey called up from below. "You've got ten minutes—no more. Get your shots and clear out. Last thing I need is some poor granny out walking her dog or a jogger stumbling on this mess."

Zack Cohen and the photographer scrambled quickly down the sand dune, followed by four paramedics who were there to take the corpses to the city morgue. Joey and the forensic boys climbed to the top of the sand dune. Meanwhile, the seagulls screeched and circled endlessly as they welcomed the incoming tide and possibly an early-morning feast.

Joey waved goodbye to Colm O'Brien, the chief of the emergency services, and told him that he'd be in touch later that afternoon. He climbed into his car and headed back to the station with Tony Jones, the forensics chief, and the two uniformed guards. The forensic team had loaded everything they needed into the Hiace van and changed back into regular clothing. All the evidence would have to be stored at the station for later analysis. Joey badly needed some rest—but he still had one crucial phone call to make and a dreaded courtesy call to Sean Doherty's widow. He decided to ask one of the guards to accompany him for moral support of sorts. They arrived at the station at 7:40 a.m. The night staff were finishing, and the day crew was just arriving, all bright and cheery. Joey headed straight to the kitchen for a black, piping-hot coffee with sugar. His head still pounded. He was going to need two more Panadols before calling Inspector Branagan.

It was 8:30 a.m., and Inspector Branagan was enjoying a window seat overlooking the countryside in Mountain View Lodge B&B in Roundwood, Co. Wicklow—his regular retreat for years. Big Jim liked the place: old, quaint, friendly staff—and the food was excellent. He was tucking into a full Irish breakfast—sausages, rashers, black and white pudding, an egg, and delicious homemade brown bread. A large pot of fresh tea meant he wouldn't go thirsty. He was reading page one of the Irish Independent as was his daily custom. The bold headline read: "Unemployment and inflation soar to historic highs." Branagan took a gulp of tea from a big mug, placed it back on the rosewood table, then looked out the window, contemplating the walk he'd enjoy after breakfast. The weather was perfect for a four–to five–hour hike. He licked his lips and spread more pudding on brown bread, thinking that despite the grim news, it was shaping up to be a fine day in the Wicklow hills. A faint smile appeared on his lips as he imagined sipping a couple of pints at the local pub later, catching up on town gossip.

Back in Dublin, Joey sat behind his old oak desk and stared at the phone number the desk sergeant had given him the night before— it was the number for Branagan's B&B. It was now 9 a.m. *Here goes*, thought Joey. *Let's get this over with.* He dialled, praying it wouldn't ring.

A plump, dark-haired, middle-aged woman answered, holding a slightly yellowed receiver. "Good morning, Mountain View Lodge—may I help you?"

"Yes, please," said Joey quietly. "I'm looking for Inspector Jim Branagan."

"Oh," replied the woman, flustered. "He's having breakfast and reading. I really wouldn't like to disturb him, sir."

"I'm sorry, but you'll have to," said Joey firmly. "It's a very urgent matter and it can't wait."

The woman placed the receiver on the desk and *waddled* to the dining room. She looked anxious as she approached Branagan. "Excuse me, Mister Branagan," she said. "There's an urgent phone call for you."

Branagan lowered his newspaper, placed his mug on the table, and glanced at the embarrassed woman, whose face was reddening by the second. He sighed deeply, rose to his full six-foot-three frame, and she led him to the reception. She pointed at the desk phone. Branagan picked up the receiver with his large hand. "Branagan here—you'd better have a good reason."

"Hello, Sir—Joey Maloney here. I'm sorry to intrude on your weekend, but there's been a series of events requiring your immediate attention." Branagan said nothing, listening. Joey relayed the night's events accurately but succinctly. When he mentioned Jack Hopkins, Branagan flinched visibly.

"Him again," he roared. "This is on your head, Maloney—do you hear me? On your head." He slammed the receiver down and stormed to his room to pack.

Fifteen minutes later, he returned dressed and with a double-shouldered haversack on his back. He rang the bell at reception. A tall, distinguished blonde woman in her late thirties—Nora, the new manager—appeared. She and her husband, Tom, had taken over from her parents years ago. Branagan had known them well.

"Checking out already, Mr. Branagan?" she asked kindly.

"Much to my regret," he replied. "An urgent matter in the city calls me back. May I have the bill, please?"

"Oh—I'm very sorry, Mr. Branagan. I hope you enjoyed your short stay." She typed up a handwritten invoice for two nights B&B plus an evening meal: £110. He pulled two fifty-pound notes and one twenty-pound note from his worn black wallet. "Keep the change—and thank you. I'll be back in the autumn, for sure."

She smiled. "Goodbye, Mr. Branagan. Have a safe trip back to Dublin."

He stepped outside through the Georgian-style door, turned right, and walked along a gravel path edged with flowers and a neat lawn. He came to the car park, slung the haversack onto the back seat of his 1966 almond-green Morris Minor 1000, and settled into the driver's seat. The seat was racked back as far as it would go—no room behind him. The car was his pride and joy, a polished collector's item. It started instantly with a pull on the choke. It was built for cruising, not speed. He'd bought it ten years before from a retired Guinness executive whose only weekend trips had kept the odometer reading low—40,000 miles then—it now showed 82,000. He turned left from the driveway and reluctantly headed for Dublin. He had a lot to explain to investigative judge John Moran. It was now just 11:10 a.m.

Branagan pulled into the tarmac car park at Store Street Garda Station, combed his hair, and exited. Desk Sergeant Pat Carolan was reviewing paperwork left by the night shift. Suddenly, the double doors burst open and Branagan strode in. The sergeant stiffened, fixing his collar and standing at attention without blinking.

"Where's Maloney?" barked Branagan.

The sergeant coughed. "He left thirty minutes ago, Sir—said he was going out on an errand."

Branagan swept by. "I don't give a damn where he is—track him down and get him back here now. I'll be in my office—and I don't want disturbances."

The desk sergeant knew exactly where Joey Maloney was. He had left thirty minutes ago on foot and crossed to the other side of the River Liffey, heading for Mulligan's Pub on Poolbeg Street. Joey had needed to escape the station—he was choking up there—and the short half-mile walk would do him the world of good. He also needed a good pint of Guinness and a toasted cheese sandwich—he hadn't eaten in over twelve hours. Mulligan's pub was famous for serving possibly the best Guinness in the city. Joey perched on a high stool at the bar. He ordered a pint and a toasted cheese sandwich and lit a much-needed cigarette as he watched the barman pull the perfect pint.

Jack climbed out of bed with great difficulty at 11 a.m. The night had been turbulent, and his body ached from top to toe. Each breath sent pain through his chest and back. He staggered painfully into the bathroom, switched on the light, and coughed up some blood into the sink. He turned the cold tap on and splashed the bruised and battered skin on his face. His reflection looked like something from a horror movie—he'd be mistaken for a professional boxer who'd taken a savage beating. Sophie's pale, drawn face appeared in the mirror behind him. She wrapped her arms gently around his muscular torso, pressing her head to his back. Warm tears slid uncontrollably down her cheeks.

"Ma pauvre chérie," she sobbed.

Jack turned, embraced her, and gently kissed her forehead.

"Let's get some breakfast," he said softly. Sophie helped him hobble to the kitchen. She filled the kettle, prepared two fresh orange juices, then poured hot water onto tea leaves in a pot and placed two slices of bread into the toaster. They were both famished. Sophie suggested visiting the Mater Hospital—Jack needed a thorough examination and X-rays to check for internal damage or bleeding. Jack knew he had cracked ribs and possibly a fractured sternum, too. They sat at the table holding hands for comfort, quietly sipping tea and nibbling hot, buttered toast.

Meanwhile, in Mulligan's Pub…

Joey had just brought the fresh pint of Guinness to his lips when the bar phone let out a sharp ring. The barman, still wearing his apron, answered: "Okay, no problem—I'll tell him."

He came over to Joey. "That was for you, Joey," he said. "Branagan's back and he's not in a good mood."

Joey merely shook his head. He was determined to enjoy his Guinness and toasted cheese sandwich before returning to the station to face the boss's wrath. Twenty minutes later, he slid off his stool, waved farewell to the bartender, and stepped through the double doors into the noisy late-morning street. He crossed the Rosie Hackett Bridge, one of the many bridges that span the River Liffey. A chilly wind whipped up; seagulls screeched, swooping in circles—a sure sign of a pressure change, and a storm brewing across the Irish Sea. It was precisely 12:20 p.m. when Joey strode through the doors of Store Street Garda Station and nodded at the desk sergeant.

The sergeant nodded back. "He's in his office, Joey, and he's fuming."

"Thanks, Pat," Joey replied, and made his way to Branagan's door. He knocked, praying for no response. His wish was short-lived.

"Enter," barked the voice from inside. Joey opened the door to find the big man seated behind his old wooden desk.

"About time—where the fuck were you?" Branagan demanded. The tone was anything but friendly.

"I needed air—clear the head," Joey replied.

"Sit down. We're calling in your ninja friend for questioning." Branagan rubbed his massive hands over his face, slammed them down on the desk, then sank back into his leather armchair. Joey flinched.

"What a fucking mess," Branagan sighed. He switched on the Sony flat-screen TV mounted on a retractable bracket opposite the desk. He wanted to watch the 1 p.m. national news on RTE 1. Joey knew Zack Cohen had probably tipped off his media contacts—it would bolster Cohen's reputation. But Joey wasn't keen on it.

At exactly 1 p.m., the ominous news jingle played. The impeccably dressed anchor sat behind a modern arc-shaped desk labelled RTE 1 News. The on-screen banner read

BREAKING NEWS

MASSACRE AT DOLLYMOUNT STRAND.

Joey silently wished he could disappear. Branagan's face grew redder by the second.

The broadcast detailed the incident while a battery of photos appeared: the blood-spattered Mercedes-S with Sean at the wheel and a blanket concealing his face; a gun-shot pajero; Jack's battered visage; the two Italian bodies lying face down in the sand. A photo of Joey appeared, too, captioned as "Detective in

Charge." Branagan slammed his colossal fist on the desk, rattling his empty tea mug.

The camera then cut to Zack Cohen sitting at the far end of the desk. He wore the latest casual fashions. The broadcaster introduced him as the investigating journalist who had uncovered the affair thanks to an anonymous, reliable tip-off. Cohen recounted in detail the gruesome scenes he encountered on arrival. He spoke of the dead detective's possible links to a known drug cartel and Jack Hopkins's presumed role in the homicide of the two Italian hit men. He went on to say that Detective Joey Maloney hadn't provided any information, but he was confident the investigating judge would reveal the truth about the night's horrific events, including connections to the local criminal underworld and possibly international drug lords. He added that many questions remained unanswered. The broadcaster then thanked Cohen for his testimony before shifting to worrying, spiralling unemployment figures and high inflation. Branagan grabbed the remote, hit the red button, and cut the broadcast. He tossed it from his big hand onto the desk as if it were red-hot.

"Get Jack Hopkins down here in a hurry," Branagan ordered.

Joey nodded, rose wearily, and exited the office without bothering to close the door. He felt worn and weary, and his day was far from over—he still had the painful task of visiting Eileen, Sean Doherty's widow. He hoped she hadn't seen the 1 o'clock broadcast, even though her husband hadn't been named. He was sure his own name would appear in that evening's edition of the Evening Herald.

The desk sergeant was deep in conversation with Gerry Meagher, one of the uniformed guards who had accompanied Joey to the crime scene. Joey called across, asking if Gerry would mind accompanying him on the difficult mission to Doherty's widow.

"Sure, no problem, Joey—whenever you're ready," Gerry said. Both men climbed into the Ford Sierra and headed in silence to the sprawling suburbs of Tallaght on Dublin's south side. They drove largely in silence. Joey had only once before delivered bad news—twelve years ago. His former partner, Con O'Flaherty, a close friend, had collapsed and died of a massive stroke while on duty. He'd been just twenty-six, newly married, healthy, a non-smoker, regular exerciser—unintended consequences.

They arrived in Tallaght around 2:30 p.m. Navigating a labyrinth of similar-looking semi-detached homes, they finally reached Sean's three-bedroom house. Some owners had built garages or rear kitchen extensions; others added bedrooms above the garage. Joey and Gerry stepped out of the car, stretching. The air felt thick, like soup. Just as Joey remembered, those seagulls signal a storm brewing. Children aged five to fifteen played and hung around in the street, chewing gum and blasting pop hits through boombox speakers. The older ones eyed the uniformed guard emerging from the unmarked car with suspicion, even whistling insults. The law wasn't welcome here.

Joey lifted the gate, and they trudged up the path to the front door. He rang—a four-note chime—then waited. No response. He pressed it again. Footsteps hurried down the stairs. The door swung open to reveal a flustered Eileen.

"Oh, my God, Joey—what's happened?" she asked, her voice cracking.

"Can we come in, Eileen?" Joey asked.

"Oh yes, of course—please come in."

They entered the parlour. Eileen sank onto a sofa and gestured to the three-seater opposite.

"There's been a very unfortunate incident, Eileen." Joey began, his voice pained. He explained what happened calmly and humanely, mentioning Sean's underworld connections. Eileen sank, frozen in shock. Joey did his best to console her. She trembled and sobbed; there's nothing harder than telling someone their loved one is dead. He offered to make tea; she nodded silently. Joey stepped into the kitchen, put on the kettle, and returned carrying a wooden tray with a teapot, three cups, milk, and sugar. He poured the tea and passed out the cups. Eileen returned slowly from her shock, curled her hands around the teacup, and sipped.

She set the cup on the bamboo-topped table. "Sean had a lot of cash recently," she said. "He spent on clothes—for himself, for me, and for the children. We went out to pubs, the cinema, restaurants more often. He bought new bikes; the kids loved them. He told me he'd won big on horse racing and poker games. I believed him—I didn't suspect anything shady. He was a good man, Joey, a loving husband and father. The family meant everything to him. May God rest his soul."

She was a full-time housewife left with a mortgage—though normally halved upon death unless a suicide clause applied—and three children: boys aged five and eight, and a daughter of eleven. Tough times lay ahead. Joey prayed her widow's pension wouldn't be compromised by Sean's criminal ties—surely the pension commission would take her situation into account.

Both men rose, took turns hugging Eileen, and wished her strength. She accompanied them to the door, thanking them for their kindness. As the door opened, the two youngest boys barreled up the path, crying, "Ma, we're hungry!"—children were always hungry, Joey thought. Eileen's task of breaking the news would be agonising. Joey and Gerry walked to the gate, turned, and waved goodbye—a gesture of relief. The hard part was done. They climbed into the Sierra, released a long, deep sigh, and felt the burden lift from their shoulders. Joey started the engine, and they headed back to Store Street. He dreamt of a hot shower, a good meal, and bed. But his day wasn't over.

Jack and Sophie finished their breakfast; a few words were exchanged—simple, everyday conversation felt impossible. Jack stood up painfully and made his way to the bathroom. Every movement and every breath was agonising. He switched on the power shower and waited for the water to heat. He stepped beneath the cascading warm water. The tonic jets pounded his bruised body—but it felt good. If only the water could wash away the horrific memories of last night, he thought. Had he woken from a nightmare, or had it really happened? As usual, Jack concluded with a cold shower. He felt invigorated.

Sophie showered next. She spent time in front of the mirror, attempting to restore her haggard face. She tried to conceal the dark circles under her eyes, applied eye shadow and under-liner. She then powdered her face with a few swipes of pale pink blush, reviving her complexion and accentuating her high cheekbones. She combed her long blonde hair into a ponytail with a red band. The result was stunning. She looked far more refreshed, even though she felt ten years older overnight.

They dressed and left the apartment. Jack leaned on Sophie to ease his pain as they descended two flights of stairs to the car park. The Fiat Spider gleamed in the afternoon sun. Sophie opened the passenger door and gently helped Jack into the seat. The car sat low, making entry difficult for him. Driving would be impossible; even turning the steering wheel would be excruciating. Sophie slid into the driver's seat and started the eager two-litre twin-carb, double overhead cam engine. She switched on the radio and found something cheerful: The Carpenters singing "Top of the World." Perfect, she thought, as Karen Carpenter sang:

I'm on the top of the world lookin' down on creation

And the only explanation I can find

Is the love that I've found ever since you've been around

Your love's put me at the top of the world

She selected first gear and glided out of the car park onto Clontarf Road, heading toward the Mater Hospital. It was only four miles—normally twenty minutes in free-flowing traffic. Fortunately, afternoon traffic was light—not the bumper-to-bumper, stop-start madness of midweek rush hour. They cruised through a green light at Clontarf Road's end into Fairview. Jack glanced left; a junior Gaelic football match was in progress. Suddenly, wind gusted, and dark clouds rolled in from the east like ominous spaceships. The air grew heavy and humid. Thunder rumbled. Darkness fell, headlights flicked on, and they hit a red light. Through North Strand, the heavens opened. Huge raindrops battered the Spider. Sophie switched the wipers to full speed. They sloshed back and forth, but the rain was winning. It hammered the soft-top and threw Sophie into tension.

Jack glanced at her and saw her knuckles whitening on the steering wheel. "Are you okay?" he asked.

"Ça va, ma chérie—just a cold chill," she replied. "Memories… last night." Jack placed a comforting hand on her leg just as the lights turned green. Sophie let out the clutch too quickly; the rear wheels spun. She regained control, and they continued from North Strand onto the North Circular Road. Visibility was poor as the rain still pounded, and cars slowed inevitably. The wipers struggled, visibility blurrier by the mile.

They turned onto busy Upper Dorset Street, then third right onto Eccles Street. The Mater Private Hospital lay just 300 yards ahead on the right. They pulled into the tarmacked car park and found a spot close to the emergency entrance. The rain eased, and the fleeting sun peered through the clouds. Sophie helped Jack out of the car; he was in agony. They climbed the steps and entered through automatic glass doors into the waiting room. Jack lowered himself into one of the many vacant seats. Sophie approached the reception to register him. Thankfully, only two people were ahead.

"Hospitals smell the same everywhere," Jack thought as the antiseptic scent wafted through his nostrils. Sophie sat beside him and took his calloused hand. Ahead in the queue were a young man in his twenties and a middle-aged woman. The young man, his arm in a makeshift sling—likely a broken collarbone or dislocated shoulder—smiled shyly at Jack's bruised, swollen face. Jack guessed the man thought he'd had a road accident. The middle-aged woman flipped through one of the magazines provided—likely to alleviate a long wait. She didn't appear to be in acute distress—perhaps a frequent "worried well" visitor.

A young, smiling nurse in an immaculate white uniform appeared. She called the woman's name and waved her through the double grey doors into an exam area. "One down, one to go," Jack thought. Ten minutes later, the same nurse called the young man into a room. She smiled reassuringly at Jack: "It won't be long now—Doctor Cronin will see you in about fifteen minutes."

At the reception, Sophie had explained that Jack was assaulted by two men with bats, but insisted Jack had driven home before checking in. She hoped the nurse understood—it wasn't fully honest, but understandable. Twenty minutes later, the smiling nurse returned with a wheelchair. She helped Sophie seat Jack and guided them through the grey doors. Sophie followed. In a white-walled exam room, Doctor Cronin—a tall, dark-haired man in his fifties stood waiting. He immediately saw Jack's discomfort and helped him out of the wheelchair. Using a footstool, he lifted Jack onto the semi-reclined examination table. He asked Jack to remove his jacket and shirt, then placed his stethoscope to Jack's chest, listening to his lungs and heart as he breathed deeply in and out.

He then went on to take Jack's pulse and was quite amazed when he found a bradycardia heart rate of 45 beats per minute, which indicated someone who worked out intensely. Most people are in the sixty to eighty bracket, and athletes are in the forty to fifty bracket. Jack went on to explain his daily physical routine to Doctor Cronin. Ah, I understand better now, he smiled warmly. He then used the palm of his hand on Jack's sternum and both sides of his rib cage. He said that X-rays would have to be taken and phoned for the portable X-ray machine to be brought down. He cleared his throat and said that he hoped that there was no internal bleeding, but there was the possibility of a cracked sternum and, most certainly, a few broken ribs and also torn rib cartilages. They certainly busted you up good, he confirmed. He asked Jack about his face, and upon hearing the gory details, he congratulated him on the resetting of his nose, saying that he had done a good job, though it must have been very painful.

Mr. Hopkins », he said quietly, « I'm going to administer a cortisone injection which will reduce the internal and external swelling. I will also prescribe some pain killers to be taken four times a day maximum ». There was a gentle knock on the door before it opened. A radiologist, a young woman in her mid-thirties, pushed a portable X-ray machine before her. She greeted Doctor Cronin, Jack and Sophie with a radiant smile. She set up the machine and proceeded to take X-rays of Jack's chest and left and right rib cage.

Results were practically instantaneous as they were digitally saved. Doctor Cronin put on his glasses and carefully inspected the screen with the radiologist. He zoomed in on the areas that were of interest to him and wrote some notes on a jotter. He looked perplexed. Sophie was standing beside Jack, holding his hand tight, afraid to let go. Doctor Cronin looked at him and took off his glasses, as they always seem to do.

He wiped his brow, « Now the situation is this Mr. Hopkins, you have a cracked sternum, a broken collar bone, the ninth and tenth ribs on the left-hand side are broken, as are the fourth and fifth ribs on the right-hand side. And to add to that, you also have two torn rib cartilages. Not exactly a pretty picture, I'm afraid. However, on the good side, there is no internal bleeding, and the lungs haven't been punctured.

You will need three months of complete rest at least, and pain will be felt up to a year from now. I hope that you have reported this matter to the police Mr. Hopkins ». He nodded his head and gave a comforting smile. « In the meantime, take your medication when necessary. Complete rest is the only solution for a quick recovery.

He and Sophie helped Jack off the examination table, and he bid them goodbye. Jack had his right arm over Sophie's shoulders for support, and she gently hugged his waist with her left arm as they pushed through the double grey doors into the waiting area. He looked down at her and smiled: Not too bad, baby, just a couple of bruises and scratches.

They picked up the painkillers from the nurse at reception and exited the automatic double glass doors into a late afternoon sun in a yellow-orange sky. The warm air was lighter and more 141 breathable. The stillness had gone, and the city was buzzing again as if someone had just flicked a switch.

They were heading toward the Fiat Spider, which was parked only a short distance from the main entrance, when suddenly two men seemed to appear out of nowhere. The first man was advancing at a rapid pace, followed by a second man who was struggling to keep pace.

He had a camera around his neck. Jack immediately recognised them as the well-known journalist Zack Cohen and his photographer. Cohen had a notebook in one hand and a pen in the other and was all business-like. The photographer had already started shooting. Talk about privacy, thought Jack as he continued walking. Mr. Hopkins, please, just a few questions for the Press, said Cohen insistently.

What are you doing at the scene of the crime? Are you responsible in any way for the death of the two Italians? What were your connections with Sean Doherty? Please, Mr. Hopkins, the people have a right to know, I have no comment to make said Jack dryly.

Now, if you don't mind, I'm under strict doctor's orders, complete rest and no stressful situations. And at the moment, you're making me restless, and you're also violating my personal space, which makes me feel stressed. If I were in good shape, I'd have already broken your photographer's arm and stuffed your notebook down your throat ».

Cohen was furious; he wasn't used to leaving a scene empty-handed. The camera was still flashing. Sophie helped Jack into the passenger seat. The photographer was in front of the bonnet, still clicking away, and Sophie pushed past him.

Allez vous faire foutre », she screamed. « Fuck off. Cohen was banging on the Spider's soft top roof. Sophie opened the passenger door and lowered herself into the comfortable leather bucket seat. She was furious. She fired up the engine and slotted the gearbox into first, revved up the engine and took off like a bat out of hell. The photographer just missed being run over by the skin of his teeth.

He ended up sprawled on the ground with Cohen helping him to his feet and making sure that the camera hadn't been damaged in the fracas. « Jesus Sophie », smiled Jack. « There's enough dead bodies without you adding to the score ». She slowed down, and she calmed down.

They exited the car park and drove out onto Eccles Street into the hub of the late afternoon traffic and headed back to the apartment in Clontarf.

Joey stopped off in O'Connell Street before heading back to the police station. He parked the car on a yellow line and put on the warning lights. He jumped out of the car and picked up the first edition of the Evening Herald from one of the street hawkers who was crying out the tragic news, read all about it, a bloodbath in Dollymount Strand.

Joey got back into the car and stared at the big bold type on the front page. The headline jumped off the page: Bloodbath in Dollymount Strand. Joey threw the paper over to Gerry.

For fuck sake, man, it's all over page one, he roared. The story filled pages one, two and three. And as he had predicted, Sean Doherty was mentioned, as were his shady connections to the underworld. Branagan is going to blow a fuse, that's for sure, thought Joey. He wasn't looking forward to seeing the big man again. He no longer felt tired, as though a concrete slab had been removed from his chest.

The adrenaline shot through him, making his heart beat faster. He would have to get Jack down to the station as soon as possible for an interview with Branagan and the investigating judge, who was more than likely to be John Moran. Jack would be taken into custody for two suspected cases of manslaughter, and he was already walking a tight rope after the Tanaka incident. Let's face it, the only eyewitnesses to Jack's actions were the lads and obviously their lips would be sealed.

The way it went was that a defendant must prove that he was in imminent danger to avoid being charged with manslaughter. Joey dropped Gerry off at Store Street Station, saying that he couldn't face Branagan again for the second time in the day. "Tell him I'm gone for late lunch," he said. Joey headed back to Mulligan's pub for a pint, a short one and some grub. With a bit of luck, there will be some Irish stew left over from today's lunch, he hoped. He was starving.

Jack and Sophie arrived back at the Clontarf apartment. The sun was still shining, and it had turned into a pleasant evening after the ferocious storm. She helped him out of the low-slung passenger seat.

They walked through the front door to the lobby and climbed the two flights of stairs to the wooden door of Jack's apartment. They were both slowly coming back down to earth after the enormous adrenaline rush they had experienced. Back to normal—if that was even possible—after what they had been through. Only time would tell.

Jack was feeling less pain after the cortisone injection and the pills, though he was beginning to feel drowsy. He sat on the couch in the living room and switched on the TV. They were both hungry. Sophie got busy checking the fridge and cupboards for their evening meal. She found pasta, fresh basil, garlic, parmesan, and olive oil.

Bingo, she said to herself—one of Jack's favourite dishes. She called into the living room, "Would you like pasta and pesto, ma chérie?"

"Just what the doctor ordered," Jack laughed—though a twinge of pain quickly reminded him of his broken ribs.

"I hope you've got a bottle of Chianti to go with it," he called back.

They were in luck. There were two bottles of Chianti, a Valpolicella, and a Bordeaux in Jack's mini wine cupboard. Jack was getting comfortably settled. A documentary was on TV about Bordeaux and the history of wine. Then, suddenly, the program was interrupted for a news flash. There it was—the ever-enthusiastic news reporter bringing viewers up to speed on the latest horrific events.

He barely managed the sentence, "Bloodbath at Dollymount Beach last night," before Jack grabbed the remote and changed the station to BBC1. He certainly didn't want Sophie hearing the gruesome details, let alone seeing the images they were likely to show. It would ruin their meal—and the evening.

Sophie came into the living room, cheerful, carrying a wooden tray with two glasses of Chianti, a small bowl of olives, and some cheese and crackers.

"Apéritif time, chérie," she said brightly.

Jack and Sophie really enjoyed their pasta al pesto and the bottle of Chianti. They talked and laughed like any normal couple, their minds freed from the grip of the previous night's horrors. They were tired, and Jack was growing drowsier after the injection, the painkillers, and the few glasses of red wine.

Hope I sleep better tonight, he thought. They decided to have an early night, not even bothering to watch *The Late Late Show* with Gary Byrne on RTE1—normally one of their Saturday night favourites. But the Sandman was calling.

Sophie helped Jack undress and propped up three pillows on his side of the bed. With broken ribs and a cracked sternum, a semi-upright position would be the least painful. Jack settled in and fell asleep almost immediately.

"Bonsoir chérie, à demain," said Sophie lovingly as she stroked his cheek.

Jack slept like the proverbial log until about 4 a.m., when he was awakened by severe pain in his ribs, chest, and back. He got off the bed gently, not wanting to wake Sophie, and made his way to the kitchen for a glass of water and two painkillers.

Would've been easier if I'd just left them on the bedside table, he thought, upon reflection.

Still, he was up and awake. He put the kettle on to boil, and a few minutes later he was sitting on the sofa with a mug of herbal chamomile tea in one hand and a book about *Bushido*—the code of honour and ideals that dictated the samurai way of life—in the other.

He read about the samurai for about an hour until the powerful painkillers dulled his senses. He dozed off, and his mind filled with memories of Okinawa and Akiko—whom he still missed dearly, as though a part of himself had been ripped away. The pain remained, even after all these years. He could see her on the beach, calling to him.

A breeze stirred at the shoreline, wrinkling the water as the waves rolled in gentle, silver lines. The ocean wind caught her snow-white kimono, making it billow like it was alive, and her long, dark cascading hair danced in the warm air, tangling around her face.

He longed to join her, but he couldn't move. Some invisible force held him back. Suddenly, he saw Joey Falconetti coming up behind her, a vile grin twisting his face. He carried a deadly commando knife in his right hand. Jack tried to cry out—to warn her—but no sound came.

He tried to move but was paralysed. Falconetti was gaining ground quickly—only twenty yards away. Akiko was still smiling and waving. Jack begged her to turn around before it was too late.

Falconetti reached her. He placed his left hand over Akiko's mouth and brought the blade to her throat.

"Too late, lover boy," he snarled.

Jack woke up in a cold sweat, shouting, "No! No! Not again—not again!"

Sophie rushed into the living room and saw Jack in a semi-trance. She cupped his face and gently kissed his forehead.

"It's okay, baby—it's okay. You just had a bad dream."

Jack finally returned to himself and clung to her tightly, as though she might vanish into thin air. Sophie gently loosened his grip and went to the bathroom. She returned with a damp face flannel and wiped his face and forehead.

Jack was suffering from a delayed aftershock reaction.

The shrill scream of the telephone shattered the silence and made them both jump.

Sophie walked over to the phone, half-hoping it would stop ringing. But it was persistent. She picked up the receiver hesitantly.

"Hello?" she said.

"Hello, Sophie—it's Joey Maloney. How are you holding up?

Hope Jack's not causing too much trouble," he laughed.

"Oh, Joey, it's you—great to hear your voice. I'm okay, still a bit shaky. Jack's relaxing on the sofa. He's been through a lot. I brought him to the hospital yesterday for a full examination.

There are broken bones, but thank God nothing too serious— nothing that won't heal, anyway. He needs a lot of rest, though. Hang on, Joey—I'll hand you over to Jack. Take care. Bye."

She walked over and handed the phone to Jack.

"How's it goin'?" chirped Joey. "Hope you're feeling better, man. Hate to disturb you on a Sunday morning, but Branagan and Judge Moran want you down at the station first thing Monday morning for questioning.

You know the drill. I'll call for you around 9 a.m. Does that work for you?"

"Hiya, Joey. Apart from feeling like I've been hit by a truck, all's good. Yeah—Monday morning works. Should I wear a suit and tie?"

Jack laughed, then ended the call. The laughter triggered pain that reminded him of his injuries, and he winced. He handed the phone back to Sophie, who returned it to the base.

There would be a lot of questions to answer on Monday morning, Jack thought. He wasn't looking forward to it.

"The goal is not to be better than the other man, but your previous self."

Dalai Lama

CHAPTER
Eleven

Okinawa, 7 years previously

Jack had settled perfectly into his new environment—like a glove to a hand, or "like a pig in shite," as the Irish would say. He went to the dojo at 5:30 as arranged for the evening class. He was introduced to the custodian of the premises, Master Saito, who received him with proper Okinawan courtesy, though he remained somewhat standoffish. It wasn't the greeting Jack had expected; he had imagined something more akin to the Irish equivalent, with lots of joking and back-slapping.

Much to his surprise, he was handed a broom and asked to sweep the traditional wooden floor before the students arrived. He bowed respectfully and took the broom from Master Saito's calloused hands. He then proceeded diligently to sweep the floor, making sure to leave it spotless and beyond reproach. Jack had done a good job. Master Saito smiled, bowed, took the broom from his hands, and beckoned him to take a seat on the bench with several other curious potential pupils who had come to observe.

"I wonder if they also passed the broom ceremony with flying colours," thought Jack.

The pupils arrived right on time at 5:50. Jack counted at least 30. Most were already wearing their karate *gi* and traditional wooden Japanese sandals called "geta."

There was, of course, a strict protocol to be respected. It was a large dojo by Okinawan standards—at least 10 yards wide and 20 yards long. Four perfect rows were formed, with the beginners at the very back and the more advanced students at the front. Jack counted 15 black belts, ranging from *shodan* (first dan) to *rokudan* (sixth dan).

Master Saito walked onto the dojo floor, his presence commanding the entire room, and proceeded to sit in the traditional *seiza* position. He bowed formally and clapped his hands twice in typical Shinto tradition—a ritual intended to chase away evil spirits—before a photo of the founder of *Shito-ryu*, Kenwa Mabuni, who was born on November 14, 1889, in Shuri, Okinawa. Mabuni had descended from the 17th generation of one of the bravest warriors of the Ryukyu Kingdom, Kenio Oshiro.

The first thirty minutes of training were devoted to warm-up exercises and various forearm-conditioning techniques. Students also practised hand and arm conditioning exercises individually, either in the dojo or at home.

Makiwara training—the use of the traditional punching board or "rolled straw," as it's officially translated—was carried out intensively. It is a common misconception to view the *makiwara* as merely a tool for producing enlarged knuckles and calluses. While the callouses are an external sign of training, the true value lies in the conditioning of the wrists, elbow joints, and fixator muscles of the armpit, chest, and back. The *makiwara* is best made from indigenous Okinawan wood called shi-ja or Japanese red oak.

The goal is to condition fists and knuckles until they become as hard as coffin nails. At first, microfractures occur in the knuckles, which then heal and harden over time. The hands are covered with a traditional balm before and after training.

The students then went on to perform the famous *Sanchin* breathing *kata*. The black belts were the first to execute the movements under the strict supervision of Sensei Saito.

Sanchin translates as "Three Battles" or "Three Conflicts." This phrase holds many meanings. Firstly, it refers to the struggle to control the body under physical fatigue. As fatigue sets in, the mind begins to lose focus, and the spirit starts to waver. Therefore, *Sanchin* develops discipline, determination, focus, perseverance, and other mental attributes. The Chinese refer to this concept as *Shen* (spirit), *Shin* (mind), and *Li* (body). Another interpretation references the "Three Burners" of the body, as described in Traditional Chinese Medicine.

Master Saito then began to slap, strike, and kick specific parts of the senior students' bodies during the execution of the *kata*. The purpose was to ensure that a correct balance, breathing, and a strong posture were maintained throughout the exercise. Mind and body were subjected to a severe and painful trial. A novice might be confused—even shocked—by what seemed like violent treatment at the hands of the Master.

Jack, however, was intrigued. He felt an overwhelming urge to try this *kata* immediately.

Nigiri-game, or gripping jars, were also used to strengthen fingers and hands. Usually made of clay with a rim around the top for the fingers to grip, sand could be added to increase their weight. Gripping these jars enhances finger strength, particularly for tearing and grasping applications. Stepping forward and backwards in various stances was also practised, with an emphasis on keeping the shoulders down and pulled back.

Jack would eventually become very familiar with the full *Hojo Undo* repertoire—the supplementary strength and conditioning exercises of Okinawan karate. Little did he know, but he would suffer both mentally and physically, as these routines were intense and gruelling. For example, there is *Chishi*—a rod with a heavy stone; *Ishisashi*—a stone padlock; *Tan*—a bar with weights; *Tou*—three bundles of cane or bamboo sticks; and *Jari Bako*—a box of sand. Each technique was used to target and strengthen a different part of the body.

The students then paired off to perform codified attack-and-defence drills, each person playing both the attacker and the defender. The class ended with a general *kumite* or sparring session, where beginners and advanced students were sometimes paired together. Each bout lasted at least two minutes, and every student sparred with at least six different partners—from novice to black belt.

Even though the class lasted at least an hour and a half, Jack felt like it passed in the blink of an eye. He was genuinely disappointed when it came to an end.

Master Saito invited him to return at the same time on Thursday evening. Jack was grateful and did his best to express his appreciation to the *sensei*. He left the dojo in high spirits and decided to head into the town centre of Naha to grab a beer.

He entered the first bar that looked like it might have a bit of atmosphere. The place was called "Bar Spade," a popular hangout for the American soldiers stationed on the island in large numbers. What Jack didn't know was that there was ongoing tension between the locals and the soldiers.

A few months earlier, a young 20-year-old woman had been raped by two GIs. As of yet, no one had been arrested or charged in connection with the alleged assault, which had caused significant anger in the local community. The military police were conducting an internal investigation.

However, there were still a few locals—both male and female—enjoying themselves in the bar. After all, one couldn't condemn an entire regiment for the actions of two bad apples.

Jack took a seat at the bar and ordered a pint of Orion, the locally brewed beer. He struck up a conversation with an athletic Afro-American named Clayton, who explained to Jack that he was stationed at the nearby army barracks and was on leave for the weekend. Clayton was in the final year of a three-year stint and was looking forward to returning to his hometown in Brooklyn. The guy was relaxed and cheerful. He looked to be in his mid-twenties and told Jack he sorely missed his beloved family and close friends.

They were getting on well together, sharing laughs and stories. Time slipped by unnoticed. Suddenly, Jack felt a pat on his back. He spun around and found himself staring into the smirking face of Joey Falconetti, who was flanked by the imposing figure of "Tank" Tommy. Jack still had fresh memories of their violent altercation in Tokyo a few weeks earlier.

"Well, look who it is," sneered Joey. "If it isn't the Karate Kid with a dressed-up monkey."

Jack's blood began to boil. The insult to his newfound friend was intolerable. Clayton immediately put a firm hand on Jack's arm.

"Let it go, Jack. This guy just isn't worth the hassle."

Jack took a deep breath and heeded Clayton's advice. He fixed his eyes on Joey.

"The next time we meet, I'll nail you to the ground, pal."

Falconetti smirked.

"Oh, I'm getting all weak at the knees, Karate Kid. I hope you've been practising, 'cause next time you might not have your gorilla to hold your hand." He let out a loud, mocking laugh.

"I'll leave you, lover boys, alone."

Clayton turned to Jack.

"How the fuck do you know that asshole?"

Jack explained in detail about the run-in he'd had with Falconetti and his cohorts in Tokyo.

"Listen up, man," whispered Clayton. "That guy is bad, bad news. He's a fucking psychopath. He's part of the infamous Falconetti mafia mob out of New York. There's a lot of talk going around about why he's here in Okinawa—some of it's true, a lot of it's bullshit. But from what I've heard, he's running an illegal drug operation using Uncle Sam's facilities, with help from some highly placed officials."

He leaned in closer. "Jack, seriously—stay well clear of that bastard and his henchmen. He's nothing but bad, bad news."

Jack nodded, appreciating the warning. He bid farewell to his new friend and promised to catch up with him for a beer or two before his departure back to the States at the end of the year. Despite Clayton's generous offer of a lift, Jack chose to walk back to his beach cabin. The walk would do him good, help him clear his mind—especially the image of Joey Falconetti's slimy, grinning face. The fabulous moonlit, starry night offered the perfect chance to gather his thoughts.

He walked the last few hundred yards to his cabin along the beach, grateful to return to his peaceful haven. All was quiet in Akiko's house next door; she and her father must have been fast asleep, he thought.

Once inside, Jack switched on a small oil lamp, brushed his teeth, and got ready for bed. It wasn't long before the Sandman came, and Jack was cradled to sleep by the gentle backwash of the ocean, with thoughts of his homeland drifting through his mind.

Jack woke up bleary-eyed to the sound of a soft tapping on his door. He looked at the bedside clock—it was 8 a.m. He had slept deeply, seven uninterrupted hours.

"Who could that be at this hour?" he wondered. He slipped into his tracksuit bottoms and opened the cabin door.

"Konnichiwa, Jack-san."

A smiling Akiko stood on the porch. She was wearing a snow-white kimono and traditional Japanese *zori* sandals with red straps. Her jet-black hair flowed over her delicate shoulders and cascaded down her back. Jack's heart skipped a beat. The image was idyllic. Was this paradise? He suddenly felt awkward.

"Ah, Akiko, what a pleasant surprise! O genki desu ka—how are you?" He felt slightly embarrassed using the bits of Japanese he'd picked up during his short stay.

"Genki desu, arigatou gozaimasu. I'm fine, thanks," she answered with grace, bowing elegantly and flashing a smile that revealed perfectly aligned white teeth.

"Please come in and take a seat," Jack offered with a smile.

She was holding what appeared to be a steaming hot, covered bowl in her slender hands.

"I've brought you miso soup with spinach," she said. "It's a breakfast speciality in Okinawa."

Jack was surprised. He hadn't expected to see Akiko so early in the morning—let alone with a homemade bowl of soup.

"You have to taste it, Jack-san," she giggled, with the innocent delight of a child.

Jack took a soup spoon from his limited cutlery collection, removed the bowl's cover, and tasted his first-ever morning miso.

He had to admit that it was both delicious and nourishing. Akiko waited with bated breath for Jack's opinion. He decided to tease her a little, making a face like someone tasting a bitter lemon. She put her hand to her face as if in shock.

"Gomen nasai, Jack-san, sore wa suki dewa arimasen—you don't like it. I'm so sorry."

Not wishing to prolong her discomfort, he smiled warmly, his blue eyes dancing as he brought another spoonful of soup to his mouth. Akiko giggled nervously, the relief on her face unmistakable. She was so happy.

She stood up and bowed.

"Sumimasen, Jack-san. Excuse me, but I have to go to the university for my economics lesson. Ja matané—see you later maybe."

Jack seized the opportunity.

"Maybe I can pick you up after your lesson. What time do you finish?"

Her face lit up.

"That would be nice, Jack-san. My lesson finishes at 12:30. Maybe we could have lunch together."

"I'd like that very much, Akiko-san." She blushed slightly, bowed elegantly, and took her leave. Jack waved to her as she walked along the shoreline in the morning sun.

It wasn't quite 9 a.m. yet, but there was already a pleasant heat in the air—at least for an Irishman more accustomed to the Emerald Isle's rainy and cooler climate. Jack had never felt better. It was the perfect time for his daily run along the beach, breathing in the pure iodine-laced air that helped him sleep like a baby nearly every night. He felt privileged.

Jack was right on time to pick up Akiko at the university. She was just exiting the main entrance as he stepped off the bus and into the sunshine. Akiko was laughing and chatting with a group of classmates. Her face lit up as soon as she saw Jack approaching. She introduced him to her friends.

They all bowed politely.

"Hajimemashite. Nice to meet you, Jack-san."

He returned the bows, taking care to honour the formal etiquette. As they said their goodbyes, Akiko explained that she had booked a table at a small, popular restaurant in the centre of Naha called Tanpopo—"the Dandelion." She told him the restaurant was well-known throughout Okinawa for its simple yet exquisite traditional cuisine.

Akiko hadn't exaggerated. The restaurant was very small—only twenty seats—and was completely full except for their elegantly set table by the window. The waiter bowed and led them to their table. A cold jug of water infused with cucumber and lime was served immediately.

The menu was written entirely in Japanese, which was unusual. Jack was more than happy to rely on Akiko's translations. He followed her recommendations, and they started with a fresh crab salad followed by Minudaru, a typical Okinawan dish of steamed pork.

Jack was beginning to truly appreciate the local cuisine—elegant, refined, and never excessive. It was a complete contrast to Irish fare, which was typically served in large portions and always came with spuds, whether one wanted them or not.

He was impressed by the refinement of the dishes. They were, in themselves, a work of art. Meals were always accompanied by herbs and spices known for their health benefits. Turmeric was omnipresent. No wonder, Jack thought, that Okinawa had the highest proportion of people over 100 years old—and they were ridiculously healthy.

Okinawans had also been found to have remarkably low rates of heart disease, stroke, cancer, and diabetes. Jack was amazed that he hadn't seen a single overweight person—though he'd noticed that teenagers were increasingly flocking to McDonald's. It wouldn't be long, he feared, before that wreaked havoc on the younger generation. A transformation was only a generation away.

Jack realized he was falling helplessly in love with Akiko. Never before had he encountered such natural, exotic beauty and charm. She had a hypnotic effect on him. After all, they say love is blind, and if that were true, Jack was a blind man without a white cane or a guide dog. He was besotted with this woman.

The meal was nothing short of excellent. Jack insisted on paying the bill despite Akiko's polite protests—he was very old-school that way.

It was a beautiful day, as was often the case in Okinawa. They decided to walk back to their quarters and make the most of the weather. What better way to end their tête-à-tête than with a coffee at the small bistro on the waterfront near Akiko's house?

The clientèle was mostly young, with a lot of students. The atmosphere was laid-back and relaxed. Akiko seemed to know many of the patrons.

They descended the wooden steps onto the white sandy beach, and Akiko linked her arm through Jack's in a completely natural manner. For a brief moment, their eyes met, and they both laughed nervously.

As they walked back to her house arm in arm, Jack couldn't remember the last time he had felt so happy and at peace with himself. Was this the new Jack? Perhaps.

And so it was, as they were bidding each other goodbye—"Mata ne, Jack-san"—that they exchanged their first furtive kiss. Jack continued back to his cabin, walking on air. He was on cloud nine and had to pinch himself to be sure he wasn't dreaming.

Jack arrived at the dojo at 5:25 p.m., five minutes earlier than the agreed time. He wanted to make a good impression and had no intention of being late. Master Saito smiled, bowed politely, and handed him the broom.

"Yoroshikereba, Jack-san," he said. "If you please."

Jack cleaned the tatamis with great diligence, ensuring they were spotless. He didn't want to leave any room for reproach.

The students were just arriving as Jack bowed and handed the broom back to Sensei Saito.

"Chakuseki shite kudasai—please take a seat, Jack-san."

Jack eagerly took his seat and waited for the session to begin.

The usual etiquette was strictly respected, followed by a twenty-minute warm-up. Little did Jack know, he was about to become the privileged spectator of a 6th dan black belt test. It would be held over two sessions and consisted of numerous katas and techniques against one or several opponents.

This would be followed by the notorious "Hyaku-nin Kumite," or the Hundred-Man Sparring ordeal, conducted over two days. Some schools completed the exhausting test in a single day, but Sensei Saito preferred to spread it over two, in order to preserve the health of the participants—some of whom would need to fight two or three times depending on the number of students present.

The ordeal was dreaded by all, leaving most participants bruised and battered—especially the main candidate. That candidate was a man named Toshiro.

He was 32 years old, in his prime, and in peak physical condition. It was as much a mental test as it was physical. Here, the notion of unity between mind and body took on its full importance. Mental fortitude would be required to fuel the battered body through the latter stages of the test.

Toshiro had started training at the young age of ten, and only now did he feel ready to face the challenge. Master Saito was like a father to him, but Toshiro knew that he wouldn't tolerate even the slightest error, nor any lack of courage or commitment. In time, Toshiro would become one of Jack's most trusted and reliable friends—a true rock in the storm, someone he could count on come hell or high water.

As Toshiro went through the motions, Jack was impressed by the man's power, agility, concentration, and precision. He was a machine—both mind and body working in perfect unison. It was poetry in motion, Jack thought. This was the kind of level he aspired to reach. It would be a long, hard journey—one that would push his body and mind to their limits.

The Hyaku-nin Kumite was next—the most gruelling test of all. That evening would consist of fifty bouts, beginning with the lower belts and culminating with the senior dan grades. Each bout would last two minutes, followed by a one-minute break before the next challenger. The second evening would follow the same format: fifty more bouts.

Toshiro began strongly, easily dispatching the less experienced opponents. Punches to the head were forbidden, but kicks were allowed. The body, however, took a terrible beating. As the rounds progressed, the accumulation of blows began to show.

For the last three bouts, Toshiro faced two 6th dans—and the final match was against the dojo's only 7th dan black belt, a forty-five-year-old powerhouse named Haru. He was as tough as they came and did not go easy on Toshiro. Yet, the respect between the two warriors was clear.

Toshiro absorbed a tremendous amount of punishment. Barely able to keep his guard up or raise his legs, he remained standing through sheer force of will. Jack watched in total admiration. One couldn't help but feel profound respect for such resilience.

At the end of the final bout, Toshiro could barely remain on his feet, yet he found the strength to kneel in seiza, bowing respectfully to his colleagues and to Master Saito. Jack could feel his pain—it was palpable. Every muscle, every joint ached. Toshiro would struggle to sleep that night. The adrenaline would continue to surge, and the aches and bruises would make any rest elusive.

But he wouldn't be alone—many of his fellow students would also be nursing their wounds, for Toshiro had dished out his share of punishment across those fifty bouts.

Jack left the dojo that evening with his head buzzing with dreams. He couldn't wait for Act Two tomorrow evening to see whether Toshiro would rise to the occasion. He headed straight back to his beach cabin. The stroll along the shore was delightful at this hour. The sea had deposited its daily offering of seaweed on the hot, white sand.

The cry of the seagulls reminded him of his beloved Dublin—of the walks and jogs along Dollymount Beach in Clontarf. Seagulls, he thought, were the same wherever you went. But the air—ah, that was something else entirely. The air in Okinawa was so pure, so free of pollution, it was almost intoxicating. Jack couldn't get enough of it.

Although it was summer, night fell quickly on the island—a rhythm Jack still hadn't quite adjusted to. He planned to wake early the next morning, just after dawn, for a run along the beach. He would also practice the katas and movements he had memorised during his dojo observations. Jack was highly observant and a quick learner, even if, for now, his training was visual only.

The cabin was plunged into darkness when he arrived. He stepped onto the terrace and lit the oil lamp he had bought at the local hardware store. The walk had left him parched, and he needed something to quench his thirst.

He opened the fridge and cracked open a cold bottle of Orion— the local beer. Jack had drastically reduced his alcohol intake since arriving in Okinawa. It had been a challenge. He allowed himself a beer most evenings, and a few more on weekends. Already, he had shed half a stone. He felt good.

Sitting on the terrace, sipping his cold Orion and listening to the soothing clap of the ocean waves, Jack's thoughts drifted back to Dublin and his old pals. What were they up to? With the eight-hour time difference, it was 1:30 p.m. in the city. Midweek. They were probably going about their usual routines.

He hadn't had much news from home. Communication wasn't easy from this distance. He had sent two postcards since his arrival, both to one of their favourite haunts—the Gravediggers Pub in Glasnevin. He'd addressed them simply as "the lads." All the barmen knew exactly who he meant.

The postcards featured stunning Okinawan landscapes—not the typical bikini-clad or topless women with model-like figures, golden tans, and Ultrabrite smiles you'd see from Spain. He was sure he'd gotten a fair slagging for it.

He could almost hear Anto's voice with that familiar grin: "For fuck's sake, since when is the Hop interested in scenery and bird life?"

The thought brought a wide smile to Jack's face. He missed them terribly—his friends, his family. But this was the price he was willing to pay to achieve his dream: to become a respected member of a prestigious Okinawan dojo and earn the rank of 6th dan.

The journey had begun. But it would be long and painful.

As he lay peacefully in bed, his mind drifted back to his beloved "lane," where he had spent much of his youth, from age seven to nearly sixteen. The lane was a hundred yards long and six yards wide. It was there that Jack had learned to play football, to fight, and to love. It was his stomping ground—a place of memories carved deep into his soul.

It was where Jack had groped his first breast. Oh yes, he remembered Mandy McDonagh only too well. He couldn't have been more than sixteen when he'd slipped her firm breast from its bra cup, fondled it, and placed the cherry-like nipple to his mouth. She had moaned with pleasure—she was no more than fifteen at the time.

It was his first experience with the pleasures of the flesh—an experience now indelibly etched into his memory. The first time— whether good or bad—is always the one that stays with you.

He recalled with amusement that, of course, he'd tried to dip into the honey pot, but that was strictly off-limits. As long as his hand stayed on the outside, everything was fine. There was no question of slipping it beneath the panties and touching the pink pearl.

Most Irish Catholic girls at the time were well-briefed by their mothers about the pink pearl. It was strictly off-limits before marriage. God forbid a girl became pregnant—it would bring shame on the family, and she would be branded a slut, an easy piece of meat.

In any case, Jack had been overwhelmed by the experience and the sheer pleasure it had provided. He felt as if he could have died a happy man that very night, he thought. His head was full of fond memories of the lane, and especially of Mr. Brady, a countryman from County Cavan.

He had a ruddy red face and always kept his hair cropped short in a crew cut. He resembled an American Marine more than a simple worker at the local airport. He wasn't an easy man—he could be quite grumpy and even violent—and had become Enemy Number One for Jack and his buddies.

All in all, there were ten of them, including Jack. They spent most of their time playing football in the narrow lane, which opened at each end into a space about twenty yards wide, or sometimes boxing with old gloves that had been handed down to them. Like most healthy young lads, they also got up to a bit of mischief and devilment. Mr. Brady was their main target for any prank they could concoct. Ever since he had burst their football—or simply confiscated it after it had gone over his door into his yard—he had been in their bad books. Mr. Brady didn't at all appreciate his garage door being used as a goalpost. Understandably so, perhaps—but not for fifteen-year-old boys.

Cradled by these fond memories, Jack slept like a baby that night and was awake at dawn the next day. He made himself a freshly squeezed orange juice, then put on his T-shirt, shorts, and runners for his daily jog along the beach. The morning was bright and calm, except for the cry of the long-billed curlews as they soared across the sea in their daily search for crabs, crayfish, or anything else to stem their hunger.

Memories of Dollymount Strand came flooding back to him—the post-work runs along the beach, down across the hard sand and back through the dunes. It had been tough going. Jack had already dropped nearly half a stone—thanks to his daily exercise, a healthier diet, and a drastic reduction in alcohol. His body transformation was underway. The mind would come later. Jack had no idea how far this body-and-mind transformation would eventually take him.

He finished his run with a sprint, continuing until his lungs were about to explode. As soon as he caught his breath, he began the breathing exercises he'd seen at the dojo, followed by a series of callisthenics and stretching movements. Then he made his way to the makeshift "makiwara" he had fashioned out of driftwood washed up on the beach and some padding he'd bought at the local hardware store.

He had decided to begin with a hundred strikes with each hand and add fifty more every week until he reached the thousand marks. It would take him at least six months—provided he didn't damage his hands in the process. It was an intensely physical practice and might seem monotonous to the uninitiated, but to Jack it was a mind-body ritual, nearly meditative in nature.

After the arduous training session, Jack was drenched in sweat, and the cold, refreshing shower was more than welcome. He had never felt so fulfilled and happy as he did at that moment. "Carpe diem," he thought to himself, to live in the present moment. It was something he knew he'd have to work at. It wasn't an easy philosophy to live by in modern society, where everything moved so fast and everyone looked constantly toward the future, always making plans, always rushing forward.

He immediately recalled a documentary he had once watched on BBC television about the Dalai Lama. When asked about happiness and fulfilment, the Dalai Lama had emphasised the importance of living in the present moment as the true path to happiness.

Jack stepped out of the shower, grabbed a towel, and threw it over his head and shoulders. Just as he made his way toward the tiny kitchen to make himself a coffee, he heard a soft knock at the cabin door, which he had left ajar. As he awkwardly reached for the towel to cover his manhood, he looked up and saw Akiko, radiant as ever, standing in the doorway. Despite her gentle smile, she was clearly mortified—she had obviously seen Jack in all his manly splendour.

"Sumimasen… excuse me, Jack-san," she said in a flustered voice. She wasn't the only one feeling awkward. Jack wished the floor would open up and swallow him whole.

He could never get over her natural beauty. She was wearing an immaculate white kimono that perfectly complemented her jet-black hair, which cascaded down her back like a waterfall. In her delicate hands, she held what looked like a small lunchbox.

"I bring you bento, Jack-san," she said with a graceful bow.

Once the awkward moment passed, Jack beckoned her inside and offered her a chair. He immediately went to his locker and threw on a clean T-shirt and a pair of black jogging pants.

Akiko extended the box to him, smiling shyly. "I make you bento. Lunch," she said.

Jack delicately opened the box and was pleasantly surprised to find a selection of finely prepared food: mini nems, shrimp, rice, noodles, and an impressive array of pickled and cooked vegetables. Not only was she beautiful and kind, Jack thought, but she was also a cook hors pair.

Everything had been so meticulously and artfully prepared—it looked like a work of art. It was so stunning that Jack didn't dare touch it at first. Then Akiko pulled a small wrapped package from the sleeve of her kimono and handed it to him with a soft smile.

He opened it to find a beautiful pair of "hashi"—jade chopsticks.

Jack was literally speechless. Never before had he experienced such delicate attention and sincere kindness. And in that moment, he realised he was slowly but surely falling in love with this extraordinary woman.

Akiko observed Jack intently as he went about tasting the contents of his bento. Jack awkwardly took one of the noodles with his beautiful chopsticks, dipped it in the appropriate sauce, and brought it to his mouth. It was deliciously mouth-watering, and it showed on his face.

Akiko giggled nervously; she was relieved. She had been so worried about Jack's reaction. Jack offered her some, which she immediately accepted, and she took out another chopstick from inside her kimono. She had been politely waiting for the invitation. They talked and laughed. In no time at all, they had finished off the exquisitely prepared lunch.

« *Domo arigato gozaimasu, oishi katta desu*, thank you, it was delicious », exclaimed Jack in nearly perfect Japanese. Akiko was more than pleasantly surprised. She clapped her hands together and giggled with glee like a child. *Sugoi, sugoi*, terrific Jack san, she exclaimed. Jack couldn't resist her contagious charm any longer.

He bent forward, taking her delicate head in his large hands and kissed her languidly. When their two tongues met, Jack felt a sudden surge of his heat in his lower abdomen. He knew that he had finally found his soulmate.

She smelt of honey and peach, and her skin was as soft as velvet. He stood up, taking her by her small, delicate hand and led her to the small bedroom. He placed his hands on her slender waist and looked into her glowing face. Her eyes were a bottomless pool of darkness where he thought he would gladly drown. Two pristine stones of onyx made by a master craftsman, like an endless stretch of midnight sky. He pulled her towards him gently and put his right hand on the back of her head.

They again kissed longingly and passionately. He felt her firm, round breasts against his chest and her mound against his thigh. It was all becoming too much for Jack as his manhood started to react. Akiko felt his sex harden and plunged her tongue in even deeper. They stopped kissing and looked at each other, panting. Jack couldn't move; he was paralysed.

Akiko took the initiative and gently cupped him. He felt his penis harden further to nearly a full erection as the blood gushed to the swollen head. He undid the belt of her immaculately white kimono and pulled it down off her shoulders. It slid silently to the floor.

She was entirely naked underneath except for a pair of laced black panties. She was perfection. Her skin was like porcelain, and her breasts, though not big, were perfectly shaped with long, dark nipples which betrayed her state of excitement. Jack took off his t-shirt. He had nearly lost all of the excess weight he had on arrival.

His torso was toned and tanned from his daily jogs on the beach. She pulled down his jogging pants to reveal a full erection. They ran their fingers along each other's bodies, discovering and exploring. Jack lowered his hand to her treasure and cupped her mound.

Akiko gasped, closed her eyes and took his bulging sex in her small hand. With his middle finger, he gently opened her and immediately felt her moistness. Like most Asian women, Akiko preferred the natural look and didn't shave.

Akiko dropped to her knees and cupped his scrotum. She licked the engorged head of his penis and then took it gently to her mouth, so gentle as though she was afraid it would melt away. She started a gentle sucking motion, increasing the pressure gradually. Jack had to fight to stop himself from exploding. He gently withdrew himself from her warm mouth and brought her to a standing position.

Their lips again met, and their tongues entangled together. Jack lifted her and placed her on the bed. She was magnificent, he thought, the perfection of Asian beauty. He lowered himself on her and kissed the side of her neck and nibbled the lobe of her ear. She felt his weight and heat.

She took his stiffened shaft and guided it to her wet vagina. Jack penetrated her softly, and she moaned with pleasure. Her juices flowed with Jack's more powerful thrusts, and her vagina clasped his swollen penis as she arched her lower back to allow for deeper thrusts. Their lovemaking was intense.

Never before had Jack felt such sexual pleasure and bonding. Their eyes met, but no words were spoken. No words were needed. Jack was reaching his climax, as was Akiko. In a last final thrust, he gasped and shuddered. His explosion was long and powerful. He hadn't made love in months. Akiko's body also quivered as her pelvis pushed against his powerful ejaculation. They had climaxed together. Jack lifted himself off her shuddering body and lay on his back. He was totally spent.

The perspiration was rolling off him. He put his hand on the back of Akiko's head and pulled her towards him. She kissed him on the cheek and placed her head and her right hand on his chest. Her right leg lay on his lower abdomen, and her knee made contact with his semi-flaccid penis. They lay together entwined for what seemed like an eternity without uttering a single word. Eventually, the backwash of the sea cradled both of them into a deep, peaceful sleep. When they finally awoke, it was late afternoon, and they were starving. Lovemaking does that.

Jack explained to Akiko that he had to be at the dojo before 7 p.m., as it was Toshiro's second phase of his 100-man kumite, « *hyakunin kumite* », and there was no way that he was going to miss that. Akiko offered to bring him to the dojo on her moped and to stop off somewhere in Naha for a small snack to stifle their hunger. Jack gladly accepted her generous offer.

They showered together quickly under the welcoming freshness of the water and stepped out refreshed and revitalised. Jack put on a blue pair of faded denim and a light short-sleeved cotton shirt. Akiko explained that she would have to change into something a little less formal and more casual than her traditional kimono. Jack couldn't argue with that.

He grabbed his black runners and walked out onto the walk with Akiko. They squinted in the sunlight, and their faces were met by a beautiful, cool sea breeze. Jack took Akiko's hand, and they started walking barefoot the five hundred or so yards to Akiko's house.

Akiko's father, Ichiro, was sitting comfortably on his porch and observed the happy young couple in the distance. His face beamed with happiness, and he smiled to himself, thinking that maybe Akiko had finally met her soul mate. At that moment, he was the happiest father on earth.

On arrival, Jack was ill at ease and felt very awkward. Akiko was still clasping his hand. She bowed, as did Jack and greeted her father. He immediately noticed Jack's discomfort and offered to make some fresh green tea – *ryokucha*. They both happily accepted Ichiro's offer. He explained that he was home much earlier than expected, as the fishing hadn't been very good.

The currents had changed, and there was little tidal movement. All in all, they had only caught a handful of fish, as had his fellow fishermen. Yet, he remained in good spirits and laughed it off, saying that better days would come. However, he proudly announced that he had caught a fine sea bass and would be honoured if Jack-san would join them later for dinner, along with his good friend Sato, the taxi driver.

Jack felt a bit embarrassed, but he was more than happy to accept the dinner invitation. He hadn't seen Sato since his arrival and was genuinely looking forward to seeing him again.

Akiko whisked off to her bedroom to change out of her kimono into something more modern. She returned in less than fifteen minutes, wearing a beautiful blue denim shirt, unbuttoned just enough to reveal a tasteful hint of cleavage—classy, but not vulgar. She paired it with a short white skirt that complemented her long, tanned, shapely legs to perfection, and the black Converse runners completed the look. Jack's eyes widened in astonishment. Talk about a transformation—from traditional to modern in the blink of an eye. She looked stunning.

They talked and laughed as they sipped green tea on the porch, overlooking the calm ocean.

Ichiro was pleasantly surprised to discover that Jack could string a few words together in Japanese and even understand certain phrases. He turned to his daughter and said,

"Watashitachi wa kare no bushi o mada watashi no aisuruhito ni shimasu."

"We will make a samurai of him yet, my dear."

Akiko smiled lovingly at her father. The only words Jack had grasped were *watashi*, *bushi*, and *shimasu*. Akiko explained that they had to leave soon, as Jack had a rendezvous at Sensei Saito's dojo.

Ichiro waved them off, telling Jack that *budo* was a way of life and not something to be taken lightly. It wasn't just a sport or hobby—it was life itself. Akiko translated her father's words as they made their way to Naha.

Jack arrived at the dojo on time, as usual. He was greeted at the door by a smiling Master Saito. Jack bowed respectfully.

"Kyo wa hoki wa arimasen, toreningu, Jack-san," smiled Master Saito. "No broom today, Jack-san. Training."

Master Saito had personally swept and polished the old pine floor that afternoon. The next beginner to tap on the dojo door would be handed the broom—just as Jack once had. Tradition was sacred in Okinawa.

He turned on his heels and returned with a gleaming white *keikogi* kimono and a white belt in hand. He bowed respectfully and presented it to Jack, who was momentarily dumbfounded.

Jack was beside himself with joy and managed to blurt out,

"Domo arigato gozaimasu, Sensei. Thank you so much."

Master Saito invited Jack to go to the dressing room to change and take a place on the *tatami*. As the other students began to arrive, Jack bowed and proudly walked onto the mat. He took a position on the far right. The order followed rank, moving from right to left, ending with the highest grades on the extreme left of the *tatami*. Jack had just realised the first part of his Okinawan dream.

The dojo filled up quickly as students took their places on the aged red pine floor. Jack counted over thirty participants. Everyone assumed the *seiza* position, arranged neatly in five rows of six or seven. Jack dared a discreet glance at the front row to his right and saw Toshiro, firmly rooted to the mat. Even with that brief look, Jack could feel the powerful aura radiating from the man—a presence of utter calm and invincibility.

Many students bore the marks of the previous night's heavy sparring—tired and bruised bodies lining the dojo. Then, Master Saito bowed and stepped onto the *tatami*. One could not help but feel the peaceful yet commanding aura he exuded. It was like standing inside a magnetic field. Uncanny.

Saito knelt with his back to the class and sank effortlessly into the *seiza* position. His hands rested lightly on his lower abdomen, right thumb tucked into his left hand. He bowed reverently before an old drawing and photograph hanging on the far wall—a portrait of Sokon Matsumura, considered the founder of Shorin-ryu, who lived to the ripe age of 92, passing away in 1889.

Photographs of other legendary masters—Choshin Chibana, Itosu Yasutsune, Higaonna Kanryu, and Mabuni Kenwa—also adorned the wall. Saito held the bow for several minutes. A calming silence enveloped the room; only effortless breathing could be heard.

He then pivoted gracefully and bowed to the class. The students responded in unison with a bow, saying, "Onegaishimasu"—please teach us.

The session began with the customary warm-up exercises. Jack was now well acquainted with the drill. The first basic *kata* was followed, then various punching and kicking techniques. These were performed individually and then with a partner. Typically, higher grades are paired with beginners.

Jack's second surprise of the evening came when Toshiro suddenly appeared before him and bowed respectfully. Moments later, they were trading punches and kicks. Master Saito then moved on to demonstrate a range of locks, holds, and choking techniques. Much to Jack's surprise and honour, he was chosen as *uke*—the partner to assist in demonstrations.

Next on the agenda was Toshiro's second bout of *hyaku-nin kumite*—the gruelling hundred-man sparring challenge. Fifty more bouts of relentless, punishing combat lay ahead. He bore the scars from the previous evening: one side of his face was badly bruised from a series of *mawashi geri* (roundhouse kicks) landed during the later stages, when fatigue dulled his reflexes. He also had two broken ribs and badly bruised shins.

Yet he betrayed no sign of weakness as he stepped into the centre of the dojo, bowed to his Sensei and fellow students, and took his stance. He waited for Master Saito to designate his first opponent.

As was customary, the bouts began with less experienced students and coloured belts. Both men bowed and waited for Sensei Saito to speak.

A monastery-like silence fell over the room. Then, Sensei shouted the word: "Hajime!"

Toshiro would lose nearly half a stone during this brutal ordeal. The first ten matches passed relatively smoothly, with each of his opponents ending up on the mat. But the last ten were punishing, physically and mentally draining. His body absorbed countless blows. Now he had a black eye, a cracked rib on the opposite side, and a fractured forearm from absorbing powerful strikes.

For his final match, sheer willpower kept him upright. He could barely stand, let alone defend himself. Yet, as tradition demanded, his opponent showed no mercy—a deep sign of respect for Toshiro's warrior spirit.

And Toshiro wouldn't have it any other way. One forges the body in the fire of will. Difficult to comprehend for the uninitiated.

He completed the trial still standing—exhausted in both body and soul—but triumphant. He had earned the respect of the entire dojo, and above all, of Sensei Saito, who presented him with the *menkyo kaiden*—the license of total transmission. This license, used by a *ko-ryū* school, signifies that the student has mastered every aspect of training within the tradition.

The dojo erupted into thunderous applause as Toshiro humbly accepted the certificate. Though his body would suffer that night and he would require weeks of recovery, he had reached the pinnacle of his art and won the eternal respect of his peers.

The class ended in the traditional way. Jack took his place in line to congratulate Toshiro on his superhuman feat—one of the most physically demanding trials known to man. Toshiro, a friend of Akiko's, had taken a special liking to Jack, appreciating his humble and discreet demeanour.

He invited Jack to join him and the other students for saké or beer at the local pub. It was dojo tradition: the person who completed the *hyaku-nin kumite* would buy a round for everyone. Jack, of course, gratefully accepted.

So twenty karateka set off in festive spirits to the local pub. The bartender, Chiko, knew Toshiro well and both admired and respected him. Toshiro came most nights after training for a mineral water or a soda, and on rare occasions, a nice cold Orion beer brewed locally.

Chiko smiled and greeted Jack, having recognised him from previous visits—either alone or with Akiko.

He guided them to a large rectangular oak table with three-legged stools on all four sides. Turning to Toshiro, he asked what they were celebrating.

"Hyaku-nin kumite," replied Toshiro.

Chiko clapped his hands in delight. Like most karate-conscious Okinawans, he understood how difficult it was to complete such an ordeal successfully.

"Sugoi! Omedetou gozaimasu, Toshiro-san!" he exclaimed. "Terrific! Congratulations, Toshiro-san."

He bowed respectfully and added, "Doitashimashite, ie no saisho no nomimono."

"It's my pleasure—the first drinks are on me."

Toshiro thanked him. It would have been very impolite to refuse such a generous offer. The order was a mixture of saké and pints of Orion beer. Jack chose a beer, as did several of his fellow students. He decided to steer clear of the strong 18-percent-proof saké—after all, the night was still young.

Jack was happier than he had ever been. He only prayed it wouldn't be fleeting. His Japanese was improving by leaps and bounds, and the local people he spoke with were both patient and helpful. After three rounds of drinks, the atmosphere was lighthearted and joyful. Songs were sung in broken English and Japanese—lyrics Jack didn't always understand.

The brave attempts to sing well-known English and American hits amused Jack to no end. He was asked to sing an Irish song, and like any true Irishman, he rose to the occasion with a heartfelt rendition of the famous Dublin tune, "Molly Malone." Everyone enjoyed it so much that he was asked to sing another. He gladly obliged with the beloved classic, "Dirty Old Town." Much to Jack's delight, some people in the bar even recognised the tune and hummed along.

Jack was just about to raise his fourth pint to his lips when he saw Joey Falconetti swagger into the bar, accompanied by "the Tank" and four other cronies. Falconetti immediately spotted Jack, and a vicious smirk twisted his face. He strutted over to where Jack was seated.

"So, the karate kid's having a good time with his gook friends," he sneered. "He even got himself a gook girlfriend, too. Don't let me interrupt your fun, guys."

Jack tried to stay calm. He didn't want any trouble.

"This is a private party, and I don't want any hassle. Just go," Jack said firmly.

"Now, where are your manners?" Falconetti scoffed. "That's no way to treat a friend. I was gonna buy you guys a round of drinks. You just don't know hospitality, Karate Kid."

Toshiro hadn't understood every word, but he noticed the anguish flicker across Jack's face. He stood up and stared directly at Falconetti. His gaze alone was enough to convince any man that this was the wrong tree to bark up. Falconetti's reptilian brain, wired for self-preservation, sensed instantly that this was not a man to mess with. Period.

"Excuse me, but this is a private party. You must go, please," said Toshiro, calmly but with firm authority.

Falconetti didn't want to lose face, so he merely laughed scornfully.

"You guys are no fun. So serious," he scoffed, then turned and walked back to his group. His cronies, who had just ordered beers all around, clapped him on the back and handed him his drink. He glared across the room at Jack and mockingly held his hand up, imitating a handgun.

"He bad man," said Toshiro to Jack. "Tomodachi ni kiwotsukete—be careful, my friend."

But Falconetti's intrusion didn't dampen their little soirée. The group carried on, enjoying the evening in good spirits. Finger food was ordered—most of them hadn't eaten in several hours, and drinking without food was never a wise choice.

As always, Jack relished the Okinawan finger food—so flavorful and offering a wide variety of dishes and tastes, all presented beautifully. It stood in stark contrast to Irish cuisine, which lacked variety and finesse, though it was always served in hearty portions.

Chiko, the bartender, sounded the gong to inform customers that closing time was in fifteen minutes—it was nearly 1 a.m. Time to head home. The day had been long, and everyone was feeling a little tipsy but content—especially Toshiro, who was both weary and sore from the dual bouts of the *hyaku-nin kumite*.

They all said their goodnights, exited the pub, and went their separate ways. Public transport had stopped at midnight, so Jack faced a six-mile walk back to his beach cabin. The cool night air and the walk would do him good. Toshiro offered to accompany him part of the way, as he lived just two miles from central Naha. Jack welcomed the company.

They hadn't gone a mile when their quiet was shattered by a blaring horn, raucous shouting, and glaring headlights. They turned toward the oncoming vehicle—Falconetti and his cronies in an army jeep. Jack noted that Falconetti seemed to enjoy certain privileges.

The jeep screeched to a halt. Jack and Toshiro shielded their eyes from the blinding headlights. Falconetti stood on the passenger side, grinning.

"Well, well, look who it is," he sneered. "It's Karate Kid and his bodyguard. Ain't that sweet. Where's your gook girlfriend, karate kid? Don't like pussy anymore?"

Falconetti jumped from the jeep, followed by the Tank—who had been driving—and the other three cronies crammed into the backseat. Jack glanced at Toshiro, whose demeanour had changed entirely.

He may have been tipsy earlier, but now he was utterly composed, alert, and tuned into his surroundings. He was in a different state of mind. The state of no-mind.

Was this *Getsumei no Michi*—the Moonlit Path Jack had read about and found so intriguing? It was a technique designed to heighten a student's awareness, enabling them to function more efficiently in life. Unlike meditation, this state allowed the mind to operate at its natural speed.

According to some beliefs, there exists a middle layer of consciousness between the subconscious and the conscious mind—a thin membrane that enabled human progress in a relatively short evolutionary span. It worked through a blend of logic, intuition, and external influences that remain esoteric and hard to explain.

As civilisation progressed, human efficiency leaned more toward logic than intuition, making this layer increasingly obsolete. *Getsumei no Michi* offered a way to re-enter this forgotten state of consciousness. The key: surrender control to imagination without focusing on any one thought. Let go.

The Tank charged directly at Toshiro. That was a critical mistake, despite being eight inches taller and fifty pounds heavier. He lunged with two shovel-like hands, aiming to grab Toshiro's shoulders.

Toshiro stepped back with his right foot and deflected the attack with a powerful middle-level forearm block—*chudan uke*. His forearms, toughened like iron, struck like a lead baton. Instantly, he countered with a *chudan tsuki*, a mid-level punch aimed at the upper ribs, powered by the precise snap of his hips and back foot.

He stepped forward and drove an elbow strike—*mae empi uchi*— again into the ribs. Then, flowing from that motion, he stepped left while drawing his right foot back, delivering a thundering *tetsui*— a hammer blow—into the Tank's right kidney.

The big man collapsed to his knees, then toppled forward with a heavy thump as his head hit the ground.

It had lasted only seconds, but it was enough to deter the others from stepping forward. It was a blur. Neutralising the main threat in such a decisive manner usually dissuades sidekicks from heroic impulses.

Everything had happened so fast that even Jack was dumbfounded. No one had expected the Tank to be taken down so easily.

Toshiro remained completely on guard. He was in *zanshin*—a state of heightened awareness, of relaxed alertness following the execution of a technique. A literal translation of *zanshin* is "remaining mind." In several martial arts, *zanshin* refers more narrowly to the posture the body assumes after a technique has been performed. It was abundantly clear that nobody was going to make a move.

It took three of them to lift the Tank and his 240-pound frame back onto his feet. They struggled to heave the giant into the passenger seat of the jeep. The big man looked worse for wear. His face was twisted in pain, he was bent over, clutching the right side of his ribcage, and his right hand rubbed the small of his back.

The injuries were obvious—broken ribs and possibly a kidney contusion, which can occur after blunt trauma or direct impact to the lower back. Such trauma can lead to internal bleeding within the kidney. He would be in serious pain for several days, and recovery from the broken ribs—always a slow and uncomfortable process—would take weeks.

Falconetti had returned to the jeep and slid into the driver's seat. But instead of gloating, he was scowling at Jack and Toshiro.

"Okay, so the gook got lucky. Next time'll be different. Say hello to your gook pussy, karate kid. *Au revoir!*" he shouted.

The jeep roared off into the night, leaving a cloud of dust in its wake. Jack and Toshiro watched in silence as it disappeared into the distance, the taillights fading until they were mere specks. Little did Falconetti realise—the Tank had actually come out lucky. Toshiro had spared him. He could have targeted more vital areas, and the big man could have ended up crippled—or worse.

Sensei Saito frowned on the use of martial arts outside the dojo. He taught that it was to be used only for self-defence and always with the minimum force necessary—unless there was absolutely no other choice.

Toshiro tapped Jack lightly on the back and raised his forefinger to his lips, saying, *"No tell Saito Sensei, Jack-san."*

"Don't worry, my friend," Jack replied. "This will remain our little secret."

The two friends continued their walk beneath a bright crescent moon and a night sky glittering like the lights of a distant city. Jack left Toshiro at his home and thanked him for the evening. He still had another four miles to cover before reaching his own haven.

It was 3 a.m. when Jack stepped off the beach onto his small wooden terrace. He still had vivid images in his mind of Toshiro slicing through the Tank like a hot knife through butter—swift, powerful, and controlled. Snuffed out like a candle in three seconds.

So this was *budo*, Jack thought. And this was what he aspired to— not for the violence, but for the mastery of self, the surrender of ego, and the unity of body and spirit. The path ahead would be long.

The moonlit sea shimmered under the jewel-studded sky, and the rhythmic backwash was a comforting sound to Jack's ears. He unlocked the door, walked into his cabin, and headed straight to the fridge, where he found a small bottle of water. He downed it in one gulp.

Jack was exhausted from the night's events. His bed beckoned. He brushed his teeth, undressed, and collapsed into bed like a felled tree. The Sandman arrived quickly, and Jack slept deeply, drifting in and out of dreams until 9 a.m.

He was awakened by a noisy flock of hungry black-tailed gulls. The tide must be in, he thought, and the gulls were on the hunt. He climbed out of bed, stretched, and went straight to his small shower.

As had become his custom, he finished with a blast of cold water. According to what Jack had read, cold water sends electrical nerve impulses to the brain, resulting in an uplifting effect. It also stimulates deeper breathing, reducing CO_2 levels throughout the body, which in turn improves concentration.

Cold showers, he had come to believe, kept you sharp and focused throughout the day.

Stepping out of the shower, he grabbed a large bath towel, dried off, then wrapped it around his waist and stepped outside onto his southeast-facing sunlit terrace. He could never get enough of the stunning ocean view.

Strong southeasterly winds sent the surf crashing against the beach and created a powerful backwash. The invigorating scent of iodine hit his nostrils—it was intoxicating. Jack fixed his eyes on the horizon, breathing deeply in and out, filling his lungs with the ocean's nectar.

The events of the previous night remained vivid in his mind, and he couldn't wait to see Akiko and tell her about the run-in he and Toshiro had with Falconetti and his gang.

Now fully dry, Jack went back inside, drank a glass of fresh orange juice, and changed into his karate gi. He began with breathing exercises and stretching, then moved to the *makiwara* punching board to perform his routine of fist, hand, and elbow strikes. The session took him a full hour to complete.

His knuckles and hands were developing calluses from the daily training. Sensei Saito had given him a special balm and instructed him to massage it into his hands after each session. It would reduce swelling, prevent injury, and promote healing. Jack followed the advice to the letter.

After his *makiwara* training, Jack was hungry and soaked in sweat. A cold shower and breakfast were in order.

Breakfast consisted of a small pot of tea, slices of buttered toast, and a boiled egg.

He needed to go to the post office in Naha to fax an article he had written about Okinawa—the people, the customs, the way of life. It was something he had discussed with Jacky Gilroy, managing director of *Independent Newspapers*, who was enthusiastic about running a monthly feature in the Sunday edition, under the "People and Places" section.

Jack had already submitted one article and a few photographs, which had been well received. He was slowly developing a loyal readership, and people now looked forward to his next submission. He intended to send in one article each month. He had now been in Okinawa for three months.

But first, he wanted to drop by Akiko's to see if she was home. Maybe she could give him a lift to Naha on her old Honda scooter, a gift from her father. She kept it in pristine condition and only used it when the weather was bad, in place of her bicycle.

Jack put on a pair of blue denim jeans, a white T-shirt, and his black trainers. One of the many advantages of living in a subtropical climate was that it was rarely cold. Even in January, temperatures dropped only to around 10°C.

This suited Jack perfectly—he wasn't exactly a dedicated follower of fashion, and his wardrobe was minimal. A few T-shirts, pullovers, one or two lightweight jackets, and a rain mac were enough.

Being subtropical, the island received its fair share of rain and wind, but it was almost always warm. And being Irish, the rain never bothered Jack. The climate he was used to was far more punishing than anything Okinawa could throw at him.

He opened the cabin door, stepped onto the terrace, and locked the door behind him. The red digital figures on his white thermometer displayed a pleasant 20°C.

He walked onto the hard sand and began the short 500-yard journey to Akiko's house. One thing he knew he'd have to invest in was a good pair of sunglasses.

The wind drove the surf to crash and roar onto the beach, and the backwash dragged the sand away like a captive. Jack felt good—and he was looking good too.

He had shed the two stone of excess weight he had been carrying when he first arrived, thanks to daily exercise, a balanced

Okinawan diet, and a significant reduction in the amount of alcohol he had become accustomed to drinking over the past year.

He also tried to follow the Okinawan principle of *hara hachi bu ne*—to eat until one is 80 percent full.

This concept originated from Confucian teachings, instructing people to leave the table slightly hungry, at just eight-tenths fullness.

> *"To live is the rarest thing in the world. Most people exist, that is all."*

— Oscar Wilde

CHAPTER
Twelve

Little Italy - Manhattan, New York, present day

It was a hazy late afternoon in Manhattan. There wasn't the slightest breeze, and the smog had lingered over the metropolis all day. The sun had made a few feeble attempts to break through, but by day's end, it was the smog and clouds that remained the undisputed winners. As usual, Little Italy buzzed with activity—especially on the ever-popular Mulberry Street, home to a host of restaurants serving traditional, high-quality Italian cuisine. Sirens wailed, and impatient drivers leaned on their horns the instant the lights turned green. It was a dangerous city for pedestrians. But then again, it was New York—the city that never slept.

The area teemed with the usual sightseers snapping photos of buildings or of each other, buying postcards or souvenirs at inflated prices. Its proximity to Chinatown only added to its allure. Business—both legal and illegal—was booming.

Joey Falconetti was seated in the back office of Caesar's Restaurant, one of the six establishments his family owned. Caesar's, however, was the oldest, founded by his grandfather, Lino Falconetti, back in the 1920s after emigrating from poverty-stricken Sicily. Lino had been just twenty-six when he walked down the gangway of the SS *Roma*, holding the hand of his young wife and stepping onto American soil for the first time. The voyage from Genoa, aboard the steamship built for the Italian line *Navigazione Generale Italiana*, had drained nearly all his hard-earned savings.

All they had upon arrival was a cousin's address, their luggage, and a fistful of dollars. Lino was a peasant, like the generations before him, but he knew the meaning of hard work—and within ten years, his circumstances would change dramatically.

In the 1920s, New York Sicilians were viewed as an inferior race—unclean, impoverished, degenerate, and criminal-minded. And that wasn't just the opinion of many Americans: immigrants from northern and eastern Europe, as well as from northern Italy, looked down on them with contempt. Sicilians were assigned the most menial tasks, paid the lowest wages, and forced to live in the worst parts of town. Prejudice against them was rampant, and at times, even deadly. But Lino rose above it all—through sweat, shrewdness, and eventually, violence, he built a modest empire.

Joey—known as Giuseppe Falconetti to his grandparents—sat back in a comfortable leather chair behind his grandfather's old oak desk. He slid open a heavy drawer to his right, flicked open a carved wooden box, and pulled out a Cohiba Cuban cigar along with a cutter. It was one of the most expensive cigars on the market—one of his daily indulgences.

Joey liked luxury. He loathed poverty—and poor people even more. As far as he was concerned, they were either too lazy to get off their asses or too stupid to make something of their lives.

He clipped the cap end of the cigar, struck a match, and held the cigar just above the flame. He was careful not to stick it directly into the fire—it would ruin the flavour, and with cigars that expensive, that wasn't an option. He let the cigar smoulder slightly to prime the tobacco before taking his first puffs.

Now, he could really unwind.

His thoughts drifted briefly to his grandfather. The old man was still alive, having just celebrated his eighty-ninth birthday. Though not very mobile, his mind was as sharp as ever—the grey matter still very much intact.

The cigar was excellent, as always. Joey smiled in satisfaction, leaned back, and blew out the first halos of smoke. They drifted upward, mixing with air particles to form a blueish-white haze beneath the artificial neon light.

Business had been thriving since Joey had taken the reins. His father had been murdered in a bloody gangland feud during the 1970s, but in the decades since, the Falconetti family had become one of the key players—controlling operations across Manhattan, the Bronx, and Harlem.

Joey held considerable power and was deeply entrenched in political circles. His brutal reputation preceded him. Few dared to cross him. No one messed with Joey Falconetti.

He had been expecting word from his Irish business associate, Christy Kelly. The news had been long overdue. Little did Joey know, he was closer to Ireland than he realised.

Ironically, Caesar's Restaurant stood on Mulberry Street—just where Kenmare Street ran through it. Kenmare was a small town in County Kerry, Ireland. The street had been named by a powerful politician, Big Tim Sullivan—the son of Irish immigrants—early in the 20th century. He'd named it after his mother's hometown.

The sudden shrill of the phone startled Joey slightly. He glanced at the screen and saw "Kelly" in bold black letters on the white display. A slimy grin crept across his face. With a flick of his pudgy middle finger, he activated the speakerphone, stood up, and took another puff of his cigar.

"How are ya, Kelly?" he said, thick Manhattan drawl dripping from every word. "I was expectin' this call, like, *years* ago. Hope you got good news for me."

"Hello, Mr. Falconetti," said Christy Kelly, his voice sounding almost apologetic. "I'm sorry, Mr. Falconetti, but the news is bad."

"So, give it to me."

"Big Toni and Paulo are dead—killed, most likely, by Jack Hopkins. And our man Doherty, the insider—he blew his own head off."

A heavy silence fell.

Baby Face Paulo had been Tony Falconetti's first cousin on his father's side. One of his father's brothers, Luigi, had three sons, and Paulo was the youngest.

"What the *fuck*," Joey bellowed. He smashed his cigar into a large glass ashtray on the desk's right side. His left fist slammed down like a hammer, shaking the oak surface. The phone base and ashtray jumped, and an empty coffee cup tipped and fell from its saucer.

On the other end of the line, Christy Kelly had clearly heard the outburst. His voice was shaky, hesitant.

"It seems... they got caught up in some kind of ambush... set up by Jack Hopkins's pals. Once the autopsies are complete, the bodies will be flown back to the States. But questions... questions will have to be answered."

"Yeah, questions," spat Falconetti. "I've got plenty of questions. I thought I was dealing with professionals here. And what do I get? Three stiffs—that's what I get. Three fuckin' body bags. This won't do, Kelly. How the hell does a bunch of amateurs kick the shit out of professionals?"

Kelly cleared his throat. "I know you're upset, Mr. Falconetti, but I think we held up our part of the deal. We supplied the guns, obtained the relevant information, and organised the kidnapping of Hopkins's girlfriend with Doherty.

Nobody expected Hopkins's buddies to get involved—we just didn't see it coming. The good news is we managed, with the help of the press, to link Doherty to the Gallagher gang. So now the cops are gonna be all over their operations for the foreseeable future. That'll keep the heat off us and allow us to expand our business."

Joey Falconetti's Latin blood was still boiling. He'd been hobbling around on a cane ever since his last encounter with Jack Hopkins years ago in Okinawa—and he craved vengeance more than anything else. He had let it go for years, until he read an article in the *New York Times* two years earlier, featuring Jack Hopkins as the Irish Ninja. The old memories came rushing back like a sledgehammer to the gut. He wanted revenge.

He slumped back into his comfortable leather chair and relit his cigar. His mind was racing. He took a puff and placed the cigar back in the big glass ashtray.

"Okay, Kelly, listen up. I'm gonna make arrangements for this asshole Hopkins, and I want you to supervise it on your side of the big pond. I'm sending two good men over to give you a hand—maybe even a cousin of mine from the old country.

That bastard Jack Hopkins will be wearing a nice pair of cement shoes real soon. I want this vermin out of my life—for good. I hope you're takin' all of this in, Kelly. I don't want any more fuck-ups. And now that Doherty blew his own brains out, we need someone reliable—and greedy—on the inside, looking after our interests. I'll consider upping the volume on the next shipment. You'd better be damn sure you can shift it."

Kelly was shaking his head, as though Falconetti were sitting right in front of him. He was tense. "Receiving your message loud and clear, Mr. Falconetti. You can depend on me. I'll do whatever it takes to get the job done. And don't worry—we can handle more volume. No problem whatsoever." Then the line went dead.

Falconetti pressed his palms flat on the desk and pushed himself to his feet. He took his gold-headed cane from the umbrella stand to the left of the desk and opened the heavy, bulletproof, soundproof wooden door. It had cost a small fortune—ten thousand dollars—but Falconetti always said it was one of the best investments he'd ever made. He knew friends and family who had been gunned down behind locked doors, thinking they were safe.

He walked across the plush red carpet of the restaurant floor and into the kitchen, where the staff were cleaning up after the mad lunch rush. The restaurant was large—two levels—and could comfortably seat a hundred guests. It was renowned for its home-style cooking, especially the caponata, lasagna, risotto, and osso buco. Falconetti's grandmother had brought the recipes from her native Sicily. She was still alive—and still a great cook.

She had worked tirelessly behind the pots and pans for years before taking a well-earned retirement. But she still came in a few times a month to cook and scold the chefs who didn't follow her prized recipes to the letter. She had set exceptionally high standards in her kitchen. Unsurprisingly, the restaurant was packed most days, both for lunch and dinner.

Joey Falconetti was hungry. He told one of the chefs to heat up some of the lasagna left over from lunch. Then he poured himself a large glass of Novello—a famous red Sicilian wine. He took a seat at the bar, and the lasagna was served piping hot and sprinkled with fresh parmesan, just the way he liked it. He took a sip of wine and smacked his lips in appreciation.

"Che piacere—what a pleasure," he thought to himself.

He then dug into his lasagna, and as he ate, his sharp mind began racing—plotting a future attempt to finally snuff out Jack Hopkins for good. He took another sip of the rich, red nectar and smiled. He knew just the men to get the job done right this time.

"If life were predictable, it would cease to be life and be without flavour."

Eleanor Roosevelt

CHAPTER
Thirteen

Dublin - present day

It was 7 a.m. Monday morning, when Lenny awoke from his deep slumber. His head hurt a bit, as he had celebrated Saturday night's events with *the* lads *for* most of Sunday evening down in the local pub. On *Sunday morning,* Lenny and the two brothers, Danger and Daragh "Sonar," had brought the Pajeros to the car wash for a special VIP treatment with a *premium* wax and polish finish. The four-wheel drives came out of the wash *gleaming, spotless.*

The rear windscreen on Lenny's Pajero had been smashed, so he had taped a strong and impermeable piece of plastic to the rear pillars of the car before putting it through the automated wash. There was also a 9 mm bullet hole in the driver's door. The other two Pajeros had bullet holes in both front and back doors. Lenny was due at work at 8:30 that morning. A lot of explaining would have to be given to his *superiors.*

"Maybe they'll just put it down to collateral damage," Lenny laughed to himself. *Wishful thinking.* But then again, it was all in a good cause.

As arranged, Danger and Daragh arrived at 8 a.m. with the two other Pajeros, and they all drank a quick coffee together before setting off on the short four-mile drive to Lenny's place of work, which was a haulage company in Dublin docks.

It was a drizzly morning with light rain, so Lenny set the wipers to lazy mode. As usual, traffic was heavy as they arrived in Fairview before turning left onto the quieter East Wall Road towards the docks. Most of the heavy traffic was making *its* way towards the city centre, where the vast majority of people worked. The temperature had dropped, and the red digits on a black background showed a cool 12°C on the four-wheel drive's dashboard. The radio was blasting out "Fast Car" by Tracy Chapman. It suited Lenny's morning mood:

You got a fast car

I want a ticket to anywhere

Maybe we can make a deal

Maybe together we can get somewhere

Any place is better

Starting from zero, got nothing to lose

Maybe we'll make something

Me, myself, I got nothing to prove

The three Pajeros arrived at 8:25 a.m., and they swished over the asphalt parking lot and came to a halt side by side. They put the gear levers into neutral and killed the big turbo diesel engines. As they closed the driver's doors, a typical pinging noise could be heard coming from the hot metal, cooling and contracting. It was a short twenty-yard walk to the offices, and Lenny felt about five feet tall.

Lenny pushed open the door to find an office alive with activity under the white fluorescent lighting. It was just like the proverbial beehive. The fax machine buzzed and then screeched to a high pitch to confirm communication had been made before spitting out thermal paper with orders, queries, and various miscellanea. The big telex machine in the corner gave it a lot of competition, with the print head moving incessantly from left to right, hissing back and forth before unleashing what seemed like an endless roll of paper filled with customs details, regulations, and backloads that weren't ready yet for pickup.

They were pleasantly greeted with a big smile by the receptionist sitting behind her state-of-the-art modern desk, who went by the name of Eileen. She was a slim, pleasant girl in her late twenties— *well-endowed,* with long dark hair and big blue eyes. She was wearing headphones and speaking into a microphone. She looked like a pilot in the cockpit of an F-16 Falcon, giving or taking instructions.

Every now and then, she smiled, as though the person on the other end of the line knew her and was paying her compliments. Maybe some guy is coming on to her. Too bad for him, as her wedding finger sported a brand-new golden wedding band, bearing testimony to someone who had just recently married.

Lenny bid hello to the two other office workers, Jimmy and Richard, who looked after logistics, outloads, backloads, and any problems that could crop up on a daily basis regarding transport. And problems were *plentiful* on a regular basis—either customs clearance, mechanical issues, angry customers, or weather problems. There was never a dull day.

Lenny then headed towards the kitchen and, at the same time, offered coffee to the lads. They nodded their heads in approval. He was in luck—coffee had been made, and the glass coffee pot showed half full. He half-filled three decent mugs with the hot black brew and proposed sugar and milk. Danger was milk with sugar, Daragh was black with sugar, and Lenny was black, *no frills.*

They walked back to the reception area and started chatting with Eileen. She asked them if they had seen the news or read the newspaper about the horrific incident down at Dollymount Strand. Needless to say, the three lads played dumb.

With that, a spanking brand-new BMW 323i glided into the parking lot and parked alongside the Pajero that Lenny had driven. Out stepped Dylan from the Bordeaux-coloured BMW. He was one of the transport company's three main partners—a high-flying, elegant executive in his early thirties. The other two associates were Arthur, his brother, and Nick. He was dressed to the nines in a grey Louis Copeland suit and wore a white shirt with a red patterned tie. His feet were decked out in a black leather pair of Clarks Derbies.

The real man-about-town image. He held a brown leather attaché case in his left hand and was scratching his head with his right while looking at the broken windscreen of the Pajero. He then walked around the three jeeps, looking intently and nodding his head. Lenny threw a worried glance at Danger and Daragh. The *storm was about to break.*

Lenny decided it would be better to retreat to the kitchen area while awaiting the inescapable encounter.

Dylan stormed into the office, barely bidding anyone good morning. He questioned Eileen: "Where's Lenny?"

She nodded towards the kitchen, which was just next to Dylan's office. He entered the kitchen like a tornado and threw his attaché case on the wooden table.

"Jesus Christ, I don't believe this. What the hell happened, Lenny? And you'd better have a good excuse. Arthur and Nick are literally going to blow a fuse when they see the damage that was done."

Lenny was literally cringing inside, and Danger and Daragh were wearing their best apologetic faces—*like dogs who had just soiled the new carpet.*

"I can perfectly understand your anger, Dylan. Can you please sit down? I'll make you a coffee and explain everything in detail," said Lenny in a meek voice. He handed Dylan a much-needed coffee and started his story from the beginning. Dylan's jaw was surrendering more and more to the law of gravity as Lenny's tale of events unfolded progressively.

Dylan was literally stunned. There was a moment's silence.

Lenny was nodding his head from left to right. "No, Dylan, there's no sweat there. We made sure to cover the registration plates once we hit the beach. And all the lads will be contributing financially for the damages incurred. If we hadn't intervened, Dylan, it would certainly have been a real carnage for Jack Hopkins. The only witnesses were Jack, Sophie, and Detective Sergeant Joey Maloney. And Joey won't be saying anything—he was only too happy that we turned up. Without our help, Jack and Joey would certainly be dead today." He let out a long sigh, a mixture of contentment and relief.

Dylan had just given up smoking. But at that moment, he needed a cigarette and another cup of coffee. Lenny gladly offered him one of his John Player Specials. Dylan put the cigarette to his mouth in an automatic gesture, and Lenny pulled a Ronson lighter from his pocket and lit him up. He pulled hard on the cigarette— *like a man who had just been told he had terminal cancer.*

The paper burned quickly, and the ash appeared. The nicotine rush provided a small high and relaxed him. He then took the cigarette from his lips, threw his head back, and blew out the blue smoke, watching it float in rings towards the ceiling.

He asked, "And tell me, Lenny—how are Jack and Sophie? I didn't even bother to ask. I was so taken up with material damage and eventual consequences."

"Well, not great," replied Lenny. "Sophie is very shaken up—it'll take time. And Jack suffered a lot of physical damage. It'll take a couple of months before he recovers fully, but he's a tough guy. He'll get over it with time and with Sophie's care and attention."

After the tension had eased off, Lenny drove Danger and Daragh to their respective homes in his company car, a Volkswagen Jetta, and told them that he would be in touch. Not many words had been exchanged in the car—everyone preferred to listen to the radio.

Joey Maloney drove his Ford Sierra into the private *macadam-paved* car park of Jack's apartment complex. It was 9 a.m. He parked in one of the four available visitors' slots. He switched off the radio and brought an abrupt end to Mick Jagger as he blasted out *"Brown Sugar."* He killed the engine and unclipped his seatbelt, which he hated wearing. The engine made the usual *tink-tink-tink* noises as the metal components started to contract.

He climbed out of his seat with difficulty—his knee was acting up, bringing back painful memories of his motorbike accident. It always gave him trouble when there was dampness in the air, causing an unpleasant stiffness in the joint. He remembered the surgeon telling him that the knee joint, along with the shoulder, was one of the most complicated joints in the human body.

The surgeon had explained that there are four major ligaments in the knee: the anterior cruciate ligament (ACL), the posterior cruciate ligament (PCL), the medial collateral ligament (MCL), and the lateral collateral ligament (LCL). These ligaments connect the femur to the tibia. *It had all sounded like rocket science to Joey.* All he knew was that the injury had ended a promising professional football career in England. He had only been eighteen at the time. Now his limp reminded him of it *every single* day.

When he finally got out of the car, he stretched and yawned. He slammed the door shut and bleeped the key; the *door-lock actuator did* the job it was supposed to do. He walked over to the main door of the apartment building and buzzed the intercom.

Sophie's voice on the other end inquired, *"Who's there, please?"*

"Hiya, Sophie, it's Joey Maloney here—as arranged."

"Oh yes, of course. Come on up, Joey."

He heard the high-pitched sound, confirming that the door was unlocked. He pushed it open and walked up the two flights of stairs to Jack's apartment. Sophie was standing at the open door, smiling. *"Great to see you, Joey. Come in. Jack's expecting you—he's in the bathroom powdering his nose,"* she laughed. *"He was up at 6 a.m. this morning. The interrogation's been on his mind all night. Would you like a cup of tea or coffee?"*

"A cup of tea would be grand, Sophie," said Joey.

They went into the spacious kitchen. Sophie poured water into the kettle and set it to boil. There was a kitchen island in the middle with four stools and three large lamps overhead. Joey pulled out one of the stools and sat down. The kettle boiled, and Sophie poured the hot water over two Lyons tea bags in the pot. She would have one herself, and perhaps Jack would join them, she thought. She let the tea steep for a few minutes before pouring out two mugs—one for herself and one for Joey. Sophie liked her tea black, and being Irish, *he liked his* with milk and sugar.

Joey took a sip from his mug. *"Ah, sure ye can't beat a cup of tea to start the day properly—just what the doctor ordered,"* he said as he placed the mug back on the counter.

Just then, Jack appeared in the kitchen. He was looking good—more relaxed and *smelling of aftershave?* His eyes were still slightly bruised from the broken nose he had sustained. His dark hair was damp from the shower and brushed back on his head. It accentuated even more his azure-blue eyes with their slight green tint, which had mesmerised many a woman. He was wearing a spotless white shirt and blue denim jeans, and he *smelled* of soap and aftershave.

"Tu veux une tasse de thé, chérie?" asked Sophie.

"I'd love a cup of tea," replied Jack.

He tapped Joey amicably on the back, grabbed a stool with his left hand, and sat beside his friend.

"How's the form, Joey?" he asked. *"You're lookin' in good fettle. How's your head after the pistol-whipping?"*

"I'm fine, buddy. I should be asking you the same thing—especially after the punishment that greaseball dished out to ye. And I feel responsible for all the trauma that you and Sophie have undergone. I got careless and paid cash for my mistakes. Anyhow, thank God we're all in one piece. What's really bothering me is my missing handgun. I'm trying to put two and two together and come up with four, but it's just not happening. It's giving me sleepless nights, Jack. And of course, needless to say, Branagan is having a canary over it. Unfortunately, I haven't heard the end of this, my friend." He took another sip from his hot brew.

Jack took a sip from his mug. Like Sophie, he liked his tea black—no sugar, no milk. It was something he had become accustomed to while living in Okinawa. The locals drank copious amounts of turmeric and Sanpin tea daily. It would be considered sacrilege to add sugar or milk to the much-appreciated beverage. He put the hot mug back on the counter and turned to face Joey.

"So what can we expect this morning?" he asked.

"Well," said Joey, scratching the back of his head. *"Inspector Branagan and the investigating judge, John Moran, are expecting us at 10:30 a.m. sharp. Sophie's presence will also be needed—she'll be required to make a deposition. They'll be asking her a lot of questions about the abduction and hoping she'll remember any details that could be relevant to the case.*

And I know it's gonna bring back horrific memories for her. You've got to make a good impression in there, my friend. But don't forget—you guys are the victims here. The judge, John Moran—I've dealt with him before. He's a stickler for protocol, plays by the book. But, having said that, he's fair. He's got a tough exterior, but he's not totally heartless."

Jack immediately saw the effect this was having on Sophie. He got up off his stool, walked around the kitchen island, placed a loving arm over her shoulders, and kissed her on the head.

"Don't worry, love—it'll be okay," he said gently. *"When all this is over, we're going on a holiday in the sun."*

Joey stood up and finished his tea. He licked his lips and put his mug back on the counter. *"Okay, it's time to go and face the music,"* he said in the most cheerful way possible.

Jack helped Sophie put on the blue leather jacket he'd bought her the previous Christmas. She was looking good, he thought—especially considering what she had been through. He put on a light grey jacket that blended perfectly with his white shirt and jeans. Then he went to the sink, poured himself a glass of cool water, and downed it in one. They were ready to go and face the music.

Traffic wasn't heavy for a Monday morning—the rush hour was over—so the drive to the station was pleasant and quick. Not many words were exchanged during the fifteen-minute ride. Jack and Sophie sat in the back and held comforting hands. Joey did his best to lighten the atmosphere, but without much success.

The station was quiet, as it usually was on a Monday morning. Joey nodded a hello to the desk sergeant and showed Jack and Sophie to the waiting room, which was drab and lacklustre. It was badly in need of a fresh coat of paint and some comfortable furniture. It was *Spartan*—and that was putting it mildly. Joey came back five minutes later and beckoned Jack and Sophie to follow him. It was a short eight-yard walk to Branagan's office. Joey knocked on the door and waited for the invitation to enter. He opened the door and waved Jack and Sophie in ahead of him.

Lambs to the slaughter, thought Jack.

Branagan and Judge Moran stood up to greet them. Branagan's face looked redder than usual, Jack noted to himself. This wasn't going to be easy-peasy. Jack tried to size up Judge Moran in one lingering glance. He was a medium-sized, bespectacled man—about five foot eight, overweight, and in his mid-fifties. His girth reflected his fondness for good food and wine—and maybe too many takeaways. He was a man who disliked most forms of exercise, except his long walks with his beloved four-legged friend, who went by the name of Barry.

He was balding with greying temples and seemed to be desperately trying to hang onto the remaining wisps of hair his head had to offer. Jack was instantly reminded of a very famous English international footballer named Ralph Coates, who combed the remaining strands of hair in such a way as to try and cover his entire head. Judge Moran was a confirmed bachelor and very set in his ways.

Branagan looked first in Sophie's direction. *"Good morning, Miss. I'm told that you are of French extraction. We haven't been formally introduced,"* he said in his most seductive manner.

"My name is Sophie Gautier," came the reply.

Branagan smiled. *"Pleased to meet you, my dear. Please, have a seat."*

Judge Moran wasn't insensitive to Sophie's undeniable charm either. He smiled and nodded. *"Je suis très heureux de faire votre connaissance, Mademoiselle,"* he said in nearly perfect French.

Branagan thrust a *ham-like* hand across the desk in Jack's direction and stared into his eyes. They clasped hands. Jack hadn't forgotten the inspector's *vice-like* grip.

Branagan held onto Jack's hand. He could also appreciate the *steel-like* grip on the other side of the table. *"We meet again, Jack Hopkins—and so soon. You were already walking a tightrope, but now you have a noose around your neck."*

He let go of his hand and invited him to take a seat.

Jack sat in the middle seat directly in front of Branagan. Joey was sitting to his left and Sophie to his right. The seats were comfortable, as they were designed for hours of questioning. People needed to feel at ease. Judge Moran was sitting to the left of Branagan at the end of the desk, in front of what appeared to be a thick file representing the police report of the fatal events.

It was going to be a long day, Jack whispered to himself.

Judge Moran addressed Sophie and asked her to tell her painful story from the beginning—and to be precise in detail, if possible.

"Just take your time, my dear. We have plenty of time. You can stop whenever you want if the memories become too unbearable, and of course, the ladies' room is available to you whenever you should feel the need." his tone was both calm and comforting.

Looking at Joey, he added gently, "Maybe Detective Maloney could fetch us a jar of iced water and five glasses. We have a lot of talking to do, and throats will eventually become very dry."

"Oh, most certainly, Sir," said Joey. He rose energetically from his seat and returned four minutes later carrying a tray with a large jar of iced water, five sparkling-clean glasses, and a generous box of tissues. Never know, he had thought, there could be a tear or two shed before the day comes to an end. He poured the glasses and served Sophie first, then Judge Moran, next Inspector Branagan, Jack, and finally himself.

Although the perpetrators of the heinous crime were deceased, both the Judge and Inspector Branagan were convinced that assistance had been provided by a third party. Their theory was further supported by the disappearance of Detective Joey Maloney's service pistol.

Sophie took the glass in her right hand and drank a large sip of the refreshing water. She then began her story from the beginning, just as the Judge had requested. Four sets of ears were poised and attentive.

She explained that it had been a routine night at the restaurant, nothing out of the ordinary. She had said a cheerful goodbye to Ms. Dom and walked into the poorly lit alley. A few yards in, a massive hand cupped her entire mouth and nose, while another wrapped around her waist. She was lifted off her feet to what seemed a great height. Screaming was impossible, and breathing became difficult. She was then bundled into the back of a large black Mercedes, and a hood was placed over her head.

She closed her eyes and sniffled slightly. Branagan offered her a tissue, which she gratefully accepted. Jack offered his large, calloused hand, which she grasped tightly, never wanting to let go. It immediately soothed her.

She recalled catching a fleeting glimpse of the driver — he had red hair, and she was almost certain she'd seen him before. But where? Little did she know it was Detective Sean Doherty playing chauffeur that fateful night. She remembered it being a short drive to the rundown apartment where she was held hostage. They had gone up two flights of stairs. Once inside, they removed her hood and threw her onto a dilapidated couch.

That was the first time she saw the two Italians: the giant Toni and the slimy Paulo. The sheer size of Toni had terrified her. She said a third man had worn a mask, clearly not wanting his identity revealed. One thing she knew: the masked man had intervened on her behalf to dissuade Paulo from having his wicked way with her. For that, she was grateful.

The wait had been excruciatingly long. She cried often, and the Italians had laughed. The masked man had been tasked with errands: sandwiches, pizzas, tea, coffee, and sometimes fish and chips. The Italians had asked for beer, so he brought back six-packs from the local pub. Time dragged. They played cards, smoked duty-free cigarettes, and drank canned beer.

She remembered being abruptly awakened. It was dark. Her hood was replaced, and she was escorted down the stairs, then bundled again into the back seat of the Mercedes. She remembered the 'like-new' smell of the car, especially the leather. It was the only pleasant memory she had from the entire ordeal. They drove slowly to the final destination.

The car stopped. She was allowed to sit upright but still wore the hood, with Paulo as her unwelcome guardian angel. She was suffocating, terrorized by the uncertainty. Then she heard a car approaching. The engine's sound was familiar — Jack's car. Even through the hood, she sensed the full beam of the headlights. A car door slammed, and voices spoke.

Suddenly, she was yanked from the car like a rag doll. No doubt, it was Toni. He removed the hood; his massive left hand gripped her throat while his right clutched her head by the hair. That's when she saw Jack, standing six yards away. He wore denim jeans and his black leather jacket. She had never seen such a distraught look on his face.

She broke down completely. The sight of her other two captors wearing hockey masks from the horror film *Friday the 13th* and pointing guns at Jack didn't ease her panic. She remembered walking like a zombie toward him as he approached. He spoke gently, but it sounded like a foreign language. She understood one word in three. He kissed her on the head and told her, "Drive and don't look back."

She drove the Fiat Spider like a zombie to the end of the road and parked it. She couldn't go any further — emotionally and physically drained, totally terrorised. Later, she heard the sound of sirens and then the sharp popping of gunfire. Tears streamed in cascades. She imagined the worst.

After what felt like an eternity, Jack opened the door of the Fiat Spider. She stared in horror at his bloodied, battered face before throwing her arms around him. Jack, back from the dead, she had thought.

Sophie made no mention of the Pajeros, as Joey had advised. She remembered only the driver and the two Italians. Branagan, Judge Moran, and Joey were clearly moved by her testimony. Judge Moran nodded sympathetically.

Branagan then turned his piercing gaze toward Jack. It was his turn. Jack glanced at Joey, knowing everything now hinged on his own account of the night's events. He drank half his glass of water and waited for Branagan's first question.

Branagan's demeanour had shifted from pity to determination. He opened the thick file Judge Moran had slid to him. He licked his thumb and extracted three A4 sheets of particular interest. Looking straight at Jack, he began:

Forensics have done a great job. They've worked around the clock. First, I'd like to know why a man in your position didn't bother to alert the lawful Gardaí forces from the beginning? Not only did you endanger your own life, but also that of Ms. Gautier. Now, we have three dead bodies — one a suicide — and we must determine whether the other two were cases of murder, voluntary or involuntary manslaughter, or self-defence."

He leaned forward. "So, we're hoping for your full and honest cooperation, Mr. Hopkins. Forensics found two bullet casings: one from a Smith & Wesson, another from Sean Doherty's Sig

Sauer. There were also multiple tyre tracks, most likely from a Japanese-manufactured Jeep. And of course, you overcame three armed men and killed two. Sean Doherty apparently abandoned the scene and took refuge in the Mercedes. Maybe you can shed some light on that for us. We'll have to start calling you Super Ninja from now on."

He slapped his massive hand on the table with a thud.

Joey's face tensed. He dared a quick glance in his friend's direction.

Jack downed another mouthful of water. Thanks to his controlled breathing, he remained calm. He placed the glass on the table and began his carefully prepared reply.

"It wasn't my intention to risk anybody's life, Mr. Branagan. On the contrary, I believed I was acting responsibly. As for the tyre tracks, they were already there when we arrived on the beach. Maybe someone was just testing out his new toy. My intensive training in Japan allowed me to come out of that situation in one piece. I managed to get the baseball bat off the giant before any guns had been pulled.

Detective Doherty fired a warning shot in my direction—it hit the sand. Just as well I ignored the warning, as both Italians then pulled their weapons, and the rest is just all a blur. My body responded instinctively to an extreme threat. When Detective Doherty saw what had happened, I guess he panicked and ran for it, knowing it was a game-over situation. He must have crossed paths with Detective Maloney on his way to the Mercedes. After that, I don't know what happened."

Inspector Branagan and Judge Moran looked at each other, bemused.

"You must move at the speed of light, my boy," retorted Branagan. "You were able to disarm two experienced hoodlums all on your own. Judge Moran and I believe that you had outside help and that you are protecting potential accessories to a crime. Be very careful, Mr. Hopkins—you could end up in prison just on false testimony. So let me ask you again: were there any other people or witnesses at the scene of the crime?"

Jack looked directly at Inspector Branagan. "No, sir. It was all down to me."

Judge Moran then interjected: "This will have to go to court, Mr. Hopkins, as there's too much conflicting evidence. However, if the opposite of what you say can't be proved, you'll be given the benefit of the doubt. In the case of self-defence, the law states that the defendant must have believed he or she was in imminent danger of harm and that the use and degree of force used was reasonably necessary to protect their safety or that of a third person.

Hence, self-defence resulting in death against two armed and dangerous assailants while your life is being threatened will result in a suspended jail sentence, normally sixteen months. We'll need to come to a mutual agreement with the state prosecutor. The last thing we want is a long, drawn-out trial at the taxpayers' expense. Until the day the hearing is set, you shall remain available at all times. I hope I make myself clear."

"I understand perfectly," said Jack. He was happy to be out of the spotlight.

It was now Joey's turn to be cross-examined. He was going to stick to the version he had already given Inspector Branagan—it coincided perfectly with Jack's testimony. Jack and Sophie were told they could take their leave. Branagan and Judge Moran thanked them for their presence and testimony. Just as they were exiting the door, Branagan's voice thundered.

Jack turned a hundred and eighty degrees to face the big man.

"Jack Hopkins, I don't want to see your ugly face in here again. You've already caused me enough sleepless nights—and possibly an ulcer. And the next time your life, or that of your family or friends, is threatened, you contact us immediately. Don't go playing sheriff again. I hope I've made myself clear, Jack."

Jack nodded in agreement. "Don't worry, sir. You won't be hearing about me again. I'll be as quiet as the proverbial mouse."

He took Sophie by the hand, and they walked out through the door. The large clock on the wall showed 12:45 p.m.

"I'm hungry," said Jack. "Let's walk down to Mulligan's and see what's cooking. The air and the walk will do us the world of good. Best of luck to Joey—they're going to put him through the mill. As long as he sticks to his guns, though, he'll come through just fine. They're going to try to trip him up along the way."

Sophie looked up at Jack. "Oui, pauvre Joey. He's a good man—and a very good friend, Jack."

The mile walk to the famous John Mulligan's pub did them both a world of good. They pushed open the old wooden doors, above which was marked in gold lettering: "Est. 1782." The first Mulligans had been established on Thomas Street, Dublin, in 1782. The Mulligan family moved their business to several different premises until finally leasing the present building on Poolbeg Street in 1854. Mick Smyth bought the pub from John Mulligan in 1932, and it was handed over to his nephews and eventually to one of the nephews' sons.

It was just 1 p.m., and the atmosphere in the pub was jovial and relaxed. Black pints of Guinness were lined up like sentries on the old wooden counter, waiting to settle before being handed over to their thirsty patrons. Jack always liked sitting at the bar whenever possible. Two customers were just vacating their much sought-after seats, which Jack, moving fast, immediately claimed.

The two seats had backrests and were more comfortable over a certain time than the traditional bar stools. And Jack's body was still recovering from the physical trauma he had endured. A backrest would be welcome. There was a choice of three meals for lunch: traditional Irish stew, lasagne, or chicken Kiev. Jack ordered a pint of Guinness and a glass—or half-pint—with a dash of blackcurrant for Sophie. The blackcurrant softened the bitter taste of the Guinness, which Sophie had never gotten used to. They both opted for the Irish stew, which they always enjoyed.

Jack was getting the odd stare here and there, as some people had recognised him from the pictures on TV and those published in the newspaper by journalist Zack Cohen. They were speaking in hushed voices. Some barely dared look at him, but those who did nodded and gave him a thumbs-up. Jack would have preferred a different kind of celebrity. A guy came up behind him and tapped him gently on the back.

"Fair play to ye," he said. "You're a brave man. Can I buy you and your wife a drink?"

Jack was more than surprised. It seemed the whole pub was looking at him with genuine admiration and awe.

"Thanks for the offer," said Jack, "but we've just ordered."

Having said that, the barman put a pint in front of Jack, saying, "That's from the gentleman at the end of the bar—he insisted on buying you a pint."

Jack looked to the end of the bar, where the man in question was waving. Jack nodded his appreciation.

He laughed. "If this keeps up, I'm going to end up like a barrel."

Sophie smiled. "Well, chérie, as the saying goes—Guinness is good for you."

The stews were served piping hot. They looked at each other and smiled. "Bon appétit." It was nice to return to a simple, normal life. Jack thought to himself: The Richer there are, the happier they are not. It was good to be alive and enjoying the simple pleasures of life.

They finished their meal, and Jack drank his second pint of Guinness—generously offered by the gentleman at the end of the bar. He then made his way to the gents to freshen up before leaving. Jack hadn't noticed, but several guys were in his wake. He had become a popular hero overnight, and everybody wanted to get close to him. Nodding heads of approval and thumbs-up signs greeted him as he made his way to the toilets.

It was just 3 p.m. when Jack and Sophie stepped out onto the pavement. They had no car. It was a pleasant afternoon, so they decided to walk the three miles or so back to the apartment rather than take public transport. Jack was still sore in a lot of places, but he felt better in an upright position and in motion.

The walk would be beneficial. He was due at the dojo that evening, and despite Sophie's caring protests, he had decided to go. He had promised her that he would only be acting in an advisory capacity. It would be a few more weeks before he could train properly. For now, exercises were limited to breathing and light stretching.

Jack's trial was set for Friday at 10 a.m. in the Criminal Court. The investigating judge, John Moran, had implied they would merely be going through the motions and that Jack would normally be acquitted with a suspended sentence—unless, of course, new evidence was brought forth during the hearing. Jack was eager for the trial to be over. He wanted to put the whole sad and nightmarish story behind both himself and Sophie—and to look toward a brighter future.

There is only one corner of the universe you can be certain of improving, and that's your own self.

Aldous Huxley

CHAPTER
Fourteen

The trial

On the morning of the trial, Jack woke up at 6 a.m. and got out of bed as quietly as he could. Sophie was still in a deep slumber, and he didn't want to awaken her. She had taken a sleeping pill the night before, as the sandman had been slow to come recently, and she was also worried sick about giving testimony at the hearing.

Jack had slept well—at least better than he had in days. He still had to sleep in a semi-upright position because of the pain he felt in his ribs and sternum. The pain was less severe but still very present, and the healing process was slow but encouraging.

He put on his tracksuit, went into the kitchen, and drank a tall glass of cool water. Sunlight filtered through the blinds on the sliding glass door to the terrace. He opened the door, which slid effortlessly and noiselessly along the aluminium rail. Sinking into the horse stance position, he began his daily breathing routine. Ten minutes later, he attempted some light stretching exercises, going only as far as the pain would permit.

After stretching, he removed the protective covering from the makiwara punching pad and went through his usual routine of open-handed and closed-fist blows. He worked out for thirty minutes using hands, fists, and elbows for different atemi. He had built up a good sweat, so he took off his tracksuit top and finished the session with the Eight Pieces of Brocade—a series of soft qigong breathing and energy techniques.

He gazed out at the horizon. The rising sun cast a rosy hue across the morning sky. Golden rays of sunlight lit up the entire bay and the incoming tide. He could hear the distinct screech of seagulls and curlews out on the hunt. And he could still taste and smell the blood that had stained the sand of Dollymount Beach. It made him shiver.

The church bell chimed seven times. It was time for breakfast, thought Jack. He stepped back into the kitchen and went about preparing an Irish breakfast, which Sophie always adored. He started by frying sausages and rashers, which he always bought from the local butcher, Patsy—a big, jovial Galway man who had arrived in Dublin in his early twenties, never losing his strong country accent. Patsy adored Jack and always gave him first-class service. Once cooked, he put the sausages and rashers in the oven to keep warm. He put the kettle on to boil and finished off the fry with eggs, Patsy's award-winning white pudding, and fried brown bread from the local bakery.

Sophie appeared in the bedroom doorway, rubbing the sleep from her eyes and yawning. "Oh, que ça sent bon," she said. "What a beautiful smell. I'm so hungry." "Well, you've come to the right place," laughed Jack.

There was nothing like the smell of a fry to get someone out of bed in the morning. Jack remembered his teenage years and the smell of the fry drifting up to his bedroom from the kitchen below, where his father always prepared the Sunday morning breakfast.

Jack took the piping hot plates from the oven and added the eggs, white pudding, and fried brown bread. The tea had infused, so he filled two mugs.

"Bon appétit. There's nothing like a good fry to start off the day," said Jack.

He nearly always prepared a fry on Sunday mornings after sleeping in until around 10 a.m. Then, after a shower, they would go for a brisk walk down the Bull Wall to help with digestion. The fry, as usual, was delicious and washed down with Lyons Tea Gold Blend Loose Leaf—what could be better?

Jack took Sophie by the hand. "Okay, love, it's time to get ready. Let's put on our glad rags and give these people something to gawk at."

Sophie looked stunning when she had finished dressing and applied her makeup. She had opted for a white blouse and a grey pencil skirt, which enhanced her feminine curves. Her black leather jacket and a pair of black high heels added the final touch. She wanted to appear alluring and sexy, but not cheap.

"Wow, you look absolutely stunning," extolled Jack. He was quite the picture himself. Jack didn't exactly have many suits to choose from—three at most. He chose a grey flannel Hugo Boss suit that he had recently bought for a wedding, a white shirt with a navy blue tie, and a pair of black slip-on loafers. He looked good, and he certainly felt good. They made quite an impression—a stunning couple.

They got into the Fiat Spider. The four-cylinder twin-carb engine fired up immediately. Regular maintenance always paid off. They headed toward the Criminal Court, housed in the famous Four Courts building on Inns Quay. It was an impressive piece of architecture and had been part of the Dublin skyline since the late 18th century. The building was initially started by Royal Exchange architect Thomas Cooley before being finished by James Gandon, who also sculpted the statues on the roof. The copper dome of the Four Courts was the building's most prominent feature, and it even appeared on the Irish £20 note.

Traffic was light—the morning rush hour was over. It was a short seven-mile drive, but there were many stops for traffic lights and pedestrian crossings. They arrived at 9:30 a.m., well in time. Jack parked the little Fiat in a side street at the back of the Four Courts. From there, it was only a short stroll to the entrance.

Sophie shuddered at the imposing sight of the building and its towering pillars. She clutched Jack's arm tighter and tighter, afraid he might vanish into thin air. The expression "the pillars of law" took on a whole new meaning.

They were greeted by a battery of photographers and journalists from both the press and television. Cameras flashed incessantly as they made their way up the steps, through the massive pillars, and past the railings toward the push-open, glass-paned wooden doors. The entrance, in contrast to the building itself, was quite small and tight. Progress toward the doors, with so many journalists and photographers crammed into the limited space, was slow and chaotic. Police officers attempted to clear a path.

Jack immediately noticed journalist Zack Cohen in all his glory. He had managed to position himself just in front of the doors with his photographer. He tried to push a microphone on an extended arm toward Jack.

"How are you feeling this morning, Jack? How do you think the verdict will go? Are you scared about going to prison?" he shouted.

"No comment," said Jack, as he pushed the microphone away from his face. The interior of the building was just as daunting as the exterior. The central block had an arched courtyard, with end pavilions on either side. The portico was supported by six Corinthian columns, and high above stood the statues of Moses, Justice, Mercy, Authority, and Wisdom. A copper-domed, collonaded rotunda rose behind.

Welcome to the corridors of power and justice, Jack thought to himself. On any other occasion, it would have been a pleasant and educational visit.

They were guided through the courtroom doors to a full and rumbling room. It was jammed. Cameras were forbidden inside the courtroom itself. Heads pivoted to face them, and mumbling voices sent incoherent messages to their ears. Jack and Sophie made their way to the front of the courtroom. Jack spotted his good friend Detective Joey Maloney, who gave him the thumbs-up sign. Sophie was placed in a seat to the right, and Jack could see a big, dark-haired man in his early forties beckoning him to take a seat beside him at a desk. Jack hadn't wanted an attorney, so he had been appointed one automatically by the State.

The man in question went by the name of Gerry Molloy, and he had built up quite a good defence record. He had a difficult task ahead of him, as he hadn't yet interviewed Jack. For the moment, he had built his defence on the details and evidence that had been handed down to him by the investigating judge. He had, of course, access to all the relevant files and the forensic results. They shook hands. Jack immediately took a liking to him.

It was bang on 10 a.m. The bailiff announced the arrival of the Judges, and he asked everyone to stand up to show respect for the Judges, the court, and the law by saying:

"All rise. This court is now in session."

Under the Irish legal system, it is always a judge (or a panel of judges in the case of the Special Criminal Court or the Court of Appeal) who imposes the sentence. The court sits with three judges and no jury, in order to avoid jury intimidation. This case had been handed over to the Special Criminal Court because of the Mafia connections.

This was followed by a lot of murmuring and the noise of people standing. The Judges arrived, sat down, and the Judge sitting in the middle told everyone to be seated and quiet. Jack looked straight over at Sophie. She caught his glance; her face bore a worried and strained look. He winked and smiled at her. The long black gowns worn by both the Judges and the attorneys were very intimidating.

There was a buzz going around the courtroom, which the Judges didn't appreciate. So, one of them had to make use of his hardwood gavel to call for attention and silence. The court was now definitely in session.

The State pathologist, Florence Leahy, a tall, slim, attractive brunette in her early forties, was first up to give precise details relating to the injuries to the two Italians. She was the only female practising pathologist in the State, and she was known for her precision and for being pedantic. She gave a detailed account which lasted a full twenty minutes.

The giant Toni had suffered a broken sternum, a broken jaw, a broken neck, and a severed spinal cord. Paulo had also sustained a broken neck and a collapsed kidney. Both men had also suffered several contusions. She pointed out that all the injuries were caused by extremely violent and powerful blows. She said that very few men would be capable of inflicting such injuries with their bare hands. It was the work of someone who had deadly skills. The Judge thanked her for her accurate testimony and released her from the stand.

The prosecution was asking for a full five-year jail sentence. The State prosecutor tried to prove that there was use of excessive and unnecessary force with the intention to kill, and that a person with such martial skills could have injured or controlled his assailants instead of killing them.

Jack's lawyer was quick to his feet and brought the Court's attention to exhibit "A," which was the baseball bat that had been used in a savage and brutal manner on his client and had caused him extensive injuries. He then brought their attention to exhibits "B" and "C" respectively.

These exhibits, he went on to explain, were the two Berettas that the Italians had intended to use against his client in a vendetta killing which had been mandated by the New York Mafia. He went on to say that his client had acted on the spur of the moment and in the heat of the action. His client's life was in immediate danger, and it certainly wasn't the moment to calculate possible restraining techniques. He was alone and unarmed against two armed and dangerous assailants, and therefore, his actions were clearly justifiable. It was a clear-cut matter of self-defence.

Jack's lawyer called Sophie to the stand. He was sure that her testimony would clear Jack and result in a not guilty decision. Sophie's testimony, along with her French accent, was poignant. The court was reduced to complete silence as she gave the details of her painful and traumatising ordeal at the hands of the two Italian henchmen and the detective Sean Doherty.

She said that she suffered from terrifying nightmares and was scared to go anywhere unaccompanied. As far as Gerry Molloy was concerned, the verdict was signed, sealed, and delivered.

The State prosecutor called Jack to the stand. He was a balding, overweight man in his mid-fifties and of average height. His face was set to flint; it expressed a hardness and the inflexibility of unwavering determination. He immediately referred to the excessive use of force that Jack had used and implied that he hadn't acted on his own but had been aided and abetted by other accomplices in these two terrible crimes. It was impossible, he said, for a single man to carry out such feats.

He was a man of great experience who had put many criminals behind bars. His speech was eloquent, and he carried out theatrical gestures to impress and win over the three Judges. No doubt about it, he was an excellent orator. He was galvanised by his self-confidence.

Despite the man's gruelling questioning and repeated innuendos, Jack didn't bat an eyelid, remaining calm and focused. He stuck to his guns and didn't change his story an iota from the one he had given to the investigating Judge and Inspector Branagan. There was no way that he was going to incriminate his buddies or sell them out.

He repeated over and over that he had acted solely and that his only intention had been to save his life against armed aggressors. The prosecutor finished his speech by declaring that Jack was a cold-blooded murderer and that the State had the obligation to put him behind bars for at least five years.

Jack's lawyer then stood up calmly and walked over to the stand. He thanked the State Prosecutor in a facetious manner for his somewhat brutal questioning and his obtuse attitude. In his cross-examination, he asked Jack to tell the Court about his years spent in Okinawa and the special skills that he had acquired from his assiduous training.

Jack addressed the court calmly and described his six years of intensive, eight-hour daily training, except for Sundays, which he liked to take off and follow the Irish tradition of no work on

Sundays. This brought a giggle from most of the people present. He described his brutal and gruelling sixth dan black belt examination, which finished with a hundred-man sparring test. There was a gasp of awe and admiration in the courtroom.

Gerry Molloy then addressed the three Judges, saying that a man of such talents could easily have carried out those amazing feats on the fatal night on Dollymount Strand on his own and without any outside help. Yes, okay, he had used excessive force. But what else does one do against two armed and experienced aggressors?

There just wasn't time to calculate the pros and the cons of the situation. He said that Jack's body had reacted naturally to an extremely dangerous situation. He thanked the three Judges and Jack and walked calmly back to his desk.

All the evidence had been heard. The State Prosecutor had no more questions; he felt the case slipping through his fingers like an oily herring. It was coming up to 1 p.m., so the session was adjourned for lunch and would resume at 3 p.m. By this time, the three Judges would have reached their final verdict.

Exiting the courtroom, even under police escort, was as difficult as it had been to enter it. Once outside, the cameras started their machine-gun-like flashing. Journalists shouted out questions to Jack and tried to push microphones in his direction. Sophie held tightly onto Jack as they tried to escape from the cacophony.

They made it back to the car. There was no way they could go to a pub or restaurant for lunch in the vicinity without being harassed. They decided to drive over the Liffey and have lunch in Sophie's restaurant, The Unicorn. There, they would find some peace and quiet and friendly faces.

It was a short ten-minute drive. Jack found a parking space on Stephen's Green, just opposite the famous and luxurious Shelbourne Hotel. The restaurant was a hundred yards away. As they arrived at The Unicorn, a couple were just leaving a table on the terrace. Jack and Sophie didn't waste any time in taking their places. Excellent—a nice cosy table and away from the public eye and all the hubbub.

Sophie stood up: "Stay here, chérie, I'll go and see Ms. Dom."

Sophie hadn't returned to work since the fatal night of her kidnapping. She had, of course, been in contact on numerous occasions by phone with Ms. Dom, the manageress of the restaurant. Ms. Dom's face lit up when she saw Sophie coming through the door.

As usual, she was discreet as ever and accompanied Sophie out the door to meet Jack—not forgetting to bring a menu with her. She showed a sincere kindness and interest in their painful situation. Being a spinster, she treated them both like the children she never had.

"Oh, Jack," she said, taking his hand, "I was so worried for you both. I was horrified when I read the newspapers and saw the news on TV. Poor Sophie—I was sick thinking about her and what she must have gone through, poor little girl. Oh, Jack, I hope those Judges have a little bit of humanity in them."

Jack cupped her small hands. "Don't worry, Ms. Dom, everything will work out okay. In a few weeks, this will all be history and old news."

Jack and Sophie scanned the menu. They both opted for the fresh tuna salad and two glasses of the famous Five Roses rosé wine from the Domaine Leone de Castris in Italy's southern picturesque peninsula. This wine was first made in 1943 and was the first rosé ever bottled in Italy. 'Five Roses' alluded to the fact that the property was then managed by five siblings.

This was Sophie's favourite rosé. She adored the brilliant cherry-red colour, the heady scent of blackberry, cherries, wild strawberries, and the fruity taste it offered. It was a perfect accompaniment for risotto, fish, and white meat. Jack had grown to enjoy it now and then with a meal, especially during the fine weather. He still preferred his pint of Guinness once or twice a week.

Ms. Dom had skipped back inside the restaurant and was back in less than ten minutes with the two salads and glasses of rosé. She placed the tray on the table and took Sophie by the hand, whispering:

"This is on me, my dear. Enjoy."

"Thank you so much, Ms. Dom. You're too kind," chimed Sophie.

A lot of kindness goes a long way in this sometimes-cruel world. It gave both of them a much-needed and well-deserved emotional uplift. The tuna salads looked amazingly appetising, and the rosé, with its cherry-red hue, just beckoned to be tasted. They were both hungry.

"This is the best tuna salad I have ever tasted," said Jack jovially. He put the rosé to his lips and tasted the nectar.

"Ah, beautiful—just what the doctor ordered," he said.

At that precise moment in time, the courtroom seemed light-years away, and his shoulders felt completely weightless. Carpe diem, he thought to himself, and he smiled lovingly at Sophie. They enjoyed their lunch in perfect anonymity. No heads turned to gawk at them—they were just any young, loving couple having lunch. The time had slipped away so fast, too fast.

As Einstein said, "Time is relative. It's only worth depends upon what we do as it is passing."

They said goodbye discreetly to Ms. Dom, thanked her again for her kindness, and headed back to face the predators of the media and to discover what fate had been decided for Jack. As expected, the journalists and photographers were on the lookout, and once they spotted Jack and Sophie, they made a beeline for their direction. The cameras started their relentless flashing.

A well-known journalist, Joe Cahill from the nation's main channel, RTE1, shouldered his way to the front and pushed a large, furry microphone in their direction.

"Any comments, Jack and Sophie? How do you think the verdict will go? Are you worried about going to jail, Jack? If he goes to prison, will you wait for him, Sophie?"

The questions were machine-gunned out in one breath.

Jack kept his usual unflappable calm. He could feel Sophie clinging tighter and tighter to his arm. He sensed the panic building in her like a volcano ready to unleash its molten lava.

Jack suddenly stopped walking.

"Okay, guys, do you want a comment?" he said with a laconic grin. "What's your name?" he asked the man holding the microphone.

"Joe Cahill, for RTE1," he replied, feeling privileged to be on the verge of broadcasting Jack's comment on live television.

Jack threw him a friendly smile. "Okay, Joe, here's what you can do. Go down to Mulligan's Pub and tell the bartender, Paddy, to pull me the best pint of Guinness he has ever pulled in his life, because I'll be there in about an hour. Oh yeah—and tell him to reserve us two seats at the bar. Good man. On your bike now."

Jack's comment triggered general laughter and helped to lighten the uncomfortable and concrete-cast atmosphere. They continued their way to the court entrance, where more journalists and camera crews were waiting in hopes of a media scoop. The courtroom, which had been like a bee's nest, suddenly fell silent as Jack and Sophie made their way to their respective seats. Jack's attorney, Gerry Molloy, nodded to him, brandishing a large, beaming smile.

The bailiff arrived and told the Court to rise. It was 3 p.m. The three Judges entered and took their seats. The chief Judge instructed the muted court to be seated. There was a lot of nervous coughing and fidgeting among the gallery. The atmosphere could be cut with a knife. Once seated, the coughing and fidgeting ceased among the members of the public.

The chief Judge cleared his throat and struck the wooden sound block with his gavel.

"Will the defendant please rise?" he said in the gravest of tones.

Sophie suddenly felt light-headed. She needed air and a glass of water. Her eyes drifted toward her lover—he was a blur. Jack and his attorney both stood together. His fate would now be sealed.

The chief Judge assumed a serious countenance.

"Mr. Jack Hopkins, we have studied all the evidence brought before us in this Court of Law with great detail, and our decision is unanimous. Taking into consideration that you acted solely in self-defence in response to what was a life-threatening situation against two armed and dangerous aggressors, myself and my two colleagues, in accordance with the laws currently in place in this State, have deemed it just that a decision of involuntary manslaughter be declared.

Manslaughter, albeit a lesser crime than murder, is a criminal offence; whereas a true self-defence killing is not a crime. Citizens have the right to use force to protect themselves from harm if necessary. This type of unintentional homicide is known as involuntary manslaughter.

However, taking it upon yourself to act outside of the law in a vigilante fashion, this Court has no other option but to condemn you to a three-year suspended sentence, taking effect from this day. You are therefore free to go. This Court is now officially adjourned."

There was general applause from the public in approbation of the Judges' decision. Jack and his lawyer embraced in a manly fashion. Sophie was being attended to by one of the Court's attendants, who had come to her rescue with a glass of water and a comforting arm. The State prosecutor, though bitterly disappointed with the judgment, congratulated both Jack and his lawyer and wished Jack all the best for the future.

Joey Maloney was immediately over to embrace and congratulate his good friend.

"It's your round, Hopkins. See ye down in Mulligan's," he said as he slapped Jack on the back.

Sitting discreetly at the back of the courtroom and going completely unnoticed was a certain Robbie Maher from the Kelly drug cartel. He had been sent by his boss to get the news of the judgment firsthand. A certain Joey Falconetti, on the other side of the Atlantic Ocean, would be only too happy to know that Jack Hopkins was out on the streets and hence an easier target than behind prison bars.

Jack had told his friends it would be better if they stayed away from the courthouse. He didn't want to get them involved or draw too much attention with the media hounds on the loose. Anyway, it would be difficult for most of them to get the day off work for a court hearing.

Sophie had recovered, and the colour had come back to her cheeks. She had the look of a woman who had just been told by her GP that the lump on one of her breasts was completely benign. The sensation of suffocation and drowning she had experienced during the hearing had completely dissipated. A blanket of lead had been lifted.

Jack and Sophie walked hand in hand out of the courtroom into the impressive, dome-shaped hall with its impeccably tiled floor and imposing pillars. The sunlight was bursting in through the bull's-eye windows, and the large clock just beneath displayed the time: 3:50 p.m.

They exited through the main courthouse doors and stepped out onto the steps, penetrating a hub of excitement. Cameras began to flash from all angles, and journalists and news reporters pushed and shoved their way closer to the now-famous couple. Questions were hurled at Jack and Sophie in a frenzy of excitement.

Jack could just about make out Trigger from "Night Owl Plumbing Ltd..," as his little business had been baptised by Bradley in his usual facetious manner. Trigger stood on the other side of the road, his back to the River Liffey and away from all the commotion. He gave Jack a thumbs-up and mimed raising a pint glass to his lips.

It was a warm afternoon. The sun played cat and mouse with fleeting clouds, and the usual late-afternoon traffic began to grow. Jack and Sophie crossed the road onto the Quays, where Trigger was waiting with a beaming smile. Jack gave him a high five, and together they began their walk down the Quays towards Mulligan's pub.

They were stalked by journalists and photographers, each one vying for the best position and hoping for a comment, no matter how trivial. Some photographers ran ahead, clutching their precious Nikon or Canon cameras that dangled from their necks. TV crews did their best to manage their bulky Panasonic video cameras amid the pushing and jostling, desperate to gather enough compelling footage for the evening news. The newspapers would have to wait until the morning editions to publish their photos—it was too late for the evening press. But come morning, page one would be dominated by Jack, Sophie, and Trigger.

Jack, Sophie, and Trigger did their best to ignore all the hubbub. It wasn't easy. Cameras were flashing, and people were calling out. They continued walking down the Quays as far as the famous Ha'penny Bridge—one of the landmarks of Dublin city and a popular meeting spot among Dubliners. They ascended the steps onto the bridge.

Halfway across, photographers and video crews were already waiting. As soon as they spotted the trio, cameras began flashing and rolling. Curious onlookers gathered quickly. The bridge wasn't large, only 47 yards long, and navigating the throng of people, press, and media crews became increasingly difficult. They went from a stroll to a dawdle, barely able to move without bumping into someone.

Some people recognised Jack from the news reels and called out to him. Others tapped him on the back and offered words of support.

"Well done, Jack! Those bastards got what they deserved!" someone shouted.

Eventually, they made it to the other side of the bridge. They descended the steps and turned left onto Burgh Quay. Cars stopped at the traffic lights honked their horns in recognition and approval as soon as they realised who was walking by. There was no doubt—Jack Hopkins, whether he liked it or not, was now famous.

They continued their stroll down the Quays, exchanging jokes and light-hearted conversation about matters of a bagatelle nature. It felt good. The recent horrors they had experienced were momentarily locked away in the amygdala—the part of the brain responsible for processing emotional memories. When a person experiences trauma, adrenaline rushes through the body, and the memory is etched into the amygdala, which registers the intensity and emotional significance of the event.

Ten minutes later, they arrived at the famous Mulligan's pub. They pushed through the wooden and glass-panelled swinging doors into a beehive of activity. As usual for a late Friday afternoon, the bar was packed with people from all walks of life. It was especially popular among civil servants, legal professionals, journalists, and theatrical actors. For many, the weekend had already begun.

As soon as Jack stepped through the doors and was recognised, the hubbub gave way to a deafening silence—as if a blanket had been thrown over a budgie's cage. Then, a few people began clapping, and soon the whole pub joined in with joyful applause.

"Good on ye, boy! Fair play to ye! Well done!" some enthusiastic punters called out.

Jack waved and nodded in acknowledgement. He then turned toward the bar, and to his great surprise, he saw two stools with 'Reserved' signs printed in white on a black background. Between them sat a pint of Guinness, already poured and waiting. Jack looked at Sophie and Trigger and laughed heartily.

"I just can't believe it," he chimed. "That TV reporter Joe Cahill is an okay guy after all. I'll have to get to know him better. After all, it would be nice to have someone in the media who isn't just there to throw you to the wolves. I must ring him sometime to thank him."

Jack and Sophie took their seats, and Trigger stood between them—there were no spare stools. Trigger ordered a pint for himself and asked Sophie what she'd like.

"A Martini," she said cheerfully.

Jack turned his gaze to the far end of the bar. A bearded, middle-aged man was waving and smiling in his direction. It was Joe Cahill himself. Jack wouldn't have to call him after all. He raised his pint of Guinness in a thank-you gesture. Cahill did likewise, and they both shouted over the din, "Sláinte! Good health!" before bringing the glasses to their lips.

Pints began arriving from all directions, courtesy of Jack's newfound fan club. Jack, of course, had no intention of drinking them all. He merely waved in thanks and left them lined up on the bar—for Trigger to enjoy.

"Don't worry, Jack. I'll look after them for ye," Trigger grinned as he brought another creamy pint to his lips.

Jack had made a pact with himself never to return to the ways he had abandoned before moving to Japan. There had been a time when he drank nearly every night for a year, gaining over two stone and falling apart both physically and mentally.

He had forged his body through sheer willpower and disciplined his mind with eight-hour daily training sessions during his six-year stay in Okinawa. Now, he limited himself to three pints two or three times a week, along with the occasional glass of wine.

However, once a year, on the anniversary of Akiko's death, he allowed himself to let go. The memories remained too painful, the emotional scars too deep to heal—at least for now. He preferred to drown his sorrows alone. He knew it wasn't right, and that Akiko wouldn't have wanted it, but the grief was stronger than him. It still haunted him. It felt as though a part of him had been amputated. Never before had he bonded so deeply—in body and spirit—with another human being. Would he ever find peace?

A little voice inside told him that someday he would come to terms with himself—but there would be a price to pay. And that price would be the death of Joey Falconetti—by his own hands. Jack now knew it was only a matter of time and patience. The wheels of fate were in motion, and there was no turning them back.

Recent events had brought the black memories thundering back like a tsunami. But Jack was ready. He knew what he had to do. And he wasn't afraid to die if necessary. It had already been filed in his mental archive under 'Things to Be Done.'

He knew Akiko wouldn't approve of his quest for revenge, but as far as Jack was concerned, he would be doing society a favour—removing one more evil from the world. It was his karma, no matter how the coin landed—heads or tails.

Joe Cahill, the news reporter, made his way over to where Jack was sitting and introduced himself formally. Jack shook his hand and thanked him for the pint and the two stools.

"You're an okay guy. I never for one second thought that you would do it," smiled Jack.

"You're more than welcome," said Cahill warmly. "I admire you, and a conviction would have been a travesty of justice as far as I'm concerned. I'd be more than grateful if you could grant me an exclusive interview. Don't worry—not about the recent events, but rather your stay in Okinawa, your sense of justice, and the way you view our modern world today, and possibly the future."

Jack finished off his second pint and wiped the froth from his mouth. "Sure thing," he said. "Once we stick to the agenda, I'm okay with it. It would be nice to have someone I can trust among the media. Just tell me when you want to schedule it, and I'll be there."

"Okay, let's shake on it," said Joe Cahill. "Be expecting a call from me in the next few days. My agenda is quite full at the moment, and I have a lot on my plate."

He thanked Jack sincerely and told him to enjoy the rest of the evening. It was coming up to 6 p.m., and the pub was now jam-packed and buzzing with early evening revellers. Some of them were just in for a drink or two after work, and others were out for the night until closing time and would possibly end their night in one of Dublin's many nightclubs.

Jack, Sophie, and Trigger were in good spirits, and they, too, had decided to carry on their festivities later on into the evening. And what better place to top off a good evening than the Unicorn restaurant, where Sophie worked? The food and wine were always good, and Sophie knew they would be absolutely pampered by Ms. Dom. The restaurant would be packed, but Ms. Dom always found a table for "special guests" down at the back of the restaurant near the wine cellar. Jack was anxious to convey the court's decision to the 'gang,' so they decided to poke their heads into O'Donoghue's pub on their way to the Unicorn in the off chance of bumping into one of the lads.

Jack lifted his third and last pint to his mouth, and Trigger, who had ploughed into the pints that Jack had gratefully received but didn't drink, put the fifth creamy pint to his smiling lips.

They left Mulligan's pub at 7 p.m. and strolled casually up to Merrion Row and the famous O'Donoghue's pub, where Jack thought they might see some familiar faces. As usual, the place was packed to the brim with locals and especially tourists—the majority of whom were American—on the trail of their Irish ancestry and roots. Jack said he'd take a look on his own. No point in the three of them trying to elbow their way through the throng of people. He came back five minutes later. There were no familiar faces to be seen, so they walked the short distance to the Unicorn.

As expected, the restaurant was jam-packed. The staff were literally run off their feet trying to keep up with the endless orders. Ms. Dom was her usual energetic self. She was like a human version of the Road Runner from the famous cartoon series—now you see her, now you don't. Her face literally lit up like a beacon when she noticed Sophie and Jack, and she was over to them at the speed of light.

She clapped her hands together with glee. "Oh, I'm so happy for you," she said.

"Wow, it's so busy," exclaimed Sophie. "This is Trigger, a friend of ours. You may remember him—he's been in here already a few times."

Ms. Dom was known as being an excellent physiognomist. "Oh, I do," she said. "Isn't he the famous plumber?"

"Spot on," said Jack. "You certainly haven't lost the touch."

The smile of a rascal played about her lips. "Now, children, follow me to the bar. I want to offer you a drink to celebrate the good news. You can relax while your table is being set. I have just the place—at the back of the restaurant near the wine cellar."

Jack smiled and winked at Sophie. Ms. Dom was her usual good-hearted self. She offered them champagne, took their orders of lasagna for three, side salads, a bottle of Chianti, and off she whisked in effortless fashion. Some people recognised Jack at the bar and dared dart-like glances in his direction before turning to their partner or friends to confirm their sighting of the 'mafia slayer.'

It wasn't long before a low drone-like hum spread across the entire restaurant as people in turn recognised the man sitting at the bar. Ms. Dom was very much in tune with the situation, and she was back in a flash to guide them to their waiting table, which had been impeccably set with an immaculate white tablecloth, napkins to match, the best of cutlery, and large tulip-like wine glasses. Hidden away nicely from the hubbub.

The wine arrived, and Ms. Dom uncorked the precious nectar in her inimitable fashion. There was nothing more convivial and inviting than the sound of a cork popping from a bottle. The lasagna arrived piping hot with the side salads—everything was perfect.

Jack raised his glass of Chianti. "Cheers—here's to happier times ahead, though I know it will be difficult to erase the horrors of that night."

They clinked their glasses, and the sound of crystal was unmistakable.

"Tchin, tchin," Sophie said, and Trigger contributed to the toast with, "Sláinte."

For nearly two hours, they wined and dined in carefree fashion, laughed, told jokes, and talked of future projects. Ms. Dom insisted on offering them a Sambuca to finish off the night—a good nightcap, as she called it—which helped the digestion and guaranteed a good night's sleep.

They were the last to leave the restaurant. They bid goodbye to Ms. Dom and thanked her for her generosity and hospitality. A blanket of clouds covered the stars, making the lane seem more sombre than usual. A cold, sudden shiver ran down Sophie's spine, chilling her to her very core. The frightening memories surged back and filled her with terror. She clasped onto Jack as though he would suddenly disappear. Jack immediately understood her distress as he put one powerful arm around her shoulder and pulled her towards him. They said goodnight to Trigger and headed towards the Quays, to where the little Spider was parked. The walk and the cool night air would be perfect companions as they set off, clinging to each other in a warm and loving embrace.

The purpose of our lives is to be happy

Dalai Lama

CHAPTER
Fifteen

A heat wave beat down on the Manhattan pavements. It was into the second week, and it showed no signs of moving on. Temperatures soared into the hundreds, and the heat from automobiles and buildings added to the already stifling atmosphere. According to weather specialists, the high-pressure belt was well anchored over the entire East Coast of the United States, and with no wind, it wasn't about to budge.

Air conditioning companies and fan outlets were overwhelmed with orders, and maintenance crews were working around the clock to install new units and repair existing ones. Those who didn't have modern AC systems had to rely on old-fashioned fans—either ceiling-mounted or standing floor models. The blades on these fans hissed nonstop, twenty-four hours a day. Many people in poorer areas had to rely on traditional Mexican-made hand fans.

New York experienced daily power cuts, especially in the most populated areas of the city, as the electricity demand had practically doubled. The city's 60 public swimming pools, scattered around the five boroughs, were constantly packed—mainly with children and adolescents enjoying their summer vacation under the blistering sun. Those who couldn't access the pools resorted to the illegal use of water from the numerous fire hydrants around the city to cool down.

It was miserable weather for overweight people and anyone working manual labour. Most companies—such as dry cleaners and construction firms—adjusted their schedules, starting at 5 a.m. and finishing by 2 p.m. to avoid the intense afternoon heat. Those working in restaurant kitchens had to grin and bear it, as eating habits weren't going to change overnight.

Ice cream vendors wore broad smiles as their sales more than doubled, and the demand for ice-cold sodas and beers exploded. Once there's a buck to be made, the American is happy.

Joey Falconetti was enjoying the air conditioning of his plush office. Being overweight, he didn't much care for the heat. He was a happy man. All his restaurants were air-conditioned and doing great business, especially with the tourists who flocked to Little Italy. He relit his Cuban cigar and settled back into his comfortable leather armchair. He blew out a puff of smoke and watched it lazily rise toward the ceiling. A smile played across his lips as he looked at the figures he had received that morning by fax. Drug sales in all areas were up by at least 20%. Business was booming.

He had just been on the phone with his first cousin Giovanni Falconetti in Sicily. Joey's uncle, Salvatore, had married into the powerful Sicilian Corleone clan through Maria Corleone. Together they had four children—three girls and one boy. The boy, the youngest, was baptised Giovanni. He was now the family's main executioner—or 'mechanic' as they liked to call it.

Although only 35 years old, Giovanni had built up quite a reputation. He had thirty 'hits' to his name and a bloody trail that included judges, magistrates, and other recalcitrant gang members. He had learned young and picked up the 'tools' of the trade at an unprecedented rate. Giovanni was an expert in all kinds of weapons—rifles, sawn-off shotguns, handguns, knives, and explosives. He wasn't bad with his hands either.

The 'family' had sent him off at 21 to Israel for a one-year course in Krav Maga and military techniques with the country's elite instructors. Krav Maga is an efficient, no-nonsense close combat method founded by Imi Lichtenfeld to protect the Jewish community from fascists. It's a practical, down-to-earth street-fighting system—and it fits Giovanni like a glove.

He returned to Sicily just after his 22nd birthday on a scorching summer day. His parents, along with all the family and clan members, were more than happy to celebrate his return, and a party was organised in his honour at the family villa that night. They couldn't believe the physical transformation he had undergone. He had left as a skinny boy and returned with an impressively built and daunting physique. His shoulders, arms, and chest were now powerfully built, exuding steel-like strength. His legs had been shaped by numerous twenty-mile hikes carrying a 60-pound backpack during training with the Israeli elite.

The Corleone family had made a generous donation to the Jewish Foundation in return for the services rendered. Giovanni's training had been intensive, with only Sundays off to relax. He looked quite the picture: six feet one inch tall, good-looking, typically Mediterranean with jet-black hair and a tanned body. The fairer sex found him extremely attractive and sexy.

There was a cruel streak in Giovanni, however, and it intensified over the years. During that summer, he would start fights in nightclubs across the island just to test his skills and impress onlookers. His victims were left with broken noses, jaws, joints—and sometimes worse. Of course, being part of the Corleone clan helped a lot. No one dared to complain or press charges, and most of the clubs were under the protection of the Cosa Nostra.

There was no doubt—Giovanni was now the alpha male, and even the mere mention of his name filled people with terror. His skills had been honed to near 'state-of-the-art' levels. Giovanni wasn't just good at his job—he was excellent. His well-padded bank account was proof to anyone who doubted his competence.

He liked fast cars and young, loose women. His garage boasted a Ferrari, a Lamborghini, and a Porsche. He also appreciated the occasional recreational smoke of a good joint. His taste for expensive wines and spirits was common knowledge—but always in moderation. Giovanni liked to keep in shape.

His sex life, however, was quite the opposite. It was outrageous. He had an insatiable sex drive and changed partners regularly—bringing two or sometimes three of the chosen few to his king-sized bed at once. Renowned for his sexual prowess and taste for luxury, young women were drawn to him like magnets, hoping for a night in the Italian stallion's bed.

Early at 8:30 a.m. on that Saturday morning, Giovanni was woken from a deep sleep—and a night of unrestrained sexual activity—by the persistent ringing of his bedside phone. He was more than surprised to hear his cousin Joey Falconetti on the other end. He didn't appreciate early morning calls. He usually arose around ten.

"Che cazzo! Ne sai che ore sono? Chi è questo?" *What the fuck! Do you know what time it is?*

"È ora di svegliarsi. Wakey, wakey, cousin!" laughed Joey Falconetti. "I have a nice little job for you abroad."

Although Joey spoke perfect Italian, he always preferred the tongue of Shakespeare unless asked otherwise.

Giovanni was all ears. He sat up in bed, slapped his latest conquest on the butt, and told her to go prepare breakfast. He liked his coffee piping hot and black, with scrambled eggs on toast.

"Cugino Joey, come stai? È da tanto che non ci vediamo. Cousin Joey, how are ye? It's been a long time."

It had been two years since the cousins last met—at a family reunion in Manhattan, at Caesar's diner. It was the perfect occasion for Joey to explain the operations on this side of the Atlantic and to strengthen the connections with his hitman cousin and the Corleone clan. The two cousins had a lot in common: a taste for luxury, women, and violence. But the main bonding factor was the cruel streak that ran in their genes.

Giovanni was interested in the contract Joey explained in detail over the phone. It sounded both interesting and amusing—he wasn't used to carrying out hits outside his native Sicily and Italy.

Joey offered to provide two reliable 'soldiers' if needed. Giovanni refused.

He worked exclusively alone. He was a lone wolf. He didn't need assistance in stalking and eliminating prey.

Joey acquiesced and said he'd put Giovanni in contact with the Kelly gang in Dublin. They would bring him up to speed regarding Jack Hopkins's whereabouts and habits. From there, he'd be on his own.

They would also supply all the materials needed to complete the mission. Money wasn't mentioned—but Giovanni knew a nice wad of notes would be waiting after the hit.

Dates were discussed. Giovanni said his schedule wasn't swamped, but he had a small job to take care of the following week in Rome.

The Mafia had a broad spectrum of illegal activity in the capital: murder, extortion, corruption of public officials, gambling, infiltration of legitimate businesses, labour racketeering, loan sharking, tax fraud, and stock manipulation schemes.

He had to convince two recalcitrant public officials to grant building contracts to a company controlled by the Corleone clan. It was a multi-million-dollar business, and Giovanni stood to earn a 10% commission.

When you did the math, it was a large sum for just a few days' work. Construction companies were extremely useful for laundering the massive amounts of money generated from drugs and prostitution, so they had to stay busy.

Usually, a few photos of the official's loved ones were enough to persuade them.

Failing that, it meant broken fingers, broken arms—or maybe a car exploding outside their office or home.

At the end of the day, they always fell in line. As Giovanni said, it was a piece of cake—a no-brainer.

Joey explained that it wasn't too urgent. Better to let things cool down and catch them off guard. So, they agreed on a date in early September—five weeks from now. Arrangements would be made.

"If you quit once, it becomes a habit. Never quit!"

Michael Jordan

CHAPTER
Sixteen

Okinawa - 6 years previous

It was autumn in Okinawa, and Jack had just passed his first year on Okinawan soil. He had made astounding progress both in karate and in the Japanese language. He could now have basic conversations, and he could read the alphabet of hiragana and katakana. The kanji, or adopted Chinese characters, were another kettle of fish, and made the reading of the newspaper a very difficult task indeed.

Kanji is a system of symbols that represent words or ideas and can have different meanings and pronunciations depending on context. A kanji can be a word all by itself, like 木 (which means "tree"), or it can be part of another word, like 木造 (which means "wooden" or "made of wood"). But Jack was determined to overcome this handicap, and Akiko was always patient and supportive.

She explained to Jack that it would take time — most Japanese themselves required years to master it. The total number of kanji exceeds 50,000. Virtually every adult in Japan can recognise over 2,000 kanji. A university-educated person will recognise around

3,000, and an exceptionally well-educated, well-read person with technical expertise might know up to 5,000.

Jack's karate training had come on in leaps and bounds — so much so that Sensei Saito wanted him to attempt his 1st dan black belt in the spring. His friend Toshiro had been more than helpful, and they worked out together two to three times during the week, performing kata and kumite, or sparring discreetly on the beach. His body was lean and had become hard as steel.

Akiko and Jack had now become a real couple. She slept over most nights, much to Jack's delight, but liked to be home now and again to prepare breakfast and the famous bento, or lunch box, for her chichi — father. Being a fisherman, her father was at the ocean's beck and call. The tide was the keeper of time for the fisherman.

It was a Saturday evening. Jack had just showered and was brushing his hair in front of the mirror in his tiny bathroom. He wanted to look his best, as it was Akiko's 22nd birthday, and the lovebirds had decided to celebrate in one of the most famous restaurants in Naha. Jack's articles on Okinawa and its people had become very popular, and he now received a generous bank transfer once a month from Independent Newspapers.

He intended to wine and dine his sweetheart in style. Jack had reserved a table for two at the famous Nuchigafu Restaurant, located in an old teahouse near Tsuboya Pottery Street — one of the best places in the city to buy Okinawan ceramics. The restaurant was renowned for its authentic Ryukyu cuisine, made with local, organic ingredients. It was also a great place to sample awamori, a traditional Okinawan liquor distilled from rice.

He stepped out onto his terrace and breathed in the briny air. He listened briefly to the waves gently breaking on the sandy beach and then headed off on the short walk to Akiko's house. It was mid-November, and temperatures had dropped drastically — unusual for this sub-tropical climate, where it rarely fell below 14°C. It was only 5:45 p.m., and the blazing orange sun bathed the sky in fire, heralding the end of another day and leaving a crimson glow in its wake. Jack pulled up the collar of his jacket to fight off the evening chill. In the distance, he could see the lanterns on

Akiko's terrace dancing gently in the breeze. Fifteen minutes later, he was knocking on her door.

To say that Jack was gobsmacked when Akiko opened the door would be putting it mildly. She couldn't stop giggling when she saw the look on his face. She was wearing a traditional Okinawan kimono of light blue, with pink and white floral patterns. The kimono was tied at her waist by a white silk obi, a broad sash. The slimness of her waist was thus accentuated.

Her long black hair was knotted and adorned with tsubaki — beautiful camellia flowers — and a tsuge gushi, a traditional and very old box comb. She carried the fragrance of flowers and vanilla. The kimono and the box comb had belonged to her mother, and she only wore them on very special occasions. Never before had Jack beheld such a refined or beautiful sight. He was walking on air. Akiko's father, Ichiro, was more than amused by the spectacle and couldn't stop laughing.

Akiko kissed him gently on the lips. "We have to call a taxi, Jack-san. Very difficult to walk," she said, smiling.

"Anata wa totemo utsukushī desu, anata wa watashi ni watashi no ai o ōini kōei ni omoimasu" — "You are very beautiful; you do me great honour, my love," Jack spoke the sentence in nearly perfect Japanese, much to the utter delight of Akiko and her father, who insisted they take a drink to toast Akiko's birthday.

He came back from the drinks closet with a bottle of 30-year-old Macallan single malt whisky. This was the Holy Grail of whisky. Macallan is the only Scotch distillery that has its own Master of Wood. It was a rare and rarefied whisky, matured in carefully selected European and American oak casks which had previously held sherry or bourbon.

The maturing process created a rich, intense liquid, with a deep colour achieved wholly naturally through the interaction between spirit and wood. This, too, was only brought out on special occasions. Akiko didn't like whisky, saying that it was too strong and that it was a man's affair. She opted for a dry martini with ice.

Ichiro, ceremoniously and with great care, poured the pale gold nectar into the Macallan whisky glasses. The man was meticulous, and Jack couldn't help noticing the look of pride on his face as the liquid flowed carefully into the drinking vessels. Jack could see tears welling in his eyes — tears of happiness. He felt honoured to share this special nectar with the man who loved his daughter.

They all raised their glasses. "Kanpai! Cheers!" they shouted in typical Japanese fashion, toasting Akiko's 22nd birthday.

Jack wasn't a whisky man, but as he raised his glass, a rich and pleasant aroma of sherry, accompanied by notes of wood smoke, nutmeg, orange, and clove, invaded his nostrils. Ichiro observed him carefully, waiting for a reaction.

"Close your eyes, Jack-san — smell and taste."

Jack obeyed. His taste buds were hit with an intense and indulgent mix of vanilla, macadamia nuts, cherry, and sandalwood. This kind of quality could certainly help in his conversion to the "hard stuff" on the odd occasion, he mused.

"So, Jack-san — good, no?" said Ichiro, impatient and anxious for Jack's opinion.

Jack placed his glass on the table and smiled at Ichiro.

"Hontoni sugoi — absolutely amazing," said Jack.

Ichiro clapped his hands together with satisfaction and glee. It would have been a great loss of face and a huge disappointment to him had the opposite been true. Hospitality and the guest's satisfaction were very important to the Japanese.

The taxi had been ordered for 7:30 p.m., and the restaurant was booked for 7:45 p.m. It was only a short eight-mile journey. A knock on the door at 7:32 p.m. interrupted their festivities. Akiko opened the door for a taxi driver with his cap in his hand, looking very apologetic.

"Sumimasen, osokunarimashita — I'm sorry for being late," he said, bowing ceremoniously.

Punctuality was a very serious matter in Japanese society. Some, however, might say that it was the virtue of the bored. It was something that Jack had come to appreciate, especially where public transport was concerned. It was in stark contrast to his native Ireland and C.I.E. (the national transport company), which was infamous for its atrocious timekeeping. Being thirty minutes late — or more — was par for the course and something the Irish people had come to accept. In Japan, on the other hand, if a train was one minute late, apologetic announcements were made over the loudspeaker.

The taxi was an old black Toyota Crown Super Saloon in impeccable condition. It was very spacious and spotlessly clean — just like the driver himself. The car was luxuriously appointed, fit for a diplomat, Jack thought to himself. And like all cars in Japan, it was right-hand drive, just like in Ireland and several other countries around the world. The seating was plush, and the legroom was more than ample. Jack was more than happy and pleasantly surprised. It was a fitting car for Akiko's exquisite attire.

Akiko gave the taxi driver the address, and they whisked off in comfort and luxury to their destination. Japanese drivers were discreet and courteous. They offered a greeting when their fare entered, and aside from confirming the route, they would not engage in small talk. The drivers could indulge in conversation, but only if spoken to first — and they were also allowed to communicate in emergency situations.

Their driver was a stocky, cheerful, and good-natured man in his mid-50s, with closely cropped, salt-and-pepper hair and a round, affable face. He went by the name Akiro and was more than happy to talk about his job and family. He had been married for thirty years and had three children—two girls and a boy. He had started off as a mechanic, but due to a severe back injury sustained during intensive training for a national judo competition, his doctor advised him to change to a non-manual profession. So he saved diligently and, with a small bank loan, was able to buy his taxi plate for his 42nd birthday.

He liked driving a taxi but missed the hands-on work of mechanics. Still, he continued to service his own car and carry out any necessary repairs. He told Akiko and Jack that they made a beautiful couple and was sure their children would be equally beautiful. He laughed heartily at his own remark. Akiko blushed and rested her head on Jack's shoulder.

Akiro had endless questions for Jack and was amazed by his long journey from Ireland, as well as the fact that he was training with the famous Sensei Saito. Akiro himself had achieved a 3rd-degree black belt in judo before being forced to retire. Now, he enjoyed long walks and fishing whenever he had the time. With little traffic on the road, fifteen minutes later, they pulled up in front of the restaurant.

Jack asked Akiro how much the fare was. He still wasn't used to the amount of yen needed even for a small purchase. Jack smiled to himself when Akiro told him the fare came to 1,600 yen—about fifteen dollars. Jack dug into his pocket and handed Akiro a 2,000-yen note, telling him to keep the change, roughly four dollars. Akiro thanked him sincerely but insisted on giving back the change.

Tipping is not customary in Japan. In fact, it can be considered rude or insulting in many situations. Most Japanese restaurants require customers to pay for their meals at the front register rather than leave money with the waiter or waitress. Tipping also isn't required for cab or bus rides and many hotel services. This was certainly in contrast to the United States—especially New York City, where everybody seems to have their hand out for the famous "tip."

Because of this, good service is expected, and there's no need to "reward" it with extra money. Leaving a tip can even be considered disrespectful, as it implies that the person being tipped doesn't earn a livable wage and needs extra money, the complete opposite of Western society.

But Jack insisted, refusing to take his change, saying it was the tradition in Ireland and that he would be highly offended if Akiro didn't accept his small token of gratitude. Akiro was apologetic, saying he had never intended to offend Jack-san, and so he accepted the tip with great humility. Then he sprang from the car with the agility of a young man to open the door for Akiko, who was sitting on the driver's side.

He bowed respectfully, saying: "Dōzo omeshiagarikudasai, enjoy your meal."

Akiko and Jack bowed in return and thanked him. Akiko asked if he could return to collect them around 22:30. A big smile spread across his face. He said it would be a real pleasure.

"Ja matane, see you later," he said as he got back into his splendid Toyota Crown.

There was a lot of shouting, howling, and boorish behaviour coming from across the street. Jack turned his head, and his eyes locked with those of Joey Falconetti and his uncouth buddies. The servicemen were on weekend leave and already well tanked up on alcohol. They were heading into a popular karaoke bar frequented by the American military.

"Well, look who it is," roared Falconetti. "If it isn't the karate kid himself with his geisha whore. I hope she's worth the money, asshole."

Falconetti mimed a handgun with his right fist in Jack's direction before turning his back to join his boisterous cohorts.

Akiko had understood the slanderous remarks and was visibly taken aback.

"How do you know this horrible man, Jack-san? Why is he so bitter and full of hate?"

Jack bent down and kissed Akiko on the forehead. "Don't worry, my love. I'll explain everything another time, but not tonight. I don't want him to spoil our evening, so let's just celebrate."

Jack had booked a table for two on the terrace. He hadn't expected the temperature to drop so drastically, but luckily, the restaurant had prepared for it. Several hibachi braziers were lit around the terrace to fight off the evening chill. Akiko clapped her hands in delight, saying it was so romantic.

They were greeted by a smiling young waitress and shown to their table. Heads turned to admire Akiko in her traditional dress—an unusual sight among the younger generation. They were handed menus along with a wine list and promptly served two glasses of Awamori, an alcoholic beverage unique to Okinawa, made from long-grain rice. It was served with a container of ice and a carafe of water. The drinks, on the house, were considered a welcome gesture.

The menu was in both Japanese and English, which Jack appreciated, as he still struggled with kanji characters. For starters, and upon Akiko's advice, they decided to share a large plate of sashimi—fresh raw fish thinly sliced and served with a mixture of sauces. The fish of the moment included tuna, salmon, sea bream, and mackerel.

For the main course, Jack had trouble deciding. He was becoming accustomed to Okinawan cuisine but was still a novice. After much thought, he opted for Pork Tamago. It was believed that Okinawan immigrants in Hawaii had created Pork Tamago and then reintroduced it to Okinawa, where it became a mainstay of the local cuisine.

Akiko chose Rafute, a traditional Okinawan dish in which chopped pork belly is slowly simmered with soy sauce or miso, brown sugar, and Awamori. The long cooking time rendered the pork tender and free of excess fat.

Jack glanced over the short wine list. Neither he nor Akiko was an expert when it came to wine. The list featured selections from France, Italy, California, and some Australian varieties. Jack decided to choose a French wine. Like most people, he had heard of Bordeaux and Burgundy. His finger moved down the short list of white wines until he came across one that rang a bell—Chablis.

He remembered a TV documentary about a famous wine critic named Robert Parker, a huge fan of Burgundy wines and especially Chablis, praising its purity of aroma and taste. The Chablis in question was a Grand Cru vintage and cost a small fortune. What the hell, thought Jack, let's break the piggy bank tonight.

When Akiko saw the price, she told Jack he was crazy to pay so much for a bottle of wine.

"Sure, we only live once," laughed Jack. "It's your birthday, so let's make the most of it. Nothing is too expensive for the girl I love."

Akiko blushed beneath her makeup and took his hand. Jack gazed into her midnight-black eyes, which seemed to reflect the light of the entire universe. He was sure he saw her divine soul and knew he was deeply, hopelessly in love with her. It is said that the eyes are the windows to the soul—Jack could now confirm it, and he could happily drown in those eyes for eternity.

The starter, main course, and wine all met and exceeded their expectations. The presentation alone was a work of art. They decided on something light for dessert, both following the Okinawan concept of hara hachi bun me—eating until 80% full. Many older Okinawans followed this tradition, but with the arrival of McDonald's and other fast-food chains, the younger generation was abandoning it. Many adolescents were now overweight.

So they ordered two generous portions each of the famous Blue Seal Ice Cream, a beloved Okinawan treat considered by many to be the best. There were more than thirty flavours to choose from, each with its own devoted following. The origin of the ice cream dates back to the end of World War II, when it was created as a morale booster for the American soldiers stationed on the island.

Jack had informed the person who took the reservation over the phone that it was Akiko's birthday. "Don't worry," the man had said, "we will prepare something special." The ice creams arrived with great ceremony, carried proudly by two smiling waitresses. In each portion of Akiko's ice cream, there was a bright yellow and red number two candle, along with tall, sparkling fountain fireworks. Naturally, heads turned and necks craned to witness the spectacle.

"O-tanjoubi omedetou gozaimasu! Happy Birthday!" cried the two waitresses in unison. The look of surprise on Akiko's face was worth a photograph in itself. She clapped her hands together in delight. The entire restaurant joined in applause and soon began singing Happy Birthday. Akiko, who did not enjoy being the centre of attention, was relieved when the moment passed and they could enjoy their dessert without an audience. They lingered over the creamy sweetness before finishing with two steaming coffees—compliments of the house.

It was approaching 22:30 when they rose from the table and went to the counter to pay. Jack smiled to himself as he dug into his pockets, producing wads of crisp hundred-yen notes. The meal and wine came to a little over two thousand yen. He insisted on leaving a tip of one hundred yen. The staff bowed deeply, smiling warmly at the gesture.

Just as they stepped away from the terrace, Akiro pulled up in his gleaming taxi—right on time. Jack was still impressed by the punctuality of the Japanese people. "They should export this to Ireland," he thought with a chuckle.

Akiro opened the rear door for the happy couple and drove slowly, asking questions about their meal. He admitted he had never eaten there—it was expensive—but he intended to save enough to take his wife for her next birthday. He dropped them off at Jack's beach cabin. Jack slipped a hundred-yen note into his hand and thanked him for the excellent service. Akiro could not stop bowing and expressing his gratitude for both the tip and their company.

"Sayonara," he called through the open window before whisking away under a star-studded sky.

The night was still young but cool. Jack put the kettle on to boil while Akiko prepared two herbal teas. They sat together on the porch bench; a plaid blanket draped over their knees to keep out the chill. The stars glittered and gleamed like scattered gemstones. Holding hands, they watched the shimmering canopy above. Jack could not remember ever seeing so many. He wondered how many there could possibly be. In that moment, he felt small and insignificant within such vastness, yet understood that every living being was part of the great equation that governed the universe—the golden ratio.

As they continued in silence, Jack felt certain that love itself was part of that equation. The gentle lapping of the tide lulled them into a meditative, alpha-like state of relaxation—true mindfulness.

Jack would later become more familiar with this mental state during training, when he would be introduced to getsumei no michi, the moonlit path. He would learn to enter and exit this mindset at will, surrendering his conscious thoughts to instinct and allowing his mind to find the best and safest course. He would notice details he had previously overlooked. It would become a true refuge, even saving his life in seemingly impossible situations.

The deep quiet, broken only by the soft backwash of the waves, gradually coaxed them into drowsiness. They folded their plaids and returned to the cosy cabin, taking a hot shower together. One by one, their hands and fingers found more intimate places. Under Akiko's skilled touch, Jack grew aroused quickly, and they made love tenderly under the warm cascade of water. They climaxed together, their entwined bodies trembling with release.

Jack turned off the shower and they stepped onto the mat, slowly towel each other dry. They were both wrapped in the rare and lingering bliss of sexual afterglow—an enhanced satisfaction neither had known before.

They went to bed drained, yet completely content. Akiko kissed Jack on the brow. "Oyasumi watashi no ai no amai yume—good night, my love, sweet dreams. And tomorrow, I have a surprise for you."

Jack fell asleep like a child, his head buzzing with questions about what Akiko had planned.

They awoke early the next morning, the afterglow still warm in their hearts. Jack glanced at the small petrol-blue mechanical clock on his bedside locker: 7:00 a.m.

He climbed out of bed and stretched. "Let's have breakfast," he said. "I'm famished."

Akiko sat up, rubbing her eyes. "No, Jack, love. This morning, we had breakfast with Father. He is waiting for us."

"Oh, is that the surprise?" Jack asked.

"Wait and see, my love—wait and see," she laughed.

They showered, freshened up, drank a glass of fruit juice, and stepped out onto the sun-drenched terrace. The air was filled with the distinctive scent of the nearby Ryukyu pine trees. It was 7:45 a.m., and the sun was rising over the horizon, replacing the moon for day duty. Hand in hand, they walked barefoot along the shore.

There was no wind, and the waves broke softly on the white sand—a reminder of man's fleeting existence compared to the eternity of nature.

They splashed each other playfully in the water, laughing like children. The water was cool at that hour. In the distance, Jack spotted a figure outside Akiko's house. The short, brisk movements reminded him of a kata, and now he could see the glint of a blade. Jack looked at Akiko, who smiled knowingly.

As they approached, Jack recognised the figure—it was Ichiro, Akiko's father. He wore a beautiful traditional kimono and hakama—pleated trousers with seven folds, five at the front and two at the back, stiffened by a rigid support. Ichiro looked at Akiko inquisitively, his hands open.

"This is Iaido, Jack—the art of drawing the sword and cutting."

Iaido placed great emphasis on being aware and ready to respond instantly to sudden attacks.

Akiko explained that her father valued not only the martial discipline of the art but also its philosophy—how the rigour of a warrior's training could be applied to everyday life. She revealed that Ichiro was a descendant of the Takeda clan, a famous samurai family, and was also an expert in kenjutsu—live-blade swordsmanship—and jiu-jitsu combat techniques.

Jack noticed the sweat glistening on Ichiro's brow, impressed by the man's concentration, precision, and effortless grace. This, Jack realised, was his introduction to getsumei no michi—letting go of the mind.

For the next thirty minutes, Jack watched in awe as Ichiro moved fluidly through the ritual: drawing the sword from its scabbard, striking, wiping the blade clean, and returning it smoothly to the saya. To Jack's untrained eye, the execution was flawless.

"Is this the surprise?" Jack asked eagerly.

Akiko smiled. "Yes, Jack-san. I hope you like it."

Jack could barely contain himself. "Sugoi! Terrific! Will your father teach me?" he pleaded.

"Yes, of course," Akiko replied. "Otherwise, he would not have let you watch."

Indeed, Ichiro had wanted to be sure of Jack's devotion to his daughter before sharing such treasured family traditions.

Jack would start with a bokken—a wooden sword—before progressing to the razor-sharp katana. Ichiro would also introduce him to tameshigiri, the ancestral art of cutting bamboo mats to simulate human limbs. The lessons would be held every Sunday from 7:00 to 9:00 a.m., and Jack would not miss a single one during his stay.

Ichiro finished his session, then smiled and bowed ceremoniously to both Jack and Akiko.

He clapped his hands. "Now—asa gohan. Breakfast," he said. "I'm hungry. Iaido practice is good for the appetite."

After a shower, Ichiro joined them in the dining area, where a low kotatsu table, covered with a futon, had been prepared. A dish warmer sat in the middle, keeping certain plates hot. There was steamed rice, miso soup, grilled fish, and various side dishes, along with coffee, tea, and fresh water. Everything smelled wonderful.

They laughed and talked freely. Ichiro wanted to hear all about the restaurant—the food, the atmosphere, and the people. He confessed he had not dined out since his wife's passing, but would be honoured to invite them both to a restaurant of their choice someday.

He praised Jack's progress in Japanese and in karate, thanked him for making Akiko happy, and said his only wish was for their continued joy. Laughing, he added that they were both ablaze with youth and vigour—"Love is a good thing," he said warmly.

After breakfast, Ichiro set the date for Jack's first sword lesson— the following Sunday at 7:00 a.m. sharp.

Not too far away, on the air force base of Kadena—the largest U.S. base among the thirty-two bases on the island and in the Pacific Ocean—Joey Falconetti was enjoying a black coffee and a cigarette. He was animatedly relating his latest sexual exploits to a rapt audience. His most recent conquest went by the name of Irene, a nurse in her late twenties based at the neighbouring military base Camp Foster. She was a tall, attractive brunette who had everything a man could want exactly where it counted, scoffed Falconetti. His audience wanted explicit details.

Falconetti took a drag from his cigarette and sent the smoke spiralling towards the harsh, white fluorescent-lit ceiling. "Listen up, guys—yez want some juicy details? What a rack she's got, and that ass—worth dying for." There were whistles, cheers, and metal coffee cups banging on the table. Falconetti continued his graphic paean to his mouth-watering audience. "What can I say, fellas? Her blowjob alone is enough to justify a man's life. Oh yeah—and her pussy—she can contract it at will: sometimes gently, with slow, irresistible pressure, sometimes with small, sharp, mischievous shakes. And that ass—she wiggled it with infinite grace before offering it to me."

Excitement was at its peak in the canteen, and one could practically smell the testosterone.

"We need some of that too, Falconetti!" they shouted.

Falconetti wore a broad, lecherous grin. "Hands off, boys—she's totally off limits to you assholes. She's now exclusively Falconetti property, capiscimi?"

Falconetti might have been in the military, but he didn't do much actual military work. He had been sent over by the Family to streamline operations and ensure that no one was dipping their fingers in the pie. Some suits and top brass had signed off on it. They were on the payroll, and it cost the Family a bagful of dollars every month, but in the end, it was worth it. Everything flowed smoothly, and there was rarely any hassle from curious customs officials.

Joey wore the uniform only to make it look official, and he didn't take orders from any superior officers. He was certainly an asshole—but a clever one. He possessed excellent organisational and logistical skills. He was a natural.

Their man on the inside, who usually looked after this end of the business, had made a few serious mistakes and become a bit too greedy for the Family's liking. So Joey had been sent over to give him a message and a final warning—which he received loud and clear. The man's name was Bob, the logistics officer for all the bases on the island. In total, there were twenty-eight military facilities in Okinawa, covering twenty-five percent of the island.

Bob was in his late forties, a stringy individual with greying, thinning hair. He was single and had been working for the Family for ten years before becoming distracted and greedy. The day Joey arrived on base, he summoned Bob to his quarters and introduced himself by breaking one of his hands with a baseball bat. Bob got the message immediately and, from that day, kept his head down. His hand took two months to heal, making even simple daily tasks difficult. Of course, Joey had broken his right—his writing—hand.

Joey was very pleased with how the drug business had increased in volume. Demand had grown so much that he had been forced to find new suppliers for heroin, opium, and the highly sought-after crystal meth. He had also discovered a new, lucrative sideline—human trafficking. Women and young children—ten-year-old boys and girls—from poverty-stricken rural areas of Cambodia, Laos, Thailand, Vietnam, and Myanmar. These countries were havens for pedophiles from the Western world and beyond.

Rich Saudis, Americans, and some Europeans were prepared to pay top dollar to satisfy their sick perversions and insatiable appetites for children. Once the children reached puberty—on average twelve years old—they were discarded like used tissues. The women, apart from being abused as sex slaves, were employed at pitifully low wages as domestics, kept as prisoners, and always escorted on their rare outings.

They were literally terrorised—living in a foreign country, not understanding the language—and of course they had no passports. Most people will do anything to escape poverty. They were considered refugees by the authorities, which made transporting them from their home countries to their new "owners" in the West or the Middle East far too easy. Questions were rarely asked—and if they were, a few wads of American dollars settled them. After all, money makes the world go round.

Falconetti didn't use drugs, and he detested the pedophiles—but the money was simply too good to ignore. With so many dollars to be made, virtue flew out the window. Falconetti never had regrets and never felt guilty. He had no problem with his conscience. Let's face it—if he didn't do it, someone else would. There was no time for do-gooders in his business.

He finished his coffee and clapped his hands. "Okay, guys, the show's over. I've got real work to do." He rose from his chair, his cigarette burning down to the butt, and left the canteen, waving to the gallery. His office was in the next building—logistics and operations—so he had to exit the main door and cross twenty yards of tarmacked yard. He had a busy morning ahead—phone calls, pickups, drop-offs. The telex machine would keep him company for most of it.

He had been toying with a new idea—arms trafficking. Working in logistics and managing inventories had its advantages. He was confident he could write off M1911 and Beretta handguns, along with the reliable but ageing Heckler & Koch MP5 submachine guns. Some were already becoming obsolete, and it would be easy to declare them non-functional. New weapons could also "go missing" in transit from the States, with the right information given to the right people.

Many South Asian guerrilla factions and drug lords would gladly pay top dollar for quality weapons. He had already received reliable feedback from a Burmese opium drug lord who was particularly interested in machine guns and landmines. A wry smile crept across his face as he flicked his cigarette butt onto the yard and headed to his office.

It was January, and temperatures along with those of the month of February were at their lowest on the island. The thermometer on Jack's little porch showed a cool 13°C. It was seven o'clock in the morning, and the temperature would rise to a pleasant 18°C later in the afternoon. It very seldom got any cooler than 14°C, and the island didn't know what frost was. Jack was used to much colder and harder weather. He was sitting comfortably in a tracksuit, sipping a piping hot coffee and watching the sunrise in the distance over the horizon. The sunlight filled the sky with a blaze of pinks, oranges and reds.

The sun was at its lowest altitude, and it cast long shadows across the ocean and the beach. Since his arrival on the island, Jack has tried never to miss a sunrise or a sunset. He had shared quite a few with Akiko. For Jack, it had become a time for self-communion and soul-searching. For him, it was practically a spiritual experience. Sunrises and sunsets, two of Mother Nature's most beautiful gifts, thought Jack, what more does a man need?

He watched wispy nebulous shapes drift silently by and dissolve slowly in the atmosphere and finally disappear, leaving no trace of their existence, completely and totally ephemeral. Screeching gulls momentarily startled Jack and woke him from his daydream. His black belt test had been set for the 2nd of April on his 24th birthday. Was it a coincidence or karma? Jack liked to believe the latter.

He was a typical Aries fire sign, energetic, passionate, motivated and confident. He had a cheerful disposition and relentless determination, which he would need on the long martial arts journey that he had set for himself. Aries were also known to be daredevils.

Akiko had important exams pending in the Spring, and she had been studying hard most evenings. She really needed these exams in order to go any further in her curriculum. So they had been seen a bit less of each other recently, three to four times a week instead of practically every day. Jack understood her situation completely and knew only too well that it was difficult to work properly with too many distractions in the way. However, that said, she still slept over every Friday and Saturday night, much to Jack's delight.

It was also all work for Jack. He still maintained his daily morning gruelling routine on the makiwara with all the additional callisthenics, katas and of course the jogging on the beach and once a week to Naha and back. He had recently purchased a second-hand bike from one of Akiko's friends who had gone back to mainland Japan after his exams. It was a light green and blue Shimano 105 road bike, and it was equipped with five gears. Ideal for the island, as most of it was flat, and especially for Jack's frequent trips to downtown Naha and to the dojo.

He who fears he will suffer, already suffers because he fears.

Michel De Montaigne

CHAPTER
Seventeen

Back to Dublin, Autumn 1990

Joey Falconetti's cousin, Giovanni, arrived in Dublin on a grey, damp Saturday morning at the beginning of October. The small "jobs" in Rome had turned into marathons, entangled with numerous complications and repercussions. As a result, his expected September arrival had been pushed back. He landed on an Air Italia flight direct from Rome. Being an early-morning, midweek flight, the plane was half empty—a convenience Giovanni welcomed, as he was sitting alone with plenty of legroom near the emergency exit at the back of the aircraft.

The flight had been pleasant, and Giovanni had taken an instant shine to one of the air hostesses—a tall, shapely, and alluring brunette in her mid-twenties. Her name was Claudia. She had even given him the name of the hotel where she would be staying for the night—the Skylon Hotel, close to the city centre. Giovanni told her he would be in touch.

"By the way, what's your family name, baby?" he asked.

"Ferrari," she laughed.

"Of course—how stupid of me. What else could it be?" he replied, smiling.

He retrieved his Gucci all-leather carry-on bag from the overhead locker above his seat at the rear of the plane and winked at Claudia as he hauled it out. Giovanni always booked seats at the rear of a plane—he believed you had a better chance of surviving a crash. At least, that's what someone had once told him. As usual, he was travelling light; this was planned as a one-week job at most.

He descended from the rear of the plane via the stairs and stepped onto the wet tarmac. A light sea mist covered the airport, muting the usual sounds of activity. Giovanni was a sunshine person, and this bleak, damp weather wasn't doing much for his first impressions. He decided he needed a cappuccino to lift his spirits.

Thanks to the EEC (European Economic Community), going through immigration control was a breeze. He even smiled at the controller as he was handed back his passport. An Italian hitman had just officially set foot on Irish soil.

Robbie Maher, from the Kelly drug cartel, was waiting patiently in the airport hall for Giovanni's arrival. He was looking forward to meeting the famous Sicilian hitman in the flesh; his reputation had long preceded him. To Robbie, Giovanni was a kind of hero.

He was holding an airport placard at chest level in his right hand. The name "Mr. Falconetti" was written in bold capital letters on a gold background. Robbie was certain he would recognise his guest immediately as soon as he came through the sliding doors. He had been given vivid descriptions by his boss and had also seen an old black-and-white photograph.

The sliding doors opened and people spilt into the hall, waving to family, friends, or colleagues—some reuniting after long separations, others meeting for the first time. Voices in various languages mixed with hugs and kisses.

The doors shut momentarily, then slid open again as Giovanni strode through. Robbie recognised him instantly and stepped forward, brandishing the sign. The Italian stood out from the crowd—tall, dark, tanned, and lean. He wore a sleek black leather

Armani jacket, blue denim Levi's jeans, and Dolce & Gabbana suede zip-up boots. "The man's got class," Robbie whispered to himself.

Giovanni walked straight over to Robbie. "I'm Giovanni," he said.

Robbie shifted the placard to his left hand and extended his right. "I'm very pleased to make your acquaintance, Mr. Falconetti." He hoped the Italian spoke some English—his own Italian was limited to ordering a "one and one" or fish and chips at the local takeaway. Instead of a handshake, Giovanni placed his leather bag in Robbie's hand. Robbie hesitated, but the green-lizard eyes bored into him, sending a chill down his spine.

"I need a cappuccino," Giovanni said flatly.

"Of course, Mr. Falconetti—no problem. I could do with a coffee myself. How was your flight? Sorry about the weather—welcome to Ireland."

Falconetti was too busy taking in his new surroundings, and besides, he hadn't understood half of what Robbie had said due to the unfamiliar Dublin accent. The cappuccino was not up to Giovanni's standards. He drank it without enthusiasm; it wouldn't have made the grade in Sicily. Few words were exchanged over the cups.

"What's the name of my hotel?" Giovanni asked in his thick Italian accent.

"Oh, it's the Shelbourne, Mr. Falconetti—the best Dublin has to offer, really top-notch."

They finished their cappuccinos, exited the bar, and stepped through the sliding doors into the damp autumn air. People bustled about—hailing taxis, queuing for buses to the city centre. Robbie wheeled Giovanni's cabin bag ahead of him and tried to make small talk, but his attempts fell on deaf ears. Giovanni was already thinking about Claudia and the pleasures awaiting him later.

Robbie had been given the boss's black Mercedes S-Class to chauffeur their Italian guest—nothing but the best. It was the first of the new S-Class models on the Irish market. Regular customers were always first in line. He pressed the key fob; the four doors and boot unlocked with a subtle clunk. He placed the cabin bag into the enormous boot and shut it with another muted thud—a testament to German craftsmanship and engineering.

The car's interior was spacious and luxurious—leather seats, polished trimmings—everything one would expect from a Mercedes-Benz S-Class. Robbie started the six-litre V12, which fired up with a deep growl as he pressed gently on the accelerator. Shifting into reverse, the car glided silently from the parking space. The power steering was feather-light and precise; a single finger could manage the tightest manoeuvres—a hallmark of Mercedes design.

He kept his foot on the brake, slid a CD into the slot, then shifted to drive. U2's "Sunday Bloody Sunday" filled the car—a tribute to the tragic events of January 30th, 1972, when British soldiers shot unarmed civil rights protesters in Derry, killing fourteen, including seven teenagers.

Much to Robbie's surprise, Giovanni suddenly lit up with enthusiasm.

"This is my favourite group!" he exclaimed.

At last, a bond had been formed, Robbie thought with relief.

Giovanni began complaining about the weather and the chill, explaining in his best English that in his Sicilian hometown, the sun shone nearly all year.

"Well, welcome to Ireland, my man," Robbie laughed. ' That's why we have the turf fires and great whisky to keep us warm. The small talk lasted until they arrived at their destination, the elegant Shelbourne Hotel. The morning traffic was light, and the ride had taken only twenty-five minutes. Robbie was happy. He had gotten through to the Italian hitman. There was a connection now; the current had passed between them. He parked the car in the designated spot right at the main entrance to the hotel. He jumped sprightly from the driver's seat, opened the boot, and took the Italian's luggage.

The Italian stepped out onto the kerb side and looked the hotel over. He nodded his head with approval and gave a thumbs-up sign to Robbie.

"Yeah, it's the best in town," laughed Robbie.

Giovanni tapped him on the back. "Grazie mille. I invite my Irish friend for a drink."

"It's a bit early in the morning for me," said Robbie, grinning. "But okay, I'll gladly accept your generous invitation."

He handed over the keys of the Mercedes to the doorman and told him he was going for a quick drink.

Giovanni checked in at the reception desk, where a smiling young woman named Nicola, according to the badge pinned to her lapel, was only too happy to hand over the room key to the charming Italian. She fell into the category of women that the Italian appreciated most—young, shapely, and of average height. He was already thinking ahead to a night of passion with the young woman. But first in line was Claudia, the air stewardess.

A janitor appeared from nowhere and took his baggage to the suite on the first floor. The Italian was equally impressed with the hotel's interior as he had been with its exterior. He followed the janitor up the plush staircase to his suite.

He was more than satisfied with the decoration and the quality of the furniture—it met his standards. He handed the janitor a crisp new fiver. The man bowed humbly, thanked him, slid the note into his trouser pocket, and departed. Giovanni decided he would check out his Signature Suite in greater detail later. For now, he needed a drink. He closed the suite door and skipped lightly down the plush staircase. Robbie was waiting for him in the lobby.

"I hope you're satisfied with the suite, Mr. Falconetti."

"Yeah, seems okay to me," he smiled. "Let's get a drink."

The two men headed to the bar. It was classy. There were people drinking coffee or tea, eating pastries, and chatting. Some were reading the morning newspaper and catching up on the latest news. An overall relaxed ambience prevailed.

Heads turned briefly as the two men entered the plush surroundings. Female glances lingered on the striking Italian while their partners weren't looking. Giovanni was always a magnet for the female eye. He was tall, tanned, with jet-black hair and an athletic build. He had that bad-boy look that many women were drawn to but wouldn't admit, preferring to suppress their natural instincts and fantasies. He was both seductive and intimidating. Robbie looked ordinary by comparison, though he possessed a certain Irish charm of his own.

They took two stools at the bar, which displayed an impressive array of alcohols. The barman, in his mid-forties, was smartly dressed in a white shirt, black tie, and matching trousers. There wasn't a hair out of place—he was impeccable.

"Good morning, gentlemen. How can I be of service?" he said with a polite smile.

"Two glasses of your best whiskey," gestured Giovanni in typical Italian style.

The dandy barman returned with two glasses of 27-year-old Redbreast whiskey. He gave a precise description of the special nectar, explaining that it was a single-pot whiskey aged in port barrels from Portugal's famous Douro Valley. He described the colour as a warm, ripe wheat hue. The nose was nutty, rich, and oily, with notes of dried peels, ginger, cut fruits, and melon. The palate was spicy with great body—nuts and citrus, hints of marzipan, dried fruits, and a hint of Sherry. "You turn it over in your mouth forever," he added. The finish, he said, was long and creamy, with custard and spice.

"Enjoy," he concluded simply.

The two men were impressed and eager to taste the golden beverage. They raised their glasses and toasted each other. One said "Salute," and the other replied "Sláinte."

The whiskey was everything the barman had promised. They nodded in unison, licked their lips, and smiled. No words were exchanged—none were needed.

When the glasses were emptied, Robbie headed to the exit to pick up his Mercedes, and Giovanni made for the stairs to his suite. Just before Robbie went through the revolving wood-and-glass doors, Giovanni called him, thumb cocked and forefinger pointed like an imaginary gun.

"Did you get my shooter as requested?"

Robbie stuck up a thumb. "No problem, Mr. Falconetti—everything is arranged. I'll call you tomorrow. Enjoy your stay."

Giovanni was more than impressed with his Signature Suite. The two windows gave magnificent views over St. Stephen's Green, one of the lungs of south Dublin. The décor and furnishings were elegant, with a separate living room and bedroom. The bathroom was opulent marble, with a soaking tub and a separate stall shower.

What interested Giovanni most was the king-size bed and the large wall mirror. As well as being narcissistic, he was also a bit of a voyeur and a total exhibitionist. He thought of Claudia, and lustful thoughts and images took over his mind. He smiled. Tonight, he would enjoy himself. He hoped Claudia would be up to his demands and tastes.

He carefully hung his shirts, two trousers, one suit, and two jackets in the walnut wardrobe and used the drawers for his socks and underwear. He then headed for the bathroom and arranged his toiletries on the marble top. He stripped naked, admiring his athletic silhouette and the scorpion tattoo on his manhood in the mirror. He stepped into the stall, equipped with a welcoming power shower. The hot water beaded his muscular torso for at least fifteen minutes before he finished with a cold shower. He felt invigorated.

He stepped out, towelled himself dry, and changed into fresh clothes—a white shirt and blue denim Armani jeans. He found his comb on the marble top, slicked back his lush black hair, and dabbed on Armani cologne. He certainly looked the part in the mirror, and he knew it.

He picked up the bedside phone, called reception, and asked to be put through to the Skylon Hotel. A young man answered.

"Skylon reception, how may I help you?"

"I want to speak to Claudia Ferrari. I don't know the room number."

"Oh, I think she's in the bar with some colleagues—I saw her enter about thirty minutes ago. Please hold; I'll page her for you."

A few minutes later, Giovanni heard a sultry voice.

"Ciao, sono Claudia. Who's speaking?"

"Ciao, baby. A taxi will pick you up in less than an hour. Don't drink too much, and dress sexy."

"Wow, speedy Giovanni," she laughed. "You're a quick mover, caro. Don't worry—I can drink, and I always dress sexy."

Happy with himself, he opened the door to his suite and skipped down the stairs to the hotel lobby. He headed to the reception, where the attractive brunette with the dancing eyes was still on duty behind her desk.

She greeted him with an open smile, clearly impressed by the virile aura he exuded. Giovanni smiled back, letting his eyes travel deliberately from head to toe. His gaze was inevitably drawn to her bosom, where the straining buttons of her immaculate white shirt seemed on the verge of surrender. She couldn't help blushing and tried to regain her composure.

« I hope you have settled in well, Mr. Falconetti. If you need anything at all, please don't hesitate to ask. I'm sure we can accommodate any of your requests, however demanding. » Little did she know.

He leaned forward, resting both elbows on the desk and lowering himself to her height, his gaze locking on hers with an air of quiet intimidation.

« I would like to order a taxi, *mia bella,* » he said with a slow smile.

She smiled back. « Oh, certainly, Mr. Falconetti. You're not dining here tonight? At what time do you wish to be collected? »

« Oh, the taxi is not for me, *mia bella*. I want it to pick up a beautiful girl named Claudia at the Skylon Airport Hotel. She'll be expecting it. »

Nicola suddenly felt a sharp pang of jealousy coil inside her. She felt momentarily betrayed and became slightly irritated, but forced herself to regain control.

She flashed him a tight-lipped smirk. « Of course, Mr. Falconetti, I shall ring a taxi immediately. Is the fare to be added to your bill? »

Giovanni straightened to his full six feet two inches. « *Si, si, mia bella*, on the bill. Oh, and please have a bottle of Dom Pérignon on ice sent to my room, along with a selection of your finest finger food. I am dining in the bedroom tonight. » He smiled with deliberate lasciviousness, turned on his heel, and took the stairs.

Jack had made a full physical recovery; his surgeon was both happy and amazed at the speed of his healing. But Jack remained psychologically marked by the events, still suffering the occasional nightmare. After all, he had killed three men bare-handed in a matter of minutes. He justified it to himself: it had been life or death — them or him. Jack had chosen life.

Still, he would wake occasionally in the early hours, drenched in sweat, calling out for Sophie or Akiko, sometimes speaking in Japanese. Sophie would soothe him gently, her voice a calming anchor until the nightmare loosened its grip.

He was back to giving lessons at the dojo five times a week. Jack had become a public figure after the tragic events — a hero, whether he wanted it or not. People flocked to the dojo for a glimpse of the "mafia slayer." Many wanted lessons, some offering large sums for private sessions. Jack turned most away; they had the wrong intentions. Beating someone was not the doctrine he followed or taught. Those who truly wished to better themselves were welcomed with open arms.

Letters and phone calls arrived daily. Requests varied: businessmen seeking bodyguards, agents wanting protection for visiting musicians, even the government inquiring about security for ministers and dignitaries. There were even marriage proposals. Jack kept one or two lucrative personal protection requests on hold.

Radio and TV invitations also piled up. He accepted just one —
an appearance on the hugely popular *Late Late Show*, hosted by
the much-liked Gary Byrne, a man Jack admired and trusted. He
hoped to use the platform to share his views on traditional karate
and the principles of *budo*, which guided his life.

What Jack hated most about his new fame was the men who
wanted to test themselves against him, like gunslingers in an old
Western. The worst were the drunken bar braggarts, egged on by
friends. Jack usually talked his way out of trouble; when that
failed, a quick application of finger pressure to a nerve ending or
joint sufficed.

Except for last week.

On his regular morning run, he sensed a presence behind him for
some time. He quickened his pace toward the old wooden bridge
on Bull Wall. The follower matched his speed. The bridge ahead
was empty. The man behind was closing in, breathing hard.

« Jack Hopkins, » a panting voice called.

Jack stopped abruptly, his mind running through possible
scenarios. The man, early twenties, ten yards away, approached
slowly. Average height, heavily muscled, biceps and chest
bulging beneath a tight T-shirt — a gym regular, maybe a boxer,
Jack thought. He noticed faint scar tissue on the man's face.

The stranger pointed a finger at him. « I want to find out for myself
just how good they say you are. »

Jack muttered to himself, *Here we go again.* He'd already gauged
him as right-handed, right-footed, and likely slow from being
muscle-bound. Now less than two yards away, the man swung a
powerful haymaker at Jack's head.

Jack slipped with the blow, dipped left into a wide knee stance,
and brought the blade of his forearm down like a baton into the
man's solar plexus. The strike knocked the wind out of him,
dropping him to one knee.

Jack shifted his stance and delivered a controlled hammer blow to
the kidney — not enough to injure internally, but plenty to end the

fight. The man gasped, eyes watering, saliva dripping from his open mouth.

Jack tapped his back lightly. « Have a nice day, my friend, » and continued his run to the end of Bull Wall, relieved he'd avoided serious harm. The man would be sore, but alive.

Claudia, the air hostess, walked into the Shelbourne Hotel lobby just as Nicola was finishing her shift. She didn't go unnoticed — especially by the men. At five feet seven, she stood above average height. Her shoulder-length dark hair gleamed, and her hazel eyes shone. A waist-length light blue leather jacket framed a white lace shirt with a plunging neckline, revealing ample breasts. She wore no bra; her taut nipples made that obvious. A black mini skirt showcased long, shapely, tanned legs, and high-heeled suede ankle boots accentuated her curves.

Nicola watched in both admiration and envy as Claudia passed. Claudia glanced at her, flashed a broad smile revealing perfect white teeth, and said, « Hello. » Without pausing, she headed up the stairs toward Giovanni's suite. Nicola would have given anything to be in her place.

Giovanni opened the door at her knock. Her beauty and erotic magnetism hit him like a wave. She'd looked stunning in uniform, but now — *wow*. His face lit with a broad smile. « *Per favore entra, bella,* » he said.

The suite glowed with candlelight. Champagne rested in an ice bucket, and a gleaming stainless steel trolley held an enticing spread of the finest finger foods the hotel could offer.

He pulled her close by the waist. Their lips met, tongues tangling, both moaning softly as they tasted each other. Her breasts pressed into his chest, nipples firm. His hands cupped her buttocks, pulling her to his groin. She placed her palms against his chest and eased back, a wicked smile curving her lips.

« I'm thirsty, *bello*. Serve me a glass of champagne. »

He obliged, popping the cork with that unmistakable sound that conjures celebration. Tilting the glasses, he poured slowly, letting the foam settle and the fine stream of bubbles — a mark of quality — rise.

When the champagne had settled, he filled both glasses. They toasted, « *Salute,* » and sipped. The champagne and finger food were exquisite. They fed each other slowly, erotically — the smoked salmon and sautéed duck particularly divine.

She asked him where he lived and what he did for a living. It was typical small talk. Giovanni told her that he lived in Sicily and worked in the wine business. He explained that he was on a business trip for a few days to visit wholesalers and wine importers. It wasn't all untrue. There was indeed a vineyard called Falconetti Vini in a small town named Linguaglossa in the province of Catania. However, the vineyard belonged to one of his cousins. The only interest Giovanni had in wine was drinking it.

She was from Florence and had an older sister and brother. Her father was an engineer, and her mother was a painter. She told him that she loved her job as an air hostess, as it gave her the opportunity to travel and see other cities and meet people.

Giovanni laughed sardonically: "A man in every city."

She drank from her glass and lifted a tapa of tapenade shrimp slowly and erotically to his mouth. "So, are you saying I'm a bad girl? I'm sure you like bad girls," she smiled mischievously.

Giovanni licked his lips and took the bottle of Dom Pérignon to pour himself a glass. It was empty. Already. He went and picked up the phone from the wooden designer bedside table and dialled reception. The phone was picked up on the other end almost instantaneously.

"This is Mr. Falconetti in the Signature Suite. I'd like another bottle of Dom Pérignon sent up immediately."

"Very good, sir. Consider it done," came the reply.

In just over five minutes, a sharp rap on the door announced the arrival of the second bottle. "Champagne for Mr. Falconetti."

He opened the door and allowed the young man, in his early twenties, to wheel in the trolley carrying the champagne in the ice bucket. He went to the closet, put his hand in his jacket pocket, and came back with a thick wad of notes. He peeled off a fiver and gave it to the young man, who smiled from ear to ear as he slipped the note into his jacket pocket.

He bowed as he walked backwards towards the door. "Thank you very much, Mr. Falconetti. Please don't hesitate if you need anything else."

Giovanni winked at the young man: "Oh, now I think I have everything I need. Wouldn't you agree?"

The young man blushed slightly and bid them both a good evening as he exited and closed the door. Giovanni filled the champagne glasses, and they tasted some more finger food. The champagne was having an effect on Claudia. She was feeling tipsy and, all of a sudden, very flushed.

She put down her glass and suggested, in a husky voice, that they should take a shower together. Giovanni was only too happy to accommodate her simple request. They stood up and kissed passionately. She sucked his lip and bit it slowly. Giovanni could feel the heat building in his groin and a tingling sensation in his scrotum.

They made their way to the spotless marble bathroom and started to undress. She had magnificent, full breasts crowned with large, dark, protruding nipples. His gaze was drawn towards her shapely legs and then to her vulva. She wasn't shaved, but just neatly trimmed. It was all very enticing.

She had been admiring his lean and athletic body as he peeled off his shirt. Then came the jeans and the Calvin Klein underwear. And then she saw it—the scorpion tattooed on his impressive manhood. He was truly blessed by nature, she thought to herself. Her gaze was fixed on the tattoo. She wanted to see it grow.

They stepped into the shower together. Giovanni adjusted it to the large nozzle above their heads. The warm liquid came crashing down as their bodies entwined. He slid a hand over her stomach and down to her mound. He cupped her gently and found her wetness. She moaned in pleasure.

She wanted to taste him. Dropping to her knees, she cupped his scrotum and, with the other hand, took his impressive shaft and brought it to her mouth. She sucked on it greedily. Possessively. The scorpion had grown and disappeared into her mouth.

Giovanni turned off the shower. He was climaxing too quickly, so he brought her to her feet and flicked her around. She placed her hands on the tiles and arched her buttocks outwards. He fingered her sodden vagina with one and then two fingers, in a gentle but continuous back-and-forth motion. She cried out with pleasure and begged him to take her. His stiff member entered her softness, and she sucked in a breath.

He pumped her slowly at first, allowing her to get accustomed to his size. The intensity increased, and he was now pounding her with long, regular strokes as he held her buttocks firmly in his large hands. She cried out with pleasure. Her orgasm was approaching. Giovanni felt the surge coming. He exploded inside her. Her body shuddered, and her vagina clamped momentarily around his member.

He slid out of her and put the shower back on—from lukewarm to practically cool. They were on fire and needed to cool down. They stepped out of the shower and towelled each other down. They then slipped into the soft designer bathrobes and headed back to the champagne and the finger food. They were hungry and thirsty. Nothing like a good bout of sex for whipping up an appetite.

When the champagne and the food were gone, they slipped out of their bathrobes and hopped into the king-size bed. The cool silk sheets caressed their bodies. It felt good. They embraced and started their second bout of intense lovemaking. As in most cases, round two was better than round one—no inhibitions whatsoever. After the second round, they were both wasted, and they slept deeply until early the following morning.

They were drawn from their deep slumber by the noise of the early morning traffic, the slightly opened window allowing the noise to invade the suite. It was 8 a.m. They were both ravenous. Giovanni picked up the receiver and phoned reception. He ordered freshly squeezed orange juice, two full Irish breakfasts, and a pot of coffee. Claudia had told him how amazing Irish breakfasts could be, so he wanted to check it out for himself. If the breakfast was anything like their finger food, well, they were in for a treat.

Breakfast arrived thirty minutes later. A smiling housemaid wheeled the stainless-steel trolley into the suite and left it at the foot of the bed. The smell of sausages, bacon, white and black pudding, along with the rest, wafted to their nostrils and stimulated their olfactory sensory neurons.

They both jumped out of bed. The desire to taste the goodies became overwhelming. They particularly appreciated the fresh orange juice, as their mouths were left tacky after the night's champagne. The coffee smelled good and tasted even better. And the breakfast was a culinary delight. Giovanni gave it ten out of ten.

They then shared the shower and engaged in a third round of raw sex. It was even better than round two. They had become very familiar with each other's bodies and sexual preferences. They dressed, and Giovanni accompanied Claudia down to the lobby and through the main door, where a throng of taxis was patiently waiting for their morning fare. She approached the first in the queue, a gleaming Mercedes Class S, and the driver was out in a flash to open the passenger door for the beautiful Italian.

She turned and waved at Giovanni. He waved back. « Ciao bella, I'll call you when I'm back in Italy ». He knew he wouldn't. For him, it had been a one-night fling. Better than he had imagined, but over. There were plenty more beauties that the scorpion wanted to sting. The fun and games were over; it was time to get down and to get serious. Giovanni was both meticulous and pedantic when preparing for a hit. He was a maniac for precision. That's what had kept him alive so far.

He walked back into the lobby to see a smiling, seductive Nicola holding the phone and calling to him. « Call for you Mr. Falconetti », she smiled alluringly. « Do you wish to take it here or shall I transfer it to your suite?

« Here is fine and so is the view », he smiled. He fixed her with his hypnotic green eyes. Another phone rang and she turned away to take the incoming call.

Giovanni turned his back to the reception desk and walked towards the main door « Falconetti here », he said into the cordless phone.

« Good mornin' I have that special order that you asked for », came the reply. «I can swing by your hotel or we can meet somewhere more discreet ».

Giovanni looked left and right. « Here is okay, just be sure that the packaging isn't conspicuous, hai capito? ».

« Yes sir, no problem. What time suits ? ».

« Come for midday, we can have lunch afterwards ». Giovanni pressed on the red button, walked back to the reception desk and handed the receiver back to Nicola. « Grazie bellezza », he said as he stroked the back of her hand. She didn't try pulling her hand away and her eyes sent messages that words could never communicate. Giovanni wasn't slow on the uptake. His smile was the response that she was waiting for.

Just before Robbie Maher walked into the lobby of the Shelbourne Hotel carrying a black guitar case. It was perfect for concealing a rifle and didn't draw any unwanted attention. Just a few glances here and there but nobody stared. Some people looked quizically half hoping to recognise a famous musician and disappointed when they couldn't. Nobody could imagine what the contents were.

He headed straight for the luxurious winding and plushly carpeted staircase and headed towards the Signature Suite on the second floor. He arrived at the door and knocked twice. « Special delivery for Mr. Falconetti », he said.

« Come in », said the voice on the other side of the door. Falconetti was drinking a coffee and admiring the view of St. Stephen's Green though the large window. He turned to greet Maher as he came into the room carrying the guitar case.

« Bravissimo », said Falconetti with a broad smile on his face. « Please put it on the bed and let's see if everything is as ordered. He had been very specific with his demands. He opened the case and carefully examined the contents. The McMillan TAC 50 calibre rifle was there along with all the accessories that he had asked for. The bipod, suppressor, ammunition and the lens. There was even a night vision lens if needed. With the proper ammunition, the TAC-50 is known for being the rifle used to achieve the longest sniper kills in the world, with Canadian snipers using the weapons making shots at over 3.5 kilometres.

He was impressed. « Perfetto Robbie, perfetto. You done well. Now let's go eat I'm famished. » They took the stairs and descended to the Saddle Room restaurant in the hotel. Business was good it was three quarters full, it was just coming up to a quarter to one. They were shown to a discreet table for two by the window. Something which Giovanni appreciated. They were shown the menus but they were quick to choose as they had other things on their minds. They both opted for the wild smoked Irish salmon with Guinness bread for starters. Giovanni chose the lamb with the usual vegetables and gravy for his main dish. Robbie preferred the roast beef with roasted potatoes and vegetables. They didn't bother with dessert. The meal was excellent and Giovanni had ordered a bottle of Château Margaux 1982 to wash it down. An excellent wine and a vintage year. He could be very generous when he was in good humour. Robbie wasn't used to drinking wine and especially not of this quality. But he thought that it was something that he could get accustomed to.

Just like any professional Giovanni wanted to test the material before he set a day and time for his hit. He took a mouthful of red ruby wine from his glass and wiped his lips with the white napkin that had been provided. « I need to test the material. Do you know somewhere discreet that we can go ».

Robbie rubbed his jaw from right to left with his right hand in pensive mood. « I know just the place in the Dublin mountains. It's called Ticknock. I go there sometimes myself for target practice and to keep sharp. Used to be an army shooting range but it has been abandoned now for years. It can be popular with strollers and hikers but if we arrive for dawn we won't be bothered. Especially at this time of the year. »

So it was decided. Robbie would swing by the hotel tomorrow morning at around 6 a.m . Tomorrow morning was a Friday so there wouldn't be many people up and about in he area. At this time of the year the sun wouldn't be on duty until about 7.45 a.m. That is if it showed up for duty at all. Robbie said that he'd bring a thermos of coffee and a few sandwiches. It could be nippy up there early in the morning.

Robbie then went on to tell Giovanni all about Jack, his daily habits and movements. He showed him clippings from the newspapers with various photos of Jack. Giovanni was very interested to hear that Jack's dojo was just ten minutes walk from the hotel in Fitzwilliam Square and that he would be present this evening in flesh and blood. They finished off their meal with a coffee in the bar and then said goodbye until early the next morning.

Giovanni like most Italians enjoyed a siesta after his meal. Especially when it was hot, which wasn't especially the case in Ireland. But he was a creature of habit. So he headed for his plush suite, undressed to his briefs and slipped into his silk sheeted bed. He set the alarm on his luxury Jaeger-Lecoultre watch for forty-five minutes and no more. He slept. The alarm went off as it was supposed to do and he awoke. It was 3.30 pm. He headed to the bathroom and stepped into the shower, put it on hot and finished on cold. He felt good. He then dressed elegantly as he wanted to visit the city.

He tread nimbly down the elegant stairs and glanced over towards the reception desk where Nicola was on duty. He winked and she smiled back coyly. The doorman nodded politely as he exited the hotel and stepped onto the footpath. As usual Stephen's Green was busy and noisy with traffic. He turned right and headed for the very trendy pedestrianised Grafton Street with it's designer shops. The street was hopping with activity. There were the usual street buskers from folk singers good and bad, traditional Irish musicians and a lone cello player. A few acrobats were also entertaining the crowds. There was of course the ever present Diceman who always attracted the tourists. He was a Scottish-Irish actor, model, and street artist specialising in mime. Born in Scotland of Irish parentage, Thom McGinty spent much of his life and career in Ireland, where he became a landmark living statue and one of the country's most popular street performers.

Giovanni was enjoying the hustle and bustle and the different entertainers. He walked towards the end of the street and female heads turned and gave him furtive glances. He smiled back. He stopped in front of the window of Brown Thomas a famous designer fashion store. He decided to take a look. Upon entry he was immediately hit by the scent of various upmarket perfumes. He headed for the designer rooms on level 1. The smell of leather attracted him like a magnet. An attractive blonde hostess in her late twenties and elegantly dressed greeted him with a beaming smile. She was hoping for a good sale and commission. With her advice and help Giovanni tried on a few leather designer jackets. He flashed on one in particular and decided to buy it. It was a magnificent black Prada leather jacket. Ideal for Autumn and Winter wear, especially in Ireland. The hostess smiled and complimented him on his choice.

Even with a ten percent discount, the jacket came to an expensive six hundred pounds. Giovanni didn't bat an eyelid and handed the smiling hostess his gold Visa card. She handed him his receipt and smiled back. She parcelled the jacket beautifully and gave him the package. He noticed she wasn't wearing a wedding band. Should he take a chance and invite her for a drink in the hotel? *No—better not*, he thought. There was already Nicola, the receptionist, he was certain to bed, and there was also work to be done. A pity, as she seemed to be waiting for an invitation. He thanked her and bid her a good day.

He wanted to check out a traditional pub, so he headed back up the street on the left-hand side towards Kehoe's Pub and turned left into Anne Street. The doorman at the hotel had recommended it, saying they served the best pint of Guinness in town. He arrived and wasn't disappointed upon entering. It was a classic pub filled with original features such as mahogany doors and wood-partitioned snug areas.

He took a stool near the snug area and sat at the bar. He was amused by the mahogany drawers behind the counter that once held rice, tea, coffee, and snuff—a reminder of a time when patrons could slip in for provisions and enjoy a pint in private. A balding, red-faced, overweight barman in an apron greeted him and asked what his pleasure was.

When in Ireland, do what the Irish do, he thought. So, he ordered a Guinness. He had never had one before, so he thought it could be an interesting experience.

"Very good, sir—nice choice," came the reply. He carefully observed the barman at work. He pulled the beer tap fully down and poured the drink into a Guinness-branded glass, holding it at a forty-five-degree angle. He continued until the glass was three-quarters full, then allowed it to settle for a few minutes because of the nitrogen. Giovanni watched, amazed, as it began to turn slowly black. The barman then topped up the glass, just proud of the rim, by pushing the tap handle back, thus creating the fabulous Guinness creamy head.

The barman brought the *masterpiece* and placed it in front of Giovanni on a Guinness beer mat.

"There you are, sir—enjoy," he smiled.

Giovanni contemplated the glass in front of him, then brought the creamy pint to his mouth and took a good gulp. It was nothing like he had ever tasted before. He had read that it was an acquired taste—but once you tasted it, you never went back. He put the glass back on the beer mat and tried to analyse what he had just experienced. There was a malty sweetness and a hoppy bitterness, with notes of coffee and chocolate.

He had taken wine-tasting lessons in his native Sicily, so he tried to apply the same protocol to the Guinness. He could also detect a roasted flavour coming through, courtesy of the roasted unmalted barley that went into its brewing. It had a sweet nose, with hints of malt breaking through, and its palate was smooth, creamy, and balanced. His analysis was spot-on. Giovanni was a fine connoisseur and would have made an excellent sommelier in another, less violent life.

He liked it, so he took another mouthful and placed the glass back on the beer mat. The big clock behind the bar told him that time was pushing on—it was coming up to six p.m. He remembered Maher telling him that Jack's dojo would be opening at 6:30 p.m. He wanted to take a look. The pub was filling up quickly, mainly with office workers. It was also a popular spot for solicitors, barristers, judges, journalists, and actors—a very mixed bunch indeed. One or two women, elegantly dressed, caught his ever-prying eye.

One was a tall brunette, magnificently classy, with curves in all the right places. The other was a blonde of average height—less classy, but dressed to kill. She wore black leather boots and a short skirt that showed shapely, false-tanned legs. Her brown suede frilly jacket suited her bronzed complexion. She seemed frivolous and playful, which suited Giovanni, but he had things to do.

He finished his pint and placed the empty glass on the table. The barman thanked him and instantly retrieved it. Giovanni recovered his jacket from the back of his stool, put it on, and made sure to take his Brown Thomas bag with its expensive contents. The blonde flashed him an alluring glance. He certainly stood out from the pack. He returned her glance and exited Kehoe's Pub. *A pity*, he whispered to himself.

He took the direction to Jack's dojo in Fitzwilliam Square, just a short stroll from his hotel. Dusk was falling, and there was a chill in the air—a stark contrast to the warm interior of Kehoe's. As he approached the address, he could hear *kiais*—sharp shouts— coming from a basement. He stopped at the small iron gate, opened it, and took the twelve steps down to the dojo. He wanted to see his prey in the flesh.

When he arrived at the open door, the smell of sweat filled his nostrils. A blood-stained *makiwara* stood in the small hall area where he paused. The dojo was a large, neon-lit space, at least sixty square yards in size. He counted at least thirty practitioners, all wearing the traditional karate *keikogi*—or *kimono*, as it is popularly known outside of Asia. The far wall was adorned with a large calligraphy scroll and icons of various Japanese karate masters. Around the room, he saw a multitude of traditional weapons, neatly stacked in corners, hanging from walls, or kept in cupboards—Bo, Kama, Sai, Nunchaku, Sansetsukon, Tekko, and especially the famous samurai's katana.

The flooring of the dojo was red pine, except for a small area set aside for the practice of *ukemi*, or break falls. Giovanni stayed well back in the dimly lit mini hallway and observed discreetly. Finally, his eyes found their future prey. All the students were in *seiza*—the standard formal way of sitting in Japan. Jack was demonstrating a traditional kata, a set of movements against imaginary opponents.

Giovanni observed intently from the doorway. Jack moved with grace and speed, emanating sheer power. He executed the movements with the elegance of a ballet dancer, thought

Giovanni—but that was where the comparison ended. The Italian could feel the *ki*—energy flowing from Jack's body as he performed the kata with precision. A shiver ran down Giovanni's spine. No way would he engage in hand-to-hand combat with such a formidable opponent. After all, Jack had put three very good men six feet under.

Jack finished the kata and bowed to his students. He then made his way toward the doorway where Giovanni stood. Giovanni could feel a block of energy moving toward him, heavy and deliberate. The man had a tremendous aura, and Giovanni felt his muscles knot. Jack appeared in front of him and bowed courteously. He stuck out his right hand and introduced himself.

"My name is Jack, the sensei of this dojo. Can I help you?"

Giovanni was taken aback. The man appeared affable and even gentle. "No, thank you," he said. "I'm on business for a few days, and I heard the kiai coming from the basement as I passed by. It stirred my curiosity, as I practise a little back home."

"Oh, I see," replied Jack. "Out of curiosity, what style do you practise?"

Giovanni thought quickly. "Shotokan. I practise the Shotokan style," he replied. Shotokan was the most popular style of karate worldwide, and the one most people were familiar with.

Jack smiled. "Ok—well, enjoy your stay in Dublin, and if you want to practise with us, don't hesitate to come back and see me."

Giovanni bowed politely. "Thank you very much for your kindness," he said, and he took the iron stairs back up to the lamp-lit street. He noticed a few cars that appeared to be kerb-crawling and eventually coming to a complete stop as a scantily clad woman emerged from the shadows and put her head through an open passenger window to propose her services. *Prostitution—it's the same the world over*, thought Giovanni.

Giovanni had been more than impressed with his encounter with Jack. As he walked the short distance back to his hotel, he thought of the energy and power that radiated from the man. No way would he engage in a physical confrontation with him—he valued his life too much. During the brief encounter, he had come to respect and even like the man. A pity Jack was his next hit, he thought. But business was business; there was no room for feelings.

He arrived at the hotel and entered the lobby. Nicola was still on duty, engaged with a client. Upon seeing him, she flashed a radiant smile. Giovanni waved back and made his way to his suite. He stripped down to his jocks and proceeded to do fifty push-ups at a slow, steady pace, followed by a hundred jackknife sit-ups and a hundred leg dips. By the end, he had worked up a good sweat, so the shower was a welcome reward. Afterwards, he felt good—and hungry. He decided to eat in tonight. He shaved, then dressed in casual attire.

As he descended the ornate staircase, he could feel the plush carpet under his feet—a small but satisfying luxury. Giovanni loved such comforts. He arrived at the hotel's reputable Saddle Room restaurant, where the clientele was a mix of residents and outsiders. The restaurant was quite full, with a blend of young, middle-aged, and mostly elderly patrons. The aroma of fine cuisine whetted his appetite. Giovanni told the smiling waiter that he was dining alone and was shown to a cosy table for two. The waiter suggested the rack of Wicklow lamb in red wine sauce, accompanied by roast potatoes and Brussels sprouts.

Giovanni accepted the recommendation and ordered an eighteen-year-old Macallan whisky along with some titbits as an apéritif. The waiter smiled at the man's discerning taste and handed him the extensive wine list. Giovanni declined politely, knowing exactly what he wanted—an eight-year-old bottle of Margaux and a small bottle of Pellegrino sparkling water.

The whisky was excellent, as was the finger food. Twenty minutes later, the main course arrived, piping hot and elegantly presented. The wine, brought earlier with the whisky, had been carefully uncorked and poured into a decanter. Beside it stood a tall Bordeaux glass with a long stem, its generous bowl slightly tapered at the rim. Giovanni knew that such a design directed the wine to the back of the mouth, enhancing each sip. The wide bowl also allowed the bouquet to develop fully.

The waiter asked if he would like to taste the wine. Giovanni nodded. He was rarely disappointed by Margaux. The waiter poured. Giovanni raised the glass and inhaled the rich, complex blend of perfumed and floral aromas. He sipped the deep ruby nectar, smiling as the silky tannins caressed his palate. The waiter bowed slightly, placed a napkin on the neck of the decanter, and filled his glass. Both the meal and the wine were superb. Giovanni left a five-pound tip as a token of appreciation—he always valued fine fare and excellent service.

It was 9:30 p.m. when he left the restaurant and passed by the reception toward the grand staircase. Nicola had finished her shift, replaced by a tall, grey-haired man in his early fifties. His name tag read "John."

He smiled and nodded. "A very good night, sir."

Giovanni returned the smile. "Thank you."

He needed an early night. Robbie, as arranged, was to come by at 6 a.m. sharp. He set his alarm for 5 a.m. and slept like a log. Giovanni awoke just before the beep-beep of his wristwatch signalled it was time to rise. He got out of bed, stretched, and did a few callisthenics before enjoying a warm, relaxing shower. Drying off, he wrapped a towel around his waist and drew the curtains. Outside, it was pitch black and misty; even with the sodium streetlights, he could barely make out the trees in St. Stephen's Green. He dressed accordingly—the mountains would be cold at this hour.

Once dressed, he opened the wardrobe and removed the guitar case containing the McMillan TAC-50 sniper rifle and its accessories. He opened the case—everything was still there. Better safe than sorry, he thought. Closing it, he donned his jacket, took the case, and slipped silently from his suite. The hotel was hushed; the plush carpet muffled his steps. The reception desk was empty—perhaps John had just finished his shift. Good. No curious eyes to question his early departure.

He crossed the chessboard-tiled hall and stepped through the wooden turnstile door onto the glass-covered porch to await Robbie's arrival. It was 5:55 a.m. The clouds of his breath in the crisp air confirmed the freshness of the morning. The streets were empty save for the occasional car, their drivers either heading to work or returning from it.

A black Mercedes S-Class rolled to a stop at the hotel entrance at 6:05. Giovanni descended the steps, opened the boot, and carefully placed the guitar case inside. The boot closed with a muffled thump. He then opened the passenger door and settled into the plush, heated leather seat.

"How's the form, Mr. Falconetti?" Robbie inquired.

"I'm good, Robbie, but you're five minutes late."

"Very sorry about that, sir—got delayed making the sandwiches. I see you're dressed for the chill."

Five minutes late might mean nothing to an Irishman, but for Giovanni it was a mark of unprofessionalism. An awkward silence followed. Robbie shrugged, shifted into drive, and the Mercedes glided away. The outside temperature read four degrees on the softly glowing blue dashboard.

The roads were empty. The radio warned of dense fog in parts of the county, urging motorists to take care. Giovanni approved of Robbie's caution.

Twenty minutes later, they reached their destination. Darkness lingered, the mist clinging stubbornly over Dublin. Robbie cut the engine; the V12 went silent. The warm cabin and heated seats made them reluctant to leave.

"Coffee and a sandwich, Mr. Falconetti?" Robbie offered.

"Sure—so long as it's not that instant crap."

"Oh no," Robbie grinned. "Percolator. Blue Mountain beans. The best."

"Bring it on," Giovanni replied. "Nothing better to start the day."

Robbie's face lit with satisfaction. He stepped out, retrieved a wicker picnic basket from the back seat, and returned. Inside was a thermos of coffee, china cups, sugar, milk, and a container of sandwiches—salmon, ham, and cheese. Giovanni was impressed; Robbie's standing had just risen, as fickle as the stock exchange.

The coffee was rich and hot, just as Giovanni liked. He especially enjoyed the salmon sandwiches; the ham and cheese were also good. They made small talk as they ate, Giovanni remarking that he'd like to bed the hotel receptionist before leaving for Sicily. Once the coffee and sandwiches were gone, they wiped their mouths with proper cloth napkins.

It was time for business. At 7:15 a.m., civil twilight began; the fog lifted slightly, and the sun—still six degrees below the horizon—cast diffused light. Giovanni pulled up his collar against the chill, opened the boot, and retrieved the guitar case. The solid thunk of its closure echoed in the quiet.

They climbed to higher ground and found the perfect spot for target practice—a large rock dominating the forest view. No one was around. Giovanni opened the case and assembled the McMillan, his hands moving with the ease of long familiarity. He clipped on the night-vision scope, attached the suppressor, and inserted the five-round magazine. Robbie watched intently; firearms were his passion, just ahead of cars. He'd even thought to bring cardboard targets and thumbtacks.

From their high-ground position, they commanded a sweeping view of the forest, comprised predominantly—about seventy percent—of Sitka spruce, with the remaining thirty percent a mix of lodgepole pine, larch, and true firs. Giovanni lifted the McMillan TAC-50 and peered through its magnified scope. His gaze settled on a magnificent Sitka spruce standing alone in a small clearing, its towering height—over fifty metres—and broad base making it an ideal target. He gauged the distance at just over six hundred metres.

Robbie understood immediately. Gathering the cardboard targets and thumbtacks, he began the descent toward the giant spruce. Seven minutes later, he was pressing the first target onto the trunk as high as he could reach. Once the task was done, he stepped clear of the clearing, ready for the demonstration to begin.

Giovanni rested the McMillan on a flat rock, the bipods providing a perfectly stable platform. Conditions were flawless—no wind at all—and the early morning light now washed the forest's edge. Assuming a prone position, he pressed the rifle stock into his shoulder and aimed. Following his well-drilled routine, he exhaled, held his breath, and squeezed the trigger. The suppressed shot didn't roar—it was more like the sharp snap of divine fingers breaking the morning stillness.

He inhaled again, repeating the same ritual for the next four rounds. Five sharp pops echoed softly across the clearing. The first three shots displeased him, but the last two were nearly dead-centre.

Robbie retrieved the perforated target and mounted another. Giovanni slid a fresh magazine into place, waiting until Robbie had cleared the area. As he settled for his next volley, movement caught his eye—on the western edge of the clearing, a large animal ambled into view. It looked like a stray dog.

"Now this could be interesting," Giovanni thought. *"A moving target—perfect."* He adjusted his position, following the dog's slow, distracted path as it sniffed the air and ground. Exhaling, he squeezed the trigger. The animal crumpled instantly—a clean, single-shot kill.

From the opposite side of the clearing, Robbie had seen the dog go down. He waved, and Giovanni returned the gesture. Crossing to the fallen animal, Robbie grabbed it by a hind leg and dragged it deeper into the forest. He estimated it weighed at least eighty pounds. Better to hide it, he reasoned—there was no need to pique the curiosity of hikers or early walkers. While it was unlikely anyone would request a canine autopsy, prudence was always the safer path.

When the carcass was well hidden, Robbie returned, replacing the target once more. Giovanni fired five more rounds. This time, all five were tightly grouped in the target's centre—near perfection. He was satisfied both with the weapon and with his own performance. Robbie collected the target and climbed back up.

"You're some shooter, Mr. Falconetti," Robbie grinned, handing over both bullet-torn sheets. Giovanni inspected them carefully. The early shots had wandered, but the final grouping—and the dog's one-shot kill—spoke volumes.

"I'm happy, Robbie—very happy." The rifle was flawless, and Giovanni's skill was as sharp as ever.

They collected the spent casings, erasing all traces of their activity. Giovanni disassembled the McMillan with practised efficiency, placing each component back into the guitar case. By now, the fog had lifted, revealing a pale, heatless sun.

Back at the Mercedes, Giovanni stored the guitar case in the boot. Settling into the warm interior, Robbie poured two more cups of rich Blue Mountain coffee, and for a while they drank in comfortable silence.

In the distance, a figure appeared—growing clearer with each step. A middle-aged woman was out with her black Labrador, the dog tugging ahead, nose to the ground. It was likely part of her morning ritual. Both men knew it was time to leave—the Labrador might well catch the scent of the dead animal. Best not to risk her noting the car's plate.

Robbie started the engine, and the big sedan eased away toward Dublin's centre. It was 8:15 a.m., and the streets were thickening with commuters.

Half an hour later, they reached the Shelbourne Hotel. Giovanni invited Robbie for a full Irish breakfast—both men were ravenous, the early mountain air and adrenaline having sharpened their appetites. Robbie found a spot on St. Stephen's Green, leaving the guitar case secured in the boot.

At the entrance, the morning porter, a slight middle-aged man, greeted them.

"Good morning, gentlemen—you're early birds," he said with a smile.

"Ah, nothing like an early morning stroll in the Green to work up an appetite," Robbie replied with a laugh.

Breakfast was excellent—more than excellent. But business awaited. Plans need to be finalised, and the date for the hit set. It was Monday, and Giovanni wanted to observe Jack's daily routine for several days before making his move.

Robbie assured him that Jack was a creature of habit—music to Giovanni's ears—but he preferred to see it for himself. Over the next two mornings, they watched from a safe distance, each equipped with high-powered Pentax SP 20×60 binoculars with night vision.

Like clockwork, just after 6:30 a.m., a light flicked on in Jack's kitchen-dining area. Moments later, Jack would slide open the aluminium patio door and step onto his balcony in a tracksuit.

They observed him perform a series of breathing and conditioning exercises, finishing with what appeared to be meditation. If Friday morning was calm and dry, Giovanni told Robbie, it would be an easy shot.

But they were wrong—Jack wasn't meditating. He had entered the state of Getsumei no Michi—the Moonlight Path—a technique designed to heighten awareness and efficiency.

Jack's teacher, Sensei Saito, had explained that the mind must be allowed to work at its natural pace. It could be frustrating at first, but persistence was essential.

Saito had gone on to say that, through mankind's evolution, some cultures believed in a thin membrane of consciousness between the subconscious and conscious levels—a layer combining logic, intuition, and mysterious external forces.

As humanity relied increasingly on logic over intuition, this layer had been neglected. Getsumei no Michi was a method to re-enter it.

On both mornings, in this heightened state, Jack had felt a dark cloud settle over his mind—a sense of an evil presence nearby.

Some instinctive, reptilian part of his brain told him something was very wrong.

A thousand days of training to develop, ten thousand days of training to polish. You must examine all this well.

Miyamoto Musashi

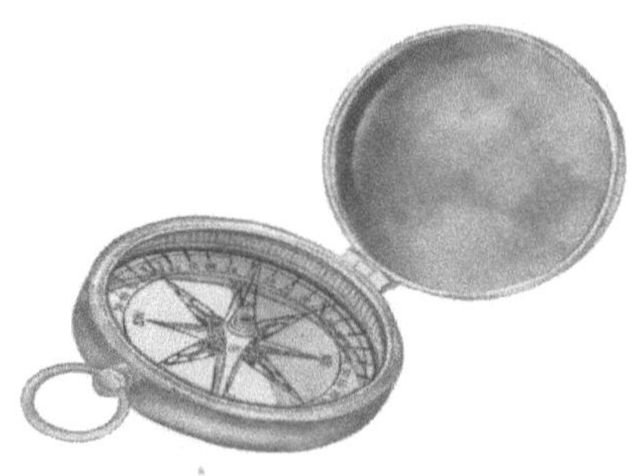

CHAPTER
Eighteen

It was D-day for Jack. He awoke from a deep sleep at 6 a.m., stirred by the loud, eerie wailing of curlews in flight. Akiko wasn't beside him — she was already in the tiny kitchen preparing breakfast, her mood unmistakably jovial. It was his birthday, and the black belt test, or Shodan — "first degree test" — was set for 5:30 p.m. that evening.

"Konnichiwa, my love. Otanjōbi omedetō — happy birthday," Akiko greeted warmly.

Jack kissed her affectionately. "That smells gorgeous. I'm starving."

Akiko had prepared a traditional Japanese breakfast: rice, grilled fish, miso soup, and a Japanese-style omelette — tamagoyaki — with extra eggs. He would need every bit of protein and vitamins for the ordeal ahead.

Jack had trained relentlessly for the occasion — twelve hours a day. The test would last about an hour and a half, beginning with katas, then various techniques with different opponents and weapons, and concluding with the twenty-man kumite — a sparring ordeal. He would first face the kohai, the junior students, gradually working his way up to the highest-ranked practitioners, including his good friend Toshiro, who had recently passed his 6th-dan test with brio. Each kumite round would last roughly ninety seconds. He would be required to win at least half of the bouts, and if knocked down, could not remain on the floor longer than five seconds. The rules were strict. Jack knew no quarter would be given — exactly as he wanted. He neither expected nor desired favours.

Akiko had to leave for an important economics lecture at 9 a.m., with crucial exams looming at the end of the month. She kissed him goodbye, wished him luck for the evening's Shodan test, and promised to attend, as would her father, Ichiro, who was deeply invested in Jack's martial journey. She skipped off in her usual good-natured, light-hearted way.

Jack changed into his tracksuit and began his usual morning routine. The briny scent of iodine in the air was invigorating. He finished with fifteen minutes of zazen meditation in the seiza position. Ichiro had introduced him to the practice, and Jack had since become addicted — he needed it. Emerging calm and focused, he changed into his bathing togs. His daily swim had become a cherished ritual. When the beach was deserted — as it often was outside of summer — he would remove his togs in the water, tying them around his arm. The sensation of complete freedom was intoxicating. The water was 20 °C, just to his liking. He'd swum in far colder waters in Ireland, though never with much pleasure. Here, he could swim for half an hour without risk of shock or hypothermia. In Okinawa, sea temperatures ranged between 20 and 30 °C, making it the only place in Japan where diving in wetsuits was possible year-round.

He emerged from the water with an intense sense of well-being, towelled off on the small wooden terrace, and prepared himself mentally for the evening's challenge. A cup of tea on the terrace, gazing at the ocean, was his reward. Jack never tired of the view, the scents, or the sounds. He intended to spend the rest of his life in this safe haven, alongside his soulmate.

Jack had left his keikogi — often incorrectly called a kimono in the West — at a dry cleaners in Naha, where they also offered an ironing service he greatly appreciated. He wanted to be immaculate for the test; a dirty keikogi signalled negligence and disrespect toward fellow practitioners. Sensei Saito tolerated neither poor attitude nor slovenliness. He himself was always immaculate — not a hair out of place.

Jack decided to cycle into Naha to collect his keikogi. It was a pleasant spring day, and the ride would be a welcome relaxation before the evening's ordeal. Just after midday, he arrived in the city centre, enjoying the seasonal shift: people had exchanged their heavy winter wear for lighter clothes — men in T-shirts, young women in blouses and skirts — a pleasant sight.

At the dry cleaners, he was greeted by a small, smiling elderly woman behind a large counter that emphasised her petiteness. Bowing, he handed over his order slip. She returned with his keikogi, pristine under its plastic covering, ironed to perfection. The price, stapled to the plastic, read 1,500 yen. Jack dug into his tracksuit pocket and gladly paid. Money well spent, he thought. The woman bowed in return — "Arigatō gozaimasu" — and wished him luck on his black belt test. Jack was momentarily taken aback. News of a Westerner attempting such a test in a traditional karate ryū clearly travelled fast; perhaps the whole island knew. Only later would he learn that the woman was none other than Sensei Saito's mother — a "young" woman in her nineties. Okinawa abounded with centenarians.

Hunger returned after the morning's training, swim, and cycle, though there was no question of a heavy meal. A miso soup and a few sushi would suffice. He cycled to Tanpopo, a small traditional Okinawan restaurant where he had often eaten with Akiko and her friends. Popular with university students, the place was known for wholesome, affordable fare.

A smiling young waitress he hadn't seen before greeted him and asked whether he wished to eat inside or out. The day was perfect — pleasantly warm, no wind — so Jack chose the little bamboo-covered terrace. Nodding to a few familiar faces on his way, he settled at a small table for two. The remaining free tables would soon be claimed; in thirty minutes, the place would be bustling with laughter and chatter.

Jack ordered miso soup with a side of fresh clams — caught that morning — followed by six pieces of freshly prepared sushi. The meal was just enough to satisfy without weighing him down. As always, the food was excellent, and he washed it down with a large glass of Pellegrino, his favourite sparkling water.

Collecting his keikogi, he went to pay the 1,400-yen bill — about twelve dollars — and, before leaving, slipped 120 yen into the waitress's hand. Tipping was uncommon in Japan, certainly unlike New York, but the young woman, though a little embarrassed, seemed pleased by the gesture from the gaijin.

Fixing his keikogi securely to the bike rack, Jack began the forty-five-minute ride back to his little paradise. The warmth, the birdsong, and the burgeoning spring filled him with an unshakable sense of harmony. For the first time in his life, he felt utterly whole, in complete accord with the universe — kokoro, the Japanese called it — when heart, spirit, soul, and mind move together in harmony with all creation.

It was 3 p.m. when Jack reached his beach cabin. After a shower and a change of clothes, he was ready. The shuttle to Naha ran every thirty minutes; he caught the 4:30 service, arriving twenty minutes later in the city centre, followed by a ten-minute walk to the dojo. Just after 5 p.m., Jack pushed open the door to the immaculate, wooden-floored hall. The kohai had done their duty, polishing the floor to a gleam, just as Jack himself once had. He and the junior students were among the first to arrive. In the changing room, he donned his freshly pressed keikogi. Ten minutes later, the place was full — thirty people, including five young women. His friend Toshiro clapped him on the back and wished him luck.

At 5:25 p.m., everyone sat in seiza, awaiting Sensei Saito's arrival. Three rows of ten lined the floor, with the senpai — senior students — on the left and the less experienced on the right. Jack could feel the tension mounting, but he was ready, body and mind. Akiko and her father sat discreetly on a wooden bench at the side, alongside a few other spectators. She caught his eye and gave him a fleeting smile.

Sensei Saito appeared, bowing before stepping onto the dojo floor, then assuming the position of seiza in the centre of the room. The entire class bowed, and in unison they called out, "Onegai shimasu," which literally meant *'do me a favour'* or *'teach me.'* The class began with the usual callisthenics and warm-up exercises, followed by basic kata and various techniques performed with a partner. Sensei Saito then clapped his hands, and everyone returned to seiza. Jack knew this was his moment.

"Jack-san," said Saito.

This was it. Jack bowed, rose, and walked to the middle of the floor. He was asked to perform five katas, which he executed with precision and poise. Next, he defended himself against an array of attacks—punches, kicks, strangleholds, and various grabs— sometimes facing one opponent, sometimes two. Then came the defences against club and knife assaults. Jack demonstrated remarkable technique, explosive power, and blistering speed. Sweat streamed down his face, and the gallery was visibly impressed.

Now came the 20-man kumite—the sparring ordeal. Each match against lower-graded opponents had to be won with *ippon* (maximum points), and against higher-ranked fighters, he needed at least fifty percent victories. If he was knocked down, he had just five seconds to get back on his feet.

The first fight proved relatively easy. His opponent, Greg, was a 21-year-old American marine biology student who had been practising for six months. Greg was fit, but Jack was sharper, faster, and far more powerful. Jack caught him with a perfectly timed foot sweep to his right leg, immediately following with a lightning-fast Mawashi geri— a roundhouse kick— to the head. Greg saw stars and was almost unconscious before hitting the wooden floor. The next four bouts were over in under a minute, each won convincingly.

Then came the more seasoned Okinawan fighters. The difficulty ramped up. Jack's cardio and stamina were pushed to their limits as he absorbed punishing blows to his body and legs. The tenth opponent was a 1st-dan black belt. Despite being knocked down once by a powerful *kari-ashi* (foot sweep), Jack scored an *ippon* to the head and won.

He took the next three bouts in style against 2nd-dan black belts, still undefeated.

His fifteenth opponent was a 3rd-dan black belt whom Jack knew well—fast, accurate, and powerful. They traded punishment for the entire match. Jack suspected at least one broken rib and felt swelling beneath his right eye, along with bruised shins. The bout ended in a draw.

Three-quarters through. The ordeal was taking its toll. The next three opponents were all 4th-dan fighters. Jack lost one match but scraped victories in the other two, each on points. In one bout, he was nearly knocked out but managed to stagger to his feet within the five-second rule.

His respect for his friend Toshiro—who had once fought a hundred opponents—deepened with every second. That was close to superhuman.

Jack's mouth was parched, sweat drenched his body, and every muscle ached. "Courage, Jack," he whispered to himself. Three brutal rounds remained.

The nineteenth match pitted him against a 5th-dan black belt. The fight went the full distance, but Jack lost on points, nursing a swollen jaw and possibly a cracked sternum.

The final bout was against his good friend Toshiro, fresh and full of energy. Out of respect, Toshiro would offer no favours, which was exactly how Jack wanted it. He shifted to a left-foot-forward stance to protect his injured ribs. But Toshiro outmanoeuvred him, landing a devastating straight right kick to his rib cage. Jack knew instantly more damage had been done. His legs felt like cotton, and a crushing blow to his left eye left it swollen shut. Still, he finished the bout on his feet, bowing respectfully to Toshiro, to all his opponents, and finally to Sensei Saito. The applause was genuine, recognising his courage, endurance, and skill.

Sensei Saito left the dojo briefly, then returned ten minutes later to formally hand Jack his *shodan* certificate—first-degree black belt—and his *kuro obi* (black belt). To his delight, a second round of applause erupted. The adrenaline had faded, and pain flared in muscles he didn't even know existed. Saito handed him a fragrant medicinal oil, instructing him to have someone rub it into his body three times daily to ease the pain and speed healing. He also told Jack to visit the hospital the next day for X-rays of his ribs and sternum.

"O tanjobi omedetō—happy birthday, Jack-san," Saito smiled. "You did very well today. I am proud of you. Now go celebrate. Now that you have mastered the basics of our system, your real training begins."

Jack bowed in gratitude and headed to the changing rooms for a much-needed shower. The pain was settling in, but he was still on a high. He set the water to lukewarm, closed his eyes, and let it cascade over his battered frame. It felt blissful. After several minutes, he finished with a cold rinse—invigorating despite the sting. Dressing carefully, he folded his sweat-soaked *keikogi* and placed it in his training bag alongside his treasured *kuro obi*.

Outside, Akiko and her father waited patiently. As soon as Jack stepped out, Akiko ran to him, unable to contain her emotion. She was radiant with joy for her bruised warrior, throwing her arms around him. He winced at the pain but welcomed her passionate kiss—a rare public display for a Japanese woman, but protocol could wait on such a day. Ichiro approached, bowing respectfully before shaking Jack's hand.

"It is a great honour to know you, Jack-san, and to see you courting my daughter," Ichiro said warmly.

Akiko linked her arm through Jack's, her eyes smiling. "I have prepared a special meal for your birthday and your *yudansha*—your dan-rank achievement. We must celebrate, my love," she said excitedly.

They walked slowly to Ichiro's car, a pristine first-generation 1972 Honda Civic he had bought new. It had never given him a moment's trouble. The happy trio arrived at Ichiro's home, laughing and joking along the way. Ichiro helped Jack out of the car, while Akiko took his bag in one hand and held him close with the other. Jack's body was stiff and sore, and he moved slowly.

"Onaka ga suita—I'm starving," Jack said with a grin. "I could eat a horse."

Inside, Jack's eyes widened in surprise. Akiko had prepared a feast fit for a king: an exquisite selection of finger foods in a dazzling array of colours, each bite-sized delicacy more mouthwatering than the last. He could hardly wait to taste them.

Ichiro had even procured a vintage Château Margaux to mark the occasion. The food was cordon bleu standard—some spicy, others sweet-and-sour, all perfectly balanced, whether vegetable, meat, or fish. Jack recognised some flavours, but others were a complete mystery. The variety was almost overwhelming.

The wine paired perfectly. After the meal, Ichiro brought out a 25-year-old bottle of Macallan whisky, knowing Jack's appreciation for a fine glass now and then. Akiko, not fond of strong spirits, chose a small glass of saké instead.

Ichiro chuckled, telling Jack the whisky would serve as an excellent anaesthetic for his aches and ensure a sound sleep. Two glasses later, Jack's pains seemed a distant memory. Peace settled over him.

Eventually, exhaustion hit like a slab of concrete. The young couple bid Ichiro goodnight and retired to Akiko's bedroom. She helped him undress and gently massaged the oil from Saito into his bruised muscles. Within minutes, Jack was asleep. He didn't stir until 7:30 a.m., waking to the smell of fresh coffee. Akiko's voice floated in from the other room as she reminded her father to be cautious on his fishing trip, with strong winds forecast for the afternoon.

Jack found sitting up difficult; the pain was intense. He slipped into a black cotton kimono he kept at Akiko's and shuffled into the kitchen, greeted by two smiling faces.

"Good morning, my love," Akiko beamed.

"Yoku nemuremashita ka?—Did you sleep well, Jack-san?" Ichiro inquired.

« Oh, I did indeed. I slept like a baby, » replied Jack.

Akiko told Jack they needed to go to the hospital so his injuries could be examined and X-rayed. "It's important," she insisted.

« Hai, » added Ichiro, « you must go to the hospital, very important. But now, good asa gohan — breakfast. Eat, Jack-san. »

The coffee was fresh, aromatic, and piping hot. Jack was hungry, and the toast and scrambled eggs slipped down a treat.

Ichiro bid them good day, explaining he had a boat to prepare and fish to catch. Akiko cleared the table, and they got ready to go to the hospital. Her father had left them his reliable little Honda car and had taken the motorbike instead. The car would certainly be more comfortable for Jack. It was a short twenty-minute drive to the local hospital, the Okinawa Central Hospital. Akiko drove slowly, carefully avoiding any bumps or potholes the road could offer. Jack was sore and stiff all over.

They arrived at the hospital, and Akiko carefully helped Jack out of the car. They walked slowly to the entrance and up the short flight of steps towards the automatic glass doors. Jack signed in at the reception, and they waited in the lounge to be called. Unlike most hospitals, the chairs were comfortable. They were third in the waiting line. After forty-five minutes, a smiling nurse in an immaculate white uniform appeared and ushered Jack and Akiko into the examination room.

They were greeted by a small, frail, elderly doctor in his late sixties. He spoke directly to Akiko in a rapid and detached manner. Jack caught only a few words. The doctor wanted to know exactly what had happened. He nodded slowly and finally began to smile as he looked at Jack.

A lot of older Okinawans still carried bitter memories of the Battle of Okinawa, which was referred to as the « typhoon of steel » — tetsu no ame (rain of steel) — in Japanese. The fighting had been ferocious, one of the bloodiest in the Pacific. At least 149,000 Okinawan people were killed or went missing — roughly half of the estimated pre-war population. It was no wonder it had left a bitter taste in the mouths of the older generation, especially those old enough to remember.

Now the little doctor's countenance shifted completely. His face lit up like a beacon. No, Jack-san wasn't American; he was Irish, and his injuries were the result of blows sustained during his black belt test in one of the oldest karate ryus on the island. The doctor knew Sensei Saito very well — they were good friends from way back. He smiled at Jack and spoke slowly in Japanese. He was delighted when Jack replied in almost perfect Japanese.

With the help of the nurse, they placed Jack on his back on the examination table. The little doctor was meticulous and gentle. He palpated Jack's entire body, smiling and nodding when Jack winced with pain. He asked a lot of questions, nodding his head in appraisal at Jack's answers. Once he had heard enough, he pushed a button, and Jack found himself in a semi-upright position. The nurse wheeled over the mobile X-ray machine.

Twenty minutes later, the doctor was holding the results. They were conclusive: Jack had sustained three broken ribs — two on the right and one on the left — a cracked sternum, and a broken cheekbone. No wonder he was in pain whenever he coughed, took deep breaths, or laughed.

The doctor lectured him, saying he would have to take it easy for a few weeks. As a rough guide, he said, fractured ribs and sternums can take about four to six weeks to heal, and even after this time, one can still feel discomfort. The bruising on his arms and legs would take between two and four weeks to clear up.

He took Jack by the hand, like a father, and said in his best English, « You take it easy, my boy. No karate for two months. »

But he might as well have been talking to a donkey in a field. Jack was Irish and stubborn. He had no intention of stopping his daily training routine. As for the pain, he would grin and bear it. As Sensei Saito said, his real training was only beginning, and Jack had no time to lose. His journey had only just begun.

The doctor gave him painkillers and anti-inflammatory tablets to be taken three times a day. They left the hospital reassured.

Luckily, the injuries were minor. There was no internal or permanent damage. They were both in good spirits.

When they arrived at the car, Jack took Akiko's head in his large hands and kissed her gently on the forehead.

Arigato, watashi no ai — thank you, my love. Now I need a beer; I'm thirsty, » he smiled.

You Irishmen, she laughed. Ja, ikimashou — okay, let's go then.

"Society exists only as a mental concept; in the real world, there are only individuals"

Oscar Wilde

CHAPTER
Nineteen

Back to Dublin - D-day

Giovanni was in the lobby of the Shelbourne Hotel at 5 a.m. sharp. An elderly gentleman at the reception desk, whom he hadn't seen before, greeted him with a polite good morning.

"You're very early, Sir. I do hope that everything is okay," he inquired.

"Perfect," replied Giovanni. "I love early morning walks in the park — just me and the little birds." A thin, sarcastic smile spread across his face.

"Oh, perfect, Sir. Do enjoy," came the reply.

As planned, Robbie was waiting exactly on time at the main entrance in an old, ragged-looking Ford Cortina. There was no point in drawing attention with the Mercedes Class S; that car was a magnet for curious eyes. Robbie had held onto the rifle and all the accessories. They were neatly packed in the boot. He had also prepared coffee and sandwiches, just like the other morning. But this time it wasn't shooting practice.

Giovanni slid into the passenger seat. The heater was on full, blowing hot air into the cabin. They greeted each other with a high five. Giovanni fastened his seat belt and settled into the seat. It wasn't Class S luxury, but it was comfortable enough. He clapped his hands together.

"Okay, let's do this and put this fucker away for good," he scoffed.

Robbie engaged first gear, and they set off. It was still pitch-black. The air was utterly still — absolutely no wind. That made Giovanni's day; it was a bonus. The wind is a major headache to snipers when it comes to long-range shooting. No wind meant there would be no need for complicated calculations, such as wind velocity and bullet trajectory. And anyway, Giovanni had completely forgotten to ask for an anemometer — a wind meter.

They passed the odd car here and there — people finishing late shifts and others just starting their early day. They slowly made their way towards Fairview, careful not to draw attention and strictly abiding by traffic laws. The last thing they wanted was a curious or overzealous Garda to pull them over and examine the contents of the boot. Robbie had a Smith & Wesson in the glove compartment to handle such a situation, should it arise.

It was just after 5:15 a.m. when they arrived in Clontarf. During the day, with traffic, the trip would have taken forty minutes. They parked the old Cortina, making sure it was out of sight. They then took the material and walked twenty minutes to the vantage point where they had observed Jack the previous day. There wasn't a soul in sight, and it was still pitch-dark.

Giovanni carefully assembled the McMillan TAC-50 and all the accessories — the silencer and the night vision. The 10-power scope with a 32mm objective lens was fixed. There was a damp chill in the morning air. When everything was set up, Robbie served two piping cups of black coffee and some salmon sandwiches. Now the waiting game would begin. They laughed and joked, trying to play down the tense situation they were about to confront.

It was coming up to 6 a.m. Both men knew it would be showtime pretty soon. The minutes before a hit were always nerve-wracking. The shooter had to remain calm; there was no time for shaky hands. Giovanni walked back and forth, slapping and rubbing his arms and shoulders to increase blood flow and stay warm. He was wearing gloves, but he would only keep a glove on his left hand when shooting. Immobilising the forward hand was important — it prevented vibration on the rifle.

They both took another cup of coffee. It was 6:10 a.m. Lights were coming on in certain dwellings, and traffic was picking up slightly. At 6:20 a.m., both men urinated — one of the inevitable side effects of coffee.

Giovanni got into position and had Jack's balcony in his sights. It was just 6:30, and both men waited with bated breath for the light to go on, the sliding door to open, and Jack to appear on the balcony to start his morning routine.

At 6:40, there was still no light and no Jack. Unlike most people, Jack didn't usually need an alarm clock to pull him out of sleep. His alarm clock was built in. But this morning, Jack was plunged into a deep sleep, and a childhood dream kept him prisoner in the arms of Morpheus.

It was 6:45 when Jack came out of his dream and opened his eyes. He looked at the clock on the bedside locker. The red digits against the black background confirmed that it was indeed 6:45 and not 6:30 a.m. He smiled. Sophie was sleeping soundly beside him. He got up out of bed, stretched, and headed for the bathroom. He urinated, washed his hands and face in cold water, and changed into his tracksuit.

It was 6:52 when the light came on and the sliding door opened. Jack stepped out onto the balcony. There was a chill in the air, but no wind. Six hundred metres away, the tension had been building to a climax. Giovanni and Robbie released audible gasps of relief when the light was switched on and when Jack stepped out onto the balcony. Jack was now moving, going through his routine.

To be on the safe side, Giovanni had decided to wait until he had a motionless target. It was a golden rule among the sniper community: when you have time, wait until the target is totally still. So Giovanni was waiting for Jack to get into his still meditation posture. That's what Giovanni thought it was — but it wasn't. Robbie lit up a John Player's Special and offered one to Giovanni, which he gladly accepted. He had given them up officially, but he enjoyed a puff every now and then — especially on occasions like this. It had a very calming effect.

Morning traffic was now more audible, and nearly every light in the apartment block was on. People were going through their daily morning ablutions and routines. It was still twilight, but light was beginning to filter, ever so slightly, through scattered nebulous clouds across Dublin Bay. It was quite magical. The cries of the curlew, hunting for small grassland animals, added an eerie atmosphere.

It was 7:50 a.m., and Jack was coming to the end of his session. It was now much brighter, and the sun was beginning to rise. Jack's apartment faced east, so it was a perfect situation for a sniper. No shooter wanted the sun reflecting in his face.

Jack stopped moving. Sophie entered the kitchen, still sleepy but smiling. She knocked on the window and blew him a kiss. Jack smiled back. He then dropped into the horse stance and slipped into getsumei-no-michi, the moonlit path. He let his mind wander. It was what scientists referred to as a sixth sense — a sense they called proprioception. An awareness of where our limbs are and how our bodies are positioned in space. Like other senses, it helps the brain navigate the universe and become aware of things that one previously had no chance of perceiving.

Giovanni took a position, striving to control his breathing. In order for a sniper to make his shot, he is required to stop breathing during the natural pause between inhalation and exhalation. The natural pause between breaths is usually two or three seconds long. By extending this pause to ten seconds, a sniper has the window he needs to make his shot and avoid any chest movement.

Jack's mind was wandering freely, jumping to every sound, sight, and smell. His mind was instinctively seeking the best and safest path. An icy cold liquid ran down the length of his spine. He felt a presence of evil — a black cloud hanging over his head.

The target was lined up, and Giovanni gently squeezed the trigger. But Jack had already begun to move. He hit the deck and scurried through the open door into the kitchen. Sophie was in the kitchen with her back to the window. The high-velocity bullet blasted through the glass, shattering it, and tore through Sophie's right shoulder blade, thrusting her forward onto the kitchen's central island.

The walls in Jack's brain caved in as he scrambled towards her. Two more shots rang out. The last one grazed the top of his skull, causing profuse bleeding. The skin on the scalp carries more blood than most of the body. He grabbed Sophie and carried her to the other side of the kitchen, away from the balcony's sliding doors and to safety. She was in deep shock. The bullet had gone straight through, shattering her right shoulder blade and clavicle. Luckily, no vital organs had been touched, and blood was just trickling. He laid her on the sofa in the sitting room with a pillow under her head and a cushion under her feet.

The blood trickled down his face and into his eyes. He rushed to the bathroom and put his head under the tap to rinse off the excess blood. He found a compress in the locker and applied it to his head. "This can't be happening," he thought.

He rushed to the phone and dialled 911, speaking quickly but clearly as he described what had happened in the simplest and most precise manner to the woman on the other side of the line.

"Is she unconscious, or is she bleeding?" the woman asked calmly.

"No, but she's in a state of shock," replied Jack.

"Alright, don't panic. Help will be there in about twenty minutes," came the reply.

Jack put down the receiver. The police were automatically notified in the case of a shooting, and they would probably arrive before the ambulance. Jack decided to ring his good friend Joey Maloney at Store Street police station. The number was listed under the J's. It was his direct line in the station. It rang for what seemed like an eternity. Time and situations were relative. Einstein was right.

"Joey Maloney here—how can I help ye?" came the response in a flat Dublin accent.

"Sophie's been shot by a sniper, Joey." Jack's voice was stripped of emotion.

"Jack, what the fuck… Is this some kind of joke, man?" There was no reply.

"Don't budge, buddy. I'm on my way." He banged down the receiver.

Joey's head was spinning. This just couldn't be happening—it was like something out of a movie. But his good friend was on the receiving end. He knew how fragile Sophie had been after the kidnapping and the attempted murder of Jack. She was on medication for the sleepless nights and frequent nightmares.

This was going to derail her completely. She was only beginning to piece it all together again and live a normal, carefree daily life. It was difficult to know how Jack was coping after the ordeal. He didn't show much emotion, clamped shut like an oyster.

He whisked past Inspector Branagan's office like Flash Gordon. The Inspector would have a kitten when he heard the news. No point in alerting him yet, thought Joey. He needed all the information and details first. He nodded to the desk Sergeant as he ran by.

"I'm off on an emergency. If anyone's looking for me, I'm not available," shouted Joey.

"Okay, message received. Take care, Joey," came the reply from the burly man behind the desk.

Joey jumped into the Ford, jammed the key into the ignition and fired up the engine. He slammed the gear stick into reverse, then first gear, and screeched out of the car park, leaving a plume of white smoke in his wake.

He reached into the glove compartment and took out the blue magnetic siren—or "Kojak light," as he liked to call it. He switched it on and banged it onto the roof. The high-pitched wailing sound left no doubt in anyone's mind concerning the urgency of the situation and the driver's desperate need to be somewhere very fast.

Cars darted out of the way upon his arrival. People on the street stopped and stared. Some shook their heads from left to right in weary confirmation of another crime being committed on the streets of Dublin. Unfortunately, it was now a daily occurrence, and Dubliners were becoming accustomed to it.

It was a short three-and-a-half mile drive from Store Street police station to Jack's apartment in Clontarf. In normal conditions with free-flowing traffic, it was a twelve-minute drive. Joey screeched into the car park in six minutes flat. Even Michael Schumacher would have been proud.

The ambulance and a local squad car were already on the scene. And as usual, the scene was like a magnet to nosy parkers and do-gooders. Joey leapt from the driver's seat, banging the car door behind him, and ran up the stairs to the apartment. The door was wide open. The medics were busy setting up a drip for Sophie, probably spiked with painkillers and a sedative.

She seemed in extreme shock. Two uniformed guards were present, one middle-aged and the other in his late twenties. The older man was questioning Jack and taking notes. The younger man was unusually attentive. Jack's face was drawn and tense, his expression completely devoid of emotion. Joey made eye contact with his good friend and saw a shimmer of feeling. The man was human after all.

Joey walked over, nodded to the two guards and flashed his ID. They shook hands.

"Okay, guys, I'll take it from here. This is a case for the homicide department," said Joey. "Cordon off the area and keep the nosy-parkers and the Press at bay. I'll ring in forensics."

"It's good to see you, Joey," said Jack blankly.

Joey tapped him gently on the back. "You need a pick-me-up, my friend."

He went into the salon and opened the drinks cabinet. He took out a bottle of Redbreast twelve-year-old whiskey. The bottle was more than half full. He took out two glasses and poured two decent measures. He came back and handed one to Jack.

"Get that into ye. It'll do you good," said Joey.

Jack stared into the glass, then knocked half of it back.

Joey took a seat opposite Jack, who was slumped in an armchair. "Okay, buddy, take it slowly from the beginning. Tell me exactly what went down here, and try to remember any small details, however trivial, leading up to the event."

Jack explained everything with incredible precision: his usual early morning routine, the sensation of something sinister through his 'sixth sense,' and the high-velocity shots shattering the sliding door's glass.

Meanwhile, the medics had carefully transferred Sophie onto a stretcher and were moving her out of the apartment.

"I have to go with her," said Jack. He emptied his glass of whiskey and put on his jacket.

"Which hospital, guys?" shouted Joey.

"The Mater, sir," came the reply from the medic.

Joey took Jack by the arm. "Ok, Jack, ride in the ambulance, and I'll see you in the hospital. Time isn't on our side, and we have to move fast."

Sophie was immediately taken into the emergency ward upon arrival at The Mater Hospital. Jack was told to wait in the lounge until further notice. Joey arrived five minutes later and found his friend sitting calmly with a coffee. Only two other people were in the waiting room.

"I could do with one of them myself," said Joey. He went to the vending machine and came back with an Americano. Joey sat next to his friend. Jack looked less tense.

Joey stirred his coffee and took a sip. "Is there anything you can think of, anything out of the ordinary, in the last week or two, Jack?"

Jack remained calm and silent. Joey observed that his friend was deep in concentration, scrolling through recent events in his mind.

Jack turned his head towards Joey. "Yes, there is. Last Monday, a guy dropped into the dojo. Said he was curious and just wanted to have a look. Said he was on a business trip in Dublin for a few days. And yes, before you ask, he was very Mediterranean-looking and dangerous. Slightly taller than me, athletic build. A bad-boy look, I'm sure, pleases the ladies."

"Okay," said Joey, excitedly. "It may be nothing, but we have to check it out. Will you be able to give a detailed description to the mugshot artist back at the station?"

"Sure, no problem, Joey. It's not a face one forgets easily."

"Okay—we'll have to get back to the station ASAP."

They both finished their coffees. A young nurse in her mid-twenties appeared in the waiting room asking for Jack. He waved, and she came over.

She had a soft country accent: "Your wife is under sedation, sir. She's not in danger, but she will need urgent surgery on her shoulder. The surgeon has arranged for an intervention at 8 a.m. tomorrow morning. She was in shock and is sleeping now. Would you like to see her, sir?"

Jack stood up. "Yes, I would like to see her." He followed her through the sliding doors.

"Don't be too long, Jack. Time is of the essence," called out Joey, fumbling in his pocket for his cigarettes.

Jack met the surgeon, a wiry, grey-haired man in his late fifties who went by the name of Doctor Molloy. He explained all the details to Jack in layman's terms, telling him how lucky Sophie was. If the bullet had been lower or even slightly to the left, it could have seriously damaged her lung and caused fatal internal bleeding.

"She must have a guardian angel," he smiled.

Jack extended his right hand. Doctor Molloy clasped it in both of his hands.

"Thank you very much, Doctor. How long will the intervention last?" asked Jack inquisitively.

"Oh, it will take at least three hours. Ring the reception in the afternoon and they'll put you through to me. But don't worry—she's in very good hands. In a few weeks, she'll be as right as rain. Now I'll leave the two of you alone. Goodbye now, and God bless. We'll talk tomorrow." He left the room.

Jack took Sophie's hand. She looked peaceful, almost angelic.

"I'm so sorry, my love. This is all my fault. I hope that in your heart you'll be able to forgive me. Had you died, I'd never have forgiven myself. I feel as though I'm reliving my nightmare in Okinawa all over again. Please, forgive me." He bent down, kissed her gently on the forehead, and left the room.

Jack found Joey waiting patiently outside the hospital. He was dragging nervously on a cigarette and fidgeting restlessly. Joey, in the meantime, had called the desk Sergeant in Store Street on the hospital's public phone and told him to get the sketch artist to the station immediately. He explained the urgency of the situation. The desk Sergeant had immediately understood.

"Send a taxi, a limo, whatever it takes—but she needs to be there yesterday," Joey had ordered. It was now 10:30 a.m.

The sketch artist in question was a young, hippy-like woman in her mid-twenties who went by the name of Suzanne, and she was very good at her job. Like most sketch artists, she was freelance.

Joey didn't pay much attention to the speed limits on the short drive back to the station. Fifteen minutes later, both he and Jack were walking through the main door.

Joey waved to the desk Sergeant.

"What's the story?" he asked.

"I sent a taxi, Joey. We're in luck—she was at home and was due to leave tomorrow on an autumn break to Rome."

"Well played. You'll be playing on the A team tomorrow," retorted Joey.

Now he would have to bring Inspector Branagan up to speed on the whole affair. He wasn't looking forward to it. As expected, Branagan hit the roof upon hearing the news. He slammed his big fist on the wooden table, making the phone jingle and knocking over a jar that contained his much-beloved pipe and a quality ball-point pen.

"A supposedly Italian hitman in my jurisdiction? I don't believe it!" he roared.

It took more than five minutes before he calmed down and his heartbeat returned to a normal rhythm. Joey had been busy getting mugs of tea ready. The sight of Jack walking into his office didn't exactly help him keep his calm.

"You again, Jack Hopkins. I might have known. You're quickly becoming my worst nightmare," he growled.

Joey was quick to defend his friend.

"It's not Jack's fault, sir. This is clearly a vendetta. If anyone should be complaining, it should be Jack. He's borne the brunt of it."

Branagan was apologetic. He was sincerely sorry to hear about Sophie and wished her a full and speedy recovery. The burly desk Sergeant appeared in the doorway, filling it with his mass and blocking the light from the corridor.

"The sketch artist has arrived, sir. Shall I send her in?"

"Yes, immediately," grunted Branagan.

It was now 11:30 a.m. She arrived at the open door, looking frail in comparison to the desk Sergeant.

"Well, don't just stand there—come in!" shouted Branagan.

Spending most of her time indoors, like most artists do, she was pale in complexion. Her auburn hair was neatly plaited, and she wore denim dungarees, which didn't do much to enhance her femininity. She appeared almost shapeless. Her face was pretty and freckled. Her eyes were a magnetic emerald green—clear and incisive. In one delicate white hand, she carried a sketch pad, and in the other, a small wooden box containing her sketch pencils. She was given a comfortable chair at the end of the big table. Jack stood beside her and began giving a detailed description of Giovanni Falconetti.

After ten minutes and a few adjustments, they were staring at a very accurate portrait of Giovanni Falconetti. Jack's description had been extremely precise, and Suzanne was clearly talented.

"Okay," said Branagan, standing up to his full six-foot-three-and-a-half. "Let's put out an all-points bulletin on this guy. Alert train stations, car ferry terminals, and airports. Send faxes to all concerned. And we need photocopies in a hurry—give that Rank Xerox machine some work to do. Let's get to it. Oh yes, and ring RTE to organise a news alert with the suspect's mug on TV." He slammed his ham-like hand onto the desk. It vibrated under the impact and startled the sketch artist.

Falconetti and Maher had long left the scene. They had made sure to collect the spent shell casings, the cigarette butts, and anything else they might have discarded. They knew forensics would be sniffing around once the ballistics team had calculated the trajectory and distance of the bullets.

They decided to hide the McMillan TAC-50 in some undergrowth. It was too risky keeping it in the car. Giovanni had cleaned it scrupulously, making sure not to leave fingerprints. His flight plans would have to be altered. He was booked on a flight the following day from Dublin Airport—that would now have to be changed. They had time, but not much. They would have to act fast.

Robbie said there were daily flights from Belfast in Northern Ireland to Rome via London with British Airways. A direct flight would have been ideal, but it wasn't to be. The drive from Dublin to Belfast was just over 100 miles. Robbie said he could do it in about two hours.

So it was back to the hotel to make a phone call and secure a flight reservation. Robbie parked on the Green and waited patiently for Giovanni's return. The Italian raced through the hotel lobby toward the staircase. Glancing at the reception desk, he recognised the affable man in his late fifties named Gerard, with whom he had already made an acquaintance.

He glided up the stairs, opened the door to his suite, and headed straight for the phone. He then rang reception and asked for the

British Airways phone number. The man at reception gladly provided the urgent information. Giovanni dialled the number and waited. The woman on the other end of the line was helpful and professional.

There was a flight to London that afternoon at 1 p.m. The flight was fully booked except for three business-class seats still available. She told him the flight time was one hour and twenty minutes. Giovanni provided her with all the necessary details and booked a seat. He asked about connecting flights to Rome—or even better, Palermo in Sicily. She asked him to be patient while she searched. He could hear her fingers deftly tapping on her keyboard. After a few minutes—bingo—there was a flight to Palermo at 4:00 p.m. with five seats remaining. He booked without hesitation and thanked her.

It was going to be tight timewise, but it was possible. All going to plan, he'd be back in his villa in Trappeto that evening. He packed in record time, hurried down the plush staircase, and headed straight to reception.

Gerard was surprised to see him carrying his designer travel bag.

"Checking out already, Mr. Falconetti?" he inquired, his face lined with surprise. "I hope you enjoyed your stay with us."

"Yes, it was excellent. But I'm afraid there's an urgency back home that needs my personal attention," he smiled.

"Oh, I hope it's not too serious, sir," came the reply.

He answered with a smile, paid his bill in cash, and left a ten-pound tip. Then he was gone, through the famous revolving doors and into the morning air. It was just coming up to 9:30 a.m. Robbie had been waiting with a John Player Special between his lips. When he spotted Giovanni, he stepped out of the car and waved. Giovanni walked across the street with large strides and threw his bag into the open boot.

"Let's move it—the flight's at 1 p.m.," he boomed.

It was a handy enough drive from Dublin to Belfast in the UK. But it wasn't all motorway, and forty-ton trucks could slow progress on national roads. On certain days, trucks were quite a hindrance, as much trade was carried out between the Republic of Ireland and the UK, their biggest trading partner.

Robbie was a good, fast, and safe driver. But he had decided to try and stick to the speed limits as best he could, not wanting to draw unnecessary attention from the Boys in Blue. Giovanni had told him about his encounter with Jack Hopkins. Robbie knew that wasn't good at all. He knew Jack wouldn't be long in putting two and two together—and bingo. Ireland was a small country, and Dublin was a small city. That would make things a lot easier for the police force. He knew time was the key factor. And luckily, it was on their side.

It was just 10:30 a.m. when they crossed the border at Jonesborough into Northern Ireland and toward Newry. Crossing the border was now a mere formality thanks to the unification of Europe. It would have been a different story before 1973 and before the accession of Ireland and the UK to the EEC. Because of the Troubles at the time, border control was stringent and time-consuming.

They drove on toward Belfast International Airport, eleven and a half miles northwest of Belfast city. It was formerly known as Aldergrove Airport, after the nearby village. With no hindrances, they'd arrive at the airport car park in forty-five minutes.

Back at Store Street Station, it was all go. Joey was waiting for the Rank Xerox to spit out the first warm sheets of photocopies. Taking a handful, he felt the heat still clinging to the paper. He called Jack, who was in deep conversation with Suzanne, the sketch artist. Jack was thanking her for her patience and for the striking accuracy of her drawing.

"Let's go, Jack," Joey shouted. "There's no time to lose. I'm heading straight to the airport to drop a few of these copies off to some of the customs and airport police lads I know. I'll drop you at the apartment—you could do with a rest."

Jack didn't disagree. He knew he needed an hour or two of complete calm to get his mind back on track and recover from the trauma.

Joey dropped him off and told him he would ring later in the afternoon. He then pointed the Ford Sierra towards Dublin Airport.

As usual, the airport was busy, people darting in every direction. Joey spotted two airport police officers he knew who were on duty. He handed out the photocopies and explained that there had been an assassination attempt and that they were urgently seeking the man in the drawing for questioning. He didn't mention Jack— that would be a breach of confidentiality.

"Okay, Joey, we'll keep our eyes open," came the enthusiastic reply.

Joey thanked them and then made his way to customs. He recognised one of the men on duty, a jovial and comical character named Tommy, who always had a story or joke to tell. Tommy, in his mid-forties, bore a beer belly that testified to his fondness for Guinness, which he drank in great quantities.

His face lit up when he saw Joey approaching. "Hey, Joey Moloney! What brings ye here—is it holidays or business?" he joked.

Joey explained the situation and handed him several photocopies.

"No problem, Joey. I'll distribute them to the lads and we'll keep our eyes open. God bless now, and take care."

Joey then headed toward the airline company desks. He had only walked twenty yards when he heard a whistle and his name being called. Spinning on his heels, he saw Tommy beckoning with a tilt of his head. Joey hurried back.

"Yeah, I saw this guy," said Tommy, scratching his chin. "He came in on a flight last Saturday from Rome. Dressed real classy, in designer clothes. He definitely stood out from the pack. Tall, tanned, athletic build, good-looking—but not the kind of fella you'd want to upset, if ye know what I mean. He had a dangerous look in his eyes… the kind that makes your skin crawl."

"Are ye sure, Tommy?"

He pointed to the drawing with his index finger. "I'm ninety-nine per cent sure, pal. That's him, deffo."

"Okay, thanks, Tommy—you're a star," said Joey, turning quickly. "I owe you a pint."

"You owe me three pints, ye little bollox," came the cynical reply.

Tommy had recently given him valuable information about a man from Finglas, north County Dublin, who was involved in a homicide and was frequently smuggling large quantities of amphetamines from Amsterdam.

Joey broke into a stride despite his hindering limp and headed straight to the Alitalia desk. A smiling brunette in her thirties printed off the passenger list from the previous Saturday and handed it to him. The list was long—the plane had been full. He scrolled patiently with his finger until, three-quarters of the way down, he stopped. The name leapt out at him. Giovanni Falconetti—typed in bold capital letters. This couldn't be a coincidence.

He thanked the hostess and hurried back to his car. He radioed the station with the precious information. Interpol would have to be alerted, and they also needed to contact the Carabinieri in Rome to see if they had any details or perhaps fingerprints on file. A translator from the Italian embassy would also be needed—it would make life a whole lot easier.

Joey's next stop was the Shelbourne Hotel. He knew it was worth checking out, as it was the nearest hotel to Jack's dojo. He pointed the Ford Sierra toward South Dublin. The traffic was dense, but he was in no hurry—thanks to Tommy's identification, he knew he was on the right track.

He arrived at Stephen's Green and circled it three times before finding a parking space. He slipped a coin into the meter and walked the hundred yards to the hotel. As he approached the revolving doors, a porter bid him good day and tipped his bowler hat.

Joey pushed through the famous doors and was immediately taken aback by the sheer class and luxury the place exuded. Pleasant memories came flooding back. Five years earlier, he had been invited to a wedding there and stayed overnight. A local businessman, John McGarry, had invited him to his eldest daughter's wedding as thanks. McGarry had been extorted by local thugs for protection money, and Joey had been assigned to the case. After months of painstaking surveillance, he had put the two main culprits behind bars for eight years. Grateful beyond measure, McGarry insisted that Joey attend the wedding. He had been booked into a luxury suite with instructions to indulge himself. For once, Joey saw how the other half lived—and he savoured every second.

At the reception desk, he was greeted by the young and pretty Nicola.

"May I help you, Sir?" she smiled.

"Hopefully," said Joey, showing his detective's badge. "We're looking for a person who might help us with a pending investigation. He may have been on your guest list."

He pulled the mugshot from his pocket and showed it to her.

"Have you seen this man? He might be a guest."

By the look of surprise on Nicola's face, Joey knew he had struck gold.

She seemed reluctant at first.

"I'd be very grateful for any information," Joey pressed gently. "This is a very serious matter."

She swallowed hard. "Yes, I recognise him—it's Mr. Falconetti. He's a guest here—or at least, he was. He checked out earlier today. He wasn't due to leave until tomorrow, but he said he had urgent family business. He was so nice. I hope it's not too serious."

Joey knew time was against him. A glance at the four clocks behind the desk—showing New York, London, Tokyo, and Sydney—told him it was 3 p.m. Greenwich Mean Time. "Do you know what time he checked out?"

"I don't know—I wasn't on duty. But I can check the guest folio," she said.

She opened the leather-bound ledger and flipped to the last page. Written neatly was: Signature Suite – Mr. Giovanni Falconetti – Bill paid in full – Check-out time 9:28 a.m.

"He checked out at 9:30, sir."

"I'd like to speak with the person who was on duty, if possible."

"Of course," she replied. "Gerry Carolan was on duty. He finished at 1 p.m. He's off for two days."

"Do you know where I can find him?"

"Well, when he finishes at 1 p.m., he usually has a sandwich and a pint of Guinness in O'Donoghue's pub down the road. He often stays into the late afternoon, especially if there's music."

"Can you describe him?" Joey asked quickly.

"Yes. Gerry's in his late fifties, with neatly trimmed salt-and-pepper hair. Slim build, above average height, distinctive looking—and as usual, he'll be wearing a suit."

With that, Joey was gone through the revolving door and into the bustling street. O'Donoghue's pub was only a stone's throw from the hotel. Joey knew it well; he had often gone for the music, the good pint of Guinness, and the banter.

He pushed through the door into the bar and down the narrow corridor that ran its length. To his right was the small space reserved for musicians. There was no music yet, just four loud Americans enjoying Irish coffees and Baileys.

The stools to the left and the barstools were only partly occupied. It was quiet. He didn't see any familiar faces or anyone who resembled Gerry Carolan. He did, however, recognise one of the barmen on duty—Ciaran. Joey nodded to him and continued toward the back room.

He walked into the dimly lit space, which received little natural light. Cigarette smoke clung heavily in the air. The atmosphere was laid back, the room half full with tourists and students. There was laughter as some sampled their first pints of Guinness. It was too early for the regulars, who were still at work.

As his eyes adjusted to the gloom, he spotted his man. In the far right corner, on a couch seat near the service hatch, sat Gerry. Nicola had been spot on—he looked every inch the distinguished, well-groomed man she described. There was no mistaking him. A pint of Guinness, minus a mouthful, rested on the table before him. A cigarette smouldered in the ashtray beside it, while Gerry, seemingly aloof to the world, was engrossed in his copy of the Irish Independent.

Joey walked towards the table where an unoccupied stool stood. "Excuse me, sir—Mister Carolan?" asked Joey softly.

The man put down his newspaper and made eye contact. His pale blue eyes beamed with intelligence. "Yes, guilty. To whom do I owe the pleasure, sir?"

He spoke the Queen's English with eloquence and clarity. Joey took his badge from his inside pocket. "My name is Detective Sergeant Maloney from Store Street. Your colleague Nicola told me that I might find you here. I'm looking for information on one of your guests, a Mr. Falconetti, who could help us with an ongoing enquiry." Joey pointed to the stool. "May I?"

"Certainly," came the reply. "How exciting. I will help you in any way I can. Can I offer you a pint of Guinness, Detective Maloney—or some other beverage?"

"It's a bit early in the day, but why not. I'll keep you company. A Guinness will be fine."

With that, Gerry stood up, put his head through the service hatch, and ordered a pint of Arthur G.

Joey shifted on his stool, trying to get comfortable. "What can you tell me about Mr. Falconetti—especially when he checked out this morning?"

Gerry took a puff from his cigarette and blew the smoke out slowly. It curled lazily into the air. "He was a charming man, always courteous and impeccably dressed. A man who seemed to appreciate the finer things in life. Strikingly handsome and of athletic build."

"One pint of Guinness coming up!" came a shout from the service hatch. Gerry reached up and placed the creamy pint in front of Joey.

"Cheers," said Joey. "Did you notice anything unusual during his stay, or when he left this morning? Did he take a taxi?"

Gerry took a sip from his pint and set it back on the table. "I saw him in the company of a young Dublin man on two or three occasions. And this morning, he checked out earlier than expected to attend to some urgent business back home. I do hope it's nothing too serious.

He was a lovely man—left me a handsome tip, too. He didn't order a taxi, but he did ring down and ask for the number of British Airways. He seemed to be in a great hurry. That's about all I can tell you, Sergeant Maloney."

Joey rubbed his chin. "Okay, so he left in a hurry and didn't order a taxi. Some acquaintance must have brought him to the airport, then."

He lifted the creamy pint from the table and took a gulp. He put the glass back and licked his lips. "Ah, there's nothing like a good pint of Guinness. You just can't beat it."

"I'll certainly vouch for that, sir," smiled Gerry, as he, in turn, brought the glass to his mouth and drank the hearty beverage.

"Could you give an accurate description of the man you saw Falconetti with?" enquired Joey.

"Oh, I certainly can. He was of average height, slim build, plain-looking, with short dark hair and a well-trimmed beard. A pleasant individual, but nothing stood out. Not someone you'd look twice at. Certainly not like Mr. Falconetti."

Joey knew immediately who he was talking about. There was no need to wade through a bunch of mug shots. It fitted the description of Robbie Maher—less the beard—to perfection.

Joey finished his pint and thanked Gerry for his cooperation and the valuable information he had provided. Gerry replied that he was more than happy to be of service and would be available for any further questions.

Joey looked at his wristwatch. It was 4 p.m. He turned his back and headed for the exit. Gerry lit another cigarette and resumed reading the Irish Independent. Joey knew that time wasn't on his side. In 1990, the world wasn't digitalised. Information was slow to travel from A to B. There were no smartphones, SMS, MMS, or internet—just landlines, telex, and fax machines that often ran out of paper. There was also the hand-held phone from Motorola, weighing over a kilogram and nicknamed *The Brick*. But it was mainly used by wealthy financiers and entrepreneurs.

Joey hurried back to the hotel. He needed a phone quickly—and he needed to contact British Airways. When he walked into the lobby, Nicola was still on duty. He rushed over to the reception.

"Did you find Gerry, sir?" she enquired.

"I did indeed, but now I need your telephone and a number for British Airways in a hurry," he gasped.

She gave him the phone number and handed him the receiver, telling him to dial 9 for an outside line. The phone rang for what seemed like hours before a soft female voice answered: "British Airways—how may I be of service?"

Joey introduced himself and explained the urgency of the situation. He asked Nicola for a pen and paper.

"Did anyone by the name of Giovanni Falconetti book a flight to Italy this morning—from either Dublin or Belfast? I'll also need departure and arrival times."

"Please hold the line, sir," said the gentle voice. Minutes passed, leaving Joey champing at the bit.

The receiver clicked and the soft voice returned: "I'm sorry, sir, but no one by that name booked a flight with British Airways to Italy—or elsewhere—this morning."

The irritation showed in Joey's voice. "Are you a hundred percent sure, miss?"

The voice remained calm: "I'm certain, sir. I even checked twice. I'm very sorry, but there's nothing else I can do."

"Okay. Thank you for your time and help, miss," said Joey, as he noted the departure and arrival times of several flights to Italy that day. *Fuck that for a game of soldiers,* thought Joey as he handed back the receiver. His wristwatch told him it was 4:30 p.m. And he was gone in a jiffy—out of the famous revolving doors and into the noisy afternoon street.

People don't realise that now is all there ever is; there is no past or future except as memory or anticipation in your mind.

Eckhard Tolle

CHAPTER
Twenty
Palermo - Italy

Giovanni Falconetti had boarded his connecting flight from London to Palermo at 3:30 p.m. The plane had taken off at 4:00 p.m., right on schedule. He was ensconced in an electric reclining business-class seat. Food and drink were available at the touch of a button, served by the very friendly air stewardesses. The flight time was just under three hours to Palermo. He ordered finger food and a double twelve-year-old Macallan whiskey.

He reclined his seat, lifted the amber-coloured nectar to his lips, and savoured the rich medley of flavours the famous whiskey had to offer. They burst across his palate—peppery clove notes rising in a grand finale as the liquid hit the back of his throat. He licked his lips, and a broad smile spread across his face. If the whiskey could be compared to music, then it belonged to the realm of the symphony orchestra.

The APB issued by the Irish police to Interpol, whose headquarters were in Lyon, as well as to their British and Italian counterparts, hadn't come up trumps. Giovanni had entered Ireland using his official Italian passport, but he had booked his outgoing flight using another. He was the owner of three passports in all—Italian, Swiss, and French.

His Italian passport bore his real name. He had used the French passport to book his flight and to pass through security. He was particularly amused by this passport, as it bore the name of Arsène Lupin—a fictional gentleman thief and master of disguise created in 1905 by French writer Maurice Leblanc. He loved using it, for it both amused and excited him.

Every time he flashed it, a little voice in his head would say: "What a neck and balls you have, Giovanni." And he would smile. He had also altered his appearance slightly, wearing a black Versace cap and dark sunglasses as he passed through security in Belfast and London. Better safe than sorry, he had thought. Nobody in security had batted an eyelid.

Giovanni descended the steps of the Boeing 737 and stepped onto the tarmac of Falcone Borsellino Airport beneath a pleasant autumn sun. It felt good to be home. With his designer bag in his right hand, he walked toward the terminal building. Security was a mere formality—he waltzed through with ease. There was no need for the cap or the sunglasses. After all, he was on home territory now, and many of the carabinieri and customs officials were on the Cosa Nostra payroll. So no sweat.

It was just after 7:00 p.m., and the airport was quite busy—mainly with holidaymakers making their way back to the Italian continent or to Europe itself. Their vacations were over. It wasn't a large airport: the structure consisted of a single terminal, a total width of 450 acres, and two runways. It ranked as the eighth busiest airport in Italy.

The walk to the car park was a short two hundred metres. His red stallion awaited patiently for its master's return. He extracted the red key from his pocket and pressed on the black stallion emblem set against the yellow background. The car doors popped open. He opened the driver's door and slung his travel bag onto the passenger seat. Lowering himself into the beige leather seat, he made himself comfortable. The scent of the leather filled his nostrils, an olfactory sensation he never tired of.

He put the key in the ignition and turned it clockwise. The Ferrari Testarossa's twelve-cylinder, 390-bhp engine fired up with a roar—the result of decades of engineering to produce a throaty rumble, connecting the lucky driver to his machine. Giovanni smiled, pushed the gear shift forward into first gear, and drove toward the exit and the parking machine. The disadvantage of a Ferrari was that it sat too low to allow him to slide the ticket into the slot from the driver's seat.

He climbed out, punched the ticket into the machine, and watched as it swallowed the slip. A four-figure price flashed up on the screen in bold letters. Tourists might have been alarmed at the amount demanded, but it was in Italian lira—about forty euros. He paid the fee with his gold credit card and slid back into the driver's seat. The barrier lifted.

He eased the Ferrari out of the car park, and a few hundred yards later, he was beyond the airport complex and on the open road to Trappeto. His villa was located on the heights overlooking the village, a few miles west, with a commanding view of the coastline. He always preferred the coast road—it was longer than the direct route but infinitely more pleasant. He was looking forward to the forty-mile drive home.

Pressing down on the accelerator, the V12 engine roared, jolting the Ferrari forward. The needle on the rev counter lurched into the red zone as Giovanni banged the gear stick into third. The enormous thrust and torque hurled him back against the leather seat. It was a crushing sensation, like a thump in the lower back—exhilarating, almost better than sex, though not quite.

It was good to be back on home soil. Yet the feeling of failure haunted him. For the first time, he had missed his target. The scene replayed over and over in his head. He had had Jack Hopkins in his sights—an easy shot. Then, in the split second he squeezed the trigger, Hopkins had vanished. As though someone had whispered in his ear to move at that precise moment. His guardian angel, perhaps.

It was uncanny. Disturbing. It spooked him. What the hell, he thought—did the guy have superpowers, like fuckin' Batman or something? Now he knew there was something special about Jack

Hopkins. He wasn't looking forward to the telephone call across the big pond to his cousin in Manhattan, nor to refunding the down payment. Yeah—that really sucked. No, not good at all.

The drive along the coast road gradually relaxed him, lifting his mood. Twenty-five minutes later, he reached Trappeto on the east side. He decided to drive through the village instead of bypassing it. To say it was quiet was an understatement. The tourists had gone, leaving the village back to its three thousand inhabitants instead of nearly thirty thousand in the summer months. He drove through and exited on the west side. It was a short ten-minute drive to his luxurious four-hundred-square-metre villa.

It was just 8:00 p.m. when he arrived. The sun was still shining, clinging stubbornly to the horizon; its shift was nearly over. He flicked a button, and the big wrought-iron gates swung inward. He drove down a tarmac slope and pressed another button. One of the double garage doors lifted upwards, sliding slowly along aluminium rails fixed to the ceiling. He parked the Ferrari behind the Porsche 911 Carrera S.

He slid out of the driver's seat, retrieved his travel bag, bleeped the garage door shut, and walked up the steps to the main entrance. The 12-by-4-metre swimming pool shimmered invitingly. He pulled the keys from his pocket and unlocked the front door.

The villa was a two-storey dwelling designed by a famous architect from Naples, whom the "family" employed regularly. A clever and tasteful mixture of concrete, glass, and steel, it was a home fit for Hollywood stars. Naturally, it was equipped with every modern convenience. The furniture was unmistakably of Italian design and manufacture. The kitchen was a state-of-the-art showcase of Carrara marble. Giovanni liked cooking, and he was good at it.

He never tired of playing gourmet chef for friends and family in his luxurious canteen, as he called it. He opened the door to the main bedroom—his bedroom—located just beside the spacious living room. He threw his travel bag onto the bed and stripped completely naked. Sliding open the bay window, he stepped out onto the tropical hardwood Ipe decking. The wooden terrace ran the length of the villa, stretching from the kitchen to his bedroom.

It was thirty metres long and six metres wide. The architect had proposed mahogany or Ipe decking because it was extremely resistant to moisture, insects, and warping—practically guaranteed for life. The choice had been between mahogany and Ipe, and Giovanni had opted for the latter. It was rarer, more distinctive.

The red sun was just dipping behind the mountains to the west, signalling the end of the day, as a soft, cool breeze suddenly stirred. He could feel the chill on his bare skin. He walked toward the blue LED-lit pool, positioned directly in front of the living room, and dived headfirst into the water kept at 25 degrees centigrade. He swam continuously for approximately thirty minutes—roughly the equivalent of a kilometre—part of his strict daily workout. He stepped out of the pool and rinsed himself under the solar shower.

Night fell quickly, descending like a curtain of asphalt, and Venus made its appearance in a cloudless sky. A couple of bats turned up for duty, flying in zigzag and circular motions through the darkness—a hunting technique used to confuse their prey. Each could devour over six thousand insects in a single night. They were the only true flying mammals, and despite their fearful appearance, they were invaluable creatures. Giovanni was thankful for their presence. Without them, the garden and house would have been infested with mosquitoes.

Giovanni thought of Jack, and a cool liquid ran down the length of his spine. He shuddered. He knew it was far from over—perhaps only just beginning. Heading into his spacious bathroom, he towelled himself dry. He was exhausted. He crashed onto his king-size bed, still bare, and slept soundly for eight hours—a deep, restorative slumber.

On the other side of the ocean, it was just after 1 a.m., and Joey Falconetti was closing up one of his Manhattan restaurants. He had just finished tallying the day's takings. Business had been good as usual—more than ten thousand dollars. Fridays, marking the start of the weekend, were always profitable. Lighting a cigar, he relaxed into his leather armchair. He plucked the phone handset from his desk and scrolled through the list of registered names. He stopped at "G" and dialled a Sicilian number.

The ringing phone pulled Giovanni unwillingly from his deep sleep. He turned his head toward the alarm clock on the bedside locker; the digital red numbers glowed: 7:10 a.m. "Who the hell is ringing at this hour?" he thought. Straightening up in bed, he lifted the Sony cordless handset from its base.

"Buongiorno, cugino," said the voice on the other end. "I hope you have good news for me."

Giovanni rubbed the sleep from his eyes. "Hello, cousin Joey. Thank you for the early morning wake-up call. I really appreciate it."

He then went on to explain, in minute detail, what had transpired. Joey listened for five minutes without once interrupting.

"So you're telling me the bastard is still alive?"

Giovanni sighed. "I know, cousin. I'll wire the money back to you first thing next week."

Joey blew out a puff of blue smoke and watched it drift slowly toward the ceiling. "No, cousin. You keep the money. But you go back there, and you finish the job. You always get the job done."

"I'm not going back there in a hurry, cousin. We have to let things cool down. I'm sure they've figured everything out. But hell, there's no proof. I'm sure they found the McMillan TAC-50. That would have been easy—we didn't have enough time to hide it properly."

Joey stubbed out his cigar in the large glass ashtray on his wooden desk and stood up. "Okay, cousin. Let me know when you're ready to move. But don't wait too long. And what if we drew Hopkins to us?"

Giovanni got out of bed, phone in hand, and walked naked toward the sliding patio door overlooking the wooden terrace. "What do you mean, cousin?"

"Leave it with me. I'll try to come up with something. Ciao, bello. I'll be in touch."

Giovanni tossed the phone onto the bed and pressed the button on the patio door, turning it green, before sliding it open. It moved silently along the aluminium rail. He stepped out onto the deck and breathed in the fresh morning air. The sun had risen, the sky a clear blue. A flock of sparrows darted across the horizon—it was mealtime. Giovanni dived into the pool. He hadn't closed the roller shutter, so the water had lost a degree or two overnight. It was brisk, refreshing. His daily routine always began with a thirty-minute swim. He wanted to wipe clean the cluttered hard disk of his conscience, overloaded with useless information. He needed to let go. Carpe diem, he reminded himself.

Our greatest glory is not in never falling, but in rising every time we fall.

Confucius

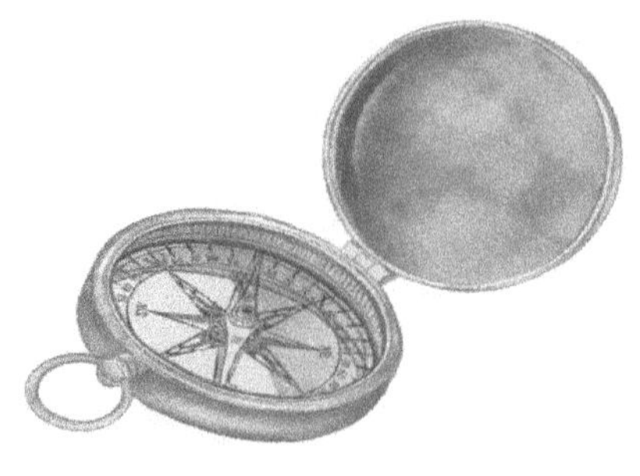

CHAPTER
Twenty-One
Dublin - Ireland

It was Saturday, and Jack awoke from a deep slumber at 6:30 a.m., just as he did most mornings. He never needed an alarm clock. He had been dreaming of Akiko and what should have been an idyllic life in Okinawa. He hadn't been in touch with his ex-father-in-law for some time now, and a pang of guilt gnawed at him. The man's phone number was etched into his mind, but Jack just couldn't make that call—too painful. Still, he resolved that he would have to change. He would ring him during the week.

He had also planned to ring the hospital later that morning to find out from Doctor Molloy how the operation had gone—hopefully well.

He got out of bed, stretched, and did a few neck exercises. Then he pulled back the curtains to discover a dark, murky morning. He put on his tracksuit bottoms and a T-shirt before heading into the kitchen, where he poured himself a glass of freshly pressed orange juice—squeezed the night before and stored in the fridge.

He then stepped out onto the balcony. A cold shiver ran down his spine as memories of the shooting flooded back. He forced the images away, slipping into the state of getsu-mei-no-michi—total awareness—before beginning his daily routine.

By 8 a.m., Jack stepped back into the kitchen. Despite the chill of the morning, sweat clung to his body and hunger gnawed at his stomach. But first, he needed a shower. He stripped off in the bathroom, stepped into the Italian shower, and set the water to hot. He gave himself a thorough scrub, then gradually twisted the dial to cold. He stayed under as long as he could bear.

Stepping out, he towelled himself down vigorously, slung a bathrobe over his shoulders, and headed for the kitchen. He set the kettle to boil, dropped an egg into a pot of water, and slid two slices of Brennan's bread into the toaster. From the fridge, he pulled Kerrygold butter and marmalade. He tossed a Lyons green label tea bag into the teapot and poured in the hot water. Breakfast was nearly ready.

It felt strange dining alone without Sophie. The sadness pressed in, but hopefully it would be only for a few days. After breakfast, replenished and feeling somewhat lighter, he flicked on the transistor radio and tuned to a station that played almost nothing but music. He had no appetite for news channels or gossip.

In the bedroom, Jack stripped off his bathrobe and studied his reflection in the full-length mirror. He had lost some weight—unsurprising, given recent events. Still, his body remained ripped, the definition of his muscles even sharper now. He looked good. He pulled on a pair of blue denim jeans, a matching shirt, and white sneakers. His black leather jacket would hold off the morning chill. He decided to walk down to the Yacht pub for coffee—and maybe some casual, friendly conversation, something he sorely needed. He would ring the hospital from there.

It was a short fifteen-minute stroll to the Yacht. The day was dank, a little depressing, but it was autumn after all. The sun was there somewhere, hidden behind a mass of dark clouds. Jack strode purposefully along the seaside of the road, inhaling the sharp scent of iodine carried from sea and seaweed alike.

Arriving at the Yacht, Jack pushed the bar door open. He preferred the bar to the lounge—especially on Saturday mornings, when the atmosphere buzzed. A cloud of smoke hung lazily in the air, and men buried their heads in newspapers opened to the horse racing column. The experts gave their tips, the patrons offered theirs, and the heated debate bounced back and forth. Someone always had a "sure winner."

Jack's entrance caused a stir. Heads lifted, conversations paused, elbows nudged. Admired and feared in equal measure, he had become a familiar face—his story splashed across television and newspapers for more than a month. Nearly everyone in Dublin recognised him now. Some even asked for his autograph—an attention Jack found deeply embarrassing.

Martin, one of the barmen, was just topping off a pint when he noticed Jack. "How are you, Jack? You're looking in great shape. I hope Sophie's alright."

"Thanks, Martin," Jack replied. "I feel good. I've got to ring Doctor Molloy later to see how the operation went."

"Can I get you a pint, Jack?"

"No thanks, Martin. Bit early in the day for me," Jack laughed. "I'll have an Americano and a glass of water when you're ready."

"Not a bother," Martin said with a grin.

A few men came over to shake Jack's hand and offer drinks, but he politely declined. He moved to the far end of the brown oak bar and perched on a high wooden stool. Picking up a newspaper, he read the bold headline splashed across page one: "Unemployment rate falls from 17% to 12.9%. Lowest since 1969."

"Well, that makes for a pleasant change," Jack thought. A welcome break from the usual drab headlines.

"One Americano coming up," Martin announced, smiling.

"Grand, thanks, Martin. Good news on page one for a change," Jack remarked.

"That's for sure—but it won't last long. Back to the usual misery soon enough," came the sarcastic reply.

Turning to page two, Jack scanned a double-column article: "Police are still investigating a shooting incident in Dollymount early Friday morning and are seeking an individual to assist with inquiries." One person had been seriously injured, another lightly. The report suggested a possible drug connection. No names were given, as the law forbade disclosure while an investigation was ongoing. The article bore the byline of Zack Cohen, the renowned crime journalist.

Jack flipped through the rest of the paper, finishing on the sports pages—a more cheerful note. He drained his coffee and glanced up at the big clock behind the bar. It was nearing 11:30 a.m.—time to call the hospital. He asked Martin if he could use the phone behind the bar, assuring him it was a local call.

"Not a bother, Jack," Martin replied with a smile, opening the hatch and waving him through.

Jack dialled the Mater Private Hospital and waited. The reply was swift.

"Mater Private, how may I help you?" chirped a jovial voice.

"Hi, my name is Jack Hopkins. Could you put me through to Doctor Molloy's service, please? I'm inquiring about my girlfriend, Sophie Gautier, who underwent surgery this morning."

"Hold the line, please, sir. I'll connect you now."

Metallic noises and electronic beeps echoed through the line. Then another voice answered.

"Hello, Doctor Molloy's surgery. How can I help you?"

Jack reiterated his request.

"Okay, Mr. Hopkins, please hold the line."

A moment later, a familiar voice came on.

"Hello, Mr. Hopkins, Doctor Molloy here. How are you this morning?"

"I'm fine," Jack replied.

"The operation went as planned, though it took longer than expected—four hours instead of three. Her shoulder was in terrible condition, with significant bone and soft tissue damage. Her collarbone was broken as well. To realign the shoulder bones, we used specialised hardware: plates, screws, and pins. We also performed bone grafting and repaired ligaments and tendons. But all in all, it went according to plan. She's back in her room now, still under anaesthetic. Come by around 1:30 p.m., and she should be fully conscious."

"Thank you, Doctor Molloy," Jack said. "How long will the healing process take?"

A cough sounded down the line.

"The collarbone should heal in about two months. Unfortunately, she'll need to wear an arm sling for that time, and she'll require help with daily tasks. The shoulder is more complicated. Given the extensive damage, I'd estimate at least six months for recovery, and a year for full strength. Regular quarterly check-ups will be needed. Physiotherapy will be essential to optimise healing. She'll also be on pain-killers for several weeks. I'll recommend an excellent physiotherapist—well known and respected in sporting circles."

"Thanks again, Doctor Molloy. We'll link up this afternoon."

Jack hung up and returned to the bar. He ordered a pint of Guinness, his thoughts heavy. The damage was worse than he'd hoped. Physical wounds were one thing, but mental scars were another battle entirely. Sophie had only just begun to recover from her first ordeal. Her nightmares had eased down to three or four a month—and she was still on Xanax. Now this would reopen everything.

What a mess, he thought. He couldn't stop blaming himself. Was Joey Falconetti going to haunt him forever? No. It was time to put that bastard away for good and end the horror story. He had already lost Akiko. He couldn't lose Sophie, too. It was time for action.

"Everything okay, Jack?" asked Martin as he placed a creamy pint of Guinness on the bar in front of him. "You look very perplexed."

"Thanks, Martin. It could be worse. Anyway, I'll deal with it." Jack lifted the pint and took a long gulp. The familiar taste instantly steadied him. A good dent in the glass already—after all, they say Guinness is good for you. Now, it was time to plan ahead, he thought.

Jack lingered over the rest of his pint, lost in thought, piecing together fragments in his mind. When he drained the last drop, he slid off the stool. The bar had grown louder, the blue haze of smoke thicker. Pints lined the counter, ready to be topped off by the barman's expert hand. Jack gave Martin a nod of farewell before stepping out through the main door.

Outside, the sun fought in vain to break through the blanket of grey clouds. When it did manage, the light was pale and lukewarm. After half a mile's walk, Jack reached his apartment, where he forced down a light lunch. His appetite simply wasn't there.

The Fiat Spider roared to life at the first turn of the key. Jack relished the gnarly carburettor growl as the twin carbs pulled in the cold morning air. Exiting the car park, he headed toward the Mater Private Hospital. Traffic was light, and twenty minutes later, he was easing the Spider into the freshly tarmacked hospital lot. The Mater was clearly thriving.

He introduced himself at the reception and was directed to Doctor Molloy's surgery on the ground floor. Molloy greeted him with a warm smile and a firm, sincere handshake. Much of what he said echoed the phone call earlier, stressing again that Sophie's recovery would demand patience and time.

"It's not every day I have patients who come in with high-calibre bullet wounds," Molloy remarked with a half-smile. "She was extremely lucky. Somebody, somewhere, was certainly saying prayers for her. The road ahead will be challenging, Jack—physically and mentally. I can recommend a sophrologist and a psychiatrist if the need arises. But for now, I'm sure you're anxious to see Sophie. She's resting comfortably in a private room on the first floor, with a view over the park. Allow me to show you the way."

Beckoning Jack, the doctor led him into the corridor. They walked in silence until they reached the lift. Molloy pressed the button and, with a soft chime, the Otis doors slid open immediately—lucky timing. A woman's voice announced their arrival on the first floor moments later, and they stepped out. Turning right, they walked down the hallway until they came to Room 92. Molloy knocked gently.

"Come in, please," called a tired voice.

Inside, Sophie was propped upright in bed, slowly spooning yoghurt while half-watching a television programme about Greece and its many islands—fashionable destinations these days. Her eyes brightened when they landed on Jack.

"I'll leave you two alone," said Molloy. "We'll keep you here a few more days, Sophie, just to be sure there are no complications or side effects after surgery. Jack, don't hesitate to reach out to me if needed."

"Thank you, Doctor Molloy. I'll bear that in mind."

Once the door closed behind the doctor, Sophie seemed suddenly smaller, frailer. Her right arm rested heavily in a sling, an IV drip in her left delivering steady painkillers. Her complexion was pale, almost translucent.

"Oh, ma chérie, I'm so happy to see you," she whispered, tears welling.

Jack perched carefully on the edge of the bed and wrapped her in his arms as gently as he could. Warm tears slid down her cheeks, and his own eyes blurred in response. He held her longer than he intended, reluctant to let go, but eventually released her and softly dabbed her face dry with a Kleenex. She smiled faintly, and their lips met in a tender, lingering kiss—a lover's kiss.

"I brought you something to pass the time," Jack said with a smile. On his way over, he had stopped at a stationery shop in Fairview and picked up a few women's magazines—fashion, home décor—the things Sophie enjoyed. He had also bought a novel much praised by critics: *Mackenzie's Mountain* by Linda Howard.

"I'll be very busy," she teased, her smile wider now.

"Hopefully it'll ease the boredom these next few days," Jack replied, leafing absently through the novel.

Sophie then broached the idea of going to France to convalesce with her parents for a few weeks. Their village near Saint-Malo in Brittany was quiet and peaceful, and she hadn't seen them in some time. It would be a chance to rest—and to relieve Jack of some of the burden of care.

Her parents had only been told she was in a minor car accident, suffering scrapes, bruises, and a mild concussion. The truth—that she had been shot—was unthinkable to share. Jack wondered how long that secret could realistically be kept. They had already insisted she be repatriated immediately, mistrusting Irish medical care. Convincing them she was in the best of hands here had taken all Jack's persuasion.

Eventually, Jack left Sophie in good spirits, promising to return at the same hour tomorrow. Outside, he breathed deeply of the cool evening air, relieved to be free of the hospital's suffocating atmosphere. To him, hospitals were oppressive places, filled with bitter memories.

Sliding behind the wheel of the Spider, Jack glanced at the dashboard clock: just before 5 p.m. After the hospital gloom, he longed for music, laughter, and a pint of Guinness. He knew exactly where to go. Steering onto the streets, he aimed for O'Donoghue's in Merrion Row near Saint Stephen's Green—a Saturday afternoon hub of music and banter, where familiar faces were always likely.

Luck was on his side: he found a space in Hume Street, right behind O'Donoghue's. After locking the car, he flicked a discreet switch under the rear wing that disabled the fuel pump—his mechanic's clever idea. Any thief who hotwired the car would make it only a few hundred yards before stalling.

Jack strode the short distance and pushed through the pub's double doors. Inside, the place was already alive. Music spilt from the little 'select' salon to his right. He immediately recognised Johnny Ryan on banjo, joined by a fiddler, a tin whistle player, and a hulking man named Finbar pounding the bodhrán. Finbar doubled as the pub's unofficial bouncer—his violent temper as notorious as his size.

Johnny, from a settled traveller family, was quiet by nature and brother to the famed piper Paddy Ryan. Sober, he was counted among the finest banjo players in Ireland. The group was in full stride, hammering out a lively jig called *The Flowing Tide*.

"The usual, Jack?" came a shout from behind the bar.

"Right on, Ciaran," Jack called back.

He made his way to the end of the counter just as a large American vacated the prime stool near the serving hatch—the perfect vantage point to watch the room. He slid into place as a creamy pint was set before him on a Guinness mat.

"That one's on the house," Ciaran grinned. "Good health to you, Jack. You've earned it."

"And *Sláinte* to you," Jack replied with a nod.

Recent events had turned Jack into a local celebrity, even a hero, in the small city. Nearly everyone wanted to shake his hand, pat him on the back, or buy him a drink. More often than not, he politely refused their generous offers. He tried to limit himself to three pints maximum, which was the legal driving limit for alcohol consumption at the time. And absolutely no drinking during the week. There was no way he was returning to his bad old habits. He now drank strictly for pleasure. He took a mouthful from the creamy pint. It hit the spot immediately. There was a well-thumbed copy of the Irish Independent on the bar. Jack picked it up and opened it to the crossword page. Bingo—he was in luck; no one had attempted to fill in any of the blank boxes. Jack smiled to himself. There was nothing more enjoyable or relaxing than a pint of Guinness and a crossword.

The pub was filling up. It was becoming difficult to move in the narrow passageway. After all, it was a hugely popular tourist destination—the place to be. A victim of its own popularity, yet a gold mine for the publican. The lads were still churning out the tunes, switching from jigs to reels, with the occasional traditional or folk song tossed in for the tourists. There were always foreign groupies eager to get better acquainted with the musicians, much to the performers' delight. They were always ready to show young maidens the true meaning of Irish hospitality—and, of course, Irish culture at its very best.

Jack saw a familiar face battling his way from the far end of the bar. It was the curly-haired, jovial-faced Eamon McCann. He was popularly known as "the mathematician," since he taught maths at a high level. He was highly intelligent, well-read, and had travelled far and wide. And he was always in good fettle, hence excellent company. As the Irish would say, he was "sound."

Jack waved, and a broad smile spread across Eamon's cherubic face. As soon as he reached within arm's distance, he pulled Jack into a heartfelt, lingering hug. Jack wondered if he was ever going to let go.

"Jesus, Jack, it's great to see you. It's been far too long. Where've you been hiding? You're looking great despite all your trials and tribulations. How does it feel to be famous?" he beamed.

"Great to see you too, Eamon. And as for the fame part— believe me, I could do without it," Jack smiled. "What are you having? A pint of Arthur G as usual, I imagine?"

"How is Sophie, Jack? She must be quite shaken after the recent turmoil."

Jack let out a soft sigh. "She sure is, Eamon, but she's on the mend. It's going to be a long, time-consuming process, and patience will be vital. My biggest fear is that there could be deep, indelible psychological scars—and that's the most worrying part."

Eamon's pint arrived, and they joyfully clinked glasses. Jack felt emotional. There was something special about renewed friendship and the deep joy true companionship could bring. The virtues of empathy, loyalty, trust, honesty, and respect—values he fondly embraced—came to mind.

They joked and bantered. Jack loved Eamon's company; he was both witty and intelligent. The time slipped swiftly by. The old clock behind the bar indicated that it was coming up to 8 p.m. Eamon ordered more pints. Jack, however, was adamant about sticking to his quota of three pints. This was his second. One more, and that was it.

Eamon had fantastic stories to tell about his summer holidays in Nepal and Tibet—the roof of the world. He always went somewhere exotic for his breaks, always for a month, and always solo. He told Jack he had been deeply shaken by the sheer poverty he'd witnessed. He had taken a bag of biros to distribute to the children in the streets of Nepal, but it had been a big mistake. The kids went wild for them, even fighting among themselves to grab the Westerner's precious gift. He had offered about a hundred biros and had quickly become the centre of attention, surrounded by more than fifty children, all clamouring and expecting more. It had turned unsafe.

Luckily, a policeman on duty came to his rescue, chasing off the kids with a few sharp whacks of his baton on their skinny legs. Eamon confessed he had felt terrible afterwards. What should have been a fulfilling and pleasurable experience had become a bad dream. The policeman advised him never to give anything, especially money. Eamon had received the message loud and clear. He admitted to Jack that he had never been so scared in his entire life.

Jack ordered two more pints. It was 9:30 p.m., and punters were still squeezing their way into the bar and down the narrow aisle. Eamon torpedoed Jack with questions about the incident on Dollymount Beach. He was fascinated by the whole affair. Whenever anyone mentioned the incident, Jack was immediately seized by a metallic smell in his memory. He had wanted to erase it from his mind completely, like wiping a hard drive. He left out the gory details and told Eamon that, thanks to his intense Okinawan training, he was lucky to be alive.

He had been bruised, battered, and broken, but he was still casting a shadow and back in form. Eamon noticed Jack's discomfort and knew it was time to stop asking. Time slipped by, and Eamon ordered two more pints.

"Not for me, my friend. I'll have a pint of Ballygowan mineral water with ice and a slice or two of lemon. That's me for the night," Jack smiled.

"Fair play to you, Jack. I admire your discipline. I wish I could emulate you," laughed Eamon.

Jack took a gulp of mineral water and set the pint glass back on the wooden counter. "So, when are you going to settle down, Eamon, and let some woman make a decent man of you?" he smiled.

Eamon laughed out loud. "Now there's a question, my friend. Sure, who'd have me? I'm a cranky old divil most of the time, too set in my ways. You only see the good side of me. I think I'll probably end up a cranky old bachelor. For the moment, an odd fling now and then suits me just fine."

"I think everyone has a soulmate waiting somewhere, Eamon. It's only a matter of time—the sooner, the better, I'd say. It's great to be able to share life with a loved one. Then again, it's nice to be single and carefree, just like yourself. The only trouble with having a loved one is losing them."

"I'll drink to that," laughed Eamon, lifting his pint to his lips.

They continued chatting and joking. Eamon ordered himself another pint of Guinness. It was 10:30 p.m. The pub was jam-packed, and people were still trying to make it through the cramped corridor. Some were there just to be able to say they had visited the world-famous pub while on holiday. Others were there for the drink.

Jack finished his mineral water and bid goodnight to his good friend. He tapped him on the back. "It was great to see you again, Eamon. Be good, and stay as good as you look."

"Slán leat, Jack. Take care, and don't be a stranger. You know where to find me."

Jack decided to leave through the back door of the pub. There was no point struggling against the oncoming traffic in the narrow corridor, he thought. He exited into the dimly lit lane and walked the short twenty yards that opened onto Merrion Row. He was in high spirits. It had been great to see an old friend again. He turned right, then right again at the traffic lights into Ely Place. He walked fifty yards and turned right into Hume Street, where he had parked his Fiat Spider. The car was parked at the end of the road, facing Stephen's Green.

What he saw put an immediate damper on what had been a very enjoyable evening. Two lads in their early twenties were checking out his car. They were peering through the windows and tugging at the door handles. Jack had arrived just in time. He was only six yards away but had not yet signalled his presence.

One of the guys was tall and powerfully built. He appeared to be holding a Stanley knife in his right hand—just the tool for slashing the soft hood of the Spider. The other was small and skinny, carrying a screwdriver in his right hand, a long scar marking the left side of his face.

Jack stopped at the car. "Did ye find what you're looking for, lads?"

They didn't panic. "What the fuck—who are you?" snarled the big guy. The smaller one stood still, smirking.

"And who do you think I am?" Jack shot back.

The smaller guy walked towards him. "We were just admiring your lovely car, Mister, that's all," he smirked.

"Yeah, sure," said Jack. "Pull the other one. I don't think the Stanley knife or the screwdriver would impress a police officer—or a judge. Do you?"

The bigger guy suddenly sprang to life. "I know you, I've seen your face on TV and in the papers. You're the fuckin' Ninja—the guy who walloped the Mafia gang on Dollymount Strand." He then shouted over to his friend, "We should be scared, Anto. He's a real killer!"

Jack opened his two hands at chest height. "I don't want any trouble, lads. Just step away from the car and we're done. I won't file a complaint, and everyone can go on their merry way."

A vicious grin lined the smaller guy's face, accentuating his scar. "Okay, Mr. Ninja, give us a tenner and we'll be on our way. Let's just call it disturbance money."

"I don't have a tenner on me, only loose change," replied Jack.

"Well, that's gonna be a problem," said the big guy. "That's a nice watch you're wearing. We'll take that and whatever is in your pockets and in the car."

"Then you're gonna have to take the watch, because it was a present from my girlfriend, and I don't intend giving it up to two scumbags," retorted Jack. He wanted to make them angry, to push them into losing their cool.

The big guy started moving forward slowly, his smaller friend in tow. Jack carefully backed off along the pavement. He wanted the railings at his back—that way, he'd have both of them in his line of vision. He couldn't risk the small guy sneaking up behind him to jab the screwdriver into one of his kidneys. He'd seen enough of hospitals recently. Passersby glanced but kept walking. Nobody was prepared to play the hero, especially with a big thug wielding a Stanley knife. "Just keep walking and mind your own business" seemed to be the credo of the day. And, as usual, there wasn't a police officer in sight.

Now the railings pressed against his back. The two men edged forward across the wide pavement. The big guy stood at least six feet three, the smaller one barely five six. Jack was just shy of six feet himself. Defending against a blade in any form was never easy—you almost always ended up cut, or worse. Sensei Saito's constant advice echoed in his mind: *walk or run away whenever possible. You lose your honour but save your life.* Jack knew, however, that if he ran, his car would be shredded to pieces. That thought didn't appeal to him.

"So you do have a pair of balls," Jack laughed as the big guy came closer. His arms stayed at chest level, palms open. The little guy lingered just behind his larger friend, slightly to the left, close enough to see what was happening. Jack had him pinned in his in-built sonar.

They were now practically within arm's reach. The big guy lowered his head to the right as a feint and suddenly lunged with a vicious inward slashing strike aimed at Jack's face.

Jack stepped diagonally in, blocking with a powerful forearm strike. The Stanley knife flew from his hand under the force of the blow. In the same instant, Jack delivered a crushing teisho—a palm heel strike—to the man's nose, fracturing the bone. He followed up with a swift step-in, driving an elbow deep into the solar plexus. The man gasped, blood gushing from his nose, before collapsing to the pavement with a heavy thud.

The smaller guy hesitated, panic freezing him, then lunged with a right-handed thrust, the long screwdriver aiming for Jack's liver. Jack shifted back to absorb the attack, blocking downward with his forearm. He advanced quickly, pivoted, and seized his opponent by the shoulders. Using kiri otoshi—"the cutting down technique"—he slammed the man hard into the pavement. His head cracked against the concrete under the sheer torque of the move. The little guy lay semi-conscious.

The big man, however, had scrambled to retrieve the Stanley knife. He came forward, cursing, slashing left and right in a wild frenzy. Jack retreated, dodging the uncontrolled arcs.

When the brute thought he had Jack pinned against the railings, he lunged, driving the blade toward Jack's gut. Jack pivoted sharply to the right, employing tai sabaki to protect his vital organs, deflecting the blow with his forearm into his waiting hand.

Seizing the inside of the man's arm, Jack locked it firmly, then smashed an elbow strike into his head. Spinning a hundred and eighty degrees, he slipped his forearm under the thug's arm just above the elbow.

Pressing downward with his right hand while forcing upward with his left forearm, he wrenched. A sharp pop signalled the elbow joint snapping. The man screamed in agony, the cutter clattering to the ground.

Meanwhile, the small guy had come to, staggering upright. His jaw dropped at the sight of his companion's ruin. Desperation pushed him forward—he charged. Jack sidestepped cleanly and unleashed a brutal right hook to the chin. The man crumpled, out cold.

Jack lifted him and propped him against a doorway. Then he dragged the big guy and set him beside his friend. Tossing a few coins onto the ground, he said coldly, "Ring for an ambulance." Jack had escaped unscathed, though the pleasant evening had been utterly ruined. He climbed into his Fiat Spider, fired the engine.

The twin carbs inhaled the cool night air. He flicked on the radio—perfect, The Doors' "Riders on the Storm" spilt through the speakers. He set off, calm as a millpond.

The music was soothing:

Riders on the storm / Riders on the storm / Into this house we're born / Into this world we're thrown / Like a dog without a bone / An actor out on loan / Riders on the storm.

The short drive back to Jack's apartment was made quicker by the absence of night traffic. He parked, climbed the stairs, and entered his flat. After switching on the light, he decided a nightcap was in order before bed.

He opened his prized drinks cabinet and withdrew a twenty-one-year-old bottle of Redbreast single pot still whiskey—a Christmas present from his parents.

They knew he cherished the finer things in life.

Pouring himself a double measure, with a glass of water on the side, he carried both to the balcony and placed them on the small bistro table.

The night was starry, Dublin Bay awash in moonlight. From the distance came the sharp whistles of curlews hunting in the dark.

Jack inhaled the fresh air and sipped the Redbreast. The sherry nuttiness and pot-still spice lingered on his tongue. His thoughts turned fondly to Sophie.

Was she asleep?

Reading?

He had planned to visit her early tomorrow afternoon. Another sip, another lick of the lips. There was no way he could tell her about tonight's incident.

She wouldn't be able to bear it. He followed the whiskey with a swallow of water, eyes fixed on the glowing full moon.

Maybe that explained why those two men had lost their minds tonight. But no—it was clear enough. With a screwdriver and a Stanley knife, they'd been up to no good from the start.

He finished his whiskey, performed his nightly ablutions, and barely had his head touched the pillow before the Sandman claimed him. Jack slipped into the arms of Morpheus and slept soundly until 6:30 a.m.

Life is more or less a lie, but then again, that's exactly the way we want it to be

Bob Dylan

CHAPTER
Twenty-Two
California, Maryland - USA

Meanwhile, on the other side of the Atlantic, business was booming for a certain Joey Falconetti—especially with his latest line of work: human trafficking. His victims, mainly children and young women, came from poverty-stricken villages in Southeast Asia—Vietnam, Cambodia, Laos, and Myanmar. At times, fifty thousand dollars for a pubescent boy or girl made it a profitable and practically risk-free business.

A U.S. Army plane had just landed in Washington, D.C., and a truck was waiting for its precious cargo. There were fifty women, all under forty, and sixty children between the ages of ten and fifteen. Demand was high, particularly for the children, who would be sold off to pedophilia rings across the country and abroad. The teenagers and some of the younger women would end up in brothels, while the others became work slaves.

They had been promised jobs as maids or servants, and their children had been guaranteed schooling. To make it even more convincing, everything was promised to be free. It never ceased to amaze Joey Falconetti how naïve, poverty-stricken people could be. A few hundred dollars to unscrupulous locals ensured that everything ran smoothly. The men were told they would join their families at a later date, once they had settled in. They were also given a few dollars—sometimes the equivalent of a year's income—which made persuasion very easy.

The pilot had been told they were refugees. A few thousand dollars was enough to convince him. The truck driver also received a few thousand dollars to keep his mouth shut and mind his own business. The "refugees" had barely touched the tarmac before being shuffled into the back of the waiting truck.

The driver had been given strict instructions and directions: he was to bring them to a warehouse in a remote part of Maryland, near California, where they would be dispatched to their new destinations. It was a short, one-and-a-half-hour drive—easy, handy money for the driver.

He had been making the same journey for the past three months, once a week. The extra money had made a major change to his lifestyle. He was content. He didn't know, nor did he want to know, what happened to his human cargo upon arrival. But he wasn't a dupe.

When he left them, they were a happy, smiling, carefree bunch of people, some even singing songs in their native tongues. But that would suddenly change.

He never witnessed the unstoppable tears flowing down the children's and women's cheeks, the heart-wrenching cries as brothers were separated from sisters and mothers torn from their children, nor the despairing screams as the horror of the situation gradually unveiled itself and the horrific truth of what they were to become finally sank in It was a living nightmare.

Their plight was comparable to that of the Jewish people during the Holocaust. They were just merchandise, to be used and abused.

As far as the driver was concerned, he was paid good money in cash to bring people from A to B. Surely, there was nothing illegal in that. What happened afterwards wasn't his concern.

Joey Falconetti never came into direct contact with the merchandise or the people involved in the operations. Communication was limited strictly to phone, fax, and telex.

He looked after the logistics—thanks to Uncle Sam—and put the dollars upfront when it was necessary. Nothing could be traced back to Joey Falconetti. And that was exactly the way he liked it. No fuss, no hassle, and especially no risk. He was both clever and extremely cunning.

And he was also very ruthless. Yet to all concerned, he was a very successful businessman and a pillar of his community.

Strategy is the craft of the warrior.

Miyamoto Musashi

CHAPTER
Twenty-Three

Okinawa - Japan 1984

Jack was now four years into life in Okinawa. For him, time had flown by at the speed of light. It felt as though he had just stepped off the plane on that autumn day. He had just earned his third-degree black belt. Nobody had ever achieved that degree of proficiency in such a short time. But Jack had. He trained relentlessly, eight hours a day, come hell or high water. The hard work had paid off. He was now regarded with great esteem in the dojo and held his place among the best. Sensei Saito had grown very fond of Jack and respected him immensely.

The feeling was mutual, and Jack considered him a second father. He was wise, intelligent, tough but fair, and an incredible martial artist. And he was always available to give advice or a helping hand whenever needed. Jack had been to Saito's house with Akiko for dinner on numerous occasions. He was now considered part of the family—a very rare privilege indeed. But that's where the privileges ended. Once he entered the dojo and stepped onto the tatami, he was afforded the same status as any other student. There were no favours given and none expected.

Akiko had finished her studies and now held her diploma in business, economics, and international trade. They were living together full-time in the little beach cabin. Things had certainly become serious—serious enough to talk about marriage and even children. Akiko's father was overjoyed at the idea. He cherished the thought of having Jack as a son-in-law, and he longed to be a grandfather.

Jack's Japanese had improved immensely, and he was now practically fluent. He could converse easily and was at ease with most topics. But writing and trying to read the endless number of kanji symbols that had been "borrowed" from China was a different ball game altogether. In total, there were around 50,000 of them, though luckily only about 3,000 were in common use. Still, that was a lot as far as Jack was concerned. Akiko's English had also improved in leaps and bounds. She even pronounced some words with a Dublin accent. This amused Jack immensely—he got a great kick out of it.

Jack was still writing articles once a week about life in Okinawa and doing his best to promote the island as a tourist destination. He sent his articles by fax without fail to the editor of the *Independent Newspaper* every Friday morning at the local post office. His articles had become quite popular back home. He also gave English lessons once a week at the university.

The combined activities ensured him a small but steady income. Akiko's father no longer demanded any rent for the cabin, due to the fact that they were now living together indefinitely. However, there weren't many work opportunities for Akiko on the island. She spoke regularly to Jack about going to mainland Japan, Tokyo in particular. With her degree, job opportunities would be available in most of the Japanese *zaibatsu* conglomerates.

Yet, the idea didn't appeal to Jack in the slightest. "Surely there has to be another solution," he would often tell her. As far as Jack was concerned, he was in paradise, and he didn't fancy leaving it. The thought of leaving his beloved dojo and Sensei Saito was unbearable. Akiko's father, Ichiro, didn't exactly embrace the idea either. He was trying his best to find an alternative solution, but for the moment, he hadn't come up trumps.

Then, one night while sitting on his terrace, admiring the moon's reflection on the ripple-less sea and sipping a glass of his favourite whisky—a Macallan 18-year-old sherry oak—he thought that he might have found the solution. He wondered why he hadn't thought of it before. Perhaps the answer had been there all along.

One of his closest and most respected friends, Saigo Nakamura, was none other than the CEO of the Orion beer brewery. The company was founded in 1957 in Nago during the American occupation of Okinawa. Orion had struggled to compete with the other major breweries until they shifted from a German-style beer to an American-style one. They had gained modest market shares in Asia but were trying desperately to expand further. With globalisation, they were hoping to conquer the Australian, European, and American markets. But it wasn't easy.

Ichiro made a mental note to talk to his good friend during their next game of Go. They played once a week, either in Ichiro's house or Nakamura's. They would order in food, drink some saké, and finish up with a glass of good whisky or cognac. There might be a job opportunity for Akiko to exercise her skills in international trade. And her command of English and Chinese would be a valuable asset to the company. Ichiro smiled, raised his glass, and took a sip from his 18-year-old Macallan.

Jack and Akiko were living a dream. Their daily life was idyllic, and their love had blossomed beyond all expectations. They were happy—something many people spent their lives trying to achieve. Their simple life suited Jack to a T. The cabin on the beach, his daily training, the wholesome foods, the fresh fish, and the locally farmed products were more than he could ever ask for. That, along with the laughter and joy he shared with his beloved, was the cherry on the cake.

Akiko had found part-time work at the Tanpopo, a restaurant they liked and frequented regularly. For the moment, there was no more talk of moving to the mainland—much to Jack's relief, and to Akiko's father's as well.

On warm evenings, they would sit outside on the terrace, admiring the incredible sunsets and enjoying a cold beer or a glass of wine. They would joke, laugh, and make wedding plans. They laughed even harder at the thought of the Irish meeting the Japanese for the first time and the problems and funny incidents the language barrier and culture shock would inevitably create.

Meanwhile, Joey Falconetti was living the life—and he had Uncle Sam to thank for that. Lavish weekends with his sidekicks in Tokyo, Seoul, or Hong Kong allowed them to live it up in the best restaurants and hotels. They could order in prostitutes, some of whom would be considered minors in the USA. But in Hong Kong, as long as they weren't under sixteen, it was all hunky-dory. And it was all done under the guise of specialised missions and fact-finding trips related to army logistics. Of course, it was all for the good of Uncle Sam.

Falconetti was in charge of logistics and had been promoted to Major. Basically, he had carte blanche with anything relating to the transit of goods or people. The drug business was running smoothly.

There were no hiccups or cock-ups. He had recently gotten into the human trafficking business, which proved even more lucrative given the vast profits to be made.

He used Hong Kong as a transit destination and, to a much lesser extent, a source territory for women and children subjected to sex trafficking. The victims included people from mainland China, Indonesia, the Philippines, Thailand, and other Southeast Asian countries. It was easy to lure them with false promises of lucrative employment.

He was now four years into Okinawa. He had arrived at the same time as Jack Hopkins. Although he was enjoying himself and had practically everything a man could wish for, he sorely missed Manhattan.

He had been able to return each year for Thanksgiving—something he had greatly appreciated. It had been nice to speak Italian again and eat the best home cooking Manhattan had to offer. Leaving family and friends was always heart-wrenching, but he had been asked to make this sacrifice for the "family business."

Upon his permanent return to Manhattan, he would be the main man—the one giving the orders, the one pulling the strings. For the moment, he was asked to grin and bear it. Business had never been better, thanks to Uncle Sam. Lots of palms had to be greased, but it paid off big in the end. The "family" now controlled high-ranking officers of the U.S. Army as well as the local police department.

And of course, they had bought the invaluable services of customs officials far and near. It had become a well-oiled machine—a machine that practically turned twenty-four hours a day.

Life is what happens when you're busy making other plans

John Lennon

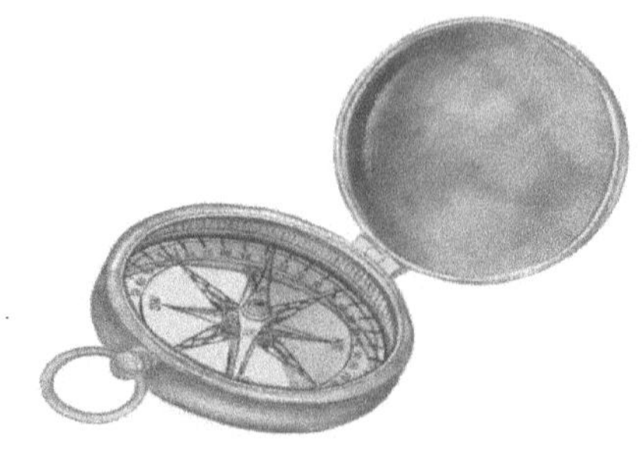

CHAPTER
Twenty-Four

Dublin, present day - November

Jack woke early as usual on a Wednesday morning. He had been sleeping on the click-clack sofa bed in the salon, as Sophie's parents, Rémy and Françoise, had taken over his bedroom—a space he had gladly offered. The sofa bed was comfortable enough and, above all, practical.

Sophie's parents had insisted on coming over to see her. They had arrived the previous Sunday at the car ferry terminal in Rosslare from Cherbourg, France, bringing their car along. The drive up from Rosslare had been a daunting experience for Sophie's father, who had never driven on the other side of the road before. Roundabouts, in particular, proved confusing. Should one turn left, or right?

In any case, they had arrived safe and sound. Rémy hadn't set any new records for the Rosslare-to-Dublin journey. Their Citroën was laden with presents, vegetables, fruit, wine, and other paraphernalia. Rémy, who kept his own vegetable patch, grew potatoes, carrots, lettuce, artichokes, onions, tomatoes, and cauliflower. He also had three apple trees and four pear trees, some of the apples used for cider and for producing a strong alcohol called *eau-de-vie*. Naturally, he had brought along bottles of cider and whatever vegetables were in season.

It was practically a mobile grocery store. Jack had laughed at the thought of him being pulled over by customs officers and having to explain what he was transporting—and why. That would have been funny, as neither Rémy nor Françoise had much English—perhaps ten words between them. They probably thought Ireland was some sort of third-world country, lacking in basic commodities.

The culture shock deepened when Jack invited them to his local pub, the Yacht. They couldn't believe the sheer number of people crowded into the place, nor the endless pints of beer being consumed, one after another. As far as Rémy was concerned, it seemed a non-stop ritual. Not to mention the whiskeys, gins, vodkas, and other spirits. They lived in a small seaside town called Saint-Malo in northern Brittany, named after a Welsh monk, Maclou, who had fled to Brittany and established his headquarters on the island in the 6th century.

The Irish pub scene was a total contrast to their French cafés, which they called simply cafés. In their town, pub culture was not ingrained in the population, and the sight of a pint of beer on a table would be rare indeed.

Jack ordered himself a pint of Guinness and tried to convince Rémy to try at least a half-pint. Rémy declined, preferring instead a glass of Harp, also brewed by Guinness. Françoise opted for a glass of Martini. They genuinely enjoyed the entirely new atmosphere. Jack's French was not too bad, so they were able to converse easily. He immediately took a liking to Rémy, a small, affable man in his early fifties, calm yet witty. By trade, he was a butcher—a horse butcher, in fact. Now *that* was a culture shock. It would be difficult to persuade an Irish person to eat horse meat, thought Jack.

Françoise, in her late forties, was unmistakably French. Her attire, mannerisms, and attitude all bore witness to her nationality. She was charming and friendly. Jack still wanted Rémy to at least taste

Guinness, so he handed him his pint glass. Rémy took a sip and immediately handed it back, his face twisted in a grimace.

"Oh, *c'est trop amer, comment tu peux la boire? — * It's too bitter, how can you drink it?"

Jack laughed heartily, as did the others.

After a typical Irish breakfast—another culture shock—Jack took them to see Sophie in hospital. They were deeply concerned about her well-being, finding her gaunt, anxious, and lacking her usual sparkle. *If only they knew,* thought Jack. He could never tell them the truth. They insisted on bringing her back to France to convalesce properly, having little faith in the Irish medical system. The French one was renowned as one of the best in the Western world. With damage to her shoulder and a broken collarbone, Sophie would be obliged to wear an arm sling for four to six weeks. She would also need regular physiotherapy treatment to recover full use of her shoulder, all of which would be covered by the French social security system. *Vive la France,* Jack thought.

Sophie played along with the plan. She needed proper rest—and safety. "Another killer could show up and finish the job once and for all," she had told Jack. The decision was made: Sophie would accompany her parents back to France on Sunday evening. The ferry left Rosslare at 5 p.m.

Sophie was to be discharged from the hospital early Friday morning. Dr. Molloy had suggested psychological treatment for her, saying it would be for the best. He had given Jack the business card of a good friend, Peadar Dunne, who worked out of the Mater Private Hospital and was known for his excellent results. For now, Sophie had been prescribed small doses of Xanax by Dr. Molloy himself. Its purpose was to relieve anxiety and treat panic disorders. It was a popular antidepressant and sedative, though dangerously addictive when used long-term.

Now, however, a French psychologist would be in the picture. Sophie could tell him the truth about what had happened, and it would remain confidential—between doctor and patient. Her parents didn't need to know. They couldn't.

Jack was up at the crack of dawn on Friday, as usual. So too was Sophie's father, Rémy, who had been an early riser all his life. He watched Jack go through his morning routine, fascinated. When Jack finished, Rémy bombarded him with questions. Jack did his best to answer and explain. Soon, Françoise joined them for breakfast. Jack had prepared fresh orange juice, freshly brewed coffee, tea, and toasted sliced pan from Brennan's, with butter and jam. Knowing the French weren't really tea drinkers—and that Sophie had told him her father loved a strong cup of coffee—he made sure to brew it well.

The sliced pan was new to them, completely different from the famous French baguette or *le pain deux livres,* both always hot and crispy from the baker's oven.

They chatted in good humour, pleased at the thought of Sophie being discharged that day. It was to be a good day. After breakfast and showers, they headed for the car park. Jack suggested that Rémy let him drive, since traffic was heavy that time of morning.

"Pas de problème," smiled Rémy. The relief was clear. As he admitted, he didn't like driving on the "wrong" side of the road. Jack had smiled at the irony: out of 241 countries worldwide, there were still 68 where people drove on the left.

Rémy's Citroën GS, with its hydro-pneumatic suspension, was a novelty for Jack, who had never driven a left-hand car before. At first, he even went to the right-hand door to get in as the driver, making Rémy laugh heartily. All in good spirits, Jack fired up the little Citroën engine.

The hydraulic suspension rose to its maximum height immediately. Ride height could even be adjusted manually with a lever in the centre console. "The car could even be driven on three wheels," Rémy proudly explained. *Some engineering feat,* Jack thought. Handy if you had a puncture and no spare.

It felt strange—steering wheel on the left, gear stick on the right. Luckily, the pedals were the same: clutch, brake, accelerator. *Thank God for that,* Jack thought. They set off into the thick morning traffic. Jack had to admit, the ride was probably the most comfortable he had ever experienced, a hallmark of Citroën's world-famous engineering and hydraulic suspension.

They arrived at the hospital after a forty-five-minute drive that usually took fifteen to twenty minutes. That's early-morning traffic for you. The light rain only worsened the congestion, as people who normally cycled instead took their cars.

At the hospital reception, the nurse told them they could go straight to Sophie's room and informed Dr. Molloy of their arrival. Sophie was sitting in an armchair beside the bed, watching TV, her right arm in a sling. She was overjoyed and elated to see them.

"Salut ma chérie," her parents said in unison. As was customary, they kissed her on both cheeks.

She looked better—more relaxed. Her complexion had improved from pasty white to a healthier golden tone, though her lightly applied makeup helped. Her bag was packed. She was excited and ready to go.

Doctor Molloy appeared at the door and offered a hearty handshake to Jack and Sophie's parents. He told Sophie that he was very happy with the results of the surgery and that she was on the mend. "You'll need plenty of rest," he added firmly. Jack had asked him not to mention the real reasons for Sophie's hospitalisation to her parents.

"Mum's the word," he had whispered, pressing a finger to his lips.

"Can I have a word, Jack?" asked Doctor Molloy, clasping Jack by the elbow.

"Certainly," said Jack. "Let's walk."

They stepped out into the corridor.

"Have you considered the psychological treatment I advised?" asked Doctor Molloy.

Jack nodded. "I have, Doctor Molloy, but things have changed since our last conversation. Sophie is returning to France with her parents to convalesce for a few months. Given the circumstances, I think it's a good idea—though I will certainly miss her."

"Oh, really?" replied the Doctor, placing a friendly hand on Jack's shoulder. "Well, she should be in good hands. They have one of the best medical systems in Europe—if not in the world," he smiled. "And how are you holding up, Jack? I know what you've gone through. It mustn't be easy. Anyway, you can always count on me for a listening ear. Don't hesitate."

"I appreciate that," said Jack. "It's very kind of you. I might take you up on it someday—over a nice pint of Guinness."

"I'll look forward to it," Doctor Molloy replied with a warm smile.

They returned to the bedroom, where Sophie and her parents were chatting joyfully.

"*Bon voyage* and have a safe trip home," smiled Doctor Molloy.

They thanked him for everything.

"Slán," said Sophie with a beaming smile.

The Doctor bowed his head, turned on his heels, and left the room.

Jack took Sophie's bag and belongings, and they headed straight to reception to fill out the necessary discharge papers.

Sophie insisted they go to the Unicorn restaurant for lunch. She wanted to say goodbye to Miss Dom and her colleagues. She also wanted her parents to see where she had been working for the past few years.

"No problem," said Jack. "Whatever makes you happy, my love. But listen—it's not even 11 a.m. yet, so let's go to Bewley's for a nice cup of coffee. I'm sure your parents will be enthralled by the ambience and the architecture."

"*Très bonne idée, ma chérie, allons-y,*" said Sophie joyfully.

Jack fired up the Citroën's little engine. The pneumatic suspension raised the car to its maximum height, and they left the hospital car park—hopefully for the last time.

Jack found a parking space on Stephen's Green. They decided to stroll through the park and show Sophie's parents the lake with its ducks and swans. They immediately loved this safe haven right in the middle of the city. Exiting the park on the west side, they arrived on the famous Grafton Street. The street was vibrant with pedestrians and shoppers; most of the big brand names had outlets there.

They strolled down the street until they arrived at Dublin's landmark, Bewley's Oriental Café. Rémy and Françoise were fascinated by the building itself. The Art Deco movement of the early 1910s had influenced Dublin architects Millar & Symes, and its façade was decorated with an Egyptian Revival mosaic—a style rare in Dublin.

They entered the large wooden doors and were greeted by a mahogany interior and tall stained-glass windows. The furniture was from another era; it felt as though they had been thrown back to the beginning of the century. Rémy and Françoise wore the faces of children in a sweet shop where everything was free. The café buzzed as usual. They ordered four large coffees and freshly baked scones—which none of them could resist. They chatted and observed, Sophie's parents especially, who soaked up the atmosphere. They loved it.

After the coffee, Sophie insisted on bringing her parents to Brown Thomas, another Dublin landmark founded in 1848. An upmarket shop dealing in designer clothes, beauty items, homewares, and gifts. Sophie knew her mother would be particularly interested, as she ran a small clothes shop of her own in a medieval town called Dinan.

Interested she was—and impressed, to say the least. Most people appreciated quality craftsmanship, and Brown Thomas offered it in abundance: Armani, Versace, Yves Saint Laurent—you name it, they had it.

Françoise's eyes lit up at a long-sleeved blouse from Yves Saint Laurent's Summer collection. One had to admit—the woman had class and taste. When Rémy saw the price of the blouse, he threw his eyes to heaven, nodded, and said defeatedly, "Les femmes..." He knew the bank card was going to take a hit.

Jack nodded back in solidarity. This was a moment all men eve-rywhere could understand—one of those rare times when commu-nication required no words.

They left Brown Thomas—the women regretfully, the men hap-pily. Jack wanted to bring Rémy to a traditional Irish pub that hadn't changed since the 19th century. They walked back up Graf-ton Street, turned left into Anne Street, and arrived at Kehoe's, the famous bar first licensed in 1803. It was an authentic Victorian shrine and one of Dublin's last great heritage pubs, a buzzing haunt for tourists, scholars, shoppers, and businesspeople alike. It was the very definition of a real pub.

They passed through the saloon-style, stained-glass mahogany doors and entered the Heritage Bar. It was unspoilt, untouched, and superbly wearing the patina of its years. Time seemed to stand still. Everything of yesteryear remained: the Victorian black bar, sumptuously carved in solid dark-grained mahogany.

Rémy had never seen anything like it in his life. The visitor was immediately struck by the austerity and subdued colourings of the Victorian age. A particular attraction was the original mahogany drawers behind the low grocery counter, once used to store rice, tea, coffee, snuff, and other provisions. In those days, shoppers could slip in and enjoy a drink in the snug while the owner pre-pared their orders.

Nothing had changed in over 100 years. The serving hatch and buzzer were still present in the snug. At the time, it had been a strict and conservative house, not overly enamoured with receiv-ing certain high-spirited literati in the '40s and '50s.

It had little effect on Sophie—she had been there many times with Jack. But her mother was in awe. "It's like stepping back into the 19th century," she said. They had a quick drink in the snug and left the pub at 1 p.m.

They walked the short distance to the end of South Anne Street, turned right into Dawson, and then up to St. Stephen's Green. They passed the famous Shelbourne Hotel—another Dublin land-mark. Rémy and Françoise were impressed by the building's façade. Jack explained that this was where Ireland's first Constitution of the Irish Free State had been drafted in 1922. He promised to invite them all for coffee there after their meal. No one disagreed.

It was a short stroll to the Unicorn Restaurant. As usual, it was jammers. Seating would be hard to find—especially without a reservation. Miss Dom was in her element, buzzing from table to table, catering to everyone's needs and whims. Some of the high-end clients could be very demanding and eccentric, wanting the same table at every lunch and the same waitress.

She turned her head briefly, and her eyes lit up when she saw Sophie and Jack standing at the entrance. She rushed over, fussing, a smile stretching from ear to ear. She was immaculately turned out as usual—not a hair out of place, her makeup next to perfect. Sophie introduced her to her parents. She was genuinely delighted to meet them.

"*Bienvenue*," she said in perfect French. "Oh, Sophie, I'm so happy to see you. I was so worried about you. Come with me— I'll set a table for you at the back of the restaurant near the dressing rooms."

She turned and set off with a light, elegant gait. They followed her. This part of the restaurant was off-limits to regular customers. Jack and Sophie had dined here on a few occasions when the restaurant was chock-a-block—or when they simply didn't want to be seen. It was the restaurant's secret little den.

She went to great efforts to explain the starters and the main courses to Sophie's parents—from the freshly made Minestrone soup and gnocchi di patate as starters to the main dishes such as lasagne alla bolognese, fettuccine al pomodoro, melanzane alla parmigiana, pollo alla cacciatora, pizza Margherita, and costoletta alla milanese.

They ordered four minestrone soups. Rémy and Françoise went for the lasagne. Sophie ordered pollo alla cacciatora—an Italian one-pot chicken stew cooked in a rich tomato sauce with vegetables and fresh herbs. Jack went for the costoletta alla Milanese, a fried, breaded veal cutlet cooked with the bone. He adored this dish.

Miss Dom insisted on offering them a glass of champagne as a "benvenuto." They ordered a bottle of Chianti with the meal. The food was excellent, and Miss Dom popped by now and then to make sure everything was satisfactory—her usual professional self.

She returned at the end of the meal for a more in-depth chat. She was sincerely saddened to hear that Sophie had decided to go back to France to convalesce for a few months. Of course, she hadn't been told the truth either regarding the cause of Sophie's injuries and the attempted murder.

"Poor Jack," she smiled. "You'll be lonely for a while. Don't worry, Sophie, I'll keep an eye on him for you." There was a twinkle in her eye.

She told Sophie that her job would always be there whenever she decided to come back. She took Sophie's left hand and gently rubbed her cheek. "You're so pretty and gentle. Take care—and see you soon."

Rémy insisted on paying the bill. They left the restaurant with Miss Dom waving and smiling from the doorstep. "Ciao bella, ciao bella!" she shouted.

"Arrivederci e grazie!" they shouted back in unison.

They walked out onto Merrion Row toward the Shelbourne Hotel for coffee. After all, a promise was a promise. They entered the famous and luxurious Horseshoe Bar and settled into the comfortable leather sofas. Jack ordered four large coffees.

A classy waiter brought the coffees on a silver tray, accompanied by a selection of small pastries. Needless to say, Sophie's parents were very impressed with both the service and the surroundings.

"This is what one can expect in a luxury five-star hotel," smiled Jack.

There were a few quick glances in Jack's direction that put Sophie ill at ease. Jack could feel her anxiety. He gently took her hand. "Ça va, ma chérie?" he asked softly.

She smiled. "Oui, ça va très bien, merci. Je suis très contente." She squeezed his hand tightly and smiled toward her parents.

One of the discreet glances had come from the well-known journalist Zack Cohen, who had covered the blood-stained and tragic events down on Dollymount Strand. He nodded discreetly in Jack's direction and received a subtle nod in return. As usual, he was impeccably attired and in the charming company of a young, lithe blonde. Wife, girlfriend, or mistress? Thought Jack. Or maybe he was working on a case.

Cohen was known to be a workaholic—sometimes working for twenty-four hours straight. Jack respected him for his sincerity and his up-front manner. He was an excellent journalist who always sought to publish the truth rather than sensationalism. His conclusions were never built on a shaky chain of assumptions, and he was a thorn in the side of Dublin's criminal underworld—especially the drug lords.

He had a very good relationship with law enforcement and had passed on crucial information on numerous occasions. There had been many threats on his life and even one car bombing, which he had miraculously survived.

Needless to say, there was a detective specially assigned to his personal safety twenty-four-seven.

The coffees and pastries were excellent. They bantered. Jack hadn't seen Sophie so cheerful and carefree in a long time. The presence of her parents seemed to be the perfect panacea. And tomorrow she was heading back to France. Jack knew he was going to miss her. They had been dating for about eighteen months and living together for nearly twelve. He also knew he was falling helplessly in love with her.

After Akiko's death, he had built an emotional firewall around himself, promising never to fall in love again. Her loss had devastated him—his world had caved in, leaving him hollow to the core. Her death had scarred him both psychologically and emotionally.

Akiko's father had introduced him to Zen meditation, which had helped immensely. It had prevented him from doing the irreparable—taking his own life by way of hara-kiri, the way of the samurai. But thanks to daily meditation, he had pulled himself together and realised that he loved life too much to let go. He now lives by the concept of carpe diem—he seized every moment of every day.

It was late afternoon when they exited the doors of the Shelbourne Hotel. Sophie was feeling a bit tired, so they headed straight back to the apartment. It was a dull evening, and a light drizzle was falling. Traffic was slow and dense. Exhaust pipes spewed their poisonous carbon monoxide fumes into the air, a headache for ecologists worried about the ozone layer and the future of planet Earth.

Sophie slept for a good hour and woke up full of energy. She suggested going to the local pub, The Yacht, for a quiet drink before the crowd arrived. Jack and her parents had no objections.

"With a bit of luck, we might bump into a few of the lads," Jack laughed.

Rémy seemed particularly happy. He was beginning to appreciate pub life in Ireland. The rain had stopped, so they decided to walk the half mile or so to the pub. It was just 7 p.m. when they entered the lounge bar, which was quite full with early evening drinkers. Most had come straight from work for a relaxing drink before heading home for dinner.

They would soon make way for the late-night drinkers, who usually arrived after 9 p.m. Some of the early crowd, however, wouldn't go home at all, making do with a few bags of crisps or a sandwich or two—much to the annoyance of their wives, who often rang the bar in frustration, dinner growing cold in the oven. That was usually when the shit hit the fan. Yet some men had a talent for inventing excuses for their tardiness—there was never any lack of imagination.

Jack scanned the bar and spotted Bradley, Lenny, and Danger sitting in one corner of the lounge. Three pints stood on their table along with a few bags of King Crisps. They won't be going home early, thought Jack. Either they'd stay until closing or move on to another watering hole. All three were single, so no one was waiting for them—and no one would be expecting them.

Lenny spotted Jack and his entourage. Standing up, he waved. "Over here, Hop!" he grinned.

Jack thought this was going to be an interesting experience. They approached the table, and the lads' faces lit up with joy at the sight of Sophie, whom they hadn't seen since the shooting. They had wanted to visit her in the hospital, but Jack had advised against it, explaining she was suffering from depression and wasn't in the right state of mind for visitors. However, Jack had kept them updated on her condition, which reassured them.

Formal introductions were made, and school French was dragged back from a long-dormant past. Bradley, of course, was the clear winner in that category. He was immediately under the charm of Sophie's mother.

"Je suis très content de faire votre connaissance, Madame. Vous êtes charmante," he said in practically perfect French.

Lenny and Danger both rolled their eyes. They knew their friend's permanent need to seduce. "There he goes," laughed Danger. "For Christ's sake, Bradley, try and keep it in your trousers, will ye? This is Sophie's mother."

Françoise smiled graciously in return. "Merci beaucoup, Monsieur Bradley. Vous êtes trop gentil et attentionné."

The lads squeezed up to make room on the couch. Bradley hoped Françoise would sit next to him, but Sophie gladly took the empty space. She was so happy to see them again; she had missed their continuous slagging and good banter.

Rémy, of course, was a bit lost for words. But the lads did their best to converse with him and put him at ease. Still, school French remained school French. They insisted on buying a round of drinks and coerced Rémy into having a pint of Harp instead of a half-pint, insisting that it was for the women. Much to Jack's surprise, he acquiesced.

The attractive young waitress arrived with the tray of drinks, and it was "tchin-tchin" and "sláinte" all around.

Lenny began to bring up the shooting, but Jack gave him a sharp kick in the shin under the table. He immediately caught on and changed the subject. Luckily, Sophie's parents hadn't understood a word.

"Thank God for that," Jack muttered under his breath.

They joked and laughed, particularly when the lads tried to converse in French with Sophie's parents—and vice versa. As the night wore on and the alcohol flowed, inhibitions dropped. Words in English and French that had seemed long forgotten were suddenly revived.

More pints arrived, along with King crisps, sandwiches, and the late-night drinkers. By 9:30 p.m., the pub was packed, and the decibel level had gone up a notch or two.

Much to Jack's surprise, Rémy was already working his way through his third pint of Harp. Although he had already visited the gents on a few occasions—unaccustomed as he was to drinking large quantities of beer in a short span of time—such was the initiation into Ireland. Françoise had just begun her second Martini.

The lads were saddened to hear that Sophie would be returning to France for a few months. Yet they understood her choice. She had endured a great deal in recent months. Though she had come out the other side in one piece, she carried scars both physical and psychological. Still, she was enjoying the evening, immersed in the laughter and craic.

"We'll look after Jack while you're away, Sophie," said a smiling Bradley in his usual sarcastic tone. "He'll be in good hands. We'll even make sure he goes to Mass every Sunday."

This remark drew a guffaw of laughter from both Danger and Lenny. Sophie had to translate for her parents, who also laughed heartily, appreciating Bradley's ironic humour. Jack simply grinned. The lighthearted atmosphere was a breath of fresh air for both Jack and Sophie. It felt good to return to normal living. But how long would it last? *Carpe diem,* thought Jack.

The night rolled on. The bell rang as the barman called last orders. A mild panic swept the lads. Lenny waved furiously at the waitress until she finally arrived, at which point he doubled their orders. He even convinced Rémy to try a whiskey—"A Jame and Pep," as he called it. A shot of Jameson with a dash of peppermint. "It takes the harsh edge off," he explained to Rémy. Of course, the purists hated it, claiming it destroyed the natural aromas and complex textures that master distillers had worked so hard to create. The smiling waitress had to make two trips to carry the drinks.

Jack suddenly felt a surge of dark, malevolent energy engulf him. A cold chill raced down his spine, and his instinctive, reptilian brain warned him that danger was near. He turned his head slowly and discreetly, scanning from right to left and then behind. That was when he spotted a smiling Robbie Maher, accompanied by his boss, Kelly and another drug lord, John Gallagher, infamously known for his violent streak. They appeared to be in a festive mood.

Jack had never met them face-to-face, but he had seen their photographs often in newspapers and on television. They had been arrested numerous times in connection with murders, thefts, and large-scale narcotics trafficking. Yet the charges never stuck. Either witnesses went missing or conveniently changed their stories.

"*Ça va, chérie?*" smiled Sophie. "You look as though you've seen a ghost."

Jack smiled back and took her hand. "No, I'm fine, love—just a bit tired, that's all."

The atmosphere shifted. People instinctively made room at the bar for Robbie Maher and his two criminal companions. They were known to all and carried an aura of fear wherever they went. The barman cheerfully served them pints and whiskeys, despite last orders having already passed. Clearly, he knew them. He shook each of their hands in turn, smiling as they patted him on the shoulder. Jack wondered if this was merely a social call or if business was being conducted. Either way, he was certain his detective friend Joey Maloney would have relished witnessing the scene.

Jack, Sophie, and her parents said their goodbyes to the lads, who were still finishing their double orders. Rémy, now in high spirits after his three pints and a whiskey, was jovial. As they left the pub,

Jack could feel Robbie Maher's eyes boring into him. Kelly and Gallagher looked him up and down, and Jack was certain there was some connection between them and Falconetti.

Outside in the chill air, night had fallen like a heavy blanket of tarmac. Lights glittered on Howth Head in the distance, and the Bailey Lighthouse cast its comforting beam across Dublin Bay, stretching outward into the darkness—a beacon of hope and safety for sailors and fishermen alike.

Across the bay, the coastline shimmered with lights from Sandymount to Dalkey, while Muglin's Lighthouse offered the same service as its Bailey counterpart. Upon returning to the apartment, they shared a cup of tea before heading to bed for a well-earned sleep.

As usual, Jack was up at dawn the next morning, slipping into his routine. He prepared breakfast: fresh orange juice and a traditional Irish fry. It would be Sophie's last Irish breakfast for some time, and he was sure she would savour it. Rémy, not usually a heavy sleeper, had to be pulled from deep slumber—but the smell of sausages and bacon did the rest.

Everyone was famished.

Rémy admitted he hadn't slept so profoundly in years.

"That's why they call whiskey a nightcap," laughed Jack.

"*Alors, il faut que je le fasse plus souvent*—so I'll have to do it more often," Rémy chuckled. Everyone laughed with him. It felt good. Laughter was indeed the best anti-stress remedy in existence—and free.

The morning dawned bright and blue, though a cold easterly breeze swept across Dublin Bay. Rémy was captivated by the view from Jack's balcony. The wind seemed to amplify the cacophony of squawking gulls, while the shrill whistles of long-billed curlews echoed in the distance. The tide was high.

Jack did his best to point out the important landmarks along the coast. His high-powered binoculars made it easier. He explained that the bay was shallow, riddled with sandbanks and rocky out-crops, and notorious in the past for shipwrecks—especially when the wind blew from the east.

The bay stretched from Howth Head in the north to Dalkey Point in the south. On such a clear day, Rémy could easily make out landmarks, especially the two towering chimney stacks of the Poolbeg Generating Station, rising 679 feet, and the famous red lighthouse.

Sophie tapped on the patio door, beckoning them inside for a warm coffee after their sightseeing. They decided that a walk around Howth Head would be perfect to digest their hearty Irish breakfast and take in the breathtaking scenery.

"It will be much better than looking through binoculars," Jack explained.

They left Clontarf in the Citroën, with Jack at the wheel. He was becoming accustomed to driving on the left. The twenty-minute drive to Howth was pleasant. Jack parked at the harbour, one of Dublin's oldest working harbours. Howth had been a fishing village and port since the 14th century, and its castle had stood for over 750 years. It remained one of the longest continuously inhab-ited private homes in Europe, still in the care of the St. Lawrence family since 1177.

Rémy and Françoise were immediately enchanted by the little fishing village. Together, they began the steep climb to the summit before taking the famous cliff walk around the head. It was a crisp, clear day—perfect for hiking. They chose the long trail, the Bog of Frogs Purple Route, which would take about three hours.

Howth Head offered stunning coastal views—a photographer's paradise. Jack pointed out Ireland's Eye, a small uninhabited is-land to the north. From the trail, they also enjoyed a magnificent view of the Bailey Lighthouse and could see as far south as Bray Head.

Jack showed them the famous Sugar Loaf Mountain, its conical shape resembling a dormant volcano. Rising 1,644 feet in the Wicklow Mountains, it overlooked the village of Kilmacanogue.

Jack glanced at Sophie. She looked radiant, her once-pale hospital complexion replaced by rosy cheeks and the healthy flush of sea air.

By the halfway mark, the brisk walk and salty breeze had whetted their appetites. Lunch at the Abbey Tavern seemed the perfect idea, Jack thought. He knew one of the owners well, a keen karate enthusiast who often attended the dojo. With luck, Jack hoped fresh sea bass or trout would be on the menu, accompanied by homemade chips. He was already licking his lips.

An hour later, they descended into Howth village and made their way to the 16th-century Abbey Tavern. Everyone felt refreshed, full of energy—and ravenous. Jack knew they would sleep like logs that night.

Inside, the restaurant was bustling. Saturdays were always good for business, and Howth was popular with tourists year-round. One of the co-owners, John, spotted Jack and hurried over with a broad smile and outstretched hand. His salt-and-pepper hair, flecked with grey at the temples, framed a friendly face lined with laughter.

He hadn't been to the dojo in two months due to back trouble and was delighted to see Jack, his sensei. He had met Sophie before and now inquired about her arm.

"Oh, just a little car accident," Sophie replied shyly.

"Ah, sure—it could've been worse," John smiled back.

He was thrilled to meet Sophie's parents and eagerly dredged up what little school French he remembered.

"Please tell me you've got sea bass on the menu today, John," asked Jack.

John patted him on the back. "You're in luck, Jack—we've a few left, but not for long. There's been a run on them since early lunch. Fresh in from this morning's catch. I went down to the pier myself to collect them." He grinned. "Helps when one of your best friends is a fisherman. Come on—I'll show you to your table."

The culinary smells from the kitchen whetted their appetites even more—if that was even possible.

"I'm so hungry," said Sophie. "This will be a change from the bland food they serve up in the hospital. Oui, j'ai très faim."

Orders were taken. It was a simple affair for the waiter: five sea bass with home-made chips and a bottle of Chablis. "Home-made" was the keyword when it came to the chips. Rémy insisted on offering everyone an apéritif and some finger food, so he splashed out and ordered a bottle of Bollinger champagne—the champagne that James Bond had made famous.

Jack had become familiar with the term *apéritif* since he began dating Sophie. But it was a concept completely alien to most Irish people. Jack thought it was one of the best customs ever.

The waiter popped the cork on the champagne, and it made that unmistakable, pleasant sound. It put everybody in party mode, and glasses clinked. "Cheers, tchin-tchin, sláinte." Happy people in happy circumstances.

The main course went down a treat. Their hunger was satiated. They ordered fresh fruit salads for dessert and coffee. Jack excused himself before the coffees arrived and headed for the gents. The toilets were in keeping with the restaurant itself—plush and spotlessly clean. Jack went to the lavatory and did his business. He felt good and airy; the few glasses of wine were having their desired effect.

He washed his hands in the white Armitage Shanks sink and sprinkled his face with cold water. Looking into the mirror, he noticed a neatly folded piece of white paper tucked behind the black frame. On it, his name was written in capital letters: "JACK."

He jerked his head backwards as if avoiding a punch. Slightly dazed, he dried his hands on the rotating cloth towel dispenser and plucked the piece of paper from behind the mirror. It unfolded into A5 size, and to his amazement, there it was, in black on white—a hand-drawing of the five-point star tattoo: *I pundi della malavita.* The points of the underworld. His eyes locked on the drawing.

The last time he had seen the tattoo was in Okinawa, on Joey Falconetti's forearm, and on one of his cronies who went by the name of Tommy "the Tank." He felt the blood slowly draining from his brain. Horrific, bloody memories gate-crashed his mind. He gathered himself and focused on his centre—the *hara*. He breathed slowly in and out until he had regained complete composure.

Was this some bizarre coincidence, he wondered. After all, a lot of people went by the name Jack. No—he had to face the truth. This was a message to him and only him. Was he being followed? He had seen nobody, nothing strange to trigger his anxiety. His primal brain hadn't alerted him to any inherent danger or menace.

Still, he had gained complete control of himself. There was no way he could show any signs of anxiety or stress to Sophie. It was just as well she was leaving tomorrow, he thought. Now he only had himself to worry about. He refolded the piece of paper and slipped it into his jacket pocket.

He exited the toilets and returned to the table wearing a big smile. The coffees had been served, along with two Rémy Martin XO cognacs—Rémy had insisted on it. Sophie was deep in conversation with her parents. Although they were talking quickly, Jack could grasp most of the conversation. Her parents were planning renovations to their house, and they were all excited.

Jack drank his coffee, sat back, and listened. The French, he thought, must be the only people in the world who give their lips such a workout when conversing. At times, it could even be sensual—depending on whose lips they were—with the exaggerated O's and U's, and of course the R's, which many foreigners found very hard to pronounce. But it was undoubtedly one of the most pleasant languages to listen to.

Rémy raised his glass of cognac: "Tchin-tchin, Jack, et merci pour ton accueil chaleureux et ton rôle comme guide touristique."

Sophie smiled. "He thanked you for your warm welcome and your role as a tourist guide."

"Yeah, I got that alright," replied Jack as he sipped his cognac. "Sláinte, Rémy. It's very good, thank you—and it's been a pleasure having you both."

They finished up, paid the bill, and headed to the car park. It was still a bright day with blue skies as far as the eye could see. The sun, however, wasn't very generous with its warmth.

Rémy and Françoise were feeling a bit fatigued after the walk and the alcohol. Their legs ached. They weren't what one would call walkers—certainly not for a three-hour stint. A lot of French people took a *siesta* after lunch, a custom that hadn't yet reached the shores of the Emerald Isle.

Back in Clontarf at Jack's apartment, he suggested a leisurely digestive stroll over to the Bull Wall via the single-lane wooden bridge. Sophie was all for it. She sighed that she had been cooped up long enough in the hospital. Despite their weary limbs, her parents agreed to tag along. Rémy asked Jack not to walk too fast.

"No problem," said Jack, laughing. "It'll be a leisurely stroll—good for the digestion."

They came to the old wooden bridge, and Jack put back on his tourist guide's cap. He explained that the bridge had been built in 1819 during the construction of the Bull Wall and that it was to be demolished after completion of the works. But thankfully, the locals had stood up for its preservation. Just as well, said Jack, as Clontarf just wouldn't be the same without it.

A brisk north-easterly wind had whipped up, encouraging them to pull their collars tight around their necks. The wind—or the rain, for that matter—never bothered Jack too much. In fact, he sometimes needed it; it enabled him to feel alive. By the time they reached the end of the bridge, their cheeks were a rosy, healthy pink from the cool wind. The tide was coming in, adding to the sensation of freshness.

They turned and headed back towards the apartment. With the wind now at their backs, it felt better. Seeing that it was their last night in Dublin, Jack suggested going to the Brazen Head Pub on the Quays. He explained that it had been established in 1198 as a coaching inn for travellers near and far, and it appeared in documents as far back as 1653.

Jack did his best to recall his history lessons, adding that it was here the United Irishmen had planned their insurrection, and that Robert Emmet had used the pub to plan the rising of 1803. Emmet had even stayed at the premises, in a room overlooking the main door, so he could watch for possible enemies. His rebellion failed, and he was hanged in nearby Thomas Street. Ironically, the hangman used to drink in The Brazen Head too. There were also strong literary connections with the pub, particularly with playwright Tom Behan and the world-famous author James Joyce.

Sophie translated the history lesson for her parents, who were all ears. Now they really wanted to visit this pub, they said, laughing.

"Great stuff," laughed Jack. "Ye won't regret it. And just to finish my story, they say the place is haunted by Robert Emmet's ghost, who still wanders the rooms of Ireland's oldest pub."

They arrived back at the apartment, had a quick coffee, freshened up, and then headed to Usher's Quay and the famous Brazen Head. Jack was back behind the wheel of the Citroën GS. He was getting used to the fantastic pneumatic suspension—just like being on a waterbed, he laughed to himself.

The Brazen Head was hopping when they arrived. Even off-season, it was busy. As usual, there were plenty of Americans eager to reconnect with their Irish roots. They dropped into the smaller bar just to the right of the entrance. They were lucky to find a table for four. It was a tight squeeze, but better than standing all night.

A shout came from behind the bar: "Jack Hopkins, for Christ's sake! Haven't seen you in decades!" Heads turned in Jack's direction. He was well known here—and even more so after his recent exploits.

The man behind the bar went by the name of Alan. He had been the pub's owner for the past eight years. A tall, broad man in his early fifties, his salt-and-pepper hair was tightly cut, and his eyes were a piercing ice blue. He was affable, as one would expect from someone working in a pub and dealing daily with the public. Recently divorced, he was now living the life of a reborn bachelor. His current female companion was fifteen years his junior. He seemed to have a new one every month—and appeared to be enjoying it.

Jack knew him well. They could easily be classified as friends. Jack hadn't been to the pub since the recent events. Alan came out from behind the bar with gusto, greeting Jack with a hearty handshake and a vigorous slap on the back. He welcomed Sophie and her parents in more than passable French. His last conquest had been from Paris, and she had obviously enriched his vocabulary and improved his accent.

"It's great to see you, Jack—it really is. You're looking as fit and as healthy as ever. How do you do it? You must give me the recipe someday," he laughed, tapping Jack on the back.

"Ah, sure, it's all down to hard work," retorted Jack. "There's no secret—just willpower."

Alan clapped his hands together. "Now, folks, what are ye having? It's on me, and it's my pleasure."

"If that's the case, I might have a glass of that fifty-year-old single malt McCallan you have stashed away in your apartment upstairs," laughed Jack.

"Jack, nothing would give me more pleasure, my friend," replied Alan.

Jack nodded his head. "Fair play to you, Alan. Maybe as a nightcap then. But for the moment, a pint of Guinness will be fine—and whatever the others are having."

Alan was back five minutes later with the tray of drinks. There were two pints of Guinness and Martinis for the women. Rémy had succumbed to Alan's persuasion to try a pint of Guinness. He was told it was the best pint to be had in Dublin.

Ballads were being churned out by the dozen, much to the joy of the tourists discovering the atmosphere of an authentic Irish pub for the first time. It was now 9:30 p.m., and people were still swarming into the pub. There was only standing room left. Many different languages could be heard—German, Spanish, Italian, French, Japanese, and Chinese. But the American accent was predominant. Uncle Sam's citizens far outnumbered the other tourists, and they weren't exactly a discreet race.

The night pushed on in a festive mood. More drinks arrived at Jack's table. The young barmaid explained they were on the house—Alan's pleasure. Jack turned towards the bar and saw Alan as busy as ever, pulling pints. He spotted Jack's gaze and flashed him a big smile and a thumbs-up sign.

Sophie's parents were thoroughly enjoying themselves, admitting they were reluctant to go home. A few more days wouldn't have gone amiss. They couldn't stop thanking Jack for all he had done to make their stay pleasant. Jack said it had been a pleasure to finally meet them, though it was a pity about the circumstances.

"Come back with Sophie when she's nursed back to full health," he smiled, placing his work-hardened hand on her knee.

The bell rang out behind the bar, and Alan shouted: "Last orders now, please, ladies and gentlemen, last orders!" It was 11:15 p.m. Jack went to the bar and ordered a final round for everyone. While waiting patiently for his order, a big, burly guy stepped up beside him.

"Hey, are you that ninja guy?" he asked in a broad Dublin accent.

"At your service," Jack replied calmly.

"Yeah, well, ye don't look that tough to me."

Jack picked up his tray of drinks. "Well, you know what they say about books, my friend?"

The big guy snorted. "Maybe I'll come down to your karate club some evening and see for myself."

"Please do," smiled Jack. "We're always seeking beginners."

He turned on his heels and headed back to his table. He was beginning to feel like a gunslinger in America's Wild West during the 19th century. There was always someone, somewhere, who wanted to test you and have their hour of glory. Man, he thought, will never change.

People were finishing their drinks and slowly leaving the licensed premises. The bar staff were very active—collecting empty glasses, washing, sweeping, and tidying. Most were anxious to get home and into bed after a long, busy day.

Jack and company were putting on their jackets and were on the point of leaving when Alan reappeared with a big smile across his face.

"Are you still on for that nightcap, Jack?"

Jack smiled back. "I sure am, Alan. Who could refuse a fifty-year-old McCallan?"

"Okay, great stuff," Alan said, clapping his hands together. "Hang on a sec, I'll be back in a jiffy—I just have to check the till."

He was back ten minutes later, more than happy with himself. It had been a great night for business. He escorted them out of the bar towards the stairs. His apartment—or penthouse, as he liked to describe it—was on the second floor. As they climbed the old, creaking stairs, he pointed out the room that was apparently haunted by Robert Emmet's ghost. He said that sometimes noises could be heard, shadows seen, and objects moved. He laughed heartily as he told his ghoulish tales.

Sophie did her best to keep her parents up to speed. Alan was amused by the anxious expressions on their faces as Sophie translated the ghostly tales and paranormal activity.

"Here we are, folks," said Alan as they reached the second floor. He tapped in a digicode and pushed open the heavy red oak door. The lights came on automatically. In a word, it was spectacular. Jack and Sophie had already been there once, on the occasion of Alan's fiftieth birthday. There was 150 square metres of living accommodation, with a sunken living room tastefully furnished with sofas in a square U-shape, abounding with cushions and centred around a low, seemingly endless mahogany table.

The living room was closed on one side by a magnificent white, natural, polished Carrara marble wall, adorned with an impressive, extra-large framed photo of the Grand Canyon. Beneath the photograph was an inset gas fire that came on with the flick of a button.

The second side was bordered by five magnificent floor-to-ceiling double-glazed bay windows, offering an impressive view of the River Liffey, the quays, and parts of the city. Birch bookshelves ran the length of the third side, flanked by two comfortable chairs.

The last side was open to a spacious, modern, American bar-style kitchen, which could seat eight people comfortably. It had suspended lighting and was equipped with everything a gourmet chef might require. In a word, it lacked nothing.

The audio system in the salon was second to none, with eight built-in Bose speakers for the ultimate sound effect. The master bedroom was en suite, with a huge tiled bathroom featuring a walk-in shower and a walk-in wardrobe. Finally, there were two medium-sized bedrooms for guests. The perfect bachelor pad.

Alan invited his guests to get comfy while he headed to the kitchen.

"Now for that McCallan I promised you, Jack," he said, opening a well-stocked drinks cabinet that some restaurants would envy. "And what can I offer the rest of you folks?"

Rémy chose a bottle of beer. He wasn't a whiskey-drinking man. Meanwhile, the girls opted for Ballygowan mineral water with a slice of lemon. Alan came back with the tray of drinks and set it on the huge mahogany table.

He opened the fifty-year-old bottle of McCallan, which was three-quarters full, and with a steady hand poured two generous measures into the Waterford Crystal Connoisseur glasses. He was pleased with himself as he raised his glass in a toast.

"Good health, all," he said. "And bon voyage for tomorrow. Have a safe trip home. It was a pleasure to meet you."

They clinked glasses and thanked him for his hospitality. Alan and Jack brought the precious nectar to their lips, anticipating a unique experience. They sipped the beverage at the same time, placed their glasses back on the table, looked at each other, and smiled. Words weren't necessary. A unique experience it certainly was. This was the holy grail in spirits terms. Alan explained that very few casks of whisky reached fifty years of age and were still drinkable—it represented only a tiny fraction of a percent.

Alan stood up, walked to the bookshelves, and returned with a large tome— the connoisseur's guide to whiskies worldwide.

"Let's see what we have here," he said, thumbing through the pages until he reached the chapter dedicated to McCallan whisky.

"Now listen to this, Jack," he said, raising his index finger. "The best whisky expert to have walked this earth, as far as I'm concerned, gave an interesting description of a fifty-year-old

McCallan. He says that if you have the chance to taste one, you've struck the jackpot. And he goes on: *the nose is spicy with vanilla, rich blackcurrants, and a subtle smell of peat. The palate brings vanilla, oak, fudge, and toffee with black pepper and orange peel. The finish is long and satisfying with lingering notes of sweet figs.* Now, let's see if we can find any of that in our next tasting."

Alan poured two more glasses of the precious nectar. Both men lifted their glasses and tasted the fifty-year-old McCallan once again. Jack thought, *Oh yes, this is the bee's knees and the cat's pyjamas all wrapped into one.* No words were necessary. Alan and Jack simply smiled and placed their glasses back on the table.

Time was pressing. It was 1 a.m., so they decided to call it a night. They finished their drinks and thanked Alan for a fascinating evening.

"No problem," replied Alan. "The pleasure was all mine."

Françoise offered to drive, as she was far from intoxicated after only two drinks. "Anyway, it will be an experience," she smiled, "driving on the other side of the road."

The road was traffic-free, and after thirty minutes of driving, they arrived at Jack's apartment. They were all quick and eager to hit the pillow, sleeping soundly until 10 a.m.—all except Jack, who had risen at eight, gone through his usual routine on the balcony, and been greeted by a gloomy, dank morning. Jack had an Irish fry ready for everyone when they arose. It gave a good kickstart to the day and lifted spirits before the drive to Rosslare Harbour to catch the ferry back to France.

One week earlier in downtown Manhattan, Joey Falconetti leaned back in his comfortable leather chair in his office and exhaled a thick cloud of blue smoke from his expensive, specially imported Cuban cigar. He observed the smoke as it rose inexorably and aimlessly toward the high white ceiling. He relished these quiet, solitary moments—it was, in a way, his manner of meditating.

Joey was a happy man. Business was doing even better than the accountant's projected annual figures, and the new venture—human trafficking—was inundated with demand. He had ordered his contacts in Asia to step up their operations, as supply wasn't meeting demand, and that meant lost money.

He smiled and took another puff from his cigar. The money that could be made from the perverts of all kinds and people's weaknesses was mind-boggling. Yes, Joey was happy. He had millions of dollars in various bank accounts and trusts, money tied up in different investments, as well as buildings and warehouses across Manhattan that brought in steady rental income.

He had a beautiful wife, Francesca, and two children—a son, Lino, six, and a daughter, Chiara, four. They were his pride and joy. And of course, he kept a mistress or two, purely for sexual purposes and certain practices he would never expect the mother of his children to perform. All in all, he was an accomplished and satisfied man. But something was nagging at him.

He sat up suddenly in his chair and doused his cigar in a glass of water. He'd finish it later.

"Fuckin' Jack Hopkins," he muttered aloud. He had nearly forgotten. When was his cousin Giovanni going to finish the job?

It was three in the afternoon. He picked up his phone and hit the number six, which dialled his contact in Dublin. Despite the distance, the ringtone sounded piercingly sharp. After a minute of ringing, a voice came on the line.

"Mr. Falconetti, what a surprise. How can I be of help?"

"Listen up. I want you to give a little reminder to our friend Jack Hopkins, just to let him know we haven't forgotten him. Nothing fancy. Something subtle. Try and draw him out a bit. Hai capito, my friend?"

The voice on the other end cleared his throat. "Yes, Mr. Falconetti. We'll do the necessary."

"Okay, ciao. Keep me up to speed." Falconetti set the phone back on the receiver and relit his cigar.

Nobody had ever lifted the lid on Falconetti's activities. If they did, they'd be opening a can of worms. Corruption, extortion, murder, human trafficking—you name it, Joey Falconetti was involved. Yet, to all appearances, he was a highly respected member of the New York Community. Joey was generous, making regular donations to several charitable organisations, including the New York Police and Fire Widows' & Children's Benefit Fund.

Of course, it wasn't genuine generosity that fueled his fire. It was the perfect way to present himself as a law-abiding, caring citizen. He never missed Sunday mass, always attending with his entire family. And it worked. His image remained untarnished. He was both respected and feared by those who knew the real Joey Falconetti but were too terrified to speak. To most people, he was simply another Italian-American who had made it big through hard work and sharp business acumen.

Joey was no fool when it came to intelligence, either. He had willingly taken part in an IQ test in college and scored a whopping 130. Nobody had been surprised. He had always been clever and cunning, and these attributes—combined with his natural flair for leadership—had been honed even further over the years. He had become a finely tuned machine.

It was Friday evening, and Joey had decided to call it a day. He was in the mood for a few glasses of Chianti. He was about to leave the office when the teleprinter came to life. It decoded the incoming pulses and sent the carriage clattering across the roll of paper. The message was short. Joey tore it from the machine:

"How are things in Manhattan? Over here, everything is running smoothly and going according to plan. The missing meat has been found in Cambodia. Lots of supplies. Negotiations are ongoing at present with the supplier. His asking figure is a bit high, but we will melt him down to a reasonable offer. All for now, will keep you up to speed. Ciao."

A large smile spread across his face, like a sunrise setting the clouds ablaze. Joey walked across his office to the filing cabinet and carefully placed the telex in the appropriate folder. He was a meticulous man—everything in its place, and a place for everything.

He opened the door and stepped onto the floor of the restaurant. This one went by the name of *Quo Vadis*, and it was both his favourite and his HQ, one of the ten restaurants he owned. He strolled to the bar where Roberto was serving beers to three thirsty construction workers who had just finished their shift.

Two young women in their early twenties—a blonde and a brunette—were sitting mid-bar, sipping Piña Coladas. They shared baby tomatoes and Parmesan cheese with Ritz crackers while talking about fashion, their boyfriends, and the price of accommodation in downtown New York. They lived in the Bronx, where rent was half the cost. They giggled often, attracting the attention of the construction workers, whose eyes were drawn like magnets to the brunette's ample bosom and luscious lips. The blonde, flat-chested but with legs that seemed to go on forever, wore a mini-skirt to prove it.

Joey snapped his fingers. "Roberto, bring me a bottle of Chianti Classico—the five-year vintage. And slice up some Parma ham, finely cut, with those olives from Puglia. They're the best. I'm in a festive mood."

Roberto took the bottle of Chianti and popped the cork. "What's the occasion, Mr. Falconetti?"

Falconetti took off his jacket and sat on one of the high stools at the bar. "I just received some very good news from abroad. Business is looking up. Join me for a drink, Roberto—I don't like celebrating alone."

Roberto cut fine slices of Parma ham and poured the olives into a bowl. He arranged the ham and olives neatly on a wooden tray along with two Chianti glasses— shaped more like Bordeaux stems— and placed them on the counter. Roberto did his job with a touch of class, and Falconetti appreciated his deft gestures and attention to detail. He was the perfect barman. Roberto poured the Chianti, half-filling the two glasses.

"Saluti," they said as their glasses clinked.

After breakfast, Jack put Sophie's two travelling bags in the boot and fired up the Fiat Spider, rewarded with the untiring roar of the twin carburettors sucking in air like a heavy smoker drawing on his last Woodbine cigarette.

Sophie travelled with Jack while Rémy and Françoise followed close behind in the Citroën Visa. It was exactly midday, and the ferry wasn't due to depart until 6 p.m.—a three-hour drive left them with time to spare.

They arrived just after 3 p.m. Time was on their side, so they decided to stop at Culleton's Bar for tea, coffee, and badly needed turkey-and-cheese sandwiches. They were hungry. Sophie said she hoped to return to Dublin in three months or so. Jack replied that he'd be waiting—he wasn't going anywhere. At least, that's what he believed.

Jack saw them off at the pier. He waved longingly as the Citroën inched forward to customs control. They were cleared, guided into the belly of the ferry, and then the car disappeared from view. Jack wiped a tear from his eye. He hated goodbyes. He decided to return to the pub for a pint of Guinness before the lonely three-hour drive back to Dublin.

Jack ordered his pint at the bar and chose a table with a comfortable club armchair facing the harbour through the large bay window. He was in a pensive mood. Darkness had fallen, and he watched the deck cabin lights flick on one by one as travellers settled in.

The bow thrusters provided the necessary lateral push, and the ferry eased away from the pier. Smoke billowed from the chimneys as the four Wärtsilä 16V31 diesel engines propelled it out of the protected harbour and into the Irish Sea.

The ferry drifted slowly into the distance until Jack could only make out the lights, which gave it the look of a floating nightclub. A wave of loneliness and mild depression swept over him. He drained his pint and headed for the public phone box. Not keen on going straight back to the apartment, he decided to call one or two of the lads to see if they were up for a last pint at the Yacht.

He was in luck. Lenny was eager for a drink and said he'd bring along Sonar, Danger, and anyone else he could round up.

"That's great, Lenny. I should be there before 10 p.m." Jack hung up the phone, headed to the gents, and then out to the car park.

His mood had lifted.

Jack reached the car and was about to open the door when he noticed a piece of paper tucked under the driver's-side wiper. He lifted the blade and unfolded the sheet carefully. Staring back at him was the five-star tattoo. This time, though, there was a message in block capitals: "DON'T WORRY, JACK, WE HAVEN'T FORGOTTEN YE. WATCH YOUR BACK."

A cold chill ran down his spine, triggering his reptilian brain into action—a brain forged over 100 million years ago. Its primary concern was survival and reproduction, and it controlled all the vital life-sustaining functions of the body. At this moment, the voice in Jack's head screamed one thing: survive. It was clear he was being stalked. He hadn't noticed anything unusual or anyone suspicious, but whoever it was, they were very discreet.

Jack fired up the engine, leaned across, and opened the glove compartment. He flipped through his CD collection until he found what he wanted—The Doors' *Riders on the Storm*, one of his favourites. He slid it into the slot. The machine sucked it in with a whirring sound, and faint music drifted through the four Pioneer speakers.

He exited the car park and hit the coast road towards Wexford. His mind was racing. The drive back to Dublin would give him time to assess the situation, consider his options, and form a game plan.

He knew he would have to act—and act quickly. This wasn't going away. It had to end. And he was going to end it. But he also knew the path ahead would be bloody.

The road back was quiet, and Jack pushed the Spider deep into the red zone. It was exhilarating—exactly what he needed. To hell with a speeding ticket.

He decided a trip back to Okinawa was what he needed most. A Spartan lifestyle for a few months would do him the world of good. He missed Ichiro, his father-in-law, and the good friends he had made there. They were a painful reminder of his suffering, but he couldn't mourn forever. It had already been too long.

Traffic built as Jack approached Bray, even more so near Shankill village. Once through, he took the roundabout onto the Stillorgan dual carriageway. As usual, it was busy and slow, with traffic lights every mile. Jack often wondered who had won the contract for all those lights. Whoever it was, they'd certainly come up trumps.

Jack turned off the dual carriageway at the Church of the Sacred Heart and headed towards Sandymount and the coast road. After a short drive, he crossed the East Link Bridge, passed to the far side of the Liffey, and continued towards Fairview, then into Clontarf.

It was exactly 9:45 p.m. when Jack eased into the car park of the Yacht Pub. He had made good time. The drive had cleared his head and given him perspective. He planned to contact his good friend, Detective Joey Maloney, and ask for information about Giovanni Falconetti, the hitman in Sicily, and his cousin in Manhattan. He was confident Joey would help however he could, as long as Inspector Branagan didn't catch wind of it—that would be disastrous. But if Jack was going hunting, he needed a head start and all the support he could gather.

As he pushed through the lounge door of the pub, he felt a weight lift off his shoulders. The place was packed, as usual. He spotted his buddies at a table, pints in front of them, having the craic. They were four: Danger, his brother Sonar, Lenny, and Bradley. He was glad to see them.

"There he is!" they clamoured as he reached the table.

"Did they get away okay?" asked Sonar.

"Yeah, no problems," replied Jack. "Bang on time."

"Get that man a pint to lift his spirits!" shouted Lenny.

"Sure, it must feel great to be free, easy, and available again," sniggered Bradley. "Dublin's female population will be delighted with the news."

"For fuck's sake, Bradley," interjected Danger.

Jack took a seat as his pint arrived. "Anyway, good to see yez all, ye shower of bastards. Thanks for coming out."

Jack laid out his plans to four pairs of attentive ears. Not all were in favour—they thought it was ambitious, risky, maybe even reckless. Except Danger, who believed it was the only solution.

"You're right, Jack. Go out and nail those bastards. Ye can't spend the rest of your life looking over your shoulder, pal."

The gong rang. It was ten minutes to last orders. They doubled their round to be safe.

Jack enjoyed the company and the usual banter. He ignored Bradley's offer to hit a nightclub in the city centre to chase what he called "dirty girls." Instead, he thanked them and said goodnight. He just wanted sleep—to reset, return to his routine in the morning, and begin planning. It would be a busy week, with old acquaintances to renew.

When he reached his apartment, another message had been thumbtacked to the door. It echoed the last:

"DON'T WORRY, JACK, WE HAVEN'T FORGOTTEN YOU."

He pulled out the tack, stepped inside, and dropped the note in the bin. He needed rest.

It is during our darkest moments that we must focus to see the light

Aristotle

CHAPTER
Twenty-Five

Okinawa 1985

Jack had just passed his third-dan (sandan) test with honours. Everybody, including Master Saito, was astonished by Jack's progress and by both his technical and physical prowess. The hard work was paying off. Six hours a day, six days a week—through hail, rain, or snow—was certainly no mean feat. It demanded an immense level of self-discipline. On Sundays, he practised kenjutsu and iaidō with Ichiro for two hours before the family lunch. This was something he particularly cherished. Ichiro had also introduced him to Zen meditation, which he now practises daily.

There were, of course, the begrudgers who felt that Jack had been awarded his dan rankings too quickly and had not respected protocol. But these were people who came to the dojo three times a week for training sessions lasting an hour and a half. The proof of the pudding, however, was in the eating, as they discovered when they faced Jack on the tatami for randori.

They were quick to change their minds when confronted with his speed, precision, power, and agility—all of which were breathtaking. To put it simply, Jack had become a fighting machine, a very dangerous man. He moved with the grace of a ballet dancer yet radiated the raw power of a tiger. Jack never went unnoticed when he entered a room, and even at a distance, he was impressive. Most people were in awe of his presence.

Akiko and Jack were now living together permanently. Like any couple, they had their ups and downs, but the ups far outweighed the downs. They had begun talking about marriage and eventually starting a family. Wedding bells were in the air, and Ichiro was over the moon at the prospect of them tying the knot and hopefully giving him a grandchild. Akiko was in her final year of business college, and nothing would be definite until she graduated and found steady employment. But that did not stop them from talking about it and making plans. They were both excited about the whole prospect.

Jack was earning an honest living through his articles on local life, which he telexed weekly to the editor of the Irish Independent. His pieces met with great success. He was also still teaching English at the local college whenever possible. Akiko, for her part, picked up shifts at the Tanpopo restaurant during lunch or in the evenings whenever her schedule allowed. She generally enjoyed the work, except on the occasions when Joey Falconetti showed up with his sleazy, loud-mouthed crew.

Akiko had been the target of roaming hands, lewd innuendos, and the occasional slap on the backside, which always drew guffaws from the gallery. The scenario was always the same, complete with the same vulgar vocabulary: "Ah, there's karate kid's piece of pussy. What a piece of arse. Wouldn't mind gettin' me some of that, boys. He doesn't deserve you, baby. You need a real man like me—Joey Falconetti, the Italian stallion." Falconetti loved being the centre of attention. He loved being the 'man.'

Akiko often had to restrain herself from jabbing a fork into his hand—or worse, into his eye. But she grinned, bore it, and took their money, especially the tips, which were always generous. It was a contradiction in terms. Perhaps Falconetti felt guilty about

his behaviour, and tipping heavily was his way of seeking for-
giveness. Akiko had never told Jack. She knew she could not. If
she did, it would be World War III.

Still, they were managing quite well. Their needs were modest.
They ate fresh fish most days, thanks to Ichiro and his catch whenever the fishing was good. Jack had completely transformed his
eating habits. Once a heavy consumer of red meat, he was now
content with a good steak once every two weeks. He did not miss
it much, though he relished it when it was placed in front of him.

Jack was now approaching his fourth year in Okinawa and had
discovered countless culinary delights he had never known existed. Indeed, he had adapted to the Okinawan lifestyle like a fish
to water. He was happy in what he liked to call his little paradise.

*I can't change the direction of the wind, but I can adjust my
sails to always reach my destination.*

Jimmy Dean

CHAPTER

Twenty-Six

Dublin 1990 December

It was a Saturday morning, just after 10 a.m., and Jack had finished his usual exercise routine. He stepped out of the shower and slipped into his black bathrobe. He felt good. Moving into the kitchen, he prepared his favourite coffee: Blue Mountain from Jamaica. Curiously, it was a coffee he had first discovered in Okinawa, where the Japanese were the largest importers of the famous bean. He had been captivated after the very first sip.

The coffee offered a sweet, rich flavour without the bitterness found in other blends. It was a smooth and popular Jamaican coffee, and once you tasted it, you understood why it was renowned for its excellence. Jack poured the piping hot beverage into his mug, added a small spoonful of brown sugar, then crossed the room, pulled open the sliding doors, and stepped out onto the balcony. It was a cool, fresh morning. The sun was shining and the skies were blue—just as Jack liked it.

Jack had spent much of his time since Sophie's departure making plans for his immediate future. He knew things would have to change—and quickly. He had telephoned his father-in-law the week before, spending over an hour on the costly call, speaking and listening intently. He had also sent a lengthy letter to him two weeks earlier. Jack was relieved to learn the letter had arrived safely. His Japanese had been hesitant for the first ten minutes of their conversation, but then it flowed back to him—just like riding a bicycle, he thought.

Jack had spoken about the possibility of visiting Okinawa in March for the sakura, the cherry blossom season. He couldn't think of a better time. Ichiro was overjoyed at the thought of his son-in-law returning. He told Jack the beach cabin was still available and that he could never bring himself to rent it out, keeping it instead as a kind of shrine to Akiko's memory. Jack knew he would be engulfed with emotion the moment he crossed the threshold of that little cabin. Even now, he could feel his eyes welling with tears. When he had finally hung up the phone, the tears flowed uncontrollably down his cheeks. It was the first time he had let his emotions truly get the better of him. And, in a strange way, he felt relieved.

Jack came in from the balcony and pulled the sliding doors shut behind him. He went to the phone and lifted the handset from the cradle. Pressing the memory button, he dialled Joey Maloney's home number. The phone emitted its usual beeps and bleeps before the ringtone sounded on the other end. Jack switched it to loudspeaker mode. It seemed to ring for an eternity before a familiar voice finally answered:

"Jaysus, Jack—can a man not enjoy a decent lie-in on a Saturday morning?"

"It's nice to hear you, too, Joey. I hope I'm not interrupting anything… intimate."

"If only," scoffed Joey. "Good to hear from you, though. What can I do for you, buddy?"

"I need a big favour, Joey," Jack replied.

Joey sat up in bed. "Oh, oh, here we go. I know I'm not going to like what comes next. Go ahead, prove me right."

Jack went on to explain his plans for the future while Joey listened attentively.

"To be honest, Jack, I don't like the sound of this at all. So, what do you want me to do, exactly?"

Jack cleared his throat. "I need Giovanni Falconetti's address in Sicily, Joey."

"For fuck's sake, man—this is suicide, complete suicide! You don't know who you're dealing with, Jack. You're talking about the Cosa Nostra—an international crime syndicate, trained killers. They don't abide by your code of budō, or whatever code you follow. These guys are paid assassins. I don't want to be standing over your grave, drinking pints of Guinness to your memory. And if I give you this info and the boss gets wind of it, my arse will be in a sling."

"Look, Joey, this is a personal vendetta against me, and I know it won't stop until I've been taken out. Joey Falconetti isn't going to back down—it's too personal now, too much a matter of pride. Believe me, I know this bastard from my time in Okinawa. He's evil personified. I have to stop it. I just need this information, Joey, nothing more. I'm begging you—as a friend."

Joey shouted into the phone, "Fuck you, Jack Hopkins! You're putting me on the spot. Alright, listen— I'll see what our Italian friends or Interpol can come up with and I'll get back to you. It's risky business, as we don't know who's on the organisation's payroll. If your pal Giovanni gets a whiff that someone is looking for him, he's going to be on tenterhooks. Wait for my call."

The phone went dead. Jack put the handset back into the cradle, went to the kitchen, and poured himself another cup of coffee. "This is good stuff," he thought. He finished his coffee, his mind racing. He needed to move. So he put on his tracksuit and decided to go for a brisk walk down the Bull Wall and back. He knew it would do him good—and maybe he'd have lunch at the Yacht on the way back. Since Sophie's departure, he had been feeling lonely and uneasy. He found it hard to get used to a solitary life.

When Jack got back to the apartment, it was just after 2 p.m. The walk had been very beneficial to his mood and had chased away much of the emotional debris that had been building up. The fish and chips made a perfect lunch, and he had enjoyed the banter and jovial atmosphere as usual. He went to the salon to switch on the hi-fi system when he noticed that the phone handset was flashing. Somebody had left a message. He grabbed the handset and hit the appropriate button.

Joey Maloney's voice came on, "Hiya Jack, just getting back to you. I put out feelers and have the info that you requested. No way I'm giving you this over the phone, so I suggest meeting in Mulligan's pub around 6:30 p.m. if that suits. Ring me back for confirmation. And don't forget, buddy—the pints are on you." There was a snigger, and the phone went dead.

Jack rang back and confirmed the rendezvous. He decided to go for a catnap, as he had a karate lesson to give at 4 p.m. It was to be a special kata session that would focus on the finer points of Kata Sanchin—the famous breathing kata that most styles of karate practice, the "three battles" between body, mind, and soul.

Jack came out of his catnap at 3 p.m. and took a quick shower. It was 3:20 p.m. when he crept out of the car park in his Fiat Spider and onto the Clontarf Road towards Fairview and the city centre. Little did he know, a set of blue eyes was observing him very closely.

When Jack arrived at the dojo, there were ten or so practitioners waiting patiently for his arrival. Some were adepts, and others had only recently taken up the art of the empty hand. After a warm-up session, Jack went straight into Kata Sanchin. It was a kata that Jack particularly liked. It was far from spectacular but emphasised the importance of deep breathing, concentration, strong stance, and balance. Sanchin is an isometric kata where each move is performed in a state of complete tension, accompanied by powerful, deep ibuki breathing that originates in the lower abdomen, the seika tanden.

It could be quite off-putting for the observer, as it appeared the instructor was inflicting punishment on the student by delivering a series of blows with his hand or foot to various parts of the body. The strong blows were simply to verify that the person doing the kata was always maintaining a state of tension and a strong stance, along with controlled breathing. The kata was also excellent for increasing blood flow. All in all, it was an excellent kata for general well-being.

At the end of the class, Jack performed the kata on his own. It was an impressive demonstration of control, concentration, power, and stability. His breathing was like a bellows and could be heard a block away. So much so that some passersby stuck their heads in the door to see what the heck was going on.

Jack locked up the dojo and headed to Mulligan's pub in Poolbeg Street. He was anxious to meet Joey and receive the precious information he had requested. It was just after 6:30 p.m. when Jack found a precious parking space in Hawkins Street, a stone's throw from the pub. Night had already fallen as Jack went through the doors of Mulligan's and into a noisy, smoky environment.

Jack scanned the bar and saw Joey sitting alone at a table at the back near the big clock. He had a pint of Guinness in front of him and was reading one of the daily evening newspapers.

Joey looked up from his edition of the Evening Herald: "Jack! Great to see you, buddy—you're a sight for sore eyes. You're looking fit as usual."

"You're looking good, too, Joey. Can I get you another Guinness?"

Joey took a mouthful from his pint. "No, Jack—get me a small Jameson. I'm in the mood for a chaser."

Jack obliged his friend, went to the wooden bar, and ordered a Guinness and a small Jameson. When he came back to the table, a Kraft envelope was waiting to be opened. Jack placed the drinks on the table, sat down, and looked at Joey.

Joey opened his hands "There you go, Jack. This is what you want. I just hope I'm not signing your death warrant. A guy I know in Interpol got me the information. He's a good guy, trustworthy— if you know what I mean? I just couldn't take a chance with the Italian police force, as a lot of it is compromised. The mob even have judges on their payroll, for Christ's sake."

Jack picked up the envelope, stared at it for a few seconds, and opened it. And there it was, in black on white: Giovanni Falconetti

– Villa Capo Bianco – Trappeto – Sicily. And there was even an unlisted telephone number. Jack put the paper on the table, took a mouthful from his pint, and said, "Thanks, Joey. I owe you one."

"You sure do, my friend. And remember—I didn't give you this information. My contact told me that this villa is safer than Fort Knox, with all kinds of alarms and cameras.

He also told me that Falconetti is suspected of having an impressive number of hits under his belt for such a young man. The list goes on and on—magistrates, Carabinieri, enemy gang members, and traitors who gave information to the police.

They can't come up with any conclusive evidence that links him to his crimes. He's the perfect assassin: a professional, a perfectionist. He's a ghost."

At the other end of the bar, the same set of blue eyes hadn't missed a detail of the encounter.

The mind is everything. What you think, you become

Buddha

CHAPTER
Twenty-Seven

Trapetto, Sicily, 1991 April

It was 11 a.m. when Giovanni Falconetti stepped out of his swimming pool under an azzurro sky. The temperature was a pleasant 20°C. Giovanni had just finished his daily one-kilometre swim—that was forty lengths of his magnificent 25-metre pool. He always finished in under fifteen minutes, which was impressive, taking into account that he usually stopped after twenty lengths for a brief breather.

He towelled himself dry before entering his well-equipped gym to perform a series of exercises that would add an extra hour to his daily routine. During the summer months, he preferred swimming in the sea; he found it more challenging and invigorating. Giovanni had also built a soundproof firing range next to the gym, where he honed his shooting skills three times a week.

He loved firearms and was a keen collector. His collection included Smith & Wessons, Glocks, SIG Sauers, Walthers, Rugers, and Berettas. But his favourite was the long-barrel Smith & Wesson Model 10. Known as the Military & Police Special in the US, it had been carried by at least 70% of the police force. He particularly liked this handgun because it was reliable, durable, very accurate, and its recoil was moderate. It had all the necessary qualities for a man in his line of work.

He liked nothing better than inviting friends over for an apéritif and a shooting contest. However, Giovanni always won. Most people thought it was just a hobby of his. Little did they know, it was a very important aspect of his trade. To most of his friends, he was in the wine business—a business that brought in a lot of money.

Giovanni had invested in the vineyard of his cousin Enzo in the province of Catania. Although he didn't participate in the daily running of the enterprise, he promoted the range of wines whenever the occasion arose. He had successfully persuaded some high-class Roman and Neapolitan restaurants to buy pallets on a regular basis. He could be a very persuasive business representative when needed. He liked to refer to it as a "business understanding" that made everybody happy. And at the end of the year, he enjoyed picking up his dividend. After all, money was money.

Giovanni stepped out of his power shower, feeling good. The wall-to-ceiling mirror he had installed specially reflected his bronzed, toned, and muscular body. At thirty-five years old, he was in his prime. He liked what he saw. He admired the scorpion tattoo—expert work by a Japanese horishi, a tattoo master during his stay in Tokyo, carried out in the traditional Japanese manner. It had hurt like hell, but he adored the craftsman's fine piece of art. It never failed to impress, whether male or female.

He dried himself and threw an Egyptian cotton bath towel around his waist. He slipped on a pair of lightweight, non-slip bath sandals and stepped into the large salon. Looking out through the sliding patio doors, he admired the view of the bay. The sun was climbing in the azzurro sky, and the incoming waves reflected the sunlight, offering a spectacular effect.

The phone rang out, suddenly interrupting his brief meditation. He picked up the handset. He saw that it was his cousin Joey from Manhattan. He's an early bird, Giovanni thought. Must be 5 a.m. over that side of the big pond.

"Ciao, cousin! Still living the dolce vita?" laughed Joey Falconetti. "What are ye doing with yourself besides having a good time with your various lady friends?"

"Come stai, cugino? What the hell are you doing up at this hour? Yeah, as always, I'm enjoying life and looking after business."

Joey Falconetti flicked the button to loudspeaker mode. "I couldn't sleep. Had Jack Hopkins on my mind—he's like a pebble in my shoe, a real pain in the ass. Ye know what I mean? And speaking of business, when are ye going to finish off the job? Remember, I gave ye fifty percent of 100G. I'm not the Vincent de Paul."

Giovanni walked out onto his teak-decked terrace and took a deep breath of air. "Don't sweat it, cousin. Ye know I always deliver. The last time was a close call. I don't fancy having Europol or Interpol on my tail. 'The Family' doesn't have many connections in those organisations. Anyway, keep me informed of his movements, and I'll make arrangements. It would be good if it happened somewhere other than that little island."

"Yeah, got ye. Just to bring you up to speed—he was seen receiving an envelope from his detective friend."

Giovanni laughed. "Maybe it was a Christmas card or a birthday card."

"Yeah, and maybe they're lovers and he gave him a love poem," snorted Joey. "Anyway, let me know soon when you've made arrangements. In the meantime, enjoy your dolce vita—and go easy on the wine, cousin." He hung up.

An unexamined life is not worth living.

Socrates

CHAPTER
Twenty-Eight
Tokyo 1991 March

Jack arrived in Tokyo in the small hours of the morning after connecting through Doha. A direct flight was far beyond his budget. The stopover in Doha airport had been a long five hours, during which Jack passed the time drinking coffee and reading a magazine he had bought specially for the flight. Much to his surprise, however, he also managed to find a beer. But Doha airport in the 1990s was not what it is today, with its many shopping facilities, restaurants, lounges, showers, museums, gyms, and spas. The list seemed endless now, and today the airport is ranked as the second best in the world.

Tokyo was exactly as Jack had left it a few years earlier—luminous, noisy, and exuberant. It was not unlike New York in that respect, a place where you could eat and drink at practically any of the twenty-four hours that make up a day.

Jack had booked into a small hotel in the touristy Roppongi area of Tokyo. It was renowned for its hectic nightlife and vast selection of restaurants and designer boutiques. He was determined to make the most of his one-night stay, as he had a train to catch on the Shinkansen—or bullet train, as it was known—the following day at 3 p.m., bound for Kyoto. He was looking forward to Kyoto, as it was sakura season, the famed cherry blossom time. He had witnessed it once with Akiko, and the memory was etched in his mind: streets and parks painted in a sea of pink and white with the Yoshino cherries in full bloom.

Jack held fond memories of Kyoto with Akiko. They had spent a whole week exploring the serene city, teeming with temples, shrines, gardens, and geisha. He had loved every moment.

One day, they had rented traditional costumes. Akiko, dressed as a geisha, had been stunning—her natural beauty magnified a hundredfold. They had giggled and laughed as Jack struggled to walk in the traditional geta. Kyoto had seemed one of the most romantic cities in the world—especially when you were smitten with love.

It was too early to check into his hotel, so Jack decided to visit an *onsen* at Spa LaQua, a hot spring facility in the centre of Tokyo that drew natural spring water from 1,700 meters underground. Jack needed to relax and wash off the jet lag. The hot spring, followed by a cold shower, would do the trick.

By midday, Jack checked into his hotel, refreshed and replenished with energy. Hungry, he set out to find a restaurant serving traditional Japanese food. He found exactly what he was looking for: a bowl of miso soup to start, followed by a seafood coddle with rice. It set him up for the day. He spent the next few hours exploring the district. The place was buzzing, living up to its reputation for lively entertainment. Tourists from around the world mingled with locals in what seemed like a never-ending flow of humanity.

It felt good to be back in the country of the Rising Sun. The language and vocabulary returned to him with ease. He went to a bar frequented by locals and ordered an Orion beer from Okinawa. Akiko had once worked in that brewery and had made great headway in the export market. Jack struck up conversations with a few locals, who were impressed with his command of the language.

They asked him endless questions—it wasn't often that an Irishman spoke Japanese so fluently in their bar. Everyone wanted to buy him a drink, but Jack politely thanked them and accepted just a second beer from the barman. It would have been impolite to refuse.

One of the men, fascinated by Jack's years in Okinawa, asked numerous questions about his karate style and training methods. He was in his mid-twenties and introduced himself as Kenzo, a second-dan black belt in Shotokan, one of the most popular karate styles in mainland Japan. Kenzo insisted that Jack visit his dojo, which happened to be near the hotel. Jack was delighted to accept. After an early night and a light breakfast, Jack was on the dojo mat by 9:30 a.m., fully dressed in his karate gi. He exchanged techniques with Kenzo and sparred for a good thirty minutes. Kenzo was more than impressed with Jack's speed, power, and overall proficiency in the art.

After the session, Kenzo invited him for a beer, which Jack graciously accepted. They showered, then headed to a local bar for a refreshing drink before saying their goodbyes. Kenzo asked Jack to stay in touch. Jack liked the young man, so he wrote his address and phone number on the back of a beer mat and handed it to him. "Dozo," he said with a bow.

With some time to spare, Jack strolled back to the hotel to collect his belongings, taking in the bustling city atmosphere. It felt good to be back on Japanese soil—it was long overdue, he thought. Deciding to walk the four kilometres to the train station, he wanted to soak up more of the unique energy. He arrived at the station at a quarter to three, awaiting his bullet train to Kyoto. The train arrived precisely on the hour. The punctuality was a stark contrast to C.I.E., the Irish transport system, which was rarely on time. In Japan, you could set your watch by the trains, and even a one-minute delay warranted apologies over the PA system. Welcome to Japan, where precision ruled. Perhaps that was why Jack loved martial arts so much—the precision in executing techniques left no room for error.

Jack boarded the Nozomi line to Kyoto and settled into one of the comfortable reclining seats. Travelling at nearly two hundred miles per hour, the trip would take less than two hours. The station master blew his whistle, and the Shinkansen glided out on time.

From his window seat, Jack watched the city flash past. With land so scarce, Tokyo's apartments were built right against the rail tracks.

Soon, the countryside and mountains came into view. Seventy-three percent of Japan was mountainous, explaining the over-crowded cities. Jack caught sight of snow-capped Fuji Yama, rising majestically against the blue sky. A hostess passed with a food cart containing snacks, drinks, and bento boxed meals. Feeling peckish, Jack ordered a bento and a cup of coffee. As he opened the box, memories of Akiko came flooding back. He recalled the first bento she had prepared for him—a true work of art, arranged with painstaking detail. It had been her discreet way of showing love without losing face.

The Shinkansen pulled into Kyoto Station right on time. Jack retrieved his bag from the overhead rack and stepped into a hive of bustling people. The air was warm, and he stretched his legs. He had booked the same ryokan in Gion where he had once stayed with Akiko. It was about an hour's walk. The city was alive, awash in pink blossoms. Narrow streets brimmed with life, and geishas in elegant, colourful kimonos drifted by. For a moment, he thought he had seen Akiko. But it was only his mind playing tricks. He remembered vividly her splendid kimono embroidered with cranes, flowers, and a red sun. The beauty and grace she radiated had been indescribable. A sudden sadness washed over him like a dark cloud.

As he walked on, the laughter of children playing made him smile, yet the gut-wrenching memory of his unborn child scarred him deeply. Eventually, he arrived at the ryokan. It was just as he remembered. He pulled the chain, and the bell announced his presence. The unmistakable sound of geta sandals approached. The large wooden door creaked open, and Madame Tamura, the owner, greeted him warmly. She was overjoyed to see Jack, bowing deeply as she invited him inside.

"Where is your beautiful wife, Jack-san?" she asked.

Jack's head dropped. "Kanojo wa shinde shimatta, Tamura-san—she is dead and gone, Tamura-san." He did not explain. He didn't need to. It would have been impolite for her to pry. Tamura-san bowed again, promising to light joss sticks in Akiko's memory. The fragrant smoke, she said, acted as a spiritual broom—cleansing impurities and creating an environment sacred for connection.

Jack was led to his room—the same one he had shared with Akiko. Incense burned on a small tatami table, its floral scent of lily, rose, and jasmine bringing calm serenity. The room featured a private *onsen*, and the sliding doors opened to a terrace overlooking a manicured garden with a koi-filled pond. A mystical stillness lingered in the air, and Jack felt a deep calm. His movements guided now by intuition, he put on his karate gi and performed the breathing kata sanchin on the terrace. With each motion, he felt the silent pulse of the universe flowing through him. He was connected.

The kata left him drenched in sweat, as if all impurities of body and mind had been expelled. Stripping down, he stepped into the 38°C onsen. It felt good. Thoughts of Akiko mingled with thoughts of Sophie. Their phone calls had grown less frequent, and Jack sensed a distance in her voice during the last one, three weeks earlier. Then a long letter had arrived. Sophie explained that she had reconnected with a teenage sweetheart named Pierre. They had been meeting regularly, "only enjoying each other's company" for now. She admitted she was emotionally confused, haunted still by the traumas of her past.

Jack understood—her scars might last a lifetime. Yet he realised that he, too, had never truly healed. His love for Akiko still burned deeply within him. Could he ever love another as he had loved her?

He was lost in thought as he stepped out of the onsen. He dried himself and put on a neatly folded nemaki robe laid out on the futon. Pulling open the sliding doors, he stepped into the small Zen garden. Breathing in the cool evening air, he felt both peaceful and sad. His thoughts turned to his upcoming flight to Okinawa in two days. He longed to be there, to see Ichiro, his father-in-law. A full month lay ahead in Okinawa—time to catch up on so much he had left behind.

The truth is what you believe.

Warren Brewin

CHAPTER
Twenty-Nine

Manhattan

Things were beginning to heat up for Joey Falconetti. The Inland Revenue had contacted him on several occasions, inquiring about his tax returns. They had been monitoring his luxurious lifestyle, his income, and his numerous restaurant businesses. Things just didn't add up, they had told him. Joey was getting very hot under the collar and increasingly pissed off.

He told his accountant to deal with it pronto, or he'd be out of a job by the end of the month. Joey knew only too well that once the Inland Revenue guys got a whiff of something bad, the Feds were never too far away. Who knows, maybe his phone had been tapped. He wouldn't put it past those bastards. As far as he was concerned, they were garbage dressed in suits. Had they nothing better to do than harass a hardworking man who paid his taxes and their wages?

Or maybe he had become careless, he thought. Was there a faulty link in the chain? The restaurants turned over a lot of legit revenue, but a lot of it was in cash that wasn't always declared. Should he grease the greedy hand of some Inland Revenue commissioner, or issue serious anonymous threats to him or his family? That always worked.

Or was it something else?

Had they caught a whiff of his illicit dealings in the drug business or the human trafficking? Impossible, as these two businesses were a strictly cash affair. Maybe someone was shooting off their mouth a bit too much. Was there a leak somewhere?

He had been extremely careful. He'd been over it a million times, and there was no way that any of this shit could make its way back to him. Or maybe somebody dropped his name somewhere along the line, and it fell on the wrong ears. He'd have to look into it. Everything had been ticking over nicely, just like a Swiss clock. In any case, he needed those cockroaches, as he referred to them, off his back.

Everything you've ever wanted is on the other side of fear

George Addair

CHAPTER
Thirty

Okinawa

Jack touched down at Naha Airport on a warm, sunny after-noon. He could already smell the ocean. He picked up his baggage from the conveyor belt and proceeded through cus-toms clearance. The police official studied Jack's Irish passport carefully, asking him several questions in broken English con-cerning the purpose of his visit, the length of his stay, and his place of residence during his time on the island. Jack replied to all of the questions in perfect Japanese, and the official's eyes lit up as his face broke into a broad smile. He stamped Jack's passport and bowed politely as he handed it back: "*Okinawa e yokoso, go taizai o tanoshinde itadakereba saiwaidesu* – Welcome to Okinawa. I hope you enjoy your stay."

Jack thanked him and walked towards the exit. Naha Airport was often busy with frequent domestic flights to and from mainland Japan, along with the constant comings and goings of the Ameri-can army, whose thirty-two military facilities occupied a com-bined 188 square kilometres of the island. Today was one of those bustling days.

In the distance, Jack could make out Ichiro. He was wearing a splendid black yukata, a type of casual kimono, along with an obi. He was tanned as always, looking fit despite his sixty years. Jack waved, and his father-in-law waved back jovially. Jack made his way through the crowd until he reached him. He put his two bags on the ground, and the two men bowed formally. In Japan, it was considered impolite to hug someone publicly. Such gestures were reserved for behind closed doors. A smile lit up Ichiro's bronzed face: "Ohisashiburi desu, Jack-san. Long time no see. You're looking well and fit. We have a lot of time to catch up, my son-in-law."

"We sure do, gifu," Jack replied with a smile.

Ichiro offered to take one of Jack's bags, and together they made their way to the car park. Jack appreciated the warmth of the Okinawan sun on his skin. He reached into his inside pocket and put on a pair of sunglasses. Ichiro's blue 1974 Toyota Corolla was waiting for them. It was in pristine condition, looking as though it had just rolled off the factory line. Ichiro had bought it as a young man and cared for it the way a samurai cared for his katana. The Corolla was an immensely popular model and would, in 1997, become the world's best-selling nameplate, surpassing the Volkswagen Beetle.

They settled into the car and left the car park. Ichiro turned to Jack. "It's so good to see you, Jack-san. I missed you so much."

"Hai, me too, gifu. I missed you deeply, and I never stopped thinking about you. But my pain was so great," replied Jack.

It was a relaxing forty-minute drive to Ichiro's beach house. During the journey, they talked casually, and Jack's father-in-law filled him in on all the latest happenings on the island. The little Orion brewery where Akiko had once worked had expanded into an international concern, exporting worldwide, including to the United States. Their turnover had more than quadrupled. Ichiro had met with his good friend Saigo Nakamura, the CEO of the brewery, who had happily shared the good news. He credited the success to Akiko's inventive and skilful communication and marketing strategies.

The memories came cascading back to Jack. He remembered how excited Akiko had been when she secured a market outside Japan. That evening, they had opened a fine bottle of wine and toasted the brewery's success and Akiko's promising career. They had been so happy.

The Corolla stopped, snapping Jack out of his semi-lucid dream. He retrieved his luggage from the boot. He could hear the sound of the ocean, smell the salt spray and seaweed. Notes of ozone, jasmine, sandalwood, and musk filled his nostrils. It felt wonderful. He hadn't realised just how much he had missed it. The cry of a curlew brought all the memories pleasantly flooding back.

They entered the house from the terrace. Jack set his bags on the floor, and the two men embraced in a warm, tender hug, neither wanting to let go. Tears slipped from their eyes, running gently down their cheeks and onto their lips. It was a joyful, intimate moment, yet filled with painful and indelible memories.

Ichiro showed Jack to his room. Everything was impeccably presented and thoughtfully arranged. The futon was neatly prepared, and towels and a kimono were carefully folded in the middle. On the floor lay a pair of uwabaki, light and flexible shoes meant for indoor use. Jack needed a shower; it had been a long, sticky, and exhausting trip. He knew the night ahead would be long and that Ichiro would have many questions.

Jack felt reborn after the refreshing shower. He dried himself off and slipped into the black kimono. His mind flashed back to the first time he had entered this house, met Ichiro, and then locked eyes with Akiko — a moment that had overwhelmed him and left him practically speechless. It seemed like a lifetime ago.

He opened his suitcase and took out a 25-year-old bottle of Redbreast single pot still Irish whiskey. He knew his father-in-law was an aficionado of fine whisky.

Jack opened the door into the dining room and was greeted by a smiling Ichiro and a majestic spread of succulent finger foods. There was a mixture of everything to tempt even the most particular palate — duck, chicken, rabbit, various fish both raw and cooked, a vast assortment of vegetable dishes, and of course, the finest rice.

Jack offered the whiskey to Ichiro, who was overcome with emotion. The two men simply smiled; no words were needed. Their body language spoke enough.

Ichiro carefully placed the bottle on the table. "We will have a glass later, Jack-san, on the terrace while watching the moon."

Jack bowed. "My mouth is already watering with anticipation," he smiled.

Both men took their places at the table in the traditional seiza position. Most Japanese could hold the posture for about twenty minutes before shifting into a more comfortable cross-legged position. Jack had once found seiza excruciating because of his stiff ankles, much to Akiko and Ichiro's amusement when he first tried. But after years in Japan and daily karate training, it had become second nature.

They toasted with a bottle of Orion beer before dipping into the delicious food. Jack hadn't eaten much all day and was eager for the treat. As expected, Ichiro was full of questions. Jack fed him the information slowly, not wanting to overwhelm him.

When Jack finished his story, Ichiro was completely speechless. He came beside Jack and embraced him warmly.

"I am so sorry, Jack-san. I had no idea you had suffered so much. But there is a pleasant surprise waiting for you in the beach cabin."

Jack looked puzzled.

"Jack-san, you remember Michyo, Akiko's cousin, who came to your wedding? She is here from Hong Kong to spend the summer on the island. She's on vacation, in the last year of her studies, and very eager to see you again. She wants you to come to the cabin for coffee tomorrow morning. She was just a teenager at your wedding, but now she has grown into a beautiful young woman. She wanted to come tonight, but I told her we needed some time alone."

Jack was momentarily lost for words. She was the last person he expected to see. Of course, he remembered her. He had been immediately struck by her uncanny resemblance to Akiko. Except for the age difference, they could have been twins, though Michyo bore faint Anglo-Saxon features from her father, a British naval officer.

The two men finished eating, satiated. It was just after midnight when Ichiro proposed a nightcap on the terrace. Jack readily accepted. Ichiro took the bottle of Redbreast that Jack had generously gifted him, and they stepped out onto the terrace, sitting together on the long bench facing the sea.

It was a perfect night. There was no chill in the air. The moon was full, and the stars burned bright. They could hear the gentle sound of the calm sea, the quiet lapping of the waves. Ichiro opened the precious bottle and poured it ceremoniously into two glasses. Both he and Jack preferred their whiskey neat — no ice, at room temperature, with a glass of water on the side to stave off dehydration and the inevitable headache the next morning. This was, after all, the proper way to drink good whiskey; ice diluted its flavours. For Jack, people who mixed it with Coca-Cola committed sacrilege, showing disrespect for the master distiller. His grandfather had explained this to him many years ago — a lesson he had never forgotten.

"*Kanpai*," said Ichiro, and the two men clinked their glasses. They lifted the golden nectar to their noses, inhaled its layered aromas, then poured it gently into their mouths, savouring the unfolding flavours. They licked their lips, locked eyes, and smiled. The smile said it all—there was nothing more to express. The master distiller had done his job. They joked, laughed, and finished their first glass of whiskey. Ichiro refilled their glasses.

"I saw *Sensei* Saito last week, Jack-san," said Ichiro as he set the bottle down. "He was asking about you. And so was your good friend Toshiro. Saito-sensei was like a father to you, and he deeply regrets the comments he made, as well as his attitude toward you after that fateful day. He hadn't known all the details—the true horror of what had really happened. You should go and visit him,

Jack-san. He will be overjoyed, ready to welcome you with open arms. And I'm sure you're eager to set foot in that old dojo again."

"Arigato gozaimasu, that warms my heart," replied Jack. "I will go to the dojo tomorrow. I've missed it terribly. The memories remain vivid, and the thought of seeing Sensei and Toshiro again gladdens my heart. It's time for me to reconnect."

Ichiro then asked about Jack's future plans. When Jack explained that he was heading to Sicily in a month or so, and then on to New York to finish his vendetta once and for all, it left Ichiro shaken. He was gravely concerned, warning Jack it would be a suicide mission. Jack thanked him for his concern but explained it was something that had to be done. He couldn't spend the rest of his life looking over his shoulder. He needed to end it, once and for all, even if it cost him his life. Only closure would bring him peace.

They finished their whiskey and retired to their futons. It was one in the morning. The moment Jack's head touched the futon, his lights went out. Whiskey was a natural sleeping pill. He slept soundly until 7 a.m., awakened only by the cries of the curlew through the open window on their early morning quest for food. Stretching, he headed to the bathroom, splashed cold water on his face, then pulled on his keikogi and stepped into the dining room. His breakfast was neatly set on the table, with fresh coffee on the stove. Ichiro had left a note saying he would see him later that evening. Being a fisherman, he had to follow the strict rhythm of the sea. "The fish don't wait for the fisherman," he had once told Jack.

Jack drank a glass of freshly squeezed orange juice, then stepped onto the terrace just as the red and orange sun rose over the horizon. He began his ninety-minute morning routine. By the end, he was dripping with sweat. Stripping off his top, he shifted into deep breathing exercises until his body cooled. Hunger soon replaced exertion.

After a shower, he felt rejuvenated, and even more so after the copious, varied breakfast Ichiro had prepared. He slipped into jeans and a T-shirt, rolled his jeans up to the knee, and headed barefoot down the beach toward the little cabin to meet Michyo.

The feel of wet sand beneath his feet brought back sharp memories. He could almost feel Akiko's hand in his—remembering how many times they had strolled here, laughing aloud when a wave surged up and drenched them to the thigh.

He reached the little cabin. It hadn't changed; it was exactly as he'd left it. His makiwara was still standing outside, well protected by Ichiro's careful maintenance. Jack climbed the three steps onto the terrace and knocked gently. A radiant, smiling Michyo greeted him.

"*Ohisashiburi desu*, Jack-san. It's so nice to see you after all these years. How are you?" she asked with a warm smile.

Jack was gobsmacked, his head reeling. For all intents and purposes, it was Akiko standing there. The resemblance was uncanny. She was slightly taller and bore softer Anglo-Saxon features from her father, a British naval officer—but otherwise, she was Akiko's mirror. Jack fought to regain his composure.

"I'm fine," said Jack. "And you look fantastic. Your resemblance to your cousin is absolutely incredible."

She blushed slightly, and Jack found it endearing.

"Oh, everyone says that," she smiled, "but Akiko was far prettier than me. Please come in, Jack-san. I've just made some coffee."

Stepping inside, Jack was assaulted by a cascade of memories— one after another, relentless.

"Are you alright, Jack-san? You seem stunned," she asked.

"Yes, I'm fine," Jack replied. "There are just so many memories rushing back."

"Yes, I understand," she said softly. "I hope you don't mind me staying here?"

Jack felt momentarily awkward. "Of course, not—you're more than welcome."

Ichiro had gifted the cabin to Jack and Akiko just after their marriage. It had been their wedding present.

Michyo asked about his plans for the day. Jack explained that he was going to the dojo in Naha to see Sensei Saito and his karate friends, and possibly share lunch with them after training.

"Maybe we could have dinner this evening," she suggested with a smile.

"I'd like that very much," Jack said. "We could go to Tanpopo. I have fond memories of that restaurant. I'll come by around 7:30 p.m., if that suits?"

"I'll be ready," she replied.

Jack rose and headed for the door. "Oh, by the way, are Akiko's scooter and bicycle still in the shed?"

"Hai," she nodded. "They're both there, though I only use the bicycle."

"Okay, great—let's go and see," Jack said as he stepped outside.

Just after their wedding, Jack and Ichiro had built the shed together. It housed the bike, the scooter, various odds and ends, and a few tools. The door creaked as he opened it. A little oil wouldn't hurt, he thought. And there it was—the old Honda 125 scooter, standing beside the bicycle. The very first time he had laid eyes on Akiko, she had been riding that same bicycle. It felt like yesterday. An angel on a bike, he had thought. Despite a few cobwebs, the scooter looked fine. Jack wheeled it out of the shed.

"Do you think it will start?" Michyo asked eagerly.

Jack ran his hand through his hair. "Let's see," he said.

First, he checked the tank. There was just enough petrol to reach the nearest station. It was the old kick-start model, stubborn after years of neglect. Jack kicked and twisted the throttle for two minutes before pausing. No point flooding the engine, he thought. After a few minutes, while admiring the ocean and the rising sun, he tried again. This time, after a minute of effort, the engine coughed, sputtered, and then roared back to life, happy to run again.

Michyo was ecstatic. She jumped, clapping her hands with delight. Jack couldn't help but be charmed. Her resemblance to

Akiko tugged at him, reminding him of his first encounter with his late wife—her innocence, sincerity, and beauty that had bewitched him so completely.

Jack stopped by Ichiro's house to grab his karate gi, then headed for Naha and the dojo. He had taken this route six times a day for nearly eight years; he could travel it blindfolded. With luck, he would make the late morning session starting at noon. He felt alive again, eager to see Sensei Saito and Toshiro. At a small family-run petrol station, he filled the scooter's tank. The owner recognised him instantly and bombarded him with questions. Jack answered politely but cut the pleasantries short before continuing.

He arrived at the dojo at 11:45 a.m.—just in time. In Japan, tardiness was never tolerated, except under extreme circumstances. Jack entered and bowed. His nostrils were immediately filled with the familiar scents of incense and polished red pine. As always, the kohai, the junior students, were still scrubbing the floor until it gleamed without a speck of dust.

Sensei Saito entered in his usual high-spirited manner. When he saw Jack, his jaw dropped. His features froze, as if he had just seen a yūrei—a ghost from folklore.

Jack bowed respectfully from a distance, then picked up his bag and approached. Still incredulous, Saito's face softened, breaking into a paternal smile.

"Jack-san, ohisashiburi desu—it's been such a long time. I missed you. Go now, quickly, and change. I hope you haven't lost your edge. Toshiro is in the locker room; he'll be overjoyed to see you. He's spoken of you every day since your disappearance. After class, we will talk, Jack-san."

Jack bowed. *"Arigato gozaimasu, Sensei."* He headed into the locker room, knocked, and opened the door. Toshiro stood alone, just finishing the knot on his kuro obi, his black belt. He turned, saw Jack in the doorway, and froze. His reaction mirrored Saito's—he looked as though he'd seen a ghost.

"Jack-san, my brother—where have you been? I missed you every single day."

He grabbed Jack in a warm and powerful embrace, unwilling to release his grip. When he finally loosened his hold, tears welled up in his dark eyes. A single tear rolled down Jack's cheek, and the two men stood in a cathedral-like silence, observing one another.

Toshiro wiped his eyes "Sensei explained everything to me, Jack-san. I am so sorry. I can't imagine the pain you have endured. But you should have kept in contact, my brother."

When Jack stepped onto the wooden dojo floor, a tingle ran down his spine. How he had missed this place, with its unique ambience and familiar scents. After the essential warm-up exercises, they went into the kata Sanchin. It was Jack's favourite breathing kata, which he practised daily. His friend Toshiro was there to control Jack's stance and posture. He delivered powerful blows to Jack's torso with his hands and feet to test whether Jack's stance was truly strong and balanced. To a neophyte's eyes, it would seem as if the man was being punished in a very brutal fashion. But Toshiro was impressed with Jack's execution of the kata. Then it was his turn to go through the motions. Jack corrected his friend's posture and, out of respect, did not pull his blows.

Jack noticed another 6th-dan black belt among the ranks —a man in his mid-thirties whom Jack had trained with during his earlier time at the dojo. Jack remembered that back then, he had just passed his test for the 1st dan. This man, Kenji, had since made tremendous progress. Saito-sensei pitted Jack against him in the first sparring session. Jack was honoured. The man was good, but not good enough. He didn't have the real-life experience Jack had endured.

He then had a *randori* with his good friend Toshiro. He was curious to see if his friend had made any progress and if he still had the edge. Jack was surprised, for Toshiro had gained both speed and power—if that were even possible. Toshiro, in turn, was also surprised at Jack's defence, accuracy, and finesse. It was as though Jack knew what his adversary was going to do before it even happened. This was called *Sen no sen*—anticipating your opponent's attack and countering immediately. In other words, you strike before your opponent has the chance to execute his movement.

After training, it was straight to the dressing room for a well-deserved shower. They were then invited to Sensei Saito's house for cool beers and some finger food. Madame Saito was overjoyed to see Jack; she had always thought of him as her own son. Jack braced himself for the barrage of questions that would inevitably come. Taking the initiative, he began to explain what had happened since his urgent departure from Okinawa.

He told them of the club he had opened in Dublin and how popular it had become, his meeting with Sophie, their romance, and their eventual falling in love. He went on to recount the pain, horror, and trauma that both she and he had endured. The gathering was dumbfounded when Jack told them about the hitmen sent from New York to exterminate him—the confrontation in the dojo, the massacre on Dollymount Beach, and the bullets fired through the balcony door.

And finally, Sophie's return to France to convalesce in her parents' home, and their eventual separation. He explained that Sophie had been psychologically scarred for life and could no longer be around Jack, despite the deep love they had shared. It was over. An awkward silence followed until Sensei Saito raised his glass. "*Kanpai*, Jack-san. It's great to see you again, and to have you back."

Jack explained that he was only staying for a month or so, as he had unfinished business to attend to. He left them all in high spirits and headed back to Ichiro's house.

On arrival, he changed into his bathing togs and grabbed a towel. He needed sunshine and a relaxing swim.

He walked down the beach towards the cabin and came across Michyo, who was sunbathing and engrossed in the novel she was reading. She was lying on her back, wearing a two-piece white swimsuit with a support under her head. Jack observed her.

She was beautiful, and at twenty-three her beauty was at its peak. Her body was lithe and toned. Her stomach was flat and tight as a drum, her breasts full and firm. Her skin had darkened under the Okinawan sun since her arrival. Jack couldn't get over her likeness to Akiko. A stirring rose in his loins. He was practically beside her before she noticed.

"Must be a good book," laughed Jack.

"Oh, Jack-san, I was lost in my book," she replied. "The book is *The Remains of the Day* by Kazuo Ishiguro. I love it."

"I'm sorry," said Jack, "but I've never heard of it—or him."

Michyo smiled. "He's a Japanese-born British author. He won the Booker Prize for Fiction. He's very good."

"Do you swim?" inquired Jack.

"Yes, I do," smiled Michyo. "I love to swim."

"Ikimashō, let's go then," replied Jack.

Jack dived straight in, as did Michyo—much to his surprise. He had seen the temperature displayed at the port: a welcoming 23°C. Quite a difference compared to the sea in Ireland, which rarely rose above 18°C.

When Jack had first arrived in Okinawa, he had been a poor swimmer. But thanks to Akiko and their near-daily swims, he had become a very accomplished one. He could now swim a kilometre with relative ease.

Michyo was also an excellent swimmer. She seemed to glide through the water effortlessly. They swam out far for about twenty minutes nonstop before taking a well-earned breather. Jack had missed the Okinawan water and sun so much. He observed Michyo. She was radiant. With her wet hair slicked back, her natural beauty was even more accentuated. He might as well have been looking at Akiko. She smiled at him innocently, and he fell a little more under her spell. He was being drawn to her, just as the moon pulls the ocean.

"Last one back has to buy a drink!" she shouted.

"Oh, you're on," replied Jack.

They swam back to the shore and exited the water practically at the same time.

"Okay, let's call it quits," said Jack, "but I'll still buy you a drink."

"*Arigato*," she smiled back.

Jack couldn't help noticing the stark contrast between his white-skinned body and Michyo's sun-kissed one. He knew it would take a few weeks under the Okinawan sun to regain the rich, berry-brown tan he had when he'd left the island three years ago.

"Would you like a beer, Jack? I've stocked some in the fridge," asked Michyo. "Well, that's a question most Irishmen would say yes to, Michyo. I'd love a beer. That swim has given me quite a thirst."

They went back to the little cabin, and Michyo brought out two ice-cold Orion beers, placing them on the small table on the wooden terrace. Jack and Akiko had spent many a day and night sipping beers there, making plans for their future.

The memories were still vivid in Jack's mind. Jack asked Michyo about her future plans. She told him she was returning to Hong Kong in six weeks to sit her final exams. She hoped to get her degree in international law and business strategy. If so, she was considering coming back to Okinawa to work for a year or so

 The brewery was looking for multilingual people, especially in the sales department, as the business had expanded internationally. Being fluent in English, Chinese, and Japanese, she felt confident about her chances.

"I'd say your boyfriend will miss you," smiled Jack. "Oh, I'm not involved with anyone," she laughed. "Not seriously, anyway. I just don't have the time, and besides, I haven't met the right person yet."

Well, that's good news, Jack thought to himself. He felt himself being drawn to her like a moth to a light bulb. He was truly smitten.

"And what about you, Jack-san? What are your plans?" Jack felt a bit uneasy. He couldn't tell her his real plans. He didn't want her involved.

"Oh, I'm just back to visit my father-in-law, my friends at the dojo, and Sensei Saito. I just didn't have the time before, and the years flew past." Michyo hadn't been told everything about Akiko's death and what followed.

"Well, thanks for the beer, Michyo. I'll pick you up about 7:30 p.m. as planned. I booked a table for eight. Now I need a shower." "I can't wait," she smiled back.

In the end, it's not the years in your life that count. It's the life in your years.

Abraham Lincoln

CHAPTER
Thirty-One
Manhattan

It was early Friday afternoon in downtown Manhattan. Joey Falconetti stretched back in his leather office armchair, puffed out the blue smoke from his favourite cigar, and put his feet on the desk. He was content. Business—both legal and illegal—was flourishing beyond his wildest dreams. He smiled as he blew out more blue smoke. He had decided to bring the family to the luxury house that he had bought in the Hamptons.

It had belonged to a wealthy New York banker who had passed away two years previously. The family had wanted a quick sale, and Joey, thanks to his sharp eye in real estate, had been very fast off the mark with an offer they couldn't refuse. The house was equipped with quality furniture, all the mod cons one could think of, a huge heated swimming pool, and the beach at the end of the garden via four wooden steps.

A knock on the door brought him out of his reverie.

"Come in," shouted Falconetti.

Roberto, the barman, entered the office looking a bit perplexed.

"Sorry to disturb you, Mr. Falconetti, but the NYPD are here and they want to talk to you."

"What the fuck?" scorned Joey. "Okay, show them in. It shouldn't take long."

Captain John McSorley entered the room, cap in hand, accompanied by two other officers.

"Very sorry to disturb you, Mr. Falconetti," he said in a doleful manner. "We were contacted by the Inland Revenue and the FBI about certain business transactions that don't seem to add up, sir, and we have a number of questions we need to ask you."

"What is this?" barked Falconetti. "Is this some kind of shake down? Do you guys know how much I donate to the widows' and orphans' funds every year?"

"We do, sir, but we're just doing our job and following orders from up above. It won't take very long, sir."

"Okay then, shoot," spat Falconetti.

Captain McSorley cleared his throat. "We can't do it here, sir. It has to be downtown. That's the procedure."

"Procedure, my ass," shouted Falconetti. "Okay then, let's go, and I'd better be back here in a hurry. This is fucking up my weekend in the Hamptons with the family. Now get out of my office and give me five minutes."

Falconetti went back to his desk and reached out for his phone. He wasn't the most patient of men at the best of times, but right now, to say that he was impatient would be quite an understatement. He hit the digit 6 on the console, and the phone dialled the direct line to Levi Cohen, who was Falconetti's chartered accountant.

The ringing tone always irritated Falconetti, but at this moment, he found it unbearable and unending. Finally, a male voice came on at the other end. It was the voice of Levi Cohen, one of the best accountants money could buy in the state of New York.

"Mr. Falconetti, what a pleasant surprise. I hope everything is okay. How can I be of service?"

"The NYPD want me downtown for questions concerning income tax returns, certain business transactions, and so on. I pay you good money, Mr. Cohen, to keep things tight and under wraps. You'd better pull something out of the hat, or you'll be losing a good-paying client."

Mr. Cohen cleared his throat. "Now, Mr. Falconetti, let's not panic. Wait and see what exactly they want to know, and we shall act accordingly. Maybe they're only letting off steam or fishing."

Mr. Cohen was a very pragmatic man. He was used to dealing with the Inland Revenue and the Feds, as most of his big customers were more than borderline.

"Okay," scoffed Falconetti, "do your bit of magic then. I'll be in touch."

Falconetti kept the phone in his hand and dialled his lawyer's number.

"Hello, Kirkland and Jones. How may I be of service?"

"Mr. Falconetti here. Tell Mr. Kirkland to get his butt down to the 19th Precinct asap."

"I'm sorry, Mr. Falconetti, but Mr. Kirkland is in court at the moment. I'll see if his partner, Mr. Jones, is available."

Falconetti was tapping his fingers nervously on his desk.

"Mr. Falconetti, Mr. Jones here. What seems to be the problem?"

"I'm being taken down to the 17th for questioning about income tax returns and some other corporate matters."

"Okay, Mr. Falconetti, they're only fishing. I'll see you down there. In the meantime, don't answer any questions until my arrival."

"You can bet on that," smirked Falconetti. He put the phone down and walked out of his office to where the police officers were waiting impatiently.

"Okay, let's go, guys. I don't have all day, and the Hamptons are calling."

Upon arrival at the precinct, Falconetti was taken into the questioning room. It was Spartan, to say the least, and the most depressing room he had ever been in. He was offered something to drink—water, fruit juice, or coffee. He opted for a coffee, knowing too well that the coffee in cop shops was far from what he was used to drinking—and that was Blue Mountain coffee from Jamaica, one of the best in the world.

He was told to sit in a chair in front of a big table. On the other side were two officers in plain clothes. One had a smile; the other looked as though he was constipated. And another guy in an immaculate white shirt and black tie stood behind them. He was smoking a Marlboro. All that was lacking was the Stetson, thought Falconetti. He politely offered a cigarette to Falconetti, who graciously turned down the offer. He never smoked that shit. He only smoked top-quality Cuban cigars.

The coffee arrived with milk and sugar. Falconetti threw one cube of sugar into the cup and stirred it. He brought the cup to his lips and took a sip. Even the smell was repulsive. It was a far cry from the Blue Mountain brand that he was used to. How could they drink that shit every day? he thought.

Falconetti's replacement lawyer, Tony Jones, entered the room. He was a tall, distinguished-looking man in his mid-fifties. He was wearing a beautiful black Armani suit. His hair, which had once been dark, had turned salt and pepper. He certainly looked the part and oozed confidence. He placed his briefcase on the table with authority.

"Okay, gentlemen, I'll take it from here. I hope you haven't been mishandling my client, Mr. Falconetti?"

The police officers threw their eyes to heaven. They were more than used to the procedure. They left the room to respect the protocol of lawyer-client privacy.

Tony Jones sat on a chair opposite Falconetti and unbuttoned his jacket.

"Now, I trust that you have said nothing, Mr. Falconetti?"

Joey Falconetti sat forward in his chair and looked Jones straight in the eye.

"I didn't say nothing, just as you advised." Falconetti liked the guy's style. He was a smooth operator, a person who inspired confidence and trust.

"Okay, very good, Mr. Falconetti. Somebody somewhere has blown a whistle, but my gut feeling is that they are just fishing for the moment and flexing their muscles. Let's invite the posse back in and see what they have to say."

So he tapped on the window and invited the three musketeers back into the room. The three detectives entered with a defeated look on their faces. They didn't have enough proof to charge Falconetti or to keep him in custody for a mandatory period of forty-eight hours with the approval of the State Prosecutor. They didn't know it yet, but the Prosecutor was one of many on Falconetti's payroll—or under threat of a nocturnal visit to his place of residence.

Tony Jones took a ballpoint pen and a notepad from his inside suit pocket. "Is my client being charged, gentlemen? If the opposite is the case, then I think he is free to leave!"

"We just wanted to ask Mr. Falconetti a few simple and informal questions," said Andy, a sandy-haired guy in his early forties.

"Okay, well, that's it, gentlemen," said Tony Jones as he stood up to his full six-foot-one height and buttoned his Armani jacket. "The next time, gentlemen, please follow procedure and come with a warrant. Myself and my client bid you all a very good day."

He picked up his leather briefcase and left the room behind Joey Falconetti. They went through the doors of the NYPD and were greeted by a boisterous late-afternoon New York City. Nothing unusual. They shook hands on the hot pavement and bid each other goodbye.

"Thanks for the way you handled that garbage back there, Mr. Jones," spat Falconetti. "Call into the restaurant sometime, and I'll treat you and your family to the best meal in Manhattan."

"I was just doing my job, Mr. Falconetti. And besides, you pay us very good money to look after your interests. It would be a pleasure to dine in your restaurant. Thank you for your generous offer, and in the meantime, enjoy your weekend in the Hamptons. Relax and enjoy the beach and the fresh sea air with your family. The weather is looking good for the weekend."

Falconetti was feeling happy again. He laughed. The NYPD were only fishing, grasping at straws. But what Joey didn't realise was that the NYPD were using a ploy. By releasing Falconetti, they were hoping to draw him out and make him lower his guard. They were building a solid case with the help of the Feds, but at present, there wasn't enough evidence to press charges. What they had would never stand up in a criminal court. They were still waiting for permission to tap Falconetti's office and home phones. They were confident that the phone tapping would provide crucial incriminating evidence—and it would be bye-bye, Mr. Falconetti. But for the moment, the authorisation wasn't forthcoming.

Falconetti hailed a yellow cab and jumped into the back seat. He gave his address to the driver, threw his head back, and settled into the seat. Traffic was dense, horns were blaring, and tempers were flaring—the usual Friday evening Manhattan ritual. After a forty-minute drive, they arrived at Falconetti's house. Joey gave the driver a hefty tip, thanked him, and got out of the taxi. He whistled as he walked up the drive to his fabulous mansion. A weekend in the Hamptons under the sun with the family was just what the doctor ordered.

The heart was made to be broken

Oscar Wilde

CHAPTER
Thirty-Two

Okinawa - present day

Jack arrived at the cabin at 8 p.m. sharp on the old Honda 125, as promised. He had barely tapped the door when it flung open. Michyo stood in the doorway. She was resplendent in a sea-green dress, a denim jacket, and white runners. Just as Akiko did, she wore a minimum of makeup, which pleased Jack.

"You look fantastic," said Jack with a smile.

"*Arigato,* Jack-san. You are also looking very handsome."

They walked to the scooter. Michyo pulled up her dress, showing her bronzed and shapely thighs as she threw her leg across the saddle. Jack swallowed hard. He was being caught up in this web of sensuality, and he wasn't looking for an escape. There was no escape.

Twenty minutes later, they arrived at the Tanpopo restaurant. It was quite full. The place hadn't changed much, and the regular staff were still there. They were all overjoyed to see Jack. He and Akiko had been regular customers over the years. Like most Japanese, they asked about his well-being without prying too much.

Jack could see from their faces that they thought they were looking at a ghost—such was the resemblance between Akiko and Michyo. But they smiled gently, trying to hide their astonishment.

They were shown to their table and offered a drink on the house. Jack took the local beer, and Michyo took an Awamori, a beverage indigenous and unique to Okinawa, made from long-grain rice.

They enjoyed a great meal of fish and shellfish and shared a bottle of French rosé wine. To say that they enjoyed each other's company would be an understatement. Michyo was curious as to why Jack had left Okinawa in such haste and why he hadn't given any news in more than three years. He did his best to explain certain things but left out the gory details. Michyo found it hard to hold back the tears. She took Jack by the hand and held it tightly.

They headed back to the cabin. Sitting on the back of the Honda, Michyo put her arms around Jack's muscular torso and pressed her head tightly to his back. They arrived at the cabin, and Michyo, slightly tipsy, ran towards the sea laughing and peeling off her clothes one by one.

"Come on, Jack," she giggled.

Jack didn't need any enticement. He stripped off, and they both dived into the warm water. The moon was huge and bright as they swam out. They giggled like children, then their lips met, and they kissed passionately as new lovers do. They couldn't get enough of each other, as though they were famished. They swam back to the moonlit beach.

Michyo threw herself onto her back on the soft sand. Her dark mound, with sea water droplets, glistened like diamonds under the moonlight. Henri Matisse would have appreciated the sight of her beauty. She giggled and beckoned Jack towards her. Her lips were like ripe cherries waiting to be plucked. He lay down beside her, and their lips met again with the same ardour.

She moaned as he cupped her firm breasts. He found one of her nipples with his mouth and teased it erect. His hand slipped slowly down, and he cupped her moist mound. She moaned again. She parted her legs, and his finger probed her gently. He then went down on her and tasted her salty wetness. She moaned loudly and begged him to enter her. Jack was now fully erect. He entered her gently.

Her legs locked around his waist, and she pulled him towards her, beckoning him on. Much to her delight, his thrusts became more and more powerful. To Jack's surprise, she was an experienced lover in spite of her young years.

She started to climax, and Jack could feel the spasms rippling through her body. He climaxed, and he came in powerful jets, which made her shudder. She cried out as she reached her orgasm, her vagina pulsing involuntarily with a pace and intensity that could not be faked. Jack gasped loudly as she released the hold on his shaft. They both lay on their backs, exhausted.

They went back to the cabin and showered together. Then they dried each other off and dressed lightly. Michyo took two cold beers from the fridge, and they stepped out onto the little moonlit terrace. They sat without saying a word and watched the star-studded sky.

"Look," cried out Michyo excitedly, pointing to the sky. "*Hoshi nagare.*" A shooting star.

It was the first shooting star that Jack had seen this year, and hopefully not the last, he thought. He had observed many shooting stars with Akiko. Each time, they had made a wish. But unfortunately, Jack's had never come true. Maybe it was a message from Akiko, thought Jack, telling him that she was alright and thinking of him. He smiled. The idea warmed his heart. If only it could be true, he wished.

Jack had told Michyo about his plan to go to Sicily and deal with Giovanni Falconetti once and for all. She tried to dissuade him, but Jack had made up his mind. No peace could be had, he explained, until his mission was finished. First Sicily, and then New York, to deal with Joey Falconetti, the devil in person.

Jack had received a registered letter a few days previously from his good friend Joey Maloney in the Dublin homicide division, as he had promised. The letter contained all the intel information concerning Giovanni Falconetti. Joey Maloney had used his Interpol contacts, and the Carabinieri had been very helpful. The latter had been trying to nail Giovanni for some time now, but to no avail. He always seemed to have a bona fide alibi.

The letter contained Giovanni's address, a list of his close friends, his daily habits, and the restaurants, bars, and nightclubs that he liked to frequent. It even revealed information about his favourite foods, drinks, and his taste in women and cars. His addiction to physical fitness, firearms, and martial arts in general was also revealed. All in all, it gave Jack a complete picture of the man he would be hunting. The last line of the letter had sent a slight chill down Jack's spine: "Take care, my good friend, you're on your own now. This man is EXTREMELY dangerous. He has a choir of fallen angels on his shoulders. I have warned you. It's in God's hands now. So tread lightly, my friend, as the next round is on you."

It was springtime in Okinawa, and Jack made the most of it with daily runs, swims, and, of course, his martial arts training. He was as fit as the proverbial fiddle. As was his habit, Jack woke early. It was 6:30 a.m., and it was a Friday morning. Michyo was in a deep sleep. He stole out of bed as quietly as smoke coming under the door. He put on tracksuit bottoms and walked out onto the small wooden terrace to view the sunrise. It had become his addiction.

He meditated silently, watching the red sun on its daily voyage and listening to the sea as the waves lapped the shore gently. He had made up his mind. This morning, he would go to the travel agency in Naha and buy a one-way ticket to Tokyo and a connecting flight to Rome. He had never visited Rome, so he intended to stay three days and visit all the famous tourist spots. It would take his mind off what was to come.

A pity that the circumstances weren't different. He would have loved to visit Rome with Michyo. He had intended going with Akiko, but it wasn't to be. Once in Rome, he would buy a ticket to Palermo in Sicily and seek out Giovanni Falconetti. He was awakened from his thoughts by two arms hugging his muscular torso. He turned around to face her. Their lips met, and they kissed.

Jack booked his flights that morning at the local travel agency. Michyo tried to talk him out of it, but to no avail. He would fly to Tokyo on the Saturday morning in two weeks and catch a connecting flight to Rome later that evening. He spent the next two weeks training intensely and enjoying his time with Michyo. At 10% body fat, Jack was in excellent physical form. He had gone down to 8% body fat when he was preparing for the extremely gruelling *Hyaku-nin kumite*, the notorious 100-man fighting test of physical and mental endurance.

Michyo and Jack had fallen deeply in love, and each day their bodies intertwined to express their love and to reach sexual peaks that Jack had only ever experienced with Akiko. Michyo had never experienced such carnal pleasures. Jack was aware that their *au revoir*—their goodbye—would be heart-wrenching. But he knew that there was no other path, especially if they wanted to live together peacefully. The Falconettis would never let go. It was a vendetta that would only end when Jack—or the authorities—took care of Joey Falconetti.

Ichiro, Jack's father-in-law, had insisted on preparing a farewell meal for Jack on the Friday evening before his departure for Tokyo. The man went out of his way and prepared a meal fit for a king. The choice of dishes was endless: miso soup, sushi, tempura, ramen, sashimi, yakitori, tonkatsu, soba, sukiyaki, and unagi.

Ichiro managed to get his hands on three bottles of Château MacCarthy, the renowned French wine, considered the second wine of the famous Grand Cru Château Haut-Marbuzet. It was a wine that Jack had come to appreciate deeply. He also invited Sensei Saito and Toshiro from the dojo. They held a special place in Jack's heart.

They wined and dined in good spirits. Sensei Saito shared numerous anecdotes from his youth growing up in Okinawa, working long days on his family's farm, and continuing his rigorous karate training even after exhausting hours in the fields. He laughed as he recalled the many challenges he had taken on as a brash young man—facing American marines, karateka from various Okinawan dojos, and even visiting karateka from mainland Japan.

He was proud to say he had lost only one fight. Of course, the fights never took place in the dojo; that was strictly forbidden. His sensei, Chosin Chibana, eventually caught wind of his extracurricular activities, which he strongly disapproved of, and suspended him from the dojo for three months. The suspension did the trick, and from that day forward, he never again accepted a challenge, fearful of being banned for life.

To finish off the night, Ichiro produced a thirty-year-old bottle of Macallan and offered everyone a nightcap. The men gladly accepted—it wasn't every day one had the opportunity to taste such a splendid beverage, rich, fruity, and full-bodied in flavor. Michyo wasn't a whiskey drinker, so she opted for a herbal tea—Japanese, of course.

The stars were out and the moon was high when Jack and Michyo walked along the beach back to the cabin. That night, they made love as though it were for the last time. Jack was up at dawn; he couldn't miss the sunrise. He had an early morning flight. They had breakfast in silence. Jack took his travelling bag, and they bade their goodbyes on the little terrace. Michyo's eyes welled with tears as she kissed Jack tenderly on the lips. She couldn't bear to go to the airport—it was emotionally impossible.

"Promise me you'll come back soon, my love," she whispered, stroking his face.

"I will return, my love. I promise," Jack replied, wiping a falling tear from her cheek.

With that, he turned his back and walked down the beach without looking back. He didn't dare to, afraid he might see Akiko standing there. Michyo stood on the terrace, waving, hoping Jack would turn around. He didn't. She continued waving until his figure diminished in the distance. Ichiro was waiting to bring him to the airport.

Jack said his goodbyes to his father-in-law in the small departure lounge of Naha's airport. He stepped out onto the tarmac and climbed the stairs onto the small propeller-powered plane bound for Tokyo. At the top of the stairs, he turned around to offer a final farewell to Ichiro, but the old man had already gone. Ichiro, too, feared it might be the last time he would see his son-in-law.

Jack settled into his window seat and waited for the plane to taxi out onto the runway. The flight would take approximately three hours.

When the plane landed in Tokyo, it was 12:30 p.m. Jack's connecting flight to Rome was scheduled for 8 p.m. that evening. He decided to take the train and spend the day in Shibuya, the busiest district of Tokyo. It was a thirty-minute ride into what many called Japan's Times Square. It was impossible to say you had truly "done" Tokyo without witnessing the human tide rolling in and out at Shibuya Crossing—often described as the world's busiest crosswalk.

Jack exited the train station into what could only be described as controlled chaos. Although he had already been here with Akiko, the hustle and bustle still hit him like a sledgehammer. It was a far cry from what he was used to. Hungry, he decided to walk to Shibuya Yakitori Food Hall, where a man could find practically everything at very reasonable prices.

The noise inside the food hall was comparable to a beehive. Jack found what he was looking for: a miso, an assortment of raw fish, and noodles. He also ordered a beer and was fortunate to find a stool at one of the numerous counters.

He watched the human tide ebb and flow. It amused him and helped pass the time, distracting him from what was to come. The big clock in the hall showed 3 p.m. The beehive was still buzzing. He laughed to himself, wondering if it was ever quiet. With time to spare, he ordered another beer.

It was just 4 p.m. when Jack left the beehive and stepped back outside into the open air and noise. With more time to kill, he decided on a pleasant stroll, immersing himself in the human tide for a short while. Despite the clamour, it was calming as he drifted into his thoughts. He remembered walking the same street hand in hand with Akiko years earlier.

He closed his eyes briefly, almost feeling her touch and hearing her laughter. They had been carefree and lighthearted. How drastically life could change, he thought. A blaring horn snapped him out of his reverie. He headed to a taxi rank and told the driver to take him to Haneda, Tokyo's international airport.

The taxi dropped him at the airport just after 6 p.m. He checked in and bought a bag of sweets and a copy of Time magazine, hoping to stave off boredom during the long flight. The journey would last just over fifteen and a half hours. It would be the first time Jack had flown directly from Japan to Europe—or vice versa, for that matter. He wasn't exactly looking forward to it.

Jack went through security, presented his ticket and passport, and received a warm smile from a female official. She bowed in the traditional Japanese fashion and handed him back his documents. After a short wait at the gate, he finally stepped onto the tarmac and climbed the stairs to his Alitalia flight. It was a clear night, calm with little or no wind.

He was greeted by four smiling, immaculately groomed, dark-haired hostesses—three brunettes and a blonde. All wore their hair in neat buns. *Top model material,* Jack thought. They looked stunning in the elegant Alitalia uniform: red cap, green-white-red scarf, red jacket, green knee-length skirt, black patent leather shoes, and crisp white blouse beneath.

Jack found his window seat in the tenth row and settled in. The seatbelt sign came on, and the hostess went through the safety drill in English, followed by translations in Italian and Japanese. The cheerful captain, Marco Bonetti, welcomed everyone aboard and wished them a pleasant flight. He explained that there were no low-pressure zones reported and that a high-pressure system stretched over Italy. All was good. Everyone was relaxed and happy.

Night had fallen as the plane taxied down the runway. Jack felt himself pressed into the seat as the turbines roared to full acceleration. The aircraft lifted, climbing swiftly. From his window, Jack admired Tokyo at night—the thousands of neon lights glowing brightly, heralding the city's nightlife.

Once airborne, refreshments were offered. Jack gratefully accepted a fresh orange juice. Later, he ordered a cappuccino, and further into the flight, he enjoyed a cool beer, followed by a second. He stood nearly every hour to stretch his legs and keep his blood circulating. Restless, like a hen on a hot griddle, he managed to read his copy of Time magazine cover to cover before falling into a deep sleep about seven hours into the flight.

He woke five hours later to a smiling hostess asking if he would like a snack. Hungry, he chose ravioli sprinkled with Parmesan cheese, accompanied by a generous glass of Chianti wine. The food hit the spot, and the wine did the rest.

It was just after 3:30 a.m. local time when the plane touched down on the tarmac of Rome's Leonardo da Vinci International Airport, better known to air travellers as Fiumicino. Some passengers clapped and cheered in nervous relief as the aircraft landed smoothly, the engines thrusting into reverse to brake and slow down the massive Boeing 747, nearly bringing it to a standstill. A flawless, safe landing.

Jack was more than happy to recover his cabin bag, walk down the steps, and step onto the tarmac. He badly needed to stretch his legs and breathe in the fresh air. Passing through security, he endured the usual questions before a tired-looking official handed back his passport. It was a short walk to the main lobby, where he spotted the exit sign.

He pushed through the revolving doors to where a string of taxis waited for potential customers. He tapped the window of the first car in the queue, a Fiat Croma, and was greeted by a smiling, dapperly dressed man in his early fifties.

"Buongiorno, signore, benvenuto a Roma," the driver said warmly in Italian as he took Jack's bag and placed it in the trunk.

Jack asked if he spoke English. The man replied that he spoke a little, explaining he liked to watch cowboy movies in the original version. Jack chuckled to himself. Yeah, he couldn't imagine John Wayne being dubbed in Italian.

Jack asked if he knew the Hotel Colosseum. Of course, he did. Off they went. Jack had chosen the hotel for its proximity to the Colosseum—only half a mile away—and because of its rooftop patio. The Colosseum was number one on Jack's list of places to visit. Not only for its historical importance, but also because it had served as the setting for the legendary fight between Bruce Lee and Chuck Norris in the film The Way of the Dragon (1972).

The taxi driver was cheerful and loquacious, reminding Jack of Irish cabbies. He pointed out historical monuments worth visiting and restaurants where one could enjoy the best lasagne and spaghetti carbonara in Rome without taking out a mortgage. He was especially keen to mention his sister's restaurant, a family-run affair renowned for traditional Italian dishes at reasonable rates. He told Jack his name was Giacomo, and if Jack went to his sister's restaurant, he should mention his name to receive a complimentary glass of wine. Even at this hour, Rome bustled with life.

The taxi dropped Jack off at his hotel. Jack gave Giacomo a decent tip and promised to visit his sister's place. Giacomo thanked him warmly and wished him a pleasant stay in the Eternal City. Jack checked into the hotel, where the woman at the front desk greeted him with a broad smile and handed him the key to his second-floor room. She spoke excellent English.

"Would you like breakfast tomorrow morning, sir? It can be served on the rooftop if the weather permits."

"That's an excellent idea," Jack replied. "It will be the perfect start to my holiday."

Jack climbed the two flights of stairs to his room. It was simple, clean, and cosy. After his nightly ablutions, he headed straight to bed. It had been a long trip, and he needed some shut-eye.

He woke at 9:30 a.m. and pulled open the curtains. Sliding open the patio doors, he stepped onto a small balcony. A cloudless blue sky greeted him, along with a stunning view of the Colosseum. He breathed in deeply. He felt good, relaxed. Down below, the city was already buzzing. Rome was awake. Yes, breakfast on the balcony it would be, he thought. He was hungry.

After a quick shower, he made his way up to the rooftop on the sixth floor. The view over Rome was breathtaking. Several couples, both old and young, were already enjoying their breakfast. Jack noticed a young couple holding hands. Honeymooners, he thought, a pang of envy catching in his chest. How he would have loved to share this moment with his beloved Akiko. A lump formed in his throat, a sharp reminder of his grief and the scars burned into his soul. Would that wound ever heal?

He chose a table facing the Colosseum. A young, smiling waitress took his order of freshly squeezed orange juice, scrambled eggs on toast, and a pot of black tea. Hungry, Jack devoured the meal, and it hit the spot. Not bad, he thought—breakfast on a rooftop overlooking one of the most famous landmarks in the world. He was still feeling the side effects of jet lag, but give it a day or two, and he'd be back to normal.

After breakfast, he walked the short distance to the Colosseum. A long queue had already formed, filled with tourists from every continent chattering away in their native tongues. Jack knew the wait would be worth it. After thirty minutes, he was through the gates and handed a pair of earphones with commentary in English, as requested. Solitary exploration suited him.

The sight that greeted him surpassed his expectations. A chill ran down his spine as he tried to imagine the crowds shouting while gladiators fought under the blazing Roman sun. One in five died in battle, most succumbing to their atrocious wounds in their mid-twenties—a shocking contrast to today's average lifespan. The thought of naval battles staged within the arena fascinated him. The only naumachia recorded in history had been orchestrated by Emperor Domitian. Staging one was ruinously expensive—but what a spectacle it must have been.

Goosebumps prickled his arms as he approached the enclosure used in the famous Bruce Lee versus Chuck Norris fight scene in The Way of the Dragon. Though only a boy when he first saw it, that film—and Bruce Lee himself—had inspired Jack and many others to embark on the long, arduous path of martial arts. Tourists crowded the enclosure, cameras flashing in a relentless frenzy.

Jack spent the next two days visiting Rome's famous landmarks, simply enjoying being a tourist. Everywhere he turned, architectural marvels stood as testaments to a once-mighty civilisation. How had such an advanced society collapsed into decadence? Who was next, he wondered—the United States? Unbeknownst to him, news of his arrival had already been leaked. He was being watched.

On his final morning in Rome, Jack was up at dawn. He made his way to the rooftop for a solid sixty-minute workout, then showered and returned for breakfast overlooking the Colosseum. He couldn't think of a better way to end his Roman holiday. At 8:30 a.m., the sun was shining, and the air was still. Perfect.

After breakfast, he packed his bags, settled his bill in the lobby, and thanked the smiling receptionist. She asked if he had enjoyed his stay. Jack told her it had been perfect, the rooftop view making it worthwhile. She smiled and, at his request, ordered a taxi to the airport. His flight to Sicily was due to take off at 11:30 a.m.

The taxi arrived promptly, and to Jack's pleasant surprise, it was Giacomo again. Curious, the driver asked if Jack had enjoyed his stay and what he thought of Rome and the Romans. Jack didn't disappoint, and Giacomo's face lit up with pride. At the airport, Jack thanked him for his kindness and tipped him generously. Giacomo tapped him on the shoulder, wishing him "bon voyage."

Jack checked in his suitcase and wandered into the lounge, ordering a cappuccino at one of the many airport coffee shops. He waited for his plane, unaware of what Sicily—or the future—had in store.

Boarding his Alitalia flight to Palermo under the blazing Roman sun, Jack was guided to his seat near the back by a smiling hostess. Within ten minutes, the plane was nearly full. The Italian captain welcomed everyone in Italian and English, announcing that the temperature in Palermo was twenty-four degrees and flight time would be one hour and fifteen minutes. A pleasant contrast to the marathon journey from Tokyo to Rome, Jack thought.

He stepped off the plane into the warm, pleasant Sicilian air. It was early May. He wouldn't need his jacket; his sleeveless T-shirt was just right. Opting for the shuttle bus to Palermo, about thirty kilometres away, Jack settled in for the fifty-minute ride—far cheaper than a taxi.

The bus filled quickly with tourists from across Europe and beyond. Comfortable and inexpensive at only five dollars, the ride passed easily. Jack leaned back, eager to stretch his legs again—and to quench his thirst with a cold beer.

The bus left him in the city centre. Jack hadn't booked a hotel yet, but for the moment, he needed a walk and a cool beer. He saw a signpost indicating the port and decided to head in that direction. After a twenty-minute walk, he found exactly what he was looking for—a bar with a terrace and a view over the port. Perfect.

He claimed a seat on the terrace and admired the lively scene. It was a bustling port, full of activity. A smiling young man with a tanned complexion and coal-black hair handed him a menu. Jack was quick to decide. He ordered a Birra Messina, first brewed in Sicily in 1923 and still one of Italy's most beloved beers, along with a plate of Prosciutto di Parma, the king of Italian hams. The young man congratulated him on his choice and rushed off to prepare the order.

Ten minutes later, the beer and ham arrived, accompanied by bread and Sicilian olives, of course. Jack asked the young man if he knew of any reasonably priced hotels in the centre. The waiter replied in perfect English, telling Jack that his aunt and uncle owned a comfortable two-star establishment called Hotel Cortese, located in the historical district not far from Via Roma.

"Tell them their nephew Paolo sent you. They'll be more than happy to accommodate you—let's just hope they have a room available."

Jack thanked him and took a long gulp of his cold beer. He had needed that. The ham was beyond his expectations—the best he had ever tasted, without a doubt. Feeling good and relaxed, he ordered another beer and watched the boats come and go. When Paolo returned with the second beer, he also handed Jack a map with precise directions to the hotel.

Jack finished his meal, left a generous tip, and made his way to the hotel, which he found easily. Its location was ideal. Pushing through the main door, he entered the lobby, where a jovial, dark-haired woman in her fifties greeted him from behind the reception desk. That must be the aunt, Jack thought. He told her that her nephew Paolo had recommended the place, and she clapped her hands together in delight.

"Oh, Paolo—he is such a nice boy," she smiled. "Let me see… yes, sir, you are in luck. We have one single room left on the third floor."

To Jack's pleasant surprise, she added that there was also a rooftop terrace on the fourth floor, where breakfast could be served between 8 a.m. and 10 a.m. if he wished. Jack handed over his passport and was given a key.

"Ah, Irlandese," she said with a smile. "I love the Irish."

A large man in his fifties with greying hair that had once been jet black offered to carry Jack's bag to the room. This must be the uncle, Jack thought.

"No, grazie," replied Jack. "The exercise will do me good."

He settled into his room, using the drawers and wardrobe to store his clothes. The décor was typically Italian—classical, old-world, and spotless. He stripped and took a cold shower, which did him the world of good. After towelling off, he slipped into light slacks, a black T-shirt, and a pair of runners.

Leaving the hotel, Jack headed to the nearest car rental, which happened to be Hertz. The man behind the desk explained they had no vehicles available on-site but could order one from their airport office. Jack requested a small Fiat 500 for three days. The rate was very reasonable, and the modest car wouldn't draw unnecessary attention. Exactly what he needed. He planned a reconnaissance trip to Giovanni Falconetti's villa the following morning and was told the car would be available at 9 a.m.

Jack left the office and spent the afternoon visiting Palermo's sights, including the Massimo Theatre and the Piazza Politeama. After three hours of playing the tourist, he headed to the harbour again, craving another cold Birra Messina. He was beginning to warm to Palermo and its people.

That evening, he dined on a terrace in a busy waterfront restaurant. He savoured an excellent lasagne, washed down with two glasses of Nero d'Avola, a robust Sicilian red wine. Little did he realise the irony—the wine was produced by Giovanni Falconetti's cousins.

The next morning, Jack rose at twilight. He splashed cold water on his face, pulled on a tracksuit, and climbed up to the rooftop terrace. He was alone. Jack loved this magical time of day, when the air glowed faintly as the sun began to rise. Facing east, with an unobstructed view of the port, he moved through his daily exercise routine. Just as he began kata Sanchin, the red-orange sun lifted slowly above the horizon on its daily journey across the sky.

When he finished, it was 7:30 a.m. He skipped back down to his room, showered, and then headed to the breakfast room, asking if his meal could be served on the rooftop. A smiling waitress assured him there was no problem. Fifteen minutes later, he enjoyed a continental breakfast of tea, coffee, cappuccino, pastries, cereal, fruit juice, and yoghurt. With the view over the port, it was the perfect way to start the day.

Jack arrived at the car rental just as the clerk was unlocking the door.

"Ah, Mister Hopkins, you are an early bird," the man laughed.

"Yes, I am indeed," Jack replied.

The clerk handed him the keys, along with a map of the island, and told him the car was parked just fifty metres away at the end of the street.

"Enjoy your stay," he called as Jack left the office.

And there it was—a sparkling red Fiat 500. To Jack's delight, it was equipped with a soft top. Sliding into the driver's seat, he pushed it back for more legroom, unclipped the roof, folded it down, and secured it. The car was basic and cramped, but it would serve its purpose. Jack studied the map and marked Trappeto with a blue biro. He decided to take the coast road—it would be longer than the direct route, but far more picturesque. The drive would take just over an hour.

He slid the key into the ignition and turned it clockwise. The little 500cc engine sprang to life. He switched on the radio. Jim Morrison of The Doors was singing *Riders on the Storm*:

There's a killer on the road – His brain is squirmin' like a toad

Take a long holiday – Let your children play

If you give this man a ride, the Sweet family will die

Killer on the road, yeah.

He put on his pair of Ray-Ban sunglasses. It was a present from Akiko after his gruelling one-hundred-man Kumite. She had said, laughingly, that it would hide the bruises on his battered face. He engaged first gear and set off. Under different circumstances, this could have been very pleasant, he thought.

The drive along the coast was breathtaking. It was a perfect day, and the little Fiat 500 hummed along joyfully. Jack had been driving for nearly an hour; he was nearing his final destination. From the information Jack had received from his good friend Joey, the villa was a few miles west of Trappeto on a cliff face overlooking the beach. The villa was about five hundred yards off the coast road along a small dirt track.

Jack parked the Fiat 500 on a small road off the coast road. It was well hidden. He would walk the rest of the way. The name of the villa was Capo Bianco. There had to be a sign at the entrance for deliveries, perhaps even a mailbox, thought Jack.

He had been walking for nearly fifteen minutes when he saw it—the mailbox. Bold letters on a white background read: *Capo Bianco Residenza Falconetti*. He started down the narrow track, hoping that nobody would be arriving or leaving. "Hope for the best, prepare for the worst," he reminded himself. After ten minutes, he reached the end of the track and the villa.

The two huge wrought-iron gates stood wide open. Two massive pillars on either side were adorned with eagles—the ultimate symbol of strength and power. The vast residence was surrounded by high concrete walls. One of the gates was equipped with a CCTV camera, as were the walls.

Jack made sure to keep out of the sight of the cameras. They weren't the 360° models; instead, they had a viewing angle of eighty degrees, leaving blind spots beyond their field of vision. The gates were open, so, sticking to the blind side and beneath the camera's range, he stole a glance inside and took a few cautious steps. There, not more than fifty yards away at the end of the pebbled driveway, stood the magnificent villa and the double garage. Three cars were parked under a large carport: a Mercedes, a Ferrari, and an Alfa Romeo. From somewhere inside, he could hear loud music, laughter, and splashing. "Somebody's having a party," thought Jack.

Entering through the main gates would be suicide, Jack realised. He would have to plan his attack carefully and meticulously. His mind turned to Miyamoto Musashi and his *Book of Five Rings.* Musashi was regarded as the greatest swordsman to have ever lived, undefeated in sixty-two duels. He was also a master strategist, as well as a skilled landscaper and painter.

Jack, like many martial artists and businessmen over the decades, had studied his book. Written in 1645, it explored the "Way of Strategy," a philosophy of using precise techniques to overcome the enemy. Because of the time it was written, its imagery relied on terms like enemy, weapon, combat, sword, cutting, and so forth. Jack decided that the best way of approach would be by the beach, scaling the villa's cliffside walls. Twilight, one of his favourite times of day, would be the ideal moment to enter.

Jack drove back to Palermo along the coast road. It gave him time to reflect on his plan of action. There would be no room for error; he would have to take Giovanni by surprise, and he knew it wouldn't be easy.

Back in Palermo, Jack parked the little Fiat 500 in a discreet side street. He then found a sportswear shop and bought a black tracksuit, a black hoodie, and black sneakers. He chuckled to himself: "This is beginning to look like ninja stuff." It was now Wednesday, and Jack had planned to strike the villa on Friday morning. The weather forecast was favourable for the coming week—clear skies and bright sun. That was good; the full moon would aid his surprise attack.

Now he needed another means of transport to leave the island, as the airport would be far too risky. In his travel guide, he found mention of a small fishing village just twenty-one kilometres away called Porticello—only a twenty-two-minute train ride.

He returned to the Fiat 500, fired up the little engine, and headed for Porticello. Twenty minutes later, he parked in the colourful port town. Feeling peckish, he found a small restaurant overlooking the harbour that specialised almost entirely in fish—fresh, of course. He ordered a glass of white wine, stir-fried gambas as a starter, followed by a fillet of sole with homemade chips. He finished with a strong cup of coffee.

Jack strolled along the port, counting about thirty trawlers. Some fishermen were busy mending nets, others chatting and joking over coffee or beer. The atmosphere was laid-back, almost timeless. Jack spotted one fisherman, mending his nets, who looked to be in his mid-sixties. His face was sun-beaten yet kind, his expression jovial. Jack approached him.

"*Buongiorno, signore,*" said Jack.

"*Buongiorno, giovanotto.* Hello, young man," the fisherman replied, smiling.

Jack knew little Italian, and the fisherman had only limited English. But with a mix of both, along with animated gestures, they managed to communicate. Jack asked if it might be possible to hire him and his boat for a trip to the mainland on Friday morning, promising to make it worth his while.

The fisherman was surprised, even taken aback. Friday, however, was convenient, as he hadn't planned to go fishing—he needed a rest. Still, it was unusual for tourists to hire fishing trawlers for such a trip. They discussed money and agreed on a price. Jack had come prepared and pulled a wad of lira from his jacket pocket.

The fisherman seemed astonished; there were thousands of lire to the dollar. Jack offered him fifty percent now and the rest on Friday morning. The man shook his head and refused the advance. "Friday will be fine—for the full amount," he said. They agreed on a time: 10:30 a.m. It couldn't be earlier, as Jack would need to return the car at 9 a.m. sharp and catch the train to Porticello.

The fisherman had been studying Jack's hands with curiosity. He pointed to them. Jack grinned. "I'm a boxer," he explained.

The fisherman laughed, revealing a mouthful of yellowed teeth. "A prizefighter!"

Jack returned to Palermo a satisfied man. The arrangement was settled. He went to the train station and bought a ticket for Friday morning at 9:45 a.m.

He spent Thursday in relative calm. Rising just before dawn, he performed his usual rooftop routine, then later jogged down to the port, enjoying a coffee at the terrace of the little restaurant he had grown fond of while watching the world go by.

That evening, he turned in early at 10 p.m., having arranged a wake-up call for 4 a.m. It was a one-hour drive to Trappeto. Just before he drifted into sleep, the events surrounding Akiko's murder—and everything that followed—came flooding back, tearing open scars that had never truly healed…

Revenge, the sweetest morsel to the mouth that ever was cooked in hell

Walter Scott

CHAPTER
Thirty-Three

Okinawa - 4 years ago

Akiko had left work on Wednesday evening at 6:45 p.m. She was one of the last to leave the office. She jumped on her bike and headed toward the cabin. She was overjoyed at the thought of telling Jack that he would be the father of their child. That very morning, she had tested positive at work. The sun was just beginning to set, and she cycled along joyfully.

She was oblivious to the army jeep closing in behind her. At the wheel was Joey Falconetti, with Tommy "the Tank" and Jimmy "the Weasel" beside him. Both were deeply involved in Falconetti's sordid affairs. They were on leave, drunk from drinking most of the day, and high on drugs. Their plan was to head to a party on the other side of the island.

Falconetti immediately recognised Akiko on the bike.

"Let's have some fun, boys," he smirked.

He smashed the jeep into Akiko's bike, driving her off the road and sending her flying. They stopped the jeep and got out, circling her like a pack of dogs. Akiko was badly shaken. She tried to run, but her ankle was sprained from the fall, and she had broken ribs where the handlebars had slammed into her chest.

They dragged her to a secluded patch of bushes. Falconetti tore at her clothes. They were in an uncontrollable frenzy.

"Well, look what we have here," shouted Falconetti. "Some gook pussy ready for the taking."

Akiko resisted with all her strength. She seemed miraculously endowed with superhuman force. She screamed and begged them to spare her, telling them she was pregnant. But instead of softening their hearts, her words only fuelled their anger.

Falconetti roared with laughter: "Well, well, the Karate Kid is going to have a gook baby."

Her resistance was so fierce that none of them managed to penetrate her. Falconetti blew a fuse in frustration. He stormed back to the jeep and returned with a baseball bat.

"So you want to play it the hard way, bitch?" he spat.

They spread-eagled her, and he drove the baseball bat deep into her vagina, bursting her womb and causing untold internal damage. She screamed in agony as tears streamed down her cheeks.

"Oh, there won't be any gook baby after all," bellowed Falconetti.

He then rammed the bat into her mouth, shattering her teeth, breaking her trachea, and tearing her larynx.

"Okay, guys, let's leave the bitch. She doesn't know what a good time she missed," shouted Falconetti.

They left her shuddering, bleeding, and barely conscious. Pain pulsed through her entire body. With superhuman effort, Akiko crawled to the roadside, praying for rescue.

It was now 8 p.m., and darkness had fallen. Jack was growing worried about Akiko's whereabouts. He rang the factory, and the night security guard answered. He told Jack that he had seen Akiko when he arrived and that she had looked fine—even radiant. Jack thanked him and hung up.

Without a car, Jack ran to his father-in-law, Ichiro and explained the situation. They set off immediately in Ichiro's old Honda Civic, searching the road Akiko always took home. Driving slowly with headlights on, they finally saw a shape moving by the roadside twenty minutes later.

They stopped, horrified. Akiko's face was so bruised she was almost unrecognisable. With great effort, she reached out a bloodied, trembling hand. Jack bent down and lifted her gently, laying her on the back seat before racing to the hospital.

There, she was rushed straight to the emergency ward. The staff had never seen anything so horrific. Akiko was sedated, given morphine for the pain, and transfused after losing massive amounts of blood from internal injuries. Jack and Ichiro refused to leave, sleeping on couches until the surgeon returned with his report.

At 4 a.m., the surgeon appeared, his face grave. The prognosis was grim. Surgery was impossible; her internal organs were irreparably damaged, and she would never speak again. She had been violated with something other than a penis—something large. The revelation that she was two months pregnant hit Jack like a sledgehammer. His head spun, and he collapsed to his knees. Ichiro helped him onto a couch; Jack's face was pale, his body trembling in shock.

By 8 a.m., Jack had regained some composure. After breakfast in the hospital, they were allowed to visit Akiko. She lay semi-conscious, several tubes protruding from her fragile body. The surgeon said she had only days left. Nobody had contacted the police, and Jack intended to keep it that way—there would be no autopsy. He couldn't bear the thought of her body being cut open. He already knew what had happened, and he knew what he had to do.

Akiko was a Buddhist. With Ichiro's approval, Jack arranged to move her to the monastery so she could pass her last hours in peace. The monks were compassionate and did everything possible to make her comfortable. Jack never left her side.

At 2 a.m. on Saturday, Akiko stirred. Her eyes lit up when she saw Jack, and she reached for his hand.

"Oh, my love, I'm so sorry," cried Jack. "What kind of monster could do this?"

She gestured for a pen. Jack handed it to her. She took his palm and traced a five-star tattoo: *i punti della malavita.* Jack understood instantly. He squeezed her hand gently and kissed her forehead. She drifted back into sleep.

At 6 a.m., a monk found Jack in the garden. "It is time," he said softly. "Her soul is leaving." Jack carried Akiko into the garden so they could share one last sunrise. Her eyes opened, and she stroked his cheek—a caress of pure love. Then, silently, she was gone.

Now Jack knew what he had to do. That vermin couldn't be allowed to live. As far as he was concerned, it was *katakiuchi*—blood revenge. It was a principle rooted in the code of the samurai.

That evening, Jack went to the bar where the Marines gathered. There they were—Falconetti, Tommy "the Tank," and Jimmy "the Weasel"—drinking beer from the bottle, smoking, and playing pool. Jack's mind shifted into another state of consciousness. His reptilian brain took over; he had entered alpha.

Falconetti spotted him immediately.

"Well, well, what do we have here? The Karate Kid himself. I suppose your wife told you about our little adventure—if she could still talk," he sneered.

Jack advanced. Falconetti nodded at "the Tank," who grabbed a snooker cue by the thin end and swung hard at Jack's head. Jack blocked with his left forearm, shattering the cue. Closing in, he delivered a crushing tetsui—a hammer-fist to the temple—stunning him. A right half-punch to the throat followed by a left finger jab to the eyes dropped the Tank to one knee. Jack spun, driving an elbow strike into his jaw.

Then, slipping behind him, he clasped both hands around the man's head and snapped his neck with brutal force. The Tank crumpled to the floor.

The bar fell silent. No one moved. Then Jack heard the flick of a knife. Jimmy "the Weasel" lunged at his abdomen. Jack, using tai sabaki, deflected with his left forearm, caught the blade in his right hand, and slammed a left elbow into the Weasel's face. Stepping back, he dragged the man's right arm across his torso in an arm bar while locking his neck with his left arm. With a swift twist, he snapped it.

Meanwhile, Falconetti had circled and stabbed Jack in the back, narrowly missing a kidney. Jack turned, meeting his smirk.

"And you didn't even know you were going to have a half-breed," Falconetti hissed.

He slashed toward Jack's face. Jack moved just as the blade passed the centre line. Gripping Falconetti's elbow with his left hand, he yanked him off balance and hammered a fist into his floating ribs. Falconetti groaned in pain. Still holding the elbow, Jack delivered a crushing downward side kick to the knee.

He heard the ligaments tear. Falconetti dropped, clutching his ruined leg. Jack wasn't finished. He stomped down hard on the Achilles tendon with his left foot. The tendon snapped.

Jack released the elbow, then drove a hammer-fist into the back of Falconetti's neck. Falconetti collapsed, finally broken.

One of the Marines in the bar knew Jack well and respected him, having practised karate alongside him in the same dojo.

"The military police are on their way, Jack — you gotta go!" he shouted.

Jack knew he had to get out of there fast. He wasn't sure whether the last blow he had delivered was fatal or not, but there was no time to check. He bolted out of the bar and began running. Back at the cabin, he packed in a hurry. He would have to leave the island before the police were on his trail. There had been too many witnesses in the bar, and word would spread quickly.

Ichiro had already made arrangements with a fisherman friend to take Jack to an island called Ishigaki. It would be a long trip, but from there, Jack could catch the ferry to Taiwan and eventually make his way back to Europe. Ichiro knew the affair would be covered up by the military police — and besides, there was no substantial proof against the Marines. Jack, on the other hand, had killed two men and maimed another, though he had acted purely in self-defence.

Ichiro also knew that his old friend Jiro, the chief police inspector, would be more than indulgent where Jack was concerned. Jiro could be counted on to slow down the investigation, eventually dismissing it entirely as a case of manslaughter rather than murder.

Jack said his goodbyes to Ichiro. He would miss Akiko's cremation two days later, but he had already bid her farewell when he cradled her in his arms for the last time. The thought of enduring a second goodbye was unbearable.

Jack made it to Taiwan and from there began the long journey back to Ireland, where he went underground. The MPs closed the case without further action, classifying it as nothing more than a bar brawl that had spiralled out of control. If the MPs were satisfied, then so too were the Japanese police — and Inspector Jiro ensured the matter was quietly shelved. Jack was in the clear.

Falconetti, however, was never suspected, never accused, and not even brought in for questioning about Akiko's horrific murder. He had no apparent motive, and his numerous alibis — all of them willing to testify under threat to their own safety — protected him completely.

Akiko and Jack had been the true victims of this horrific incident. Jack had managed to make amends in his own way, to exact revenge, and to carry out justice in the only manner left to him. But Joey Falconetti was still breathing, still walking free.

Jack was alive too, but inside he felt like nothing more than an empty shell…

Pain is inevitable. Suffering is optional.

Haruki Murakami

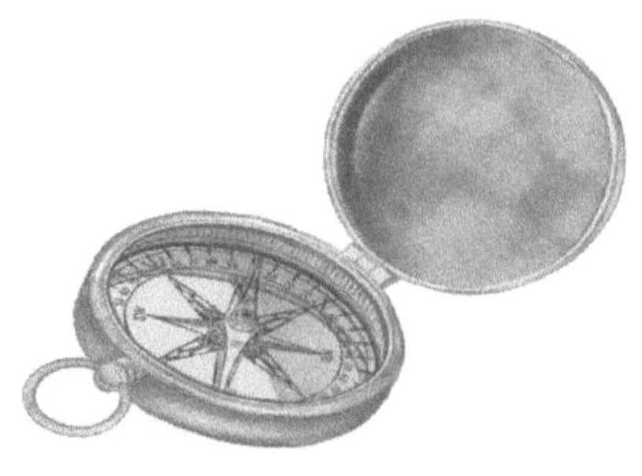

CHAPTER
Thirty-Four
Back to Palermo

Jack awoke at 3:45 a.m. without the need for an alarm. He headed straight to the bathroom, took a quick cool shower, and changed into his gear. He was fired up and ready to go. He stole down the stairs without making the slightest sound, moving like smoke slipping under a door. He was lucky — there was no one at reception. He stepped out onto the unlit street.

Not a soul in sight. He jogged the three hundred metres to where the little Fiat 500 was waiting, jumped in, and started the small engine. He set off for the hour's drive to Trappeto. Jack had the road entirely to himself.

He parked the Fiat on a dirt track about five hundred metres from the villa and made his way down to the beach. It was 5:15 a.m. The night was clear, the moon full and bright. Jack jogged along the beach as the waves broke gently onto the shore. It was deceptively peaceful.

He climbed up a small cliff face, scaled the two-metre wall of the villa, and dropped quietly into the garden. The villa was in darkness, but the big swimming pool glowed pale blue. Jack scanned the grounds and the house, listening. Not a sound. He continued towards the villa, stepping off the grass onto the teak wooden deck, and approached the patio doors.

Suddenly, a bullish-looking man appeared from nowhere, shining a flashlight in his face. Jack was caught off guard but quickly composed himself. The guy must weigh at least 120 kilos, Jack thought.

Jack moved fast — stepping in with his left, he blocked powerfully upward, sending the flashlight flying. At the same time, he delivered a gyaku-zuki, an explosive reverse punch, to the big man's sternum with his right fist. The man gasped, dropped to his right knee, and Jack followed with a reverse knife-hand strike to the groin. The big man cried out, bending slightly. As Jack rose back to his feet, he applied a ripping motion to the man's scrotum with his right hand, then shifted stance, stepped in with his right foot, and delivered a brutal elbow strike to the head. The man hit the deck with a heavy thud, left in a semi-conscious state.

Suddenly, the lights came on inside and outside the villa, and the patio doors slid open. Giovanni stood there — shirtless, bronzed, and barefoot. Jack couldn't help but notice his athletic build. Giovanni's hypnotic green lizard eyes bored into him.

"I've been expecting you, Jack. I was informed the day you set foot in Rome, and you've been watched ever since. I received a phone call at five this morning telling me you were on your way. That's one of the advantages of having a large family."

He glanced at Roberto, sprawled on the terrace. The man was breathing heavily and clearly in great pain. Giovanni went to him, helped him to his feet, and eased him onto a sun lounger.

"I'm glad you didn't kill him, Jack. Roberto is no fighter. Oh, he can handle himself, but not against a man of your particular talents. You're a real fighting machine, Jack. Roberto is my handyman. He looks after the villa, the pool, the garden, and fixes what needs fixing — even cars. He's a good guy."

Jack was taken aback by Giovanni's cool, calm attitude.

"I never wanted to kill that poor guy," said Jack. "He was just in my way to get to you."

"So you want to kill me, Jack? You know that if I'd wanted you dead, you'd already be gone. But I wanted to meet you once again, face to face. By the way, I'm sorry about your girlfriend. She took the bullet that was meant for you. I had you in my sights, Jack — and then you moved. Uncanny. As though someone told you to step aside."

"That would be too difficult to explain, Giovanni," said Jack. "I'm tired of being hunted, so I decided to become the hunter. I can't spend the rest of my life looking over my shoulder. This has to end."

Giovanni moved closer. "The man you want is my cousin Joey. I'm just a mechanic. I get paid to eliminate people. I've killed many, and I've been cruel and vicious. But I had to be. It's not an easy job, despite what you might think. I accepted the hit on you as a personal favour to my cousin. But I was out of line.

Listen, I've spoken to my uncle, and he didn't approve of my actions. It was outside business interests. He's what's known as the Capomandamento — the Godfather, in your language. He decides who lives, who dies, and what business strategies we follow. Joey is a capo bastone, an underboss. But recently, he's gone off the rails, getting involved in business we don't tolerate. There are lines we don't cross — and one of them is child prostitution. Let's just say we have a code of honour, like your Bushido. Joey is selling off poor Asian children into the sexual slave market and pedophilia rings."

Jack opened his hands. "So what's all this got to do with me?"

"Hear me out," pleaded Giovanni. "The situation has changed. Joey is drawing too much heat from the Feds and the Internal Revenue. He's become a thorn in the family's side. He doesn't listen anymore. Let's go inside and talk. I'll get us some cappuccino."

Jack sat down at a long, low coffee table in the luxurious salon. A few minutes later, Giovanni returned with two cappuccinos.

"I've done some digging," said Giovanni. "I know what happened to your wife in Okinawa. And frankly, I find it repulsive. I can't imagine how much you've suffered."

Jack had been prepared for many things, but not this — sitting at a table, sipping cappuccino with the man who had once tried to kill him. Could Giovanni really be trusted?

"So listen, Jack," Giovanni continued. "My uncle — the Don — and I understand your desire to avenge your wife's murder. If you pay Joey a visit, you'd be doing us a favour. We can help you in your mission. In the meantime, I'll tell Joey you came to see me and that you met with an unfortunate accident. He'll be satisfied with that. You walk away knowing there'll be no more contracts on your head. We don't want to intervene because he's still family, after all. And he's got two kids, for fuck's sake. So — do we have a mutual agreement, Jack?"

Jack rubbed his chin. "How do I know I can trust you?"

Giovanni laughed. "You don't, Jack. You have my word — that's all. And by the way, I saw you training at the Cortese rooftop hotel. The owners are part of the family, too. I could have wasted you that morning with ease. It was an easy fifty-metre shot. If that's not proof of my good faith, I don't know what is."

Jack thought it over. He had felt a presence one morning on the rooftop, but it hadn't carried the same threat as the day of the shooting on his balcony. That day, there had been no intent — only observation.

"Okay, Giovanni," said Jack. "You've got a deal."

Giovanni stood up. Jack did the same.

"Let's shake on it, Jack."

So, Jack shook hands with the man who had once tried to murder him, a man who now entrusted him with the promise of eliminating his cousin in Manhattan. The whole situation felt surreal, but Jack was strangely satisfied with the outcome.

"I would have liked to test your martial skills, Jack, but I suspect you would have been far too good for me. Come—I want to show you something."

Giovanni led him downstairs into his private gym, moving towards a large, code-protected cabinet. With practised ease, Giovanni entered the code and swung open the doors, revealing an arsenal that would impress any soldier. Inside were Uzi submachine guns, high-calibre rifles, various handguns, and an imposing collection of knives. But Giovanni's eyes were fixed on one treasure in particular. From the top shelf, he carefully took down one of the five katanas proudly displayed.

Jack had never seen such a weapon in his life.

Giovanni extended the sword to him. "*Onegaishimasu*—please," he said with surprising reverence.

Jack accepted the sword, and Giovanni gave a solemn nod. As Jack unsheathed it, the blade revealed a beauty beyond words.

"Yes," said Giovanni softly. "Magnificent, isn't it? This is a Shintō katana from the sixteenth century, forged by the legendary swordsmith Horikawa Kunihiro himself. I won't insult you with its price. Let's just say I'm well compensated for what I do."

Jack placed the scabbard carefully on a nearby table, gripping the sword with both hands. Its balance was flawless. He executed a precise *shomen-uchi*, a vertical strike, followed by a *kesa-giri* diagonal cut. The craftsmanship was exquisite—perfection made of steel.

Giovanni watched him intently, his piercing green eyes gleaming.

"You could end me right now, Jack, with a single cut. That's why I consider us even. I've shown you my good faith."

Jack inclined his head, slid the blade back into its sheath, and returned it with gratitude.

"No," said Giovanni, shaking his head. "Keep it. Consider it a gift—a bond between us. Besides, I don't practice Iaido. You'll make far better use of it than I ever would."

Jack was momentarily speechless. He bowed respectfully and accepted the gift.

"*Kokorokara kansha shimasu*—my heartfelt thanks," he said.

They returned upstairs and stepped out onto the deck just as the sun began to rise. The view from the villa was breathtaking, gilded in golden light. Roberto had recovered enough to stand, and the two men shook hands before Jack departed through the main entrance. He felt light, almost weightless—as though an enormous burden had lifted. The dark cloud that had shadowed him for so long seemed finally to dissolve.

The drive back to Palermo was a joy. Every turn of the coastal road filled him with wonder. Still, he couldn't shake the strangeness of what had just transpired. "Talk about a turn of events," he muttered to himself. It was 8 a.m. when he walked past reception. The woman at the desk was checking out guests and didn't even glance at the katana in his hand.

Back in his room, he slid the sword under the bed, then returned to reception to order breakfast on the rooftop. The freshly pressed orange juice, scrambled eggs on toast, and Earl Grey tea were perfect. Gazing over the port, Jack let his thoughts drift. Only two days earlier, Giovanni had been watching him from across the street. A chill crept up his spine.

After finishing breakfast, Jack returned to his room and called reception for access to an international line. He dialled a number in Hong Kong—it was 3 p.m. there. After a brief wait, a woman's voice answered.

"Hello, Michyo here."

"Hi, Michyo. It's Jack. How are you?"

Her voice brightened instantly. "Oh, my love! How are you? Where are you? I've been worried sick."

"Everything's fine, better than I expected. I'm in Sicily but leaving tomorrow for Rome. I'll explain everything when we meet. I have to go to Dublin, but I'll be back in Okinawa at the end of the month. Can you make the trip?"

"Oh, Jack, it's wonderful to hear your voice. I had almost given up hope. Yes, of course—I'll come at the end of the month. We'll talk soon to finalise details. Take care, Jack. I love you."

"Me too. *Mata ne*—see you." He hung up, feeling warmth spread through him.

Jack then called the airport and booked an Alitalia flight to Rome for the following morning at 11 a.m. At the reception, he extended his stay by one more night and asked if they had a long cardboard box and some tape. The woman smiled as she handed him both.

"I hope that does the job."

"Thank you. È perfetto," he replied.

In his room, Jack carefully packed the katana into the box and sealed it securely. Time was moving quickly, and he hadn't forgotten his promise to the fisherman—a trip he now no longer needed.

Carrying the package under his arm, he left for the post office, where he arranged for it to be shipped to his address in Okinawa, adding extra insurance against loss or damage. From there, he stopped at the car rental office to extend his lease.

"No problem," said the man behind the counter. "*Ci vediamo domani*—see you tomorrow, sir."

By 10 a.m., Jack was back behind the wheel of the Fiat 500, heading for Porticello. He arrived just before 10:30 and found the fisherman enjoying an espresso and laughing with a friend.

"Ah, there you are, my boy, right on time. All right then, let's go," the fisherman chuckled.

"There's been a change of plan," Jack told him. "I don't need to go to the mainland after all."

The fisherman grinned, showing yellowed teeth and a mischievous glint in his eye. "So, you're not in such a hurry to leave the island after all."

"No, I'm not," Jack admitted. "But I'd like to tour the coastline—for the same price—if you're willing to play tourist guide."

"No problem, my friend. It would be a pleasure. And perhaps we can do some fishing along the way. If the catch is good, I'll invite you to my humble home for dinner."

"Sounds good to me," said Jack. He was beginning to like the old man.

The fisherman proved to be an excellent guide. As they sailed, he narrated Sicily's long history with passion, pointing out landmarks and sharing local legends. He also fished, and in just over an hour caught three sea bass and four sole.

"Which do you prefer?" he asked.

"I like both," Jack replied, "but I have a preference for sea bass."

"Then sea bass it is for dinner tonight," the fisherman laughed.

By early evening, they were back at port. It had been a remarkable day. The fisherman carried the catch to the restaurant where Jack had dined on his first night on the island. The same young man greeted them warmly.

"Ah, Marco," he said. "Come stai, old man?"

"I'm well," Marco replied, handing him the sole. "I don't like freezing fish," he explained to Jack.

"Can I buy you a drink?" Jack asked. "And if I'm not mistaken, we haven't been properly introduced."

The old man's eyes twinkled. "Marco Falconetti, at your service, young man."

Jack froze for a moment, masking his reaction. Could it be a coincidence?

"Something wrong, my friend?" Marco asked.

"No," Jack said quickly. "Just thinking of something I have to do. A pleasure to meet you. I'm Jack."

They shared two glasses of crisp white wine on the house, paired with crostini.

"Okay, andiamo a casa," Marco said cheerfully, and they set off.

Four hundred metres later, overlooking a quiet beach, they reached Marco's "humble abode." Jack couldn't help but think it was anything but humble. Doubts about Marco's true identity began to form. Inside, he was introduced to Maria, Marco's wife, a striking woman in her late fifties who still radiated charm. She ushered Jack to the terrace while Marco poured two glasses of wine. Soon, Maria reappeared with trays of finger food before returning to the kitchen to prepare the sea bass.

Dinner was superb—sea bass with homemade chips and a fresh salad. The conversation flowed easily, filled with laughter, as if they had known each other for years. Maria, an English teacher at the local primary school, was as gracious a host as her husband.

By 11 p.m., Jack thanked them for a wonderful evening and walked back to where the Fiat was parked. But he couldn't shake the thought—Falconetti. Could Marco really be connected to the family? The question would haunt him for the rest of his life.

Back at the hotel, Jack slept soundly. At dawn, he rose, completed his rooftop training, and enjoyed his last breakfast overlooking the port. As he sipped his tea, he wondered what Marco Falconetti was doing that morning—mending nets, out fishing, or something else entirely. Who could ever know?

He checked out of the hotel and returned the Fiat 500 to the rental company. The clerk thanked him and asked if he had enjoyed his stay on the island. Jack replied that it had been an interesting experience. Then he boarded the shuttle bus that carried him to the airport.

Jack stepped onto the tarmac of Leonardo da Vinci–Fiumicino Airport in Rome beneath a clear, welcoming sky. He collected his bags, passed through customs with nothing to declare, and moved toward the uscita—the exit. Yet before leaving the terminal, he glanced up at the departure screens. An American Airlines flight to New York was boarding at 1 p.m. Instantly, Giovanni Falconetti's words echoed in his mind:

"Pay Joey a visit, Jack. You'll actually be doing us a favour."

But Jack wasn't ready. For now, he needed peace, quiet, and a return to something resembling normal life. His thoughts turned to Michyo—how deeply he longed to see her again, to hold her in his arms. Taking a bus to the train station, he grabbed a quick meal to satisfy his hunger. Yet there was one thing he had to do before leaving Italy. At the ticket office, he bought a one-way ticket to Florence.

For years, he had wanted to see Michelangelo's masterpiece, the statue of David, and this was the perfect chance. The next train wasn't for two hours, so Jack purchased a copy of the New York Times to pass the time.

What he read nearly knocked him over. The front-page headline blazed in bold capitals:

"PRESUMED MAFIA BOSS JOEY FALCONETTI DIES IN HORRIFIC CAR ACCIDENT."

Jack sat down hard, absolutely stunned. "Well, I'll be damned," he muttered. Another weight lifted from his shoulders.

Yet he couldn't help but regret not avenging Akiko's murder personally—not making Joey Falconetti suffer before his end.

He devoured the article. According to reports, a massive Kenworth truck had ploughed straight into Falconetti's car, sending it off the road. The vehicle exploded, and Falconetti was burned alive. CCTV footage and multiple witnesses confirmed the crash. A statewide all-points bulletin had been issued in search of the truck and its driver. The body, burned beyond recognition, required an autopsy, but all evidence suggested that Falconetti had been behind the wheel. The New York PD was investigating. Staff at his restaurant confirmed that he had left around midnight, likely heading home when the accident occurred. Jack could hardly believe it. Had someone done him—and the Sicilian Falconettis—a favour? Or had the driver been *hired* for a mission?

Then again, maybe it hadn't been Joey in the car at all. His head spun with possibilities. "No—it has to be him," Jack tried to reassure himself. "It has to be."

Arriving in Florence, Jack stepped off the train and made his way toward the vibrant city centre in search of a place to stay. The energy of the streets struck him immediately—alive with voices, footsteps, and the hum of life. Reaching the Piazza del Duomo, he stopped and craned his neck, breath catching at the sight of the soaring Cathedral.

Its grandeur was staggering—an architectural triumph that seemed almost beyond human capability. Jack thought with awe that, if the doors were large enough, a jumbo jet could fit inside. Tourists—mostly Americans and Asians—buzzed around, their voices blending in a lively chorus that added to the city's energy.

He found a modest two-star hotel near the Accademia Gallery and booked in for two nights. Rising early the next morning, he discovered there was no rooftop terrace for his workout, so he donned his tracksuit and ran along the Arno River. The streets were unusually calm. For an hour, he jogged through Florence, discovering hidden corners before the city awakened fully.

Back at the hotel, he showered quickly and went down for breakfast, but didn't linger. The museum opened at 9 a.m., and he knew the queues would be long. He grabbed a coffee to go and joined the line of early visitors outside the Accademia. After an hour of waiting, he finally stepped into the gallery, overwhelmed by the sheer volume of masterpieces.

Then came the moment he had been waiting for. Entering a long corridor, Jack felt something stir inside him, as if drawn by an invisible force. He turned his head—and there it was. Michelangelo's David, illuminated and majestic, stood at the end in all its glory. Marble turned to flesh, perfection made stone.

Jack froze, his breath shallow. Slowly, almost reverently, he walked forward, each step pulling him closer—not only to the statue, but to something eternal and spellbinding. The attention to detail defied comprehension. Every chiselled vein, every ripple of muscle seemed infused with life itself. Respect was the only possible response to such genius.

He recalled what he had read about Michelangelo: a workaholic, a perfectionist, rumoured to work sixteen-hour days, often sleeping in his clothes with his boots still on. He cared little for appearances or food. Like many visionaries, he was notoriously irascible, short-tempered, and utterly consumed by his craft.

When Jack finally left the gallery, his mind was spinning. The magnitude of what he had witnessed left him dazed, almost breathless. He needed to walk, to let the experience settle.

Florence had awakened in his absence. The once-quiet streets now buzzed with tourists wielding cameras, locals zipping by on scooters, and shopkeepers greeting the day. Jack headed back toward the Arno, seeking calm. The gentle murmur of the river and the sun sparkling on the water helped clear his thoughts. He strolled until he reached a small bar near the Ponte Vecchio, where he sat outside and ordered a cold draught beer.

The first sip was heaven—refreshing, grounding. He gazed across the river, letting the hum of the city and the taste of the beer tether him back to the present.

When the glass was empty, he wandered through Florence's winding streets with no destination in mind. The midday sun bathed the terracotta rooftops in golden light, and the cobbled lanes glowed with history. The city was intoxicating. It wasn't just beautiful—it was alive. Every corner whispered stories from centuries past, while the people breathed a youthful, creative spirit into the air.

Jack felt himself falling for Florence. And then her name rose unbidden: Michyo. He could picture her eyes wide with wonder in front of a Botticelli, hear her laughter over a glass of Chianti in a tucked-away trattoria. He knew she would love it here.

Before leaving Florence, he decided, he must see Botticelli's masterpiece, *The Birth of Venus*. So, the next morning, he queued outside the Uffizi Gallery. The line stretched on, but he waited nearly two hours with patience. It was a small price to pay for the works inside—over fifty rooms of genius, a three-hour journey through art history.

The Uffizi did not disappoint. It surpassed every expectation. Jack wandered through vast halls, pausing before paintings that spoke to him, absorbing their stories in silence. Finally, after nearly two and a half hours, he stood before Botticelli's *The Birth of Venus*, painted in the mid-1480s.

There she was: the goddess Venus, arriving at shore fully grown, borne on a giant scallop shell. The flowing lines, the delicate beauty, the luminous pastels—all shimmered with divine grace. Jack stared not just at the painting but *into* it, feeling centuries dissolve in the presence of such timeless wonder.

Eventually, Jack tore himself away from Botticelli's masterpiece, reluctantly weaving through the final galleries towards the exit. By the time he stepped back out onto the bustling Florentine Street, the midday sun was high and the city throbbed with life.

He checked his watch. It was just after 1 p.m., and his stomach reminded him that he hadn't eaten since early morning.

Following his instincts more than any map, he wandered into a quieter side street, away from the crowds. The sound of clinking glasses and laughter led him to a small trattoria shaded by vines. A chalkboard menu listed the day's specials: pici cacio e pepe, ribollita, and tagliata di manzo.

He took a table outside, letting the breeze cool his skin as he ordered a simple plate of pasta and a glass of house red.

As he waited for his meal, Jack leaned back in his chair, soaking in the atmosphere—waiters chatting in rapid Italian, the aroma of garlic and olive oil drifting from the kitchen, and the faint hum of a street musician playing classical guitar nearby. Florence wasn't just beautiful—it was generous. It fed your senses as well as your soul. He thought of Michyo.

It was Jack's last day in Florence. He had a flight to Dublin the following morning, and after a hectic round of packing and tying up loose ends, he found himself in need of quiet and calm.

He had heard about the Boboli Gardens—how peaceful they were, tucked just beyond the bustle of the city. It seemed like the perfect way to say goodbye.

He paid his bill at the trattoria and set off on foot, crossing the Ponte Vecchio with its glittering rows of goldsmiths' shops, their windows catching the afternoon light. As he climbed the gentle slope toward the gardens, the city's rhythm seemed to slow. The narrow, winding streets gradually opened into wide, serene spaces, offering glimpses of Florence spread out below—domes, towers, and a sea of warm, sunlit rooftops.

The Boboli Gardens were just as he had hoped: vast and quiet, a world apart from the museum crowds. He wandered aimlessly along shaded paths lined with towering cypress trees, passing centuries-old sculptures and trickling fountains.

Every so often, he paused—sometimes to take in a panoramic view of the city, other times simply to sit on a worn stone bench and breathe. He hadn't felt this light-hearted in a long time.

Florence, for all its intensity and history, knew how to offer stillness too.

Jack eventually made his way back to the hotel, slipping once more into the familiar bustle of the city. The streets buzzed with life—tourists with shopping bags, the distant hum of scooters, the clatter of cups from sidewalk cafés.

Back in his room, he stepped into the shower, letting the cool water wash away the dust and heat of the day. The grime of the city slid off his skin, leaving him feeling renewed, though tinged with a faint bittersweetness.

Tomorrow, he would leave Florence behind. But for now, he let the water run and held on to the feeling of the place just a little longer.

Feeling refreshed, Jack dressed and stepped out once more as the sun began to dip behind the rooftops. The air had cooled, and the city had taken on a softer, golden glow. Evening in Florence had a different kind of magic—less spectacle, more soul.

He wandered without direction, letting his feet find their way. Eventually, he settled on a quiet trattoria tucked into a narrow side street, away from the clamour of the main piazzas. A few locals sat outside, speaking in low tones over glasses of wine. It felt like the right place.

Jack ordered a simple meal—grilled vegetables, fresh bread, and a glass of red. As he waited, he went over what he had witnessed in the past few days: David, the Birth of Venus, the Ponte Vecchio at sunset, the sweeping view from the Boboli Gardens. Each image carried a weight now, layered with feeling.

It was a pity that Michyo wasn't with him. He knew she would have loved this city. The waiter brought his wine, and Jack raised his glass in a quiet toast—to Florence, to good timing, and to whatever came next.

The night was warm and still, and somewhere in the distance, a violin played.

Back at the hotel, Jack's head had barely touched the pillow before he drifted into a deep, dreamless sleep.

But soon, the past began to stir. He found himself back in the narrow lane where he had played as a boy, the place where he'd grown up—scraped knees and scuffed shoes, a football always nearby. The cracked pavement, the rusting fences, the laughter echoing off brick walls and garages—it all came rushing back with the clarity of a memory long buried but never forgotten.

That lane had been his world. His safe haven. It was there he learned what friendship meant, how to stand up for himself, how to take a fall and get back up. It was where he first tasted the bittersweet edge of growing up.

In his dream, he saw the faces of old friends—some he hadn't thought of in years. They were all there, younger, untouched by time, grinning at him as if no one had ever left.

And for a little while, Jack was home again—in the place where it had all begun.

Jack woke to the soft grey light of early morning filtering through the curtains. For a moment, he lay still, disoriented, caught between the echo of childhood laughter and the unfamiliar quiet of the hotel room.

The dream lingered, vivid and aching. He could still see the lane, hear the shouts of boys chasing a ball, girls skipping, feel the worn stone beneath his feet. It had been so real.

He sat up slowly, running a hand through his hair. There was a strange comfort in having visited that part of himself, even in sleep—a reminder of who he was before the years layered on responsibility, distance, travel, and change.

He got up, opened the window slightly, and let the cool air rush in. Somewhere below, the city was stirring to life—the clatter of bins, a dog barking, a lorry backing up.

Jack smiled faintly. The past was still there. Florence was still with him. And he had a plane to catch.

Let what comes come. Let what goes go. Find out what remains
...

Ramani Maharshi.

466

CHAPTER
Thirty-Five

Dublin

The plane touched down in Dublin just after noon. The skies were overcast, the air cool and damp—typical of late spring in Ireland. Jack stepped out of the terminal and into a different rhythm altogether: less romantic, more grounded, more familiar. The city greeted him not with Renaissance beauty, but with its own kind of charm—gritty, witty, alive.

He took a cab to his apartment in Clontarf, watching the landscape shift through the rain-smeared window. Florence already felt like a dream, but the feeling it stirred in him—that quiet urgency to see, to feel, to connect—was no illusion. It was real, and it had come back with him.

When he opened the door to his apartment, he was met by a stale, stuffy smell. The place hadn't been aired out since he'd left. He dropped his bags just inside the door and walked straight to the patio doors. Sliding them open, he stepped out onto the small balcony overlooking Dublin Bay. The fresh, salty air hit his face like a reset button.

He inhaled deeply, filling his lungs, letting the chill of the Irish coast cut through the fog of travel. Despite the grey skies and the drizzle hanging in the distance, he felt good—clearer, lighter somehow. Something in him had shifted, and he knew it wasn't only the change of scenery.

Nobody knew Jack was home—not yet. And that was just the way he wanted it, for now. But soon, he'd have to do the rounds: visit family, check in with old friends, let people know he was back—if only briefly, before returning to Okinawa.

One stop, in particular, was already on his mind. He'd have to call into the dojo, which he had left in the capable hands of Gerry McCarthy, now a second-degree black belt—young, sharp, and full of fire.

Jack felt a flicker of pride.

The dojo had been more than a training space—it was community, discipline, and a kind of spiritual grounding. Leaving it behind hadn't been easy, but knowing it had continued to grow in his absence was a comfort.

That evening, Jack kept things simple.

He unpacked slowly, methodically—shirts folded into drawers, books returned to their shelves, a small Florentine notebook placed carefully on his desk. The apartment felt quiet, almost too quiet, but he welcomed the silence. It gave him room to think.

He made himself a light dinner: pasta with olive oil, a few cherry tomatoes, and some pecorino he had brought back in his luggage. A nod to Florence, a thread to keep the memory alive.

With the meal done and the dishes rinsed, he poured a glass of red wine and stepped out onto the balcony again. The sea air was colder now, tinged with salt and the far-off scent of turf smoke. He could hear the cry of the curlew. The lights of Dublin twinkled in the distance, and the occasional car passed below, but otherwise, the city seemed to settle with him.

He leaned on the railing, glass in hand, and let the day ease out of his bones.

He thought of the Uffizi. Of David. Of the dream that had pulled him back to that old lane. And, yes, of Michyo. He would ring her tomorrow.

He wasn't searching for answers tonight. He didn't need to plan or decide anything. He was just being. And for the first time in a long while, that felt like enough.

He took another sip of wine and made a mental note: tomorrow, he'd stop by the dojo unannounced. See how things were running. He needed to feel the dojo floor under his feet again.

But tonight, the stillness held. And he let it.

The next morning, Jack rose early and went through his usual routine on the balcony. The air was crisp and damp, the kind of Irish morning that carried the smell of earth and salt.

He finished his session and took a welcoming shower. He then dressed simply—in track pants, a hoodie, and an old pair of runners—and decided to make his way across town to the dojo. But first, there was one call he needed to make.

The phone rang once. Twice.

Then her voice—bright, familiar, unmistakably hers.

"Jack!"

A smile spread across his face. "Hey, Michyo."

She laughed softly, the sound wrapping around him like sunlight. "I'm so happy to hear your voice. I've missed you."

"I've missed you, too," he said quietly.

They talked easily, falling into that gentle rhythm only people who know each other well can manage. Jack told her he'd be back in Okinawa by the end of May. They agreed to meet then—no rush, just certainty.

"I can't wait to see you," she said.

Neither could he.

When the call ended, Jack stood there for a moment, phone in hand. The world felt a little softer now. A little more alive.

And with that, he set off across town in his Fiat Spider.

Jack paused at the entrance to the dojo, his hand resting on the door handle. He could already hear movement inside—feet sliding on the polished wood floor, the occasional sharp *kiai*, and Gerry's steady voice leading the session.

He stepped inside quietly.

The dojo looked good. Clean. Ordered. The same old banner hung above the mirrors, its calligraphy faded but proud. The air held the faint scent of sweat, wood polish, and purpose.

Gerry spotted him almost immediately. For a moment, his voice faltered, then broke into a grin.

"Look who the wind dragged in," he called out, stepping off the mat.

Jack bowed lightly, smiling. "I thought I'd drop in. Didn't want you getting too comfortable."

The students—half of whom didn't recognise him—glanced curiously at the exchange. A few of the older ones did and offered respectful bows.

"Still remember how to tie a belt?" Gerry teased, handing him a black one from the shelf.

Jack slipped off his hoodie and stepped onto the mat barefoot. The floor welcomed him like an old friend. He bowed to Gerry, then to the class.

"I might be a little rusty," he said.

Gerry smirked. "We'll see about that."

Jack chuckled. "Alright. Let's see what you've got, Sensei."

They bowed, then assumed fighting stances. The dojo fell silent as the others stepped back to watch.

Gerry struck first—fast, controlled, testing. Jack blocked, countered, and shifted his weight. Within seconds, they were moving in a fluid exchange of strikes, parries, and sidesteps. Nothing showy. Just clean, efficient movement.

It wasn't about winning. It was about presence. Precision. Respect.

Gerry's technique had matured—more disciplined, more thoughtful. Jack noticed it with quiet pride even as he narrowly dodged a well-placed roundhouse.

The bout lasted five minutes, but it felt like no time at all. Breathless, they both stepped back and bowed.

"Not bad for a rusty old man," Gerry said, grinning and catching his breath.

Jack laughed. "You've come a long way."

The students clapped quietly, impressed.

Jack looked around the room—at the faces watching, the energy alive in the space.

He felt something settle inside him—not nostalgia exactly, but gratitude. The dojo was still right. Still part of him.

Still home.

After the session, Jack headed to the changing room and took a long, welcoming shower. The heat worked its way into tired muscles, washing off the sweat and dust of the dojo—and something else too, something heavier. It felt good. Grounding.

Jack said goodbye to Gerry with a firm handshake and a smile. "I don't know when I'll be back," he admitted.

Gerry nodded, understanding more than Jack said out loud. "You'll always have a place here."

With that, Jack stepped out into the Dublin air, a mix of past and future tugging at him. It was time to reconnect.

He rang his parents and his only sibling, Brynn. They were surprised but delighted to hear his voice. After a few minutes of warm conversation and a bit of scolding for not calling sooner, they made plans to meet that evening for dinner at Clontarf Castle.

Something quiet. Something familiar.

The idea of sitting down with them—of being surrounded by those who knew him from the start—suddenly felt necessary. Anchoring.

He'd fill them in on recent events, of course: the museums, Florence, the return to Dublin, the upcoming trip back to Okinawa. And of course, his romance with Michyo. But not everything. Sicily would stay unspoken, at least for now. Some stories needed time.

Others didn't need telling at all.

He looked at the time.

Still a few hours until dinner.

Jack tucked his hands into his hoodie pockets and began walking toward his car.

He arrived home and parked the Fiat Spider. A nice walk down the Bull Wall was what he needed—the wind from the bay brushing against his face. There was something soothing about letting the day unfold one step at a time.

That evening, Jack arrived early at Clontarf Castle.

The old building, with its ivy-draped stone and warm interior lighting, still held a quiet grandeur. He stood in the lobby for a moment, soaking it in. The familiar mix of old-world charm and Irish hospitality made him feel oddly at ease—like slipping on a coat he hadn't worn in years, but that still fit just right.

His parents arrived first in their little Nissan Micra.

"A great little car," his father often said.

His mother greeted him with a tight hug that lingered just a second too long, as if to make up for all the months they hadn't seen each other. His father clapped him on the shoulder in his usual understated way and said, "You're looking leaner. Japan suits you."

Brynn swept in soon after with an unexpected guest, arms wide and a teasing grin in place. "Well, well—look who's graced us with his mysterious world-travelling presence."

Jack laughed and pulled her into a hug. "I missed this."

"This is Bryan, my boyfriend. I wanted you to meet him," she grinned.

"B&B," laughed Jack. He extended his hand and gave Bryan a solid handshake. He seemed like a nice, decent fella, Jack thought.

"He sings and plays guitar," said Brynn.

They sat at a quiet table near the window, candles flickering, soft music playing in the background. The menu was familiar—Irish staples with a touch of flair—and the comfort of it all helped settle Jack's nerves.

He told them about Florence: about the art, the early morning runs by the Arno, the beauty of the city, and how it had stirred something in him. He talked about Dublin, about visiting the dojo, about seeing Gerry, and how proud he was of the progress there.

He kept it light, warm, real—but careful. No mention of Sicily. Just enough to reconnect.

His mother asked if he was eating well. His father asked if he was training hard. Brynn asked if there was anyone "interesting" in Japan.

Jack only smiled and said, "There might be."

After dinner, they moved to the bar and shared a quiet drink—his dad with a pint, his mum a glass of white wine, and Brynn with something pink and fizzy. Jack sipped a whiskey, letting the warmth settle in his chest.

For a moment, time slowed. They laughed, reminisced, talked about old neighbours, about summer plans. It wasn't dramatic or life-changing. But it was exactly what it needed to be—a reminder of who he was, and where he came from.

Brynn wasn't one to let things go easily. She wanted to know everything about the new girl in Jack's life.

As they sat in the castle bar, her glass of Prosecco now nearly empty, she leaned in with a grin and narrowed eyes. "Alright, enough dodging. Who is she?"

Jack raised an eyebrow. "Who?"

She gave him a look. "Michyo. You said 'there might be someone' and then went quiet like a guilty teenager."

Their mother perked up slightly. "Michyo?" she repeated.

Jack laughed, gently swirling the amber in his whiskey glass.

"You don't miss a thing, do you?"

Brynn grinned. "Not when it comes to you, brother."

He took a breath. "Her name's Michyo. She hopes to get a job teaching at the university in Okinawa. Literature, mostly. She's… calm. Smart. She listens in a way that makes you feel like your words matter."

His voice softened. "We met on my last trip back to Okinawa. She was staying with my father-in-law, Ichiro. She's a cousin of Akiko and lives in Hong Kong."

"Ah," Brynn said, nudging him.

His mother looked pleased. "And is it serious?"

Jack hesitated, not because he didn't know, but because saying it aloud made it more real.

"Yes," he said at last. "It is."

Brynn nodded slowly, her teasing fading into something gentler. "Well, she'll have to be someone special to keep up with you."

Jack met her gaze. "She is."

The conversation drifted on from there, but something had settled—something peaceful. For the first time that evening, Jack felt like he wasn't just visiting home. He was sharing the direction his life was truly taking.

Later, when they stepped out into the cool evening air, Brynn hugged him a second time—this one quieter, tighter.

"Tell her I said hi," she whispered.

Jack said his goodbyes with warm hugs and promises not to leave it so long next time. As he stepped out of Clontarf Castle, the night greeted him with a cool breeze and a sky clear enough to reveal a scattering of stars.

The walk back to his apartment was quiet, the streets hushed, the city winding down. He liked it this way. Dublin had a different kind of magic at night—less showy, more honest. You could hear your thoughts.

And tonight, his thoughts were with Michyo. There was comfort in knowing they would see each other again soon.

He reached his building, climbed the stairs, and let himself in. The air was cooler now, the space less stale since he'd aired it earlier. He poured a glass of water, stepped out onto the balcony, and looked out over the dark sea, the city lights twinkling behind him.

Tomorrow would be a different kind of reunion—catching up with the lads: beers, jokes, stories. But tonight was his. A quiet moment to carry the weight and warmth of the evening.

He breathed in deeply, letting it all settle: the stars above, the sea below, the pull of Okinawa on the horizon.

Michyo felt closer than ever now—her voice still echoing gently in his mind, her laughter tucked away in some quiet corner of memory. There was comfort in knowing she was waiting for him.

But not all homecomings were easy.

His thoughts drifted to Akiko.

Her presence came with warmth and silence. He had loved her once—truly—but time and change had taken their toll. Still, her death had left a mark. And now, her ashes were waiting for him in Okinawa. He had been putting it off for some time, but now it was time to say goodbye.

She had left simple instructions: no ceremony, no speeches.

Just the wind. The sea.

He had promised he would do it himself.

Standing on his balcony under the starlit sky, Jack felt the weight of that promise press gently against his chest. He would find the right moment. The right place. And he would let her go—finally, fully.

He would say goodbye.

Not with regret, but with respect.

The city was silent now. A light blinked far out at sea. Jack watched it, unmoving, for a long time.

Two women. Two stories.

One ending. One beginning.

And somewhere in the space between, Jack stood—ready, at last, to walk forward.

Before the evening's laughter and pints, Jack had one more stop to make.

The Garda station on Store Street hadn't changed much: same pale walls, same smell of coffee and floor polish, same undercurrent of weariness that clung to most police stations. Jack signed in at the front desk and was directed upstairs to the small, cluttered office of Detective Inspector Joey Maloney.

Joey was leaning back in his chair, sleeves rolled up, glasses perched halfway down his nose as he squinted at a file.

"Well now, I'll be damned," he said without looking up. "I hear rumours. A certain globe-trotter back on home soil? I never thought I'd see you alive again, my friend."

Jack smiled. "Thought I'd drop in before the lads got their claws in me."

Joey stood up, extended a hand, and pulled Jack into a bear hug. "Good to see you, mate."

They sat, the mood easy, familiar. A kettle boiled quietly in the corner. Joey poured them both tea—strong, the way Jack liked it.

"You look different," Joey said, studying him. "Something's shifted."

Jack shrugged. "Been through a bit. Travelled. Let go of some ghosts."

Joey didn't press. He never did. They had history—cases closed, secrets kept, mutual trust earned over years. He couldn't believe it when Jack told him all that had happened in Sicily.

"You still carrying, Jack?"

Jack shook his head. "Not anymore. Different life now."

Joey nodded. "Good. You deserve some peace." There was a pause.

"I've been seeing someone," Jack said. "Her name's Michyo. She's... special."

Joey raised an eyebrow. "From Okinawa, right? Heard whispers."

Jack chuckled. "You hear everything, don't you?"

"Occupational hazard."

They talked for another half hour—about the state of the city, old colleagues, the quiet moments that mattered. When it was time to leave, Joey walked him to the door.

"Whatever's ahead, Jack—don't look back too much. Sometimes what we leave behind should stay there."

Jack nodded, clapped Joey on the shoulder. "I'll hold onto that."

And with that, he stepped out into the soft Dublin evening, ready for the night, the laughter, and the stories waiting at the pub.

Jack made his way into town to meet the lads. They'd chosen a spot just off Grafton Street—a pub that had seen better days but still poured a solid pint and knew how to keep the music low enough for conversation.

Inside, it was already buzzing.

Lenny was there early, holding court at the usual corner table. Beside him sat Anto, Bradley, Danger, and Sonar, pints in hand, faces lighting up as Jack approached.

"Well, well," Lenny said, rising to clap him on the back. "Look what the wind blew in!"

"You're late," Anto grinned. "We were about to toast to your mysterious disappearance."

Jack laughed and shook his head. "It's good to see you too, lads. Where's Trigger?"

"Your guess is as good as mine," Bradley drawled.

And with that, the door swung open and in walked Trigger—late as usual and cool as a cucumber.

Jack ordered a pint and took his seat, falling into the rhythm of old friendships as if no time had passed at all. They asked about what he'd been up to since the last time they met.

He talked about his trip to Italy and his encounter with Giovanni Falconetti. The lads couldn't believe their ears.

"Jaysus, Jack, you're a lucky man to still be alive," said Bradley.

He wanted to keep things light, so he talked about Okinawa's sun, the discipline of teaching again, and the stillness he'd found there.

When Michyo came up, they leaned in.

"Tell us about her," Danger smirked.

"She sounds like someone you wouldn't meet in Clondalkin," Anto added.

Jack smiled quietly. "She's… different. Grounded. Brilliant, really. We understand each other without needing a lot of words."

They nodded, offering approving looks and raised brows. They were happy for him—even if their way of showing it was wrapped in sarcasm and jabs.

The night rolled on. Pints emptied and refilled. Stories grew taller. Laughter grew louder. Someone brought up their wild trip to Amsterdam years ago, and the entire table nearly cried with laughter.

But between the banter and the beers, Jack felt something deeper—gratitude. These were his people. No matter how far he'd travelled, how much he'd changed, this would always be a part of him.

Later, as they spilled out onto the damp Dublin pavement, arms slung around shoulders, someone shouted, "Next one's in Okinawa, yeah?"

Jack grinned. "Anytime, lads. First round will be on me."

As usual, it had been a great night—full of banter, laughter, and the kind of effortless camaraderie that only years of shared friendship could bring. Jack felt lighter, even with the pints settling in his stomach. The faces, the jokes, the inside references—they were familiar, grounding.

He strolled toward the taxi rank in the cool Dublin night, the city damp with a misty drizzle that hadn't quite become rain. The pavement glistened under the amber streetlights, and his breath rose in small clouds.

The streets had quieted. A bus rumbled in the distance, and a few late-night revellers laughed their way past him, arms locked together, heels clacking on the wet concrete.

Jack reached the taxi stand and climbed into the first cab.

"Clontarf, please," he said, leaning back into the seat.

The driver gave him a nod and pulled away from the curb.

The city slipped past the window in a blur of light and shadow. Jack watched it all with a distant gaze—half here, half already gone. The buzz of the evening still hummed in his chest, but his thoughts were elsewhere. Okinawa—Michyo—Akiko.

His next chapter was waiting. And he was ready now, steadied by the laughter of old friends, the warmth of family, and the quiet certainty that came from knowing who he was and where he was going.

The cab turned onto the coastal road. Out over the water, the black sea stretched into nothingness. Jack stared at it, thinking of the wind, the ceremony he still had to carry out, and the woman who would be waiting on the other side of the world.

He felt something shift in him—quiet, small, but real.

He was ready to go home.

The morning of his departure came quietly.

Jack rose before dawn and went through his workout. The city was still wrapped in sleep. His bags were already packed—he had never unpacked much to begin with. Just a few clothes, a couple of gifts.

He took one last look around the apartment. He had placed it with a local real estate agency, which would find a tenant during his absence. The incoming rent would be appreciated. The place felt empty again, but this time he didn't mind. It had served its purpose—a place to rest, to reconnect, to remember. Now it was time to move forward.

The taxi arrived right on time. The driver, an older man with a strong Dublin accent, helped him with his bags and made small talk on the way to the airport. Jack mostly listened, content to let the city speak through someone else's voice one last time.

At the terminal, everything moved as it always did—queues, announcements, the hum of travellers in motion. Jack moved through it all with quiet purpose, pausing once at a café for a black coffee. He stood by the window, watching the grey morning slowly lighten, and took a long sip.

Dublin had given him what he needed: familiar faces, laughter, a reminder of who he had been. But the call of Okinawa—the life he had chosen, the love waiting for him, and the promise he had yet to fulfil—pulled at him more strongly now.

As the plane taxied onto the runway, Jack looked out at the green fields disappearing beneath the rising fuselage. He thought of his parents, Brynn, the lads, and Gerry. And he felt no sadness, only gratitude.

Above the clouds, the sun finally broke through. The sky was clear, endless. He leaned back in his seat, closed his eyes, and let the light wash over him. Home was still ahead. But he was on his way.

He landed at Heathrow Airport in London and waited five hours for a direct flight from London to Tokyo. Jack slept most of the time on the flight. When he touched down in Tokyo, he checked into a small hotel and found a small restaurant for a bite to eat. He was hungry. He was early to bed, as he had a flight the next day to Naha Airport.

The soul always knows what to do to heal itself. The challenge is to silence the mind.

Caroline Myss

CHAPTER
Thirty-Six

Okinawa

The air in Okinawa hit him the moment he stepped off the plane—warm, heavy with humidity, thick with the scent of salt and lush tropical greenery. It felt like stepping into another skin, one he had once shed and was now reclaiming.

Jack moved through the small airport with ease, nodding politely at the familiar customs officers, collecting his bag with practised efficiency. Everything here felt slower, softer—time seemed to move differently in Okinawa, as though the island itself breathed more deeply than the rest of the world.

Outside, the light was golden, the sky wide and untroubled. A soft breeze stirred the palm trees, and in the distance, he could already hear the sea.

He hailed a taxi and gave the driver his address in quiet Japanese. The cab wound its way along the coast, past roadside shrines and low-tiled houses, the deep blue of the ocean keeping pace beside them.

When the driver dropped him off at his beach cabin, Jack paused before unlocking the door. It looked just as he'd left it—simple, still, serene. He stepped inside, greeted by the faint scent of wood.

He opened the windows, letting the light pour in, the sea breeze flow through.

But the moment he'd been quietly bracing for was waiting.

On the low table in the corner sat a simple wooden box—Akiko's ashes. There was no note, no message. Just the box, and the unspoken weight of a final request.

Jack walked over, placed a hand gently on it, and closed his eyes.

"I'm back," he whispered.

Outside, the waves rolled in, steady and endless. He would rest tonight. And tomorrow, he would say goodbye to Akiko with Ichiro by his side.

Jack stood for a long while in the quiet of the cabin, the sea breeze shifting the curtains gently. He hadn't seen Ichiro since the funeral. They hadn't spoken much—grief had wrapped itself around them both like a heavy fog. But there was a bond between them, forged not just through Akiko, but through shared silence, shared pain. There were things that didn't need words.

Jack lit a single incense stick and placed it beside the box. The smoke curled upward, fragile and wandering, like memory. He sat cross-legged in front of it for a few minutes, not praying exactly, but being still—thinking of the laughter that once lived here, the quiet evenings, the long walks they had taken after dinner. The sunrises and the sunsets they had watched together. He thought of what had been lost and what was still waiting to be found.

Tomorrow would be a ritual, a release.

Michyo was due to arrive in two days. He already felt the quiet anticipation of her presence—her calm voice, the way she listened without interrupting, the warmth in her smile. She would understand. She always did.

For now, the cabin was silent but full of memories, of meaning, of transition. Jack could almost hear Akiko laughing, could nearly feel her hand stroking his face.

He rose slowly and slid the balcony door open. The moon hung low over the sea, casting silver light on the water below.

He exhaled deeply.

The waves kept rolling in.

The morning arrived soft and grey, with a quiet wind moving through the trees.

Jack rose early, dressed simply, and placed Akiko's ashes carefully into a cloth bag he had prepared the night before. He stepped out into the morning, the scent of the sea already in the air, and began the walk to Ichiro's house.

Ichiro was waiting at the gate.

He looked smaller than Jack remembered—thinner, more stooped—but his eyes still held that steady, unreadable depth. He gave Jack a quiet nod, and they bowed to each other without a word.

The walk to the cliffs was made in silence.

The two men moved side by side along the narrow path that wound through pine trees and low stone walls, up toward the headland that looked out over the East China Sea. Akiko had loved it here. They had come often in the early days—just the two of them, sitting on the rocks, watching the waves chase each other to the shore.

At the edge, the wind picked up.

Jack placed the bag gently on the rock before them and unwrapped the box. Ichiro stepped forward and placed both hands on it for a moment, bowing his head. Then he stepped back.

Jack opened the lid.

The ashes were pale and fine, like powdered bone and scattered memory. He stood holding the box, the wind tugging at his sleeves, and for a moment he said nothing. Then, softly:

"Thank you, Akiko. For everything you gave. For all that we shared. For your grace—even when things were hard."

His voice caught, but he didn't fight it. He turned the box slowly, and the ashes caught the wind.

"Goodbye, my love."

Jack stood motionless, his eyes tracing the path of the ashes as they vanished into the horizon. The breeze brushed his cheeks like a final caress, soft and knowing. For a fleeting moment, the air shimmered—and there it was.

The ideogram for love.

Just a whisper of a shape, delicate and precise, drawn in dust and air, hovering against the blue before fading into the sky. Jack blinked, unsure if it had been real. But it didn't matter. It was what he needed to see. What she had needed to say.

He lowered the empty box and bowed his head once more.

Ichiro, silent at his side, placed a hand gently on Jack's shoulder— a rare gesture, light but solid. The gesture of a father not only letting go of a daughter, but acknowledging the man who had loved her.

They said nothing on the walk back.

At the edge of the village, they parted with a respectful bow.

Jack returned to the cabin, a deep stillness within him. He washed his hands, lit another stick of incense, and opened the windows wide to the sea.

That night, he sat on the porch under a sky scattered with stars. The moon had risen again, silver and calm, casting its light on the waves as they curled endlessly toward the shore.

He was alone now. But not lost. Tomorrow, Michyo would come. And something new would begin.

The sun was already high when Jack heard the sound of the taxi slowing outside.

He stepped out onto the porch, heart beating a little faster, and watched as Michyo stepped from the car, shielding her eyes against the bright Okinawan light. She wore simple linen trousers and a navy-blue top, her hair tied back. She looked calm, collected, but when her eyes met his, they softened instantly.

She smiled—and Jack felt something inside him loosen.

They walked toward each other without words.

When they embraced, it was without urgency. Just two people who understood each other, holding space for everything that had passed and everything still to come.

"It's good to see you," Jack said finally, his voice low.

"It's good to be here," Michyo replied. She looked past him to the sea. "I could feel the wind from the plane window. I knew you were nearby."

Jack managed a quiet laugh. "She's at peace now."

Michyo nodded. "And you?"

"I'm getting there."

They went inside. Jack made tea the way Akiko had taught him—green, gently steeped, no words needed. They sat across from each other in the quiet cabin, sharing small sips and long glances, the kind that asked no questions but offered presence.

Later, they walked to the cliff where the ashes had been released. Jack showed her the spot, pointing to the rocks and the line of the horizon.

"She loved this view," he said. "I think part of me does too, now."

Michyo stood beside him, silent. She reached out and took his hand.

"I didn't know her very well," she said softly, "but I'm grateful for her."

Jack looked at her, a lump rising in his throat.

"Me too."

They stood together, the sea breathing below them, two shadows in the sun.

Whatever lay ahead, it would begin from here—not in forgetting, but in remembering well.

And in moving forward, together.

That night, under the hush of the Okinawan sky, they lay together in the dim light of the cabin, the scent of salt and night-blooming flowers drifting through the open windows. The silence between them was not empty—it was charged, deep, alive.

When their lips met, it was with a hunger that had been waiting quietly, patiently. There were no words—only touch, only breath. They undressed each other slowly, reverently, as though peeling away all that had come before: the grief, the distance, the waiting.

Their bodies moved in rhythm, urgent and tender all at once. It was not just desire—it was release. It was the need to feel alive again, fully, fiercely. Jack moved with her like a man rediscovering a part of himself that had been buried, while Michyo held him with the steady fire of someone who understood loss—and chose love anyway.

They moved as if time had slipped away, as if the world outside no longer existed.

And when it was over, Jack lay beside her, breathless and quiet, a hand resting gently on her bare shoulder.

He felt emptied—yet whole.

It was the first time in so long that he had let go completely.

In the dark, Michyo traced circles on his chest with her fingertips. "You're home now," she whispered.

And Jack, eyes closed, simply nodded. At last, he was.

The morning sun filtered gently through the rice-paper screens, casting soft golden light across the wooden floor. The air was still, warm, and carried the distant cry of seabirds. Jack woke first, his body wrapped in a warm tangle of limbs and cotton sheets. For a long moment, he lay there watching Michyo sleep, her jet-black hair falling loosely across the pillow, her breath steady and calm.

Peace. That was the word that came to him—not just in the silence, but deep within himself.

Eventually, she stirred, eyes fluttering open. She smiled the moment she saw him.

"Morning," she said, her voice husky with sleep.

"Morning," he replied, brushing a strand of hair from her face.

They stayed in bed a while longer, talking softly, laughing now and then—about nothing and everything. There was no pressure, no weight—just the comfort of being together, finally, without shadows between them.

Later, Jack made breakfast—grilled fish, miso soup, and rice the simple Okinawan way. Michyo joined him on the porch with two cups of tea in her hands.

They ate in silence, watching the waves shimmer under the late morning sun. A gentle breeze stirred the trees. Everything felt slow, grounded, real.

"I've been thinking," Jack said, breaking the silence.

Michyo looked at him, curious.

"I hope to stay longer this time. Maybe... find a way to make it work here."

She didn't answer right away. Instead, she reached across and placed her hand over his.

"Then we'll make it work. I love you, Jack," she said.

Jack looked out to the sea, feeling the truth of it settle into his bones.

The past was behind him now. The path ahead is uncertain, but shared.

And that was enough.

--The End--